P9-DYY-807

STAR WARS

FORCES OF DESTINY™

Facebook: **facebook.com/idwpublishing**
Twitter: **@idwpublishing**
YouTube: **youtube.com/idwpublishing**
Tumblr: **tumblr.idwpublishing.com**
Instagram: **instagram.com/idwpublishing**

ISBN: 978-1-68405-228-8   21 20 19 18   1 2 3 4

COVER ARTIST
ELSA CHARRETIER

COVER COLORIST
MATT WILSON

COLLECTION EDITORS
JUSTIN EISINGER
and ALONZO SIMON

COLLECTION DESIGNER
CLYDE GRAPA

PUBLISHER
GREG GOLDSTEIN

STAR WARS: FORCES OF DESTINY. APRIL 2018. FIRST
PRINTING. © 2018 Lucasfilm Ltd. & ® or ™ where indicated. All
Rights Reserved. © 2018 Idea and Design Works, LLC. The IDW
logo is registered in the U.S. Patent and Trademark Office. IDW
Publishing, a division of Idea and Design Works, LLC. Editorial
offices: 2765 Truxtun Road, San Diego, CA 92106. Any
similarities to persons living or dead are purely coincidental.
With the exception of artwork used for review purposes, none
of the contents of this publication may be reprinted without
the permission of Idea and Design Works, LLC.
Printed in USA.
IDW Publishing does not read or accept unsolicited submissions
of ideas, stories, or artwork.

Originally published as STAR WARS FORCES OF DESTINY—
LEIA, STAR WARS FORCES OF DESTINY—REY, STAR WARS
FORCES OF DESTINY—HERA, STAR WARS FORCES OF
DESTINY—AHSOKA & PADME, and STAR WARS FORCES OF
DESTINY—ROSE & PAIGE.

Greg Goldstein, President & Publisher
Robbie Robbins, EVP & Sr. Art Director
Chris Ryall, Chief Creative Officer & Editor-in-Chief
Matthew Ruzicka, CPA, Chief Financial Officer
David Hedgecock, Associate Publisher
Laurie Windrow, Senior Vice President of Sales & Marketing
Lorelei Bunjes, VP of Digital Services
Eric Moss, Sr. Director, Licensing & Business Development

Ted Adams, Founder & CEO of IDW Media Holdings

Lucasfilm credits:
Jennifer Heddle, Executive Editor
Michael Siglain, Creative Director
Leland Chee, Joshua Rimes, James Waugh
and Matt Martin, Story Group

LEIA
Writers: Elsa Charretier & Pierrick Colinet
Artist: Elsa Charretier
Colorist: Sarah Stern

REY
Writer: Jody Houser
Artist: Arianna Florean
Colorist: Adele Matera

HERA
Writer: Devin Grayson
Artist: Eva Widermann
Colorist: Monica Kubina

AHSOKA & PADMÉ
Writer: Beth Revis
Artist & Colorist: Valentina Pinto

ROSE & PAIGE
Writer: Delilah S. Dawson
Artist & Colorist: Nicoletta Baldari

Letterer: Tom B. Long
Series Assistant Editor: Peter Adrian Behravesh
Series Editors: Bobby Curnow & Denton J. Tipton

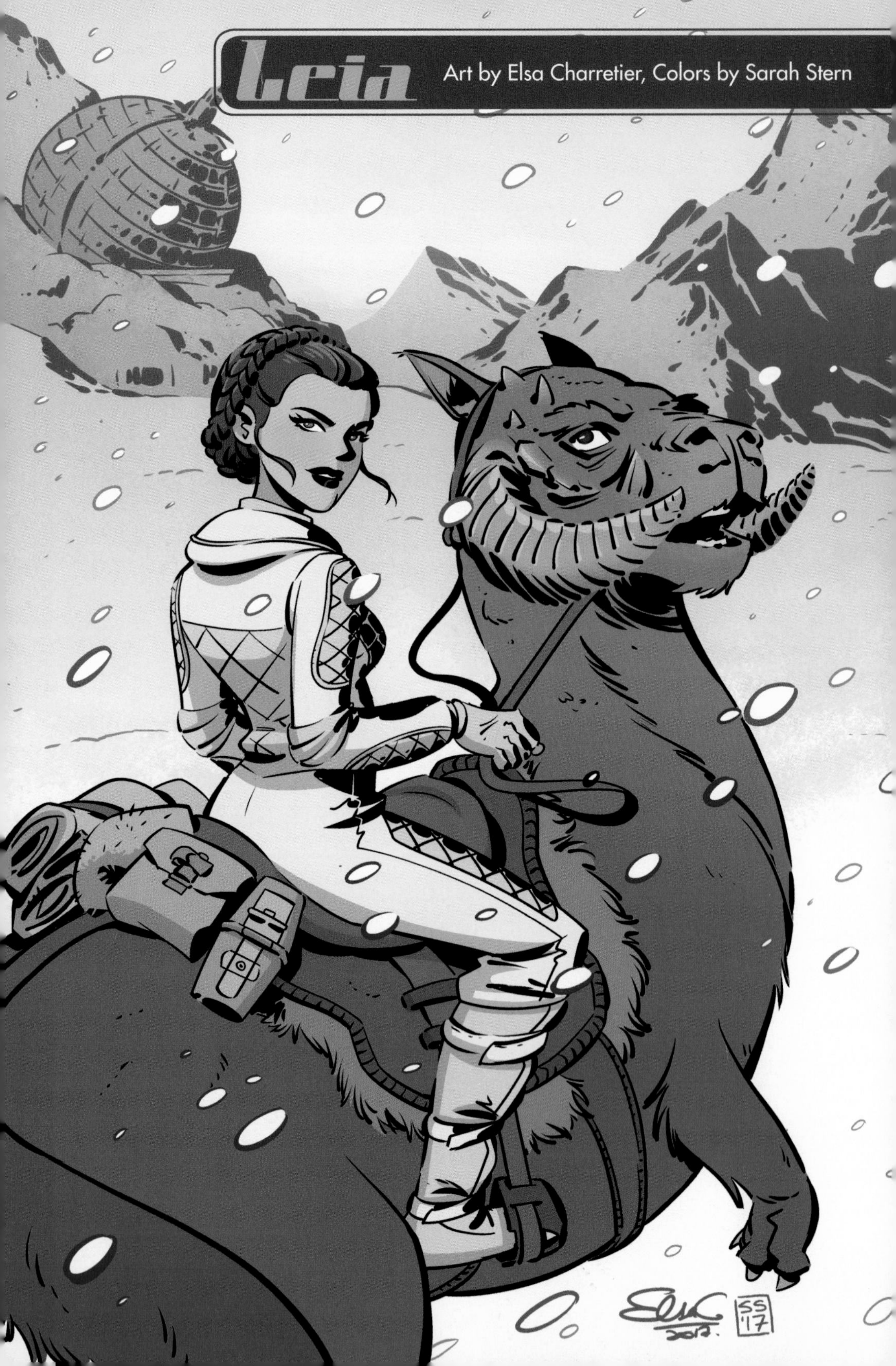
Leia
Art by Elsa Charretier, Colors by Sarah Stern
SS '17

SOME DAYS, IT FEELS LIKE MY DESTINY IS NOT OF MY OWN CHOOSING.

I MOVE FORWARD ONE WAY, AND GET PUSHED BACK ANOTHER.

I TRY TO RESIST, BUT ONLY GET PUSHED BACK HARDER.

EACH NEW STEP BECOMES A CHALLENGE, EVERY CHOICE A QUESTION.

I'M EQUIPPED. I'VE PREPARED FOR THIS. FOR THIS MOMENT WHEN, MAYBE, I'LL BE PUSHED TO MY LIMITS.

COME ON!

IS EVERYTHING ALL RIGHT, LEIA?

DOES YOUR HIGHNESS NEED A BREAK?

GRUNCH CRUNCH

BUT I NEVER EXPECTED THAT I WOULD BE DRIVEN TO THE EDGE BY...

RESTING IS A LUXURY I CAN'T AFFORD, HAN.

...AN UNBRIDLED...

BESIDES, I HAVE THIS PERFECTLY UNDER CONTR—

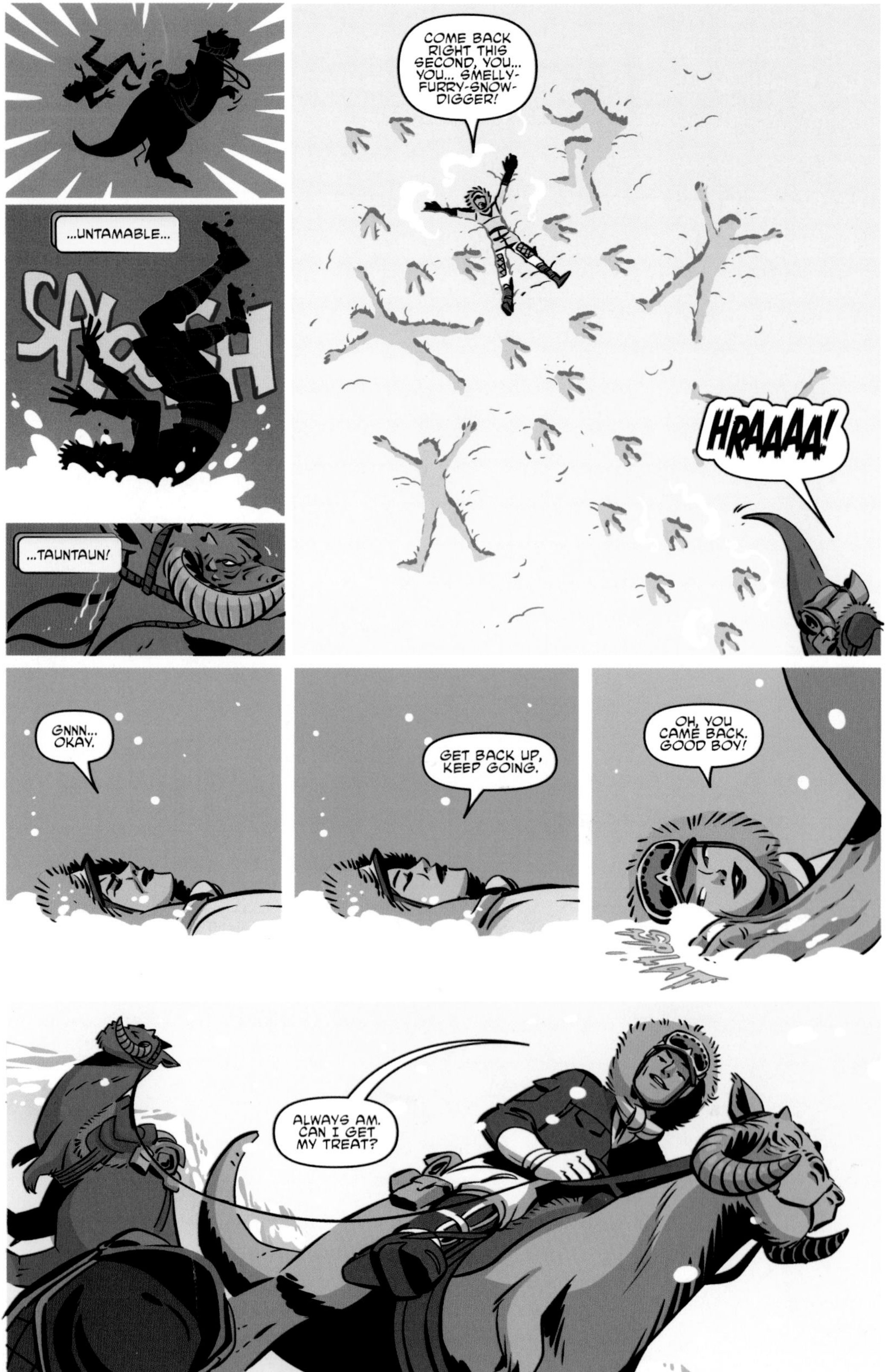
...UNTAMABLE...
SPLOOSH
...TAUNTAUN!
COME BACK RIGHT THIS SECOND, YOU... YOU... SMELLY-FURRY-SNOW-DIGGER!
HRAAAA!
GNNN... OKAY.
GET BACK UP, KEEP GOING.
OH, YOU CAME BACK. GOOD BOY!
ALWAYS AM. CAN I GET MY TREAT?

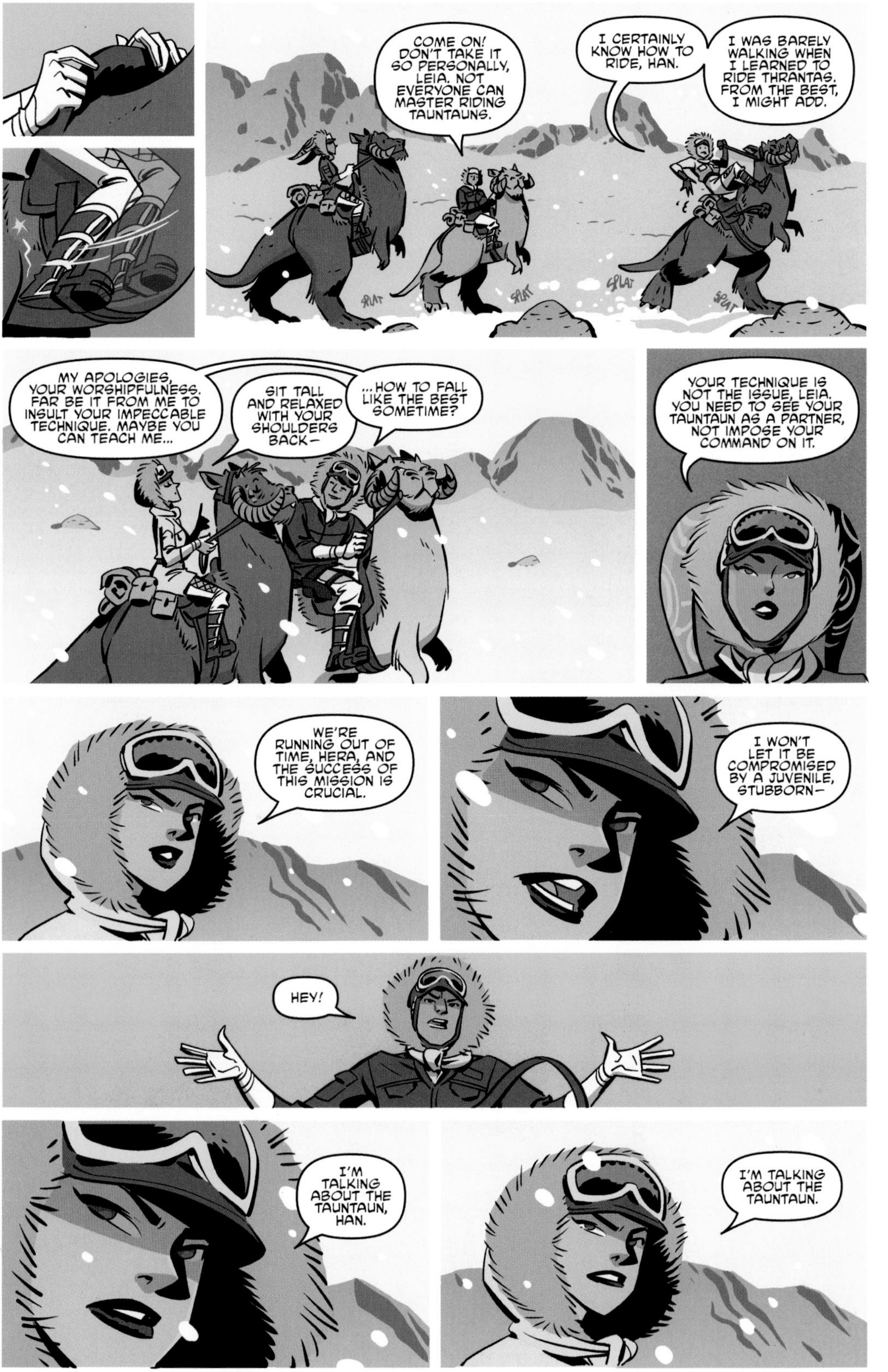

COME ON! DON'T TAKE IT SO PERSONALLY, LEIA. NOT EVERYONE CAN MASTER RIDING TAUNTAUNS.
I CERTAINLY KNOW HOW TO RIDE, HAN.
I WAS BARELY WALKING WHEN I LEARNED TO RIDE THRANTAS. FROM THE BEST, I MIGHT ADD.
SPLAT
SPLAT
SPLAT
SPLAT
MY APOLOGIES, YOUR WORSHIPFULNESS. FAR BE IT FROM ME TO INSULT YOUR IMPECCABLE TECHNIQUE. MAYBE YOU CAN TEACH ME...
SIT TALL AND RELAXED WITH YOUR SHOULDERS BACK—
...HOW TO FALL LIKE THE BEST SOMETIME?
YOUR TECHNIQUE IS NOT THE ISSUE, LEIA. YOU NEED TO SEE YOUR TAUNTAUN AS A PARTNER, NOT IMPOSE YOUR COMMAND ON IT.
WE'RE RUNNING OUT OF TIME, HERA, AND THE SUCCESS OF THIS MISSION IS CRUCIAL.
I WON'T LET IT BE COMPROMISED BY A JUVENILE, STUBBORN—
HEY!
I'M TALKING ABOUT THE TAUNTAUN, HAN.
I'M TALKING ABOUT THE TAUNTAUN.

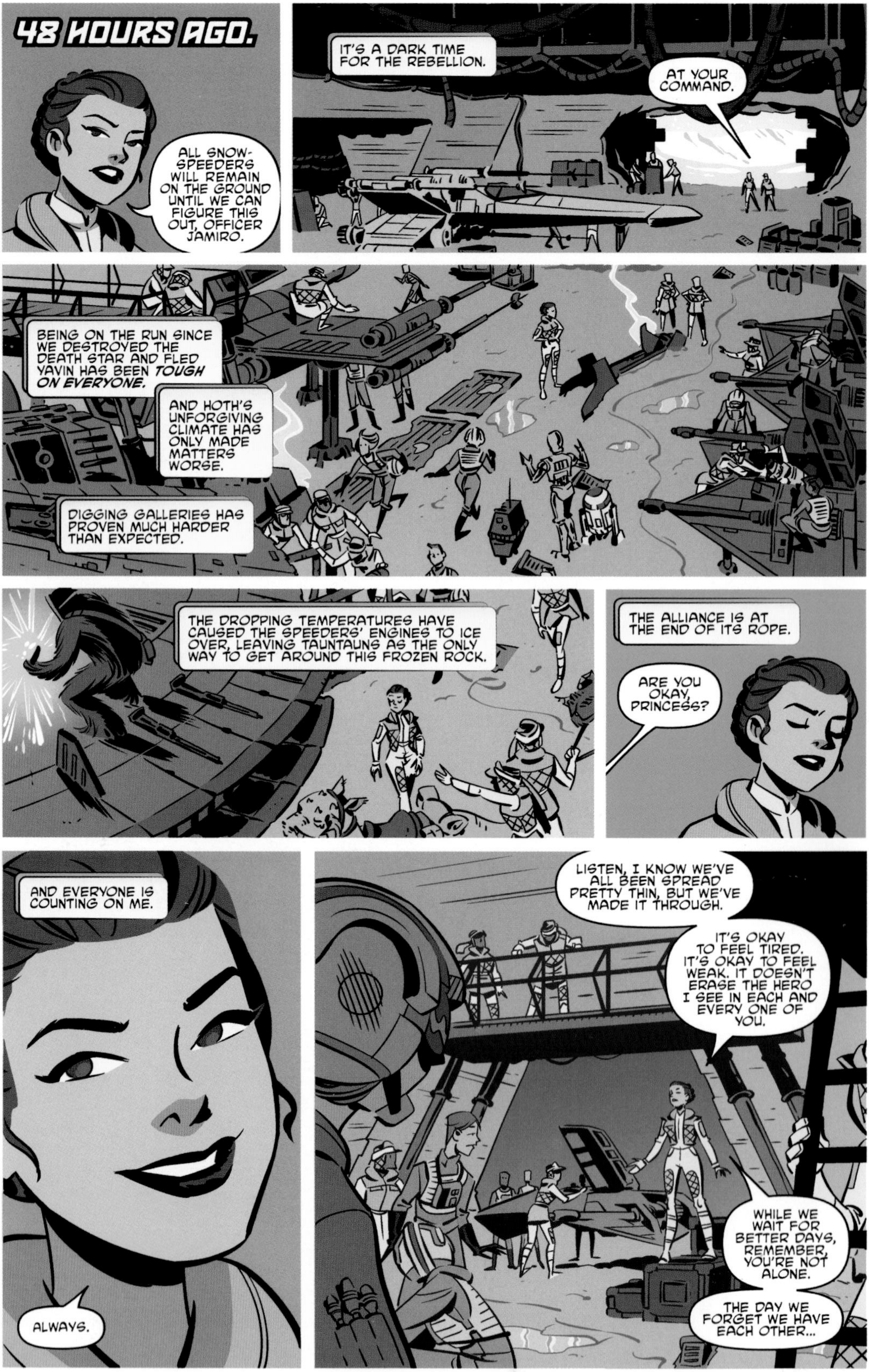
48 HOURS AGO.
ALL SNOW-SPEEDERS WILL REMAIN ON THE GROUND UNTIL WE CAN FIGURE THIS OUT, OFFICER JAMIRO.
IT'S A DARK TIME FOR THE REBELLION.
AT YOUR COMMAND.
BEING ON THE RUN SINCE WE DESTROYED THE DEATH STAR AND FLED YAVIN HAS BEEN *TOUGH ON EVERYONE.*
AND HOTH'S UNFORGIVING CLIMATE HAS ONLY MADE MATTERS WORSE.
DIGGING GALLERIES HAS PROVEN MUCH HARDER THAN EXPECTED.
THE DROPPING TEMPERATURES HAVE CAUSED THE SPEEDERS' ENGINES TO ICE OVER, LEAVING TAUNTAUNS AS THE ONLY WAY TO GET AROUND THIS FROZEN ROCK.
THE ALLIANCE IS AT THE END OF ITS ROPE.
ARE YOU OKAY, PRINCESS?
AND EVERYONE IS COUNTING ON ME.
ALWAYS.
LISTEN, I KNOW WE'VE ALL BEEN SPREAD PRETTY THIN, BUT WE'VE MADE IT THROUGH.
IT'S OKAY TO FEEL TIRED. IT'S OKAY TO FEEL WEAK. IT DOESN'T ERASE THE HERO I SEE IN EACH AND EVERY ONE OF YOU.
WHILE WE WAIT FOR BETTER DAYS, REMEMBER, YOU'RE NOT ALONE.
THE DAY WE FORGET WE HAVE EACH OTHER...

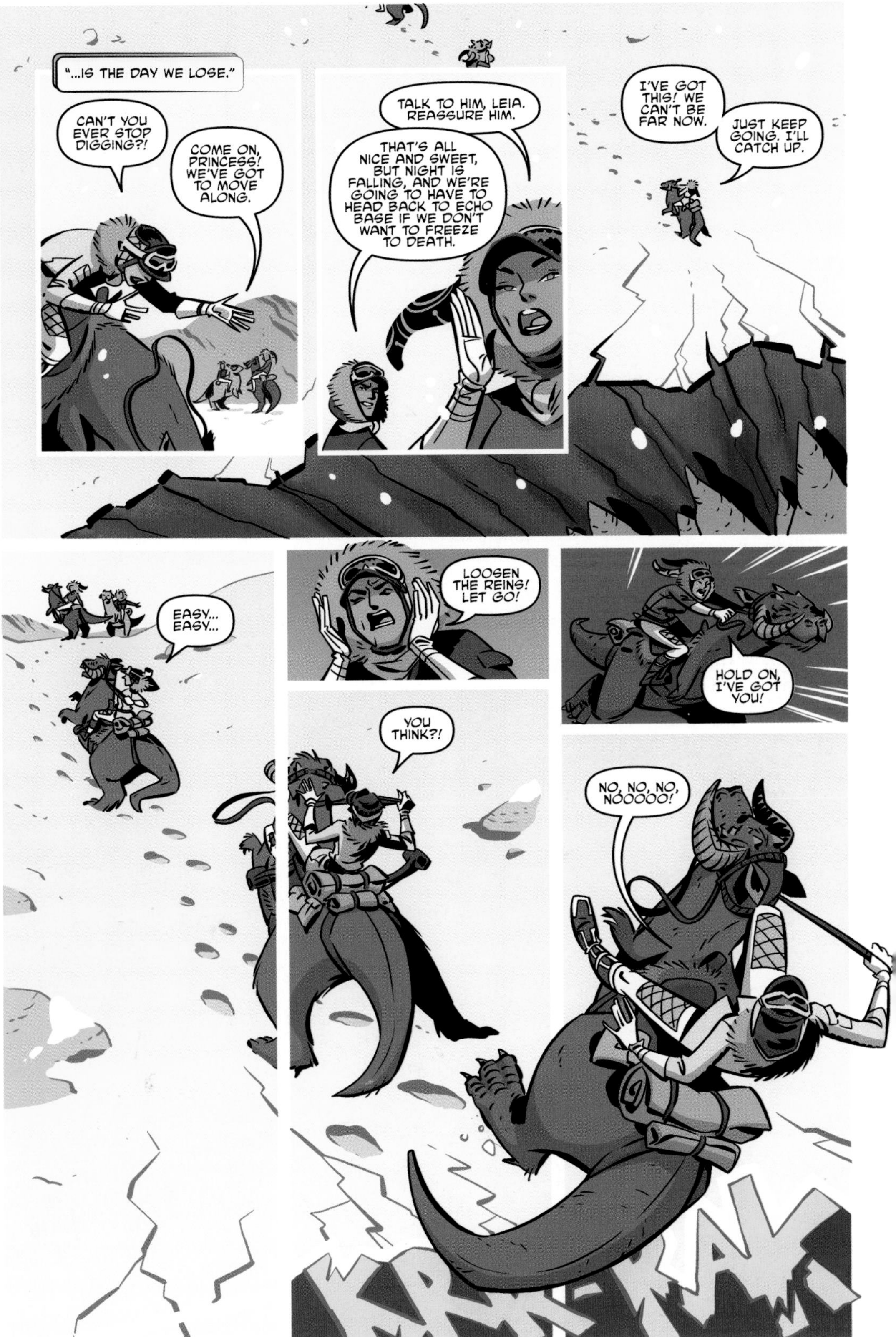
"...IS THE DAY WE LOSE."
CAN'T YOU EVER STOP DIGGING?!
COME ON, PRINCESS! WE'VE GOT TO MOVE ALONG.
TALK TO HIM, LEIA. REASSURE HIM.
THAT'S ALL NICE AND SWEET, BUT NIGHT IS FALLING, AND WE'RE GOING TO HAVE TO HEAD BACK TO ECHO BASE IF WE DON'T WANT TO FREEZE TO DEATH.
I'VE GOT THIS! WE CAN'T BE FAR NOW.
JUST KEEP GOING. I'LL CATCH UP.
EASY... EASY...
LOOSEN THE REINS! LET GO!
HOLD ON, I'VE GOT YOU!
YOU THINK?!
NO, NO, NO, NOOOOO!
KRK-RAK!

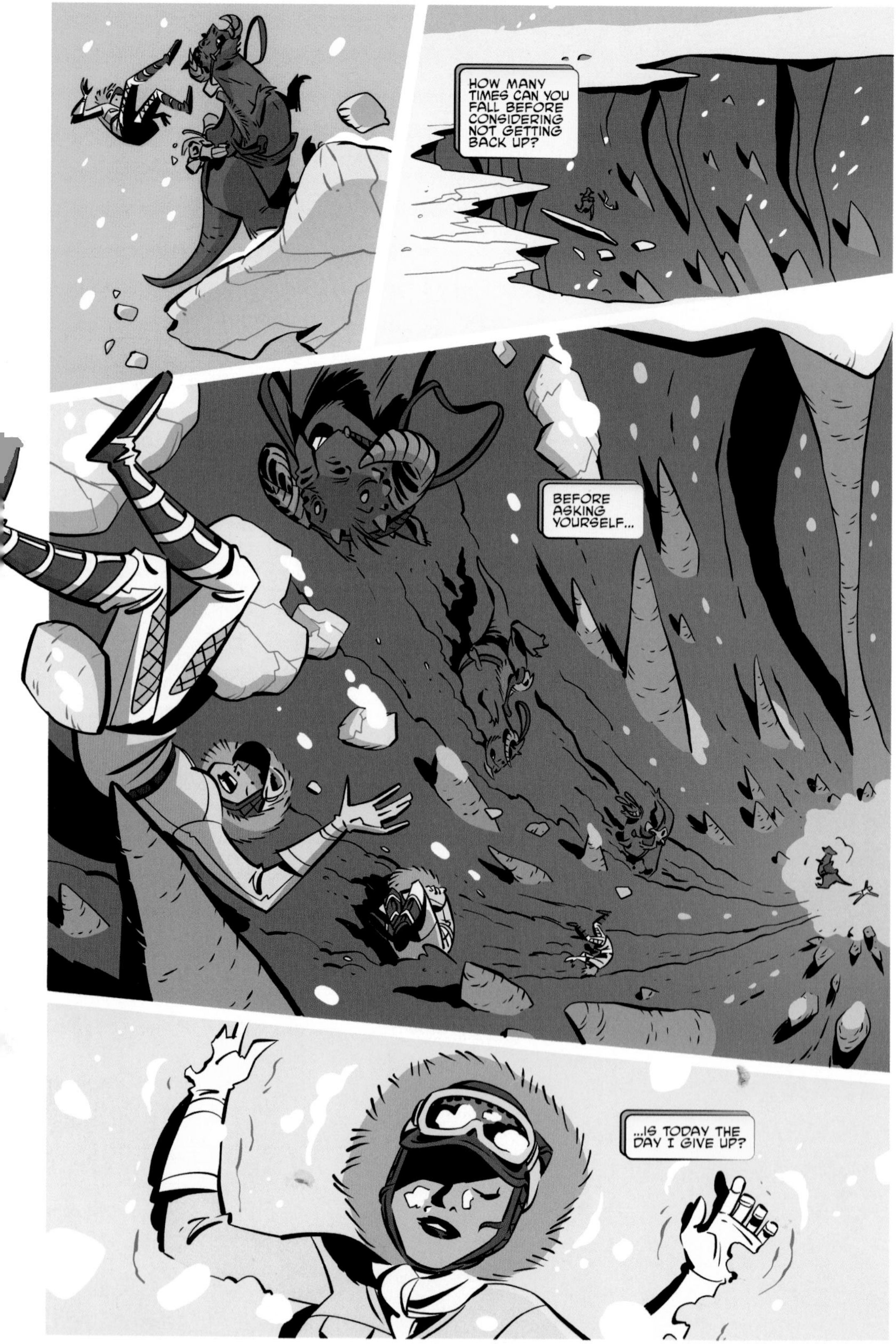
HOW MANY TIMES CAN YOU FALL BEFORE CONSIDERING NOT GETTING BACK UP?
BEFORE ASKING YOURSELF...
...IS TODAY THE DAY I GIVE UP?

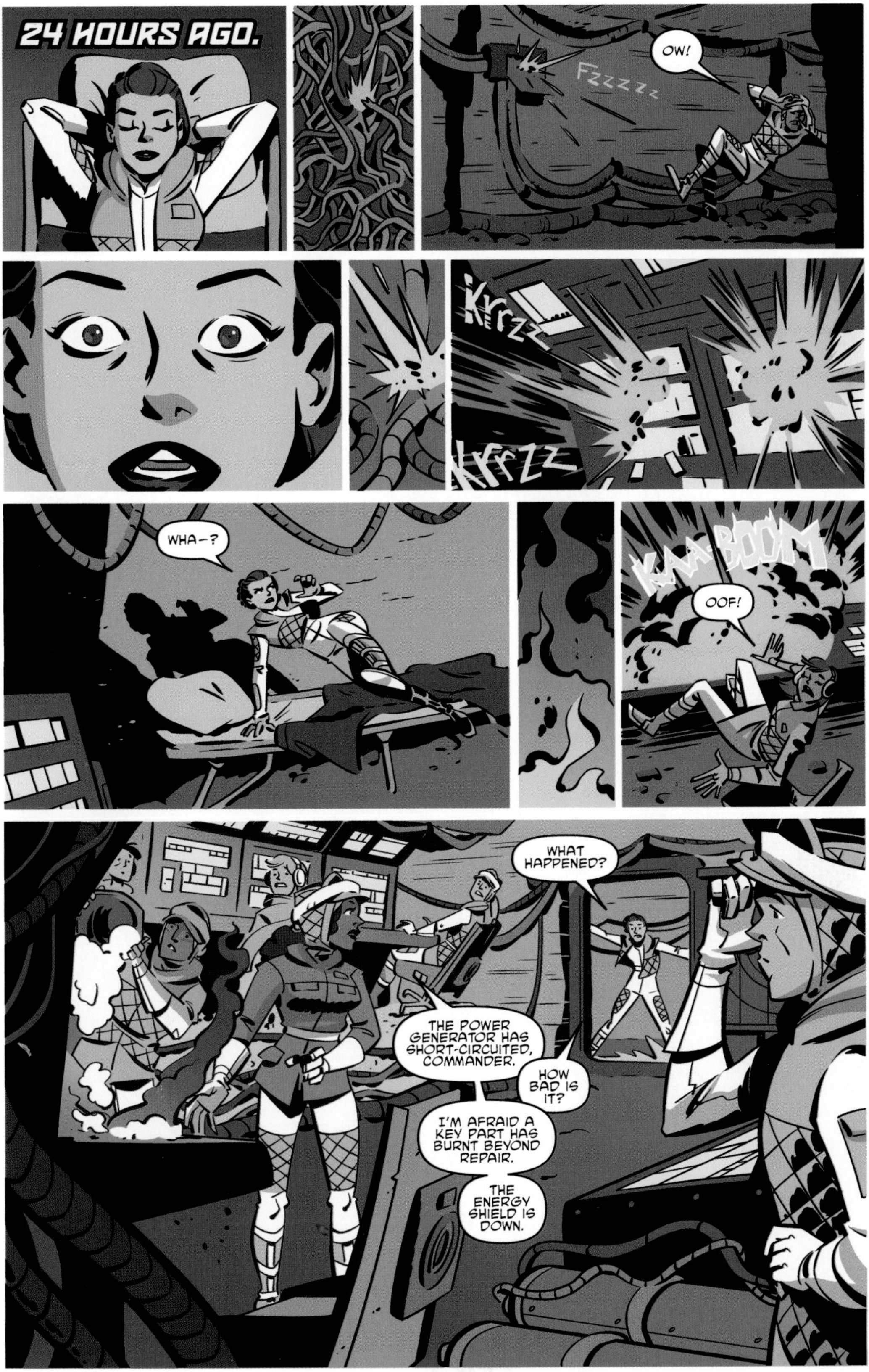
24 HOURS AGO.
OW!
Fzzzzz
Krrzzz
Krrzzz
WHA--?
KAA-BOOM
OOF!
WHAT HAPPENED?
THE POWER GENERATOR HAS SHORT-CIRCUITED, COMMANDER.
HOW BAD IS IT?
I'M AFRAID A KEY PART HAS BURNT BEYOND REPAIR.
THE ENERGY SHIELD IS DOWN.

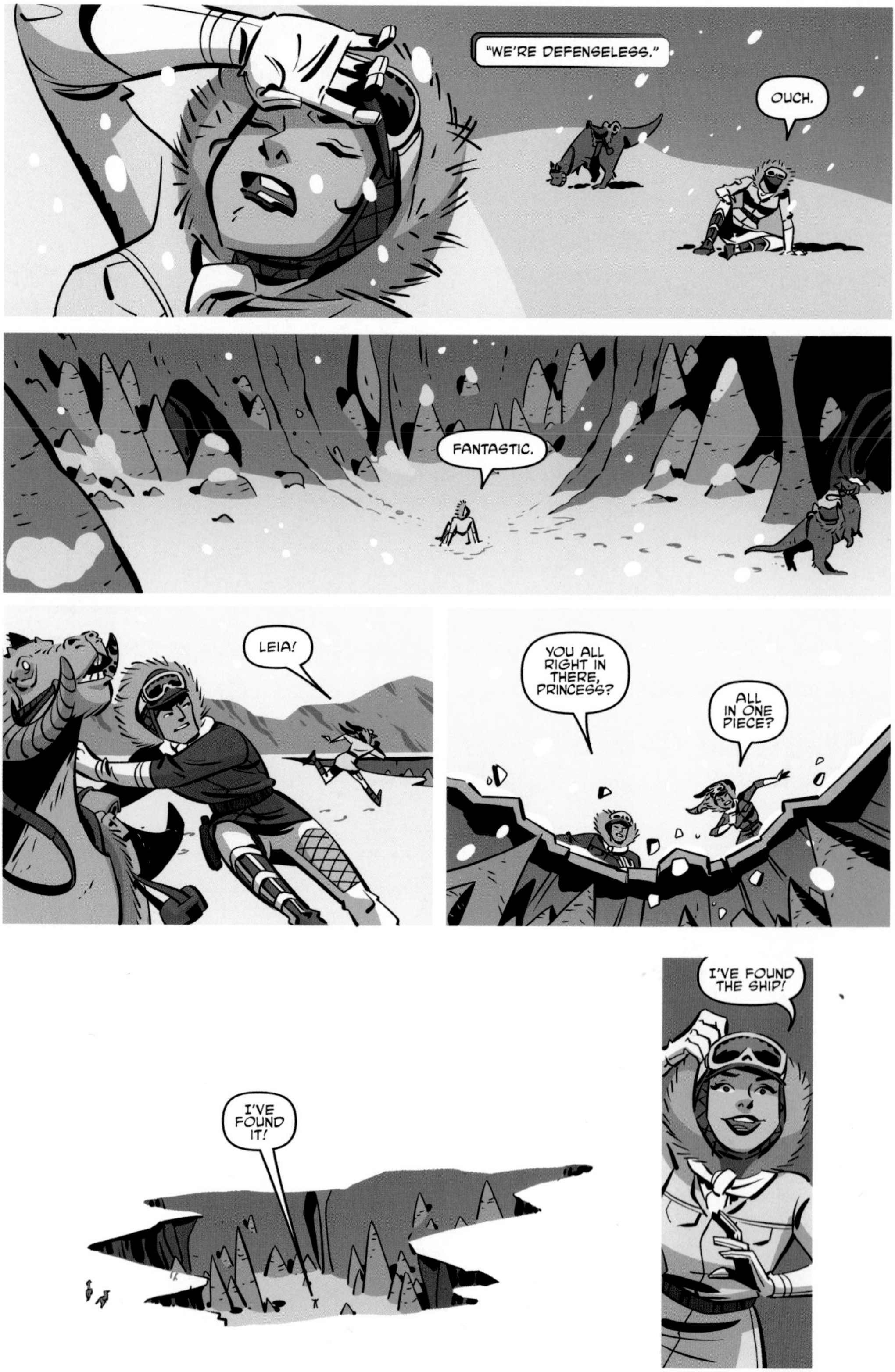
"WE'RE DEFENSELESS."
OUCH.
FANTASTIC.
LEIA!
YOU ALL RIGHT IN THERE, PRINCESS?
ALL IN ONE PIECE?
I'VE FOUND IT!
I'VE FOUND THE SHIP!

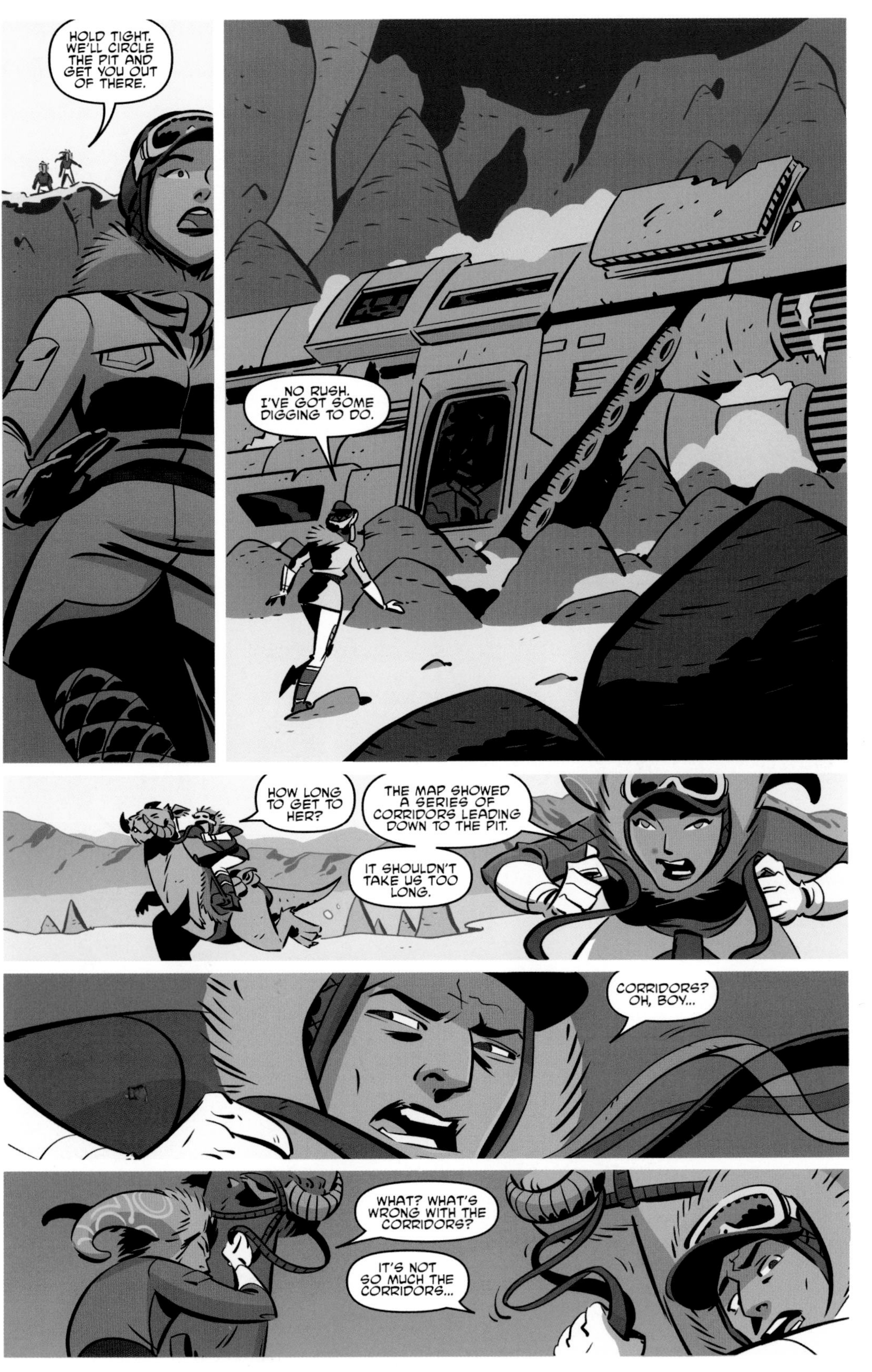
HOLD TIGHT. WE'LL CIRCLE THE PIT AND GET YOU OUT OF THERE.
NO RUSH. I'VE GOT SOME DIGGING TO DO.
HOW LONG TO GET TO HER?
THE MAP SHOWED A SERIES OF CORRIDORS LEADING DOWN TO THE PIT.
IT SHOULDN'T TAKE US TOO LONG.
CORRIDORS? OH, BOY...
WHAT? WHAT'S WRONG WITH THE CORRIDORS?
IT'S NOT SO MUCH THE CORRIDORS...

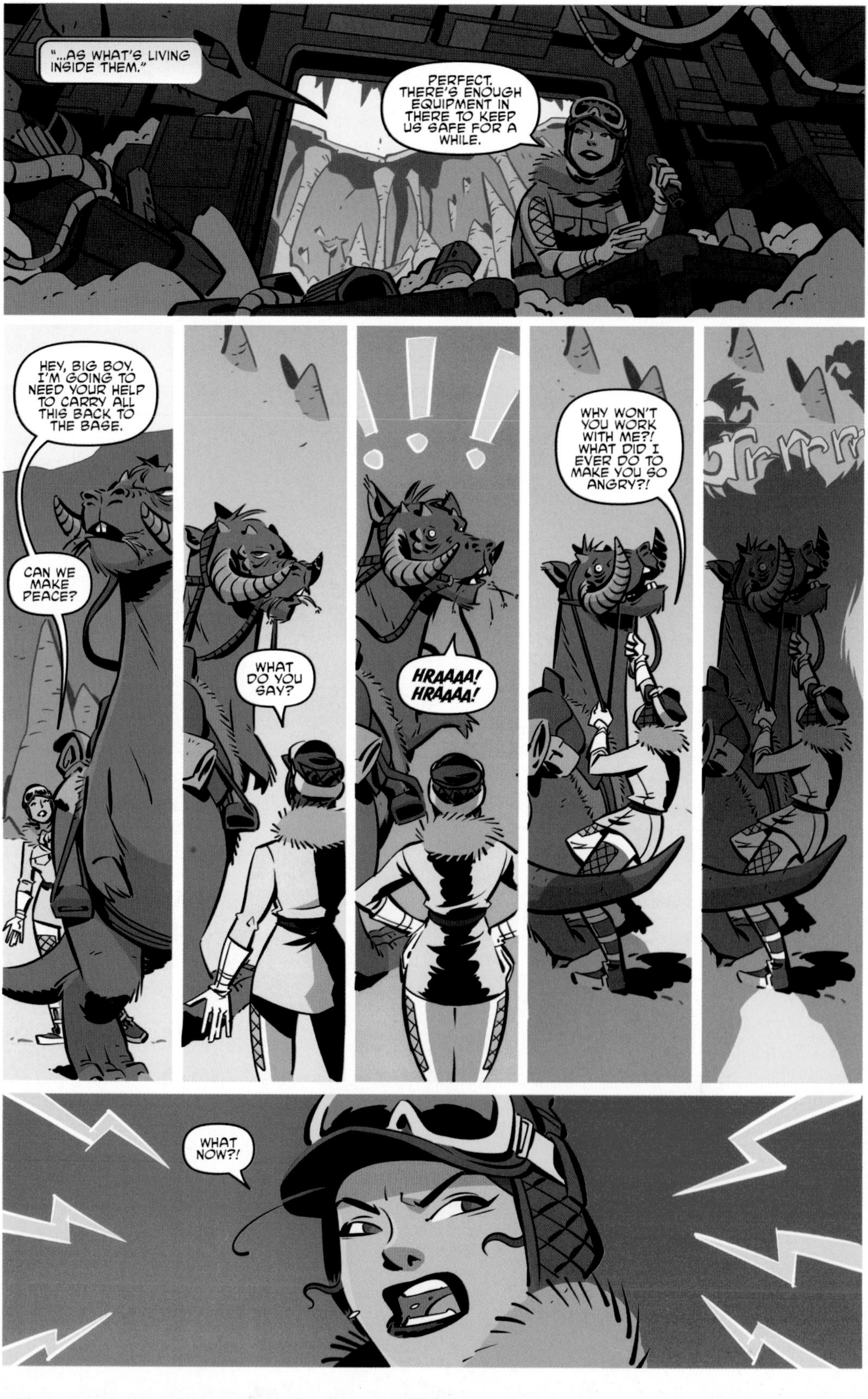
"...AS WHAT'S LIVING INSIDE THEM."
PERFECT. THERE'S ENOUGH EQUIPMENT IN THERE TO KEEP US SAFE FOR A WHILE.
HEY, BIG BOY. I'M GOING TO NEED YOUR HELP TO CARRY ALL THIS BACK TO THE BASE.
CAN WE MAKE PEACE?
WHAT DO YOU SAY?
HRAAAA! HRAAAA!
WHY WON'T YOU WORK WITH ME?! WHAT DID I EVER DO TO MAKE YOU SO ANGRY?!
WHAT NOW?!

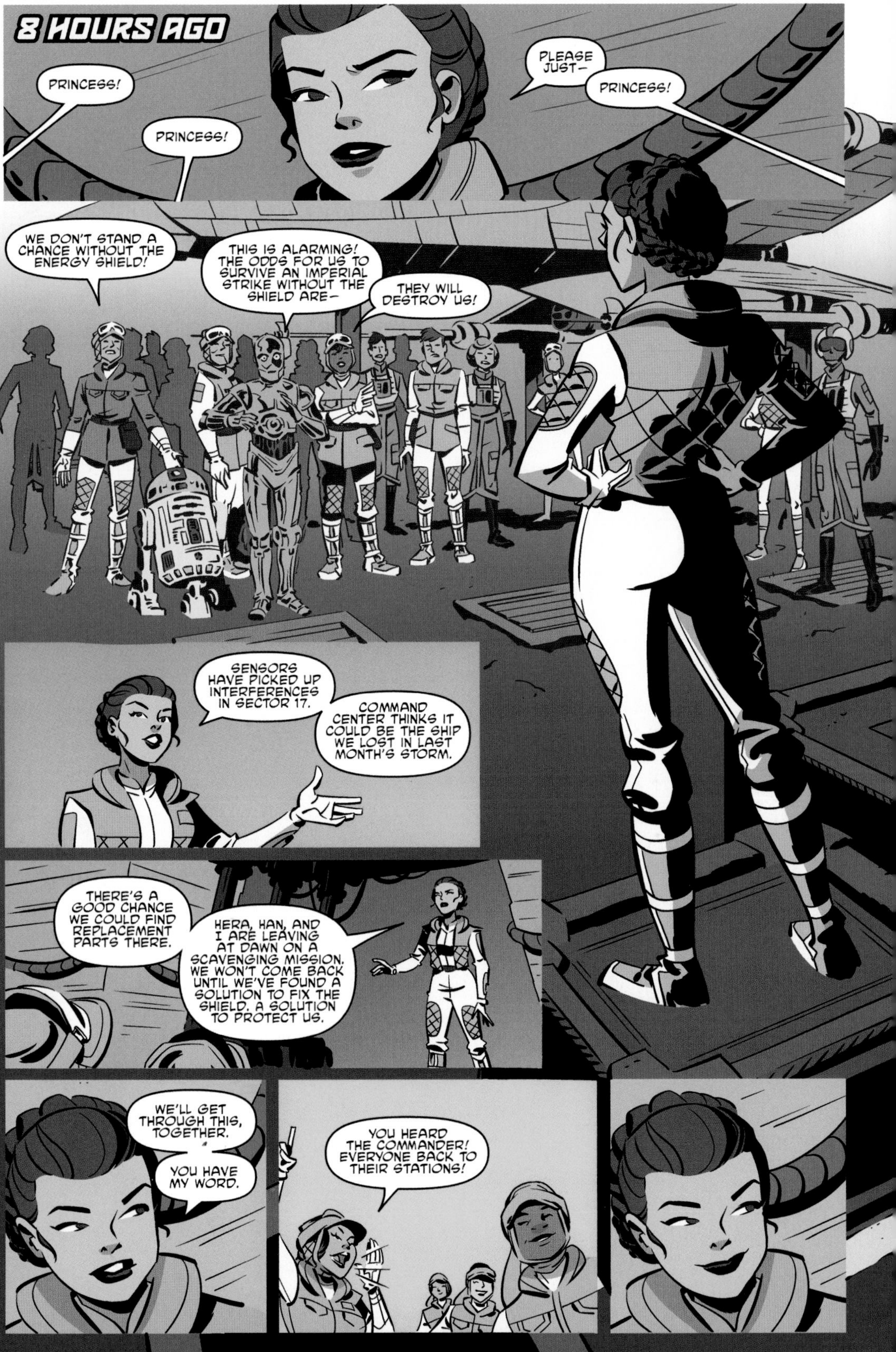
8 HOURS AGO
PRINCESS!
PRINCESS!
PLEASE JUST—
PRINCESS!
WE DON'T STAND A CHANCE WITHOUT THE ENERGY SHIELD!
THIS IS ALARMING! THE ODDS FOR US TO SURVIVE AN IMPERIAL STRIKE WITHOUT THE SHIELD ARE—
THEY WILL DESTROY US!
SENSORS HAVE PICKED UP INTERFERENCES IN SECTOR 17.
COMMAND CENTER THINKS IT COULD BE THE SHIP WE LOST IN LAST MONTH'S STORM.
THERE'S A GOOD CHANCE WE COULD FIND REPLACEMENT PARTS THERE.
HERA, HAN, AND I ARE LEAVING AT DAWN ON A SCAVENGING MISSION. WE WON'T COME BACK UNTIL WE'VE FOUND A SOLUTION TO FIX THE SHIELD. A SOLUTION TO PROTECT US.
WE'LL GET THROUGH THIS, TOGETHER.
YOU HAVE MY WORD.
YOU HEARD THE COMMANDER! EVERYONE BACK TO THEIR STATIONS!

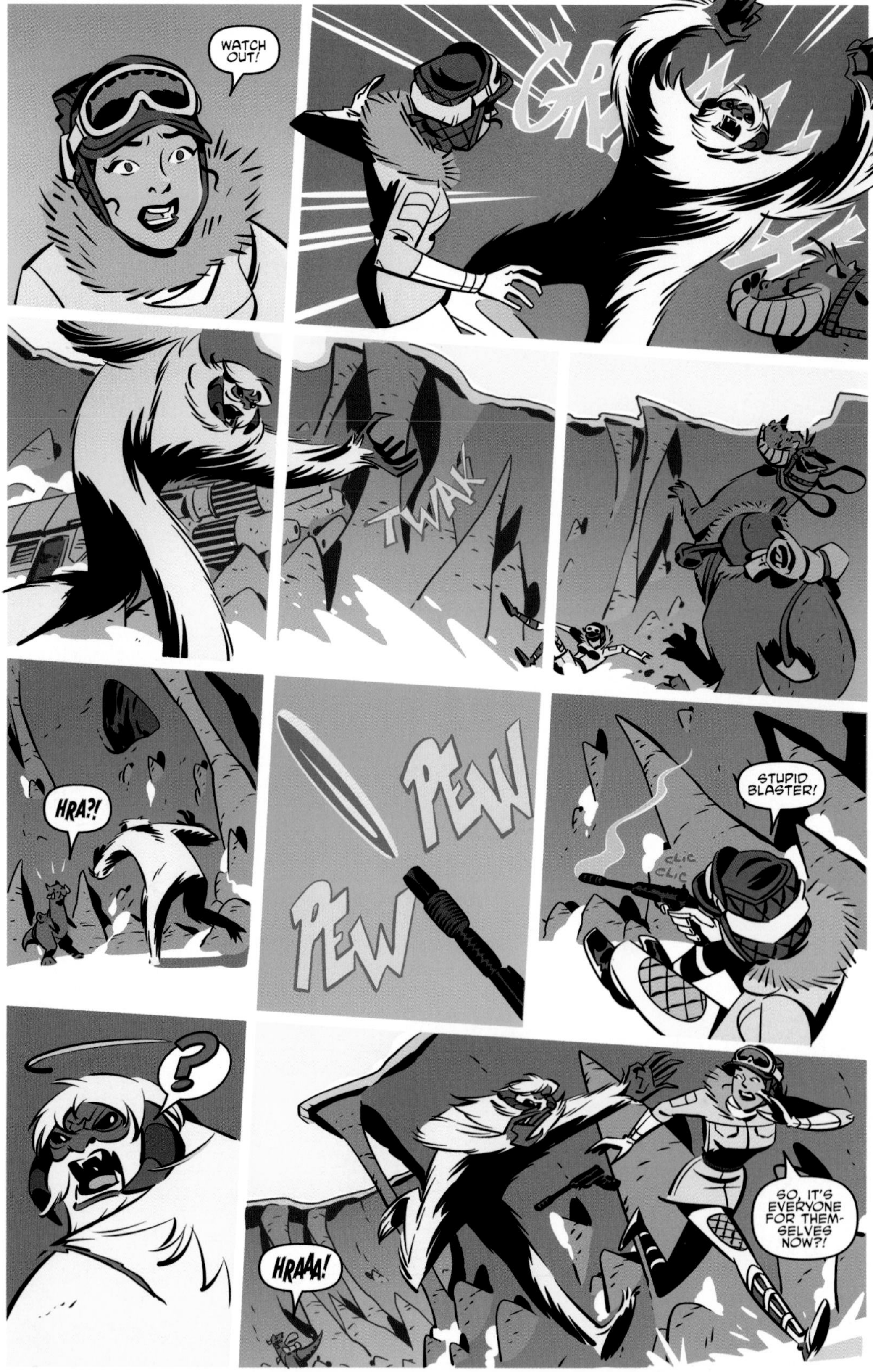

WATCH OUT!
GRAAAAH
TWAK
HRA?!
PEW
PEW
STUPID BLASTER!
CLIC CLIC
?
HRAAA!
SO, IT'S EVERYONE FOR THEM-SELVES NOW?!

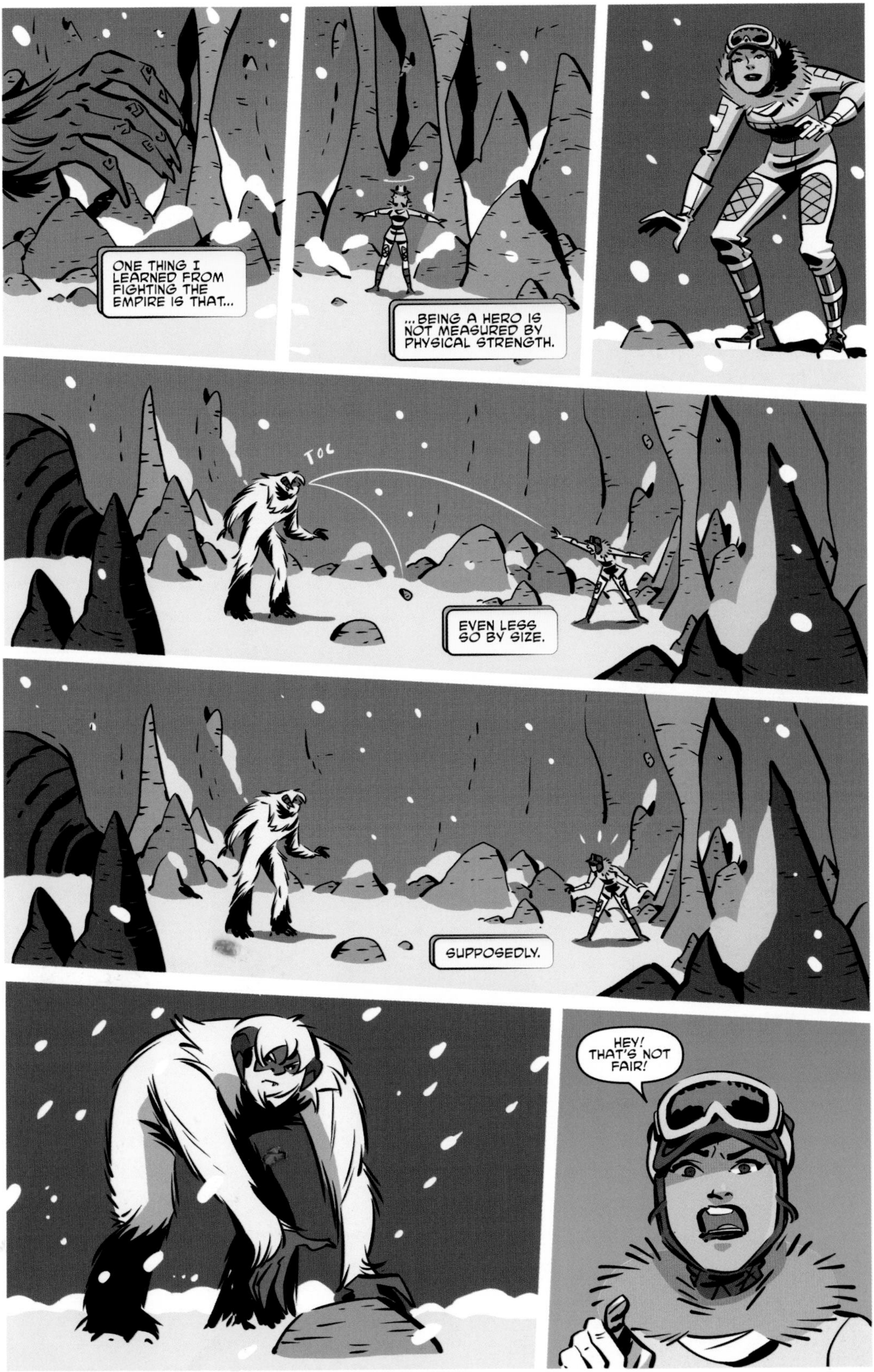
ONE THING I LEARNED FROM FIGHTING THE EMPIRE IS THAT...
...BEING A HERO IS NOT MEASURED BY PHYSICAL STRENGTH.
TOC
EVEN LESS SO BY SIZE.
SUPPOSEDLY.
HEY! THAT'S NOT FAIR!

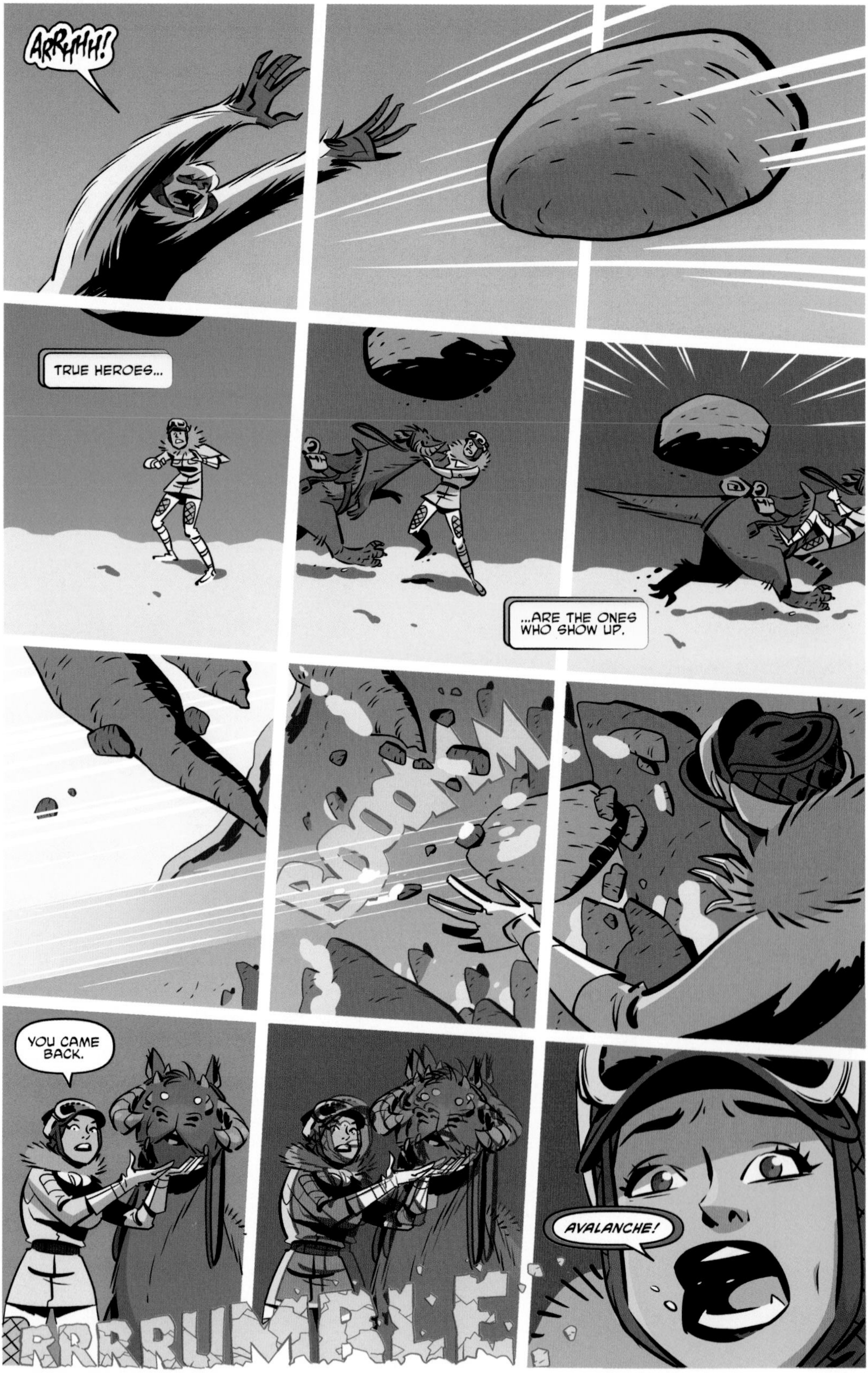

ARRHHH!
TRUE HEROES...
...ARE THE ONES WHO SHOW UP.
BOOM
YOU CAME BACK.
AVALANCHE!
RRRRUMBLE

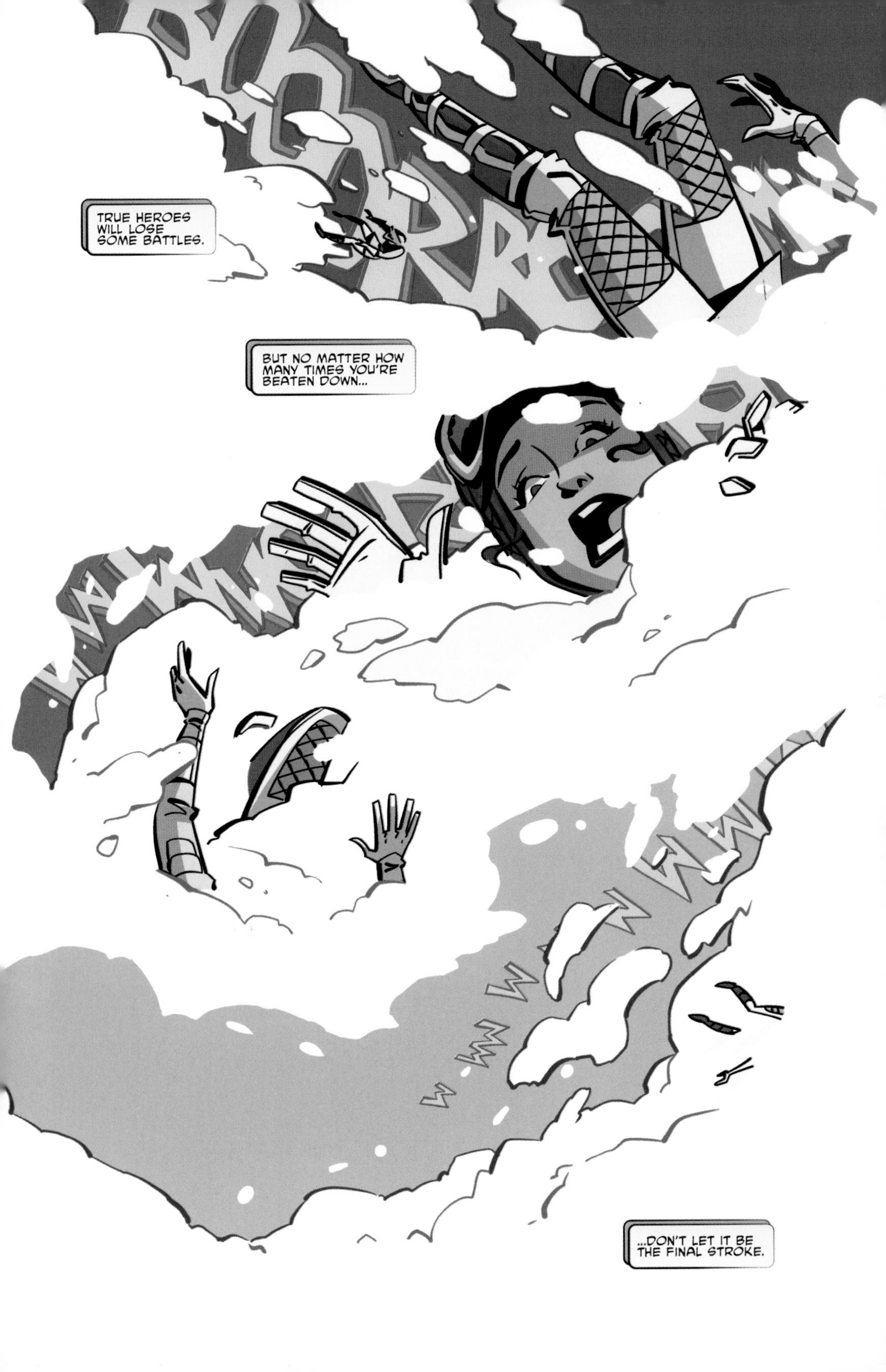
TRUE HEROES WILL LOSE SOME BATTLES.
BUT NO MATTER HOW MANY TIMES YOU'RE BEATEN DOWN...
...DON'T LET IT BE THE FINAL STROKE.

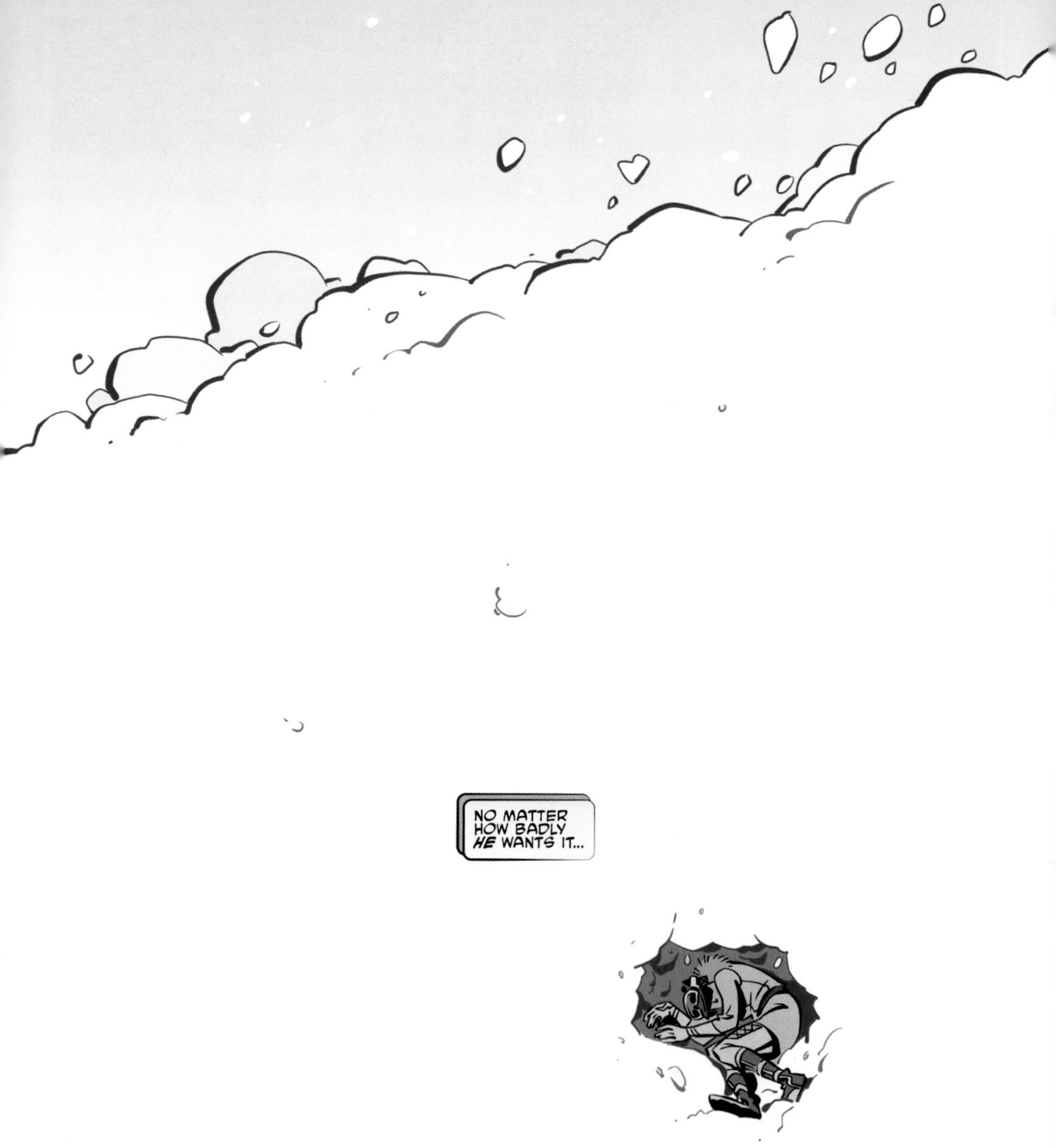
NO MATTER HOW BADLY *HE* WANTS IT...

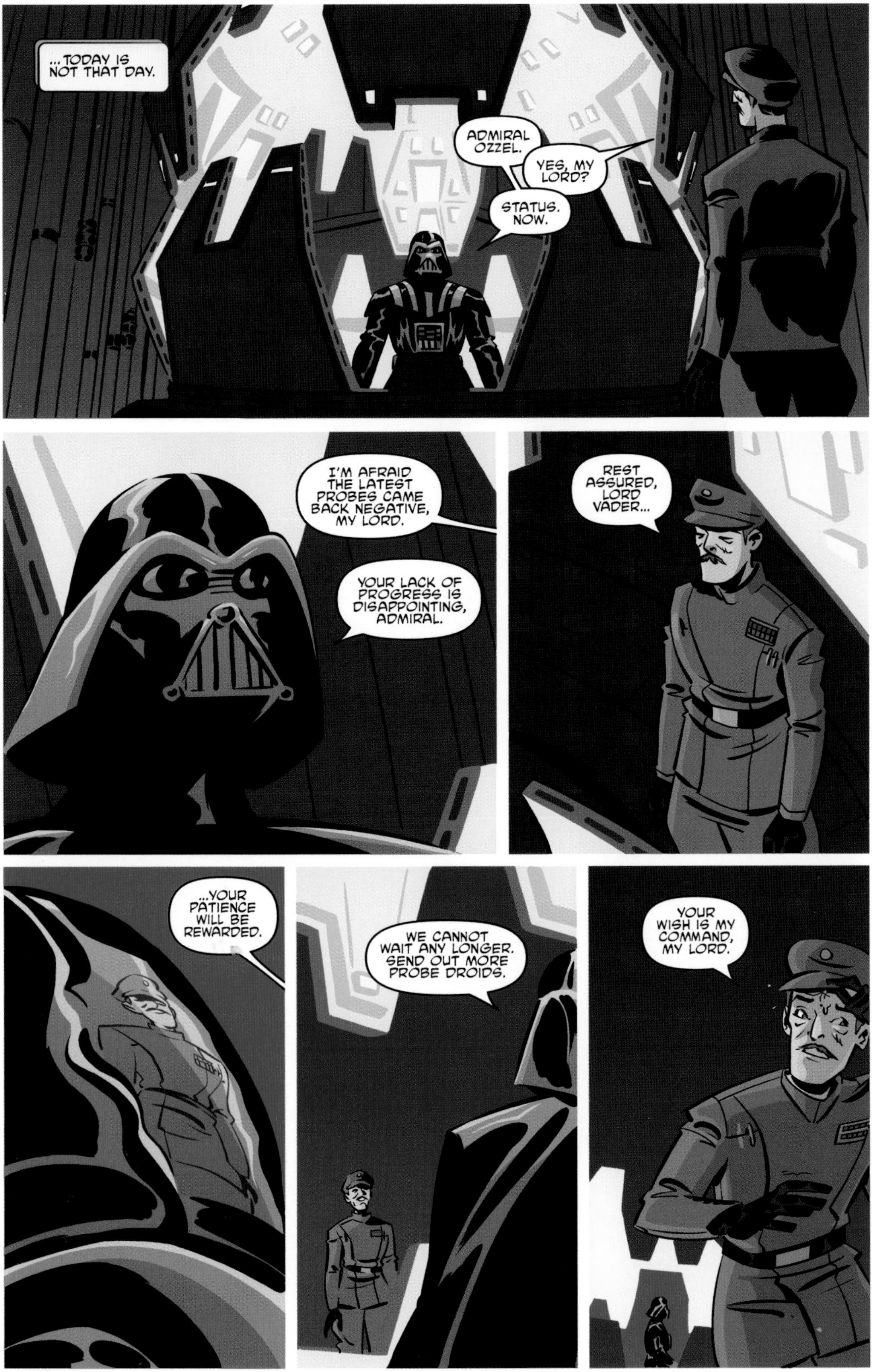
...TODAY IS NOT THAT DAY.
ADMIRAL OZZEL.
YES, MY LORD?
STATUS. NOW.
I'M AFRAID THE LATEST PROBES CAME BACK NEGATIVE, MY LORD.
YOUR LACK OF PROGRESS IS DISAPPOINTING, ADMIRAL.
REST ASSURED, LORD VADER...
...YOUR PATIENCE WILL BE REWARDED.
WE CANNOT WAIT ANY LONGER. SEND OUT MORE PROBE DROIDS.
YOUR WISH IS MY COMMAND, MY LORD.

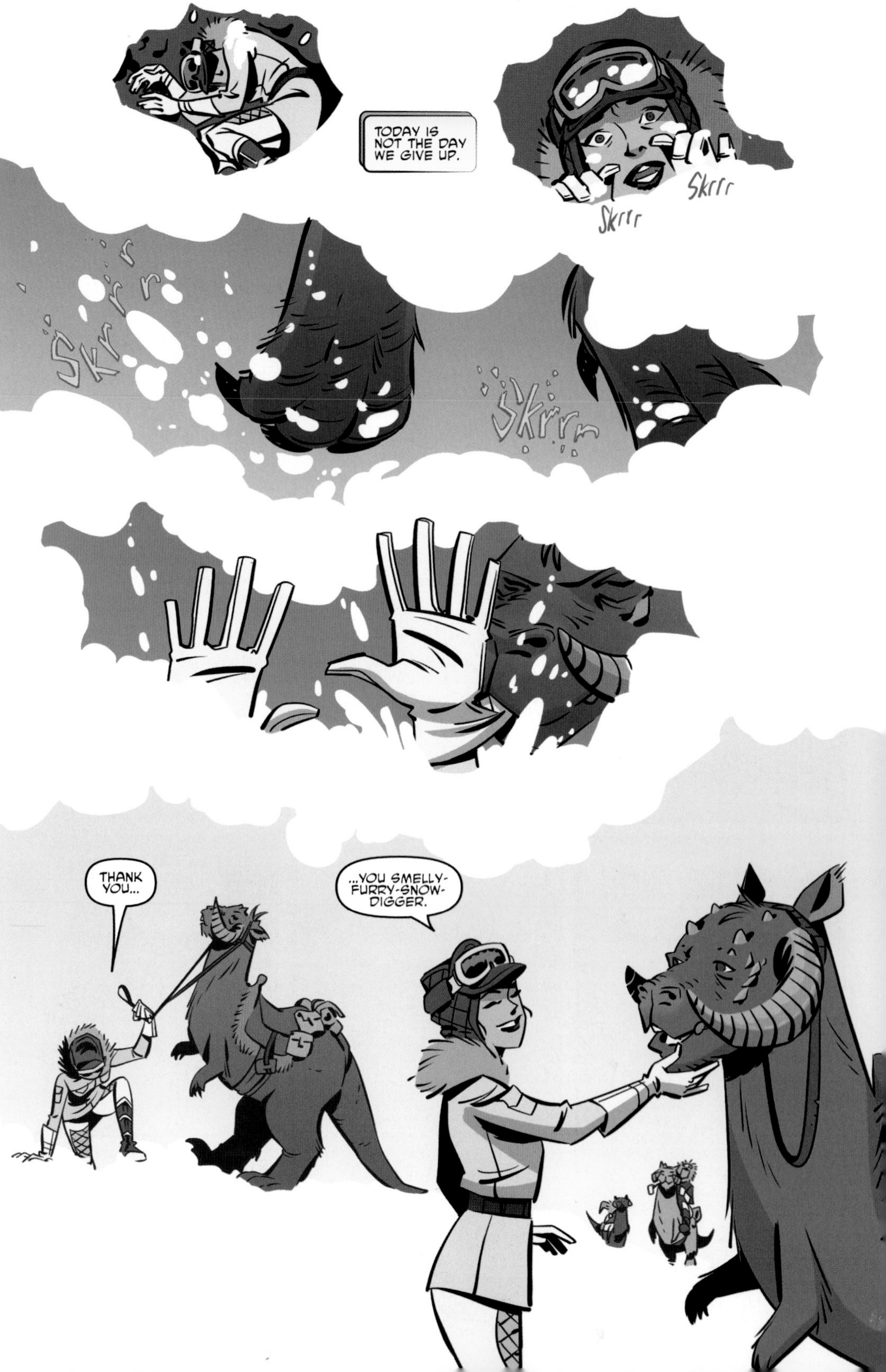

TODAY IS NOT THE DAY WE GIVE UP.
Skrrr
Skrrr
Skrrr
Skrrrn
THANK YOU...
...YOU SMELLY-FURRY-SNOW-DIGGER.

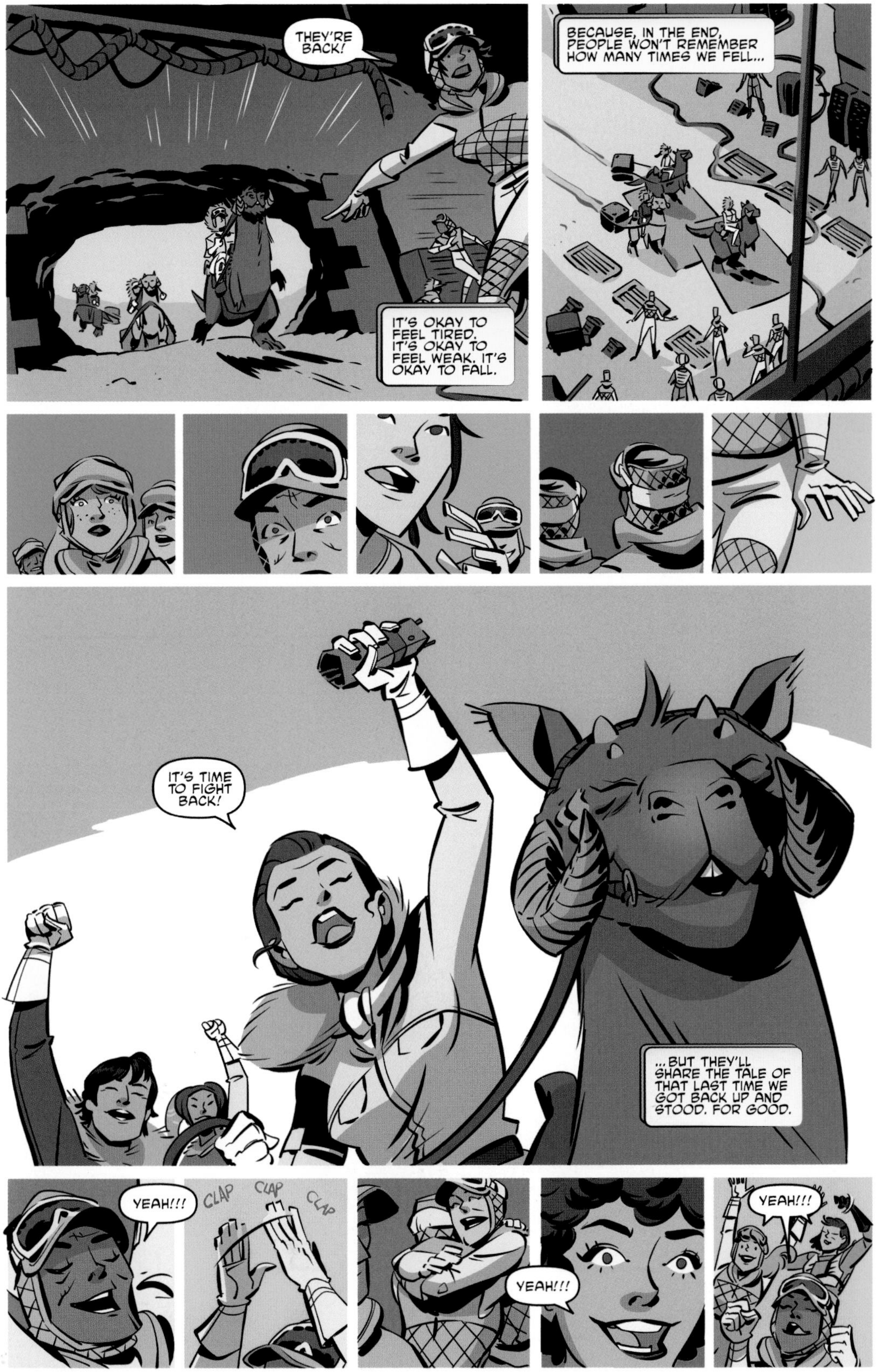
THEY'RE BACK!
IT'S OKAY TO FEEL TIRED. IT'S OKAY TO FEEL WEAK. IT'S OKAY TO FALL.
BECAUSE, IN THE END, PEOPLE WON'T REMEMBER HOW MANY TIMES WE FELL...
IT'S TIME TO FIGHT BACK!
...BUT THEY'LL SHARE THE TALE OF THAT LAST TIME WE GOT BACK UP AND STOOD. FOR GOOD.
YEAH!!!
CLAP CLAP CLAP
YEAH!!!
YEAH!!!

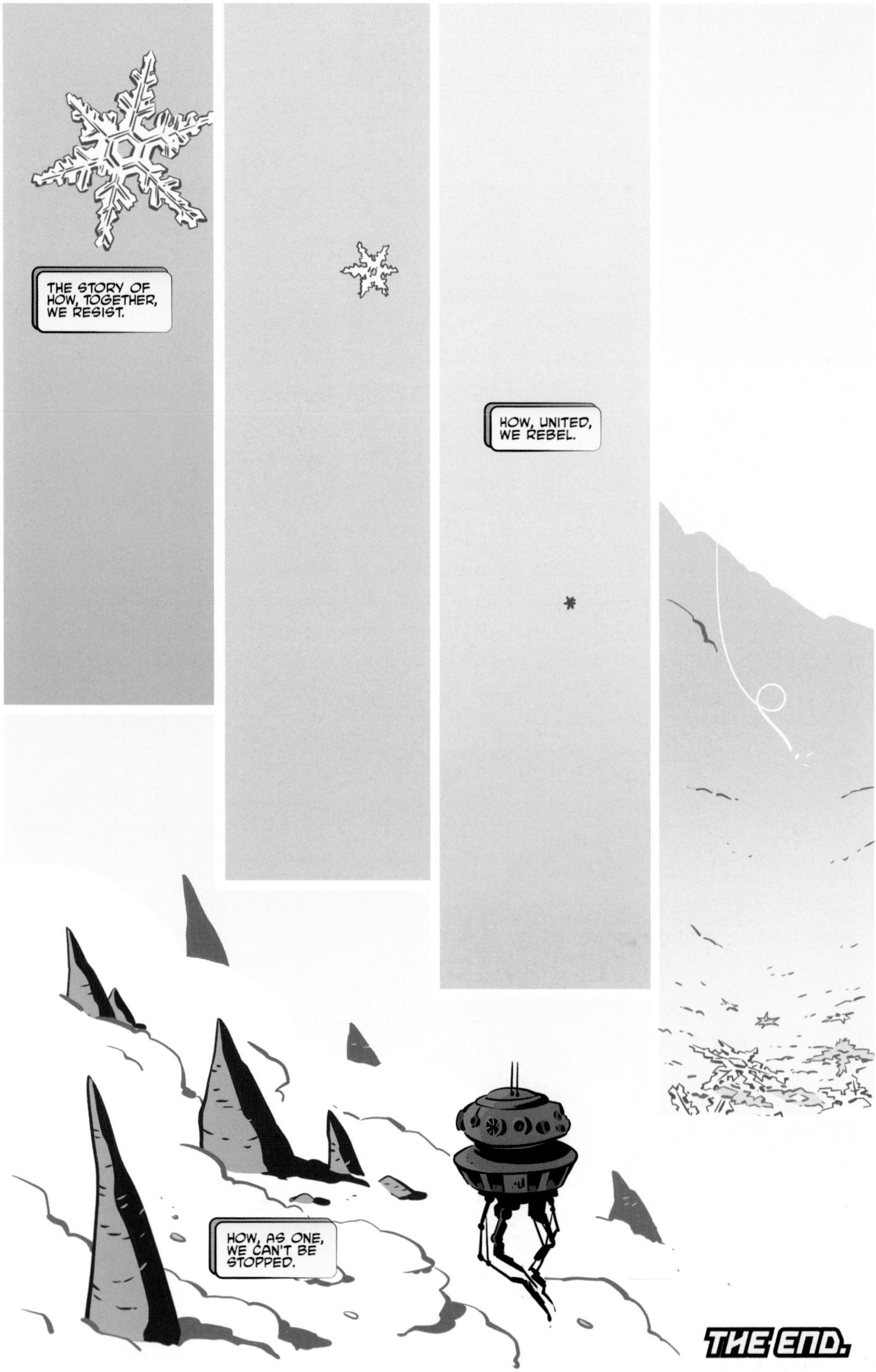
THE STORY OF HOW, TOGETHER, WE RESIST.
HOW, UNITED, WE REBEL.
HOW, AS ONE, WE CAN'T BE STOPPED.
THE END.

Art by Elsa Charretier, Colors by Matt Wilson

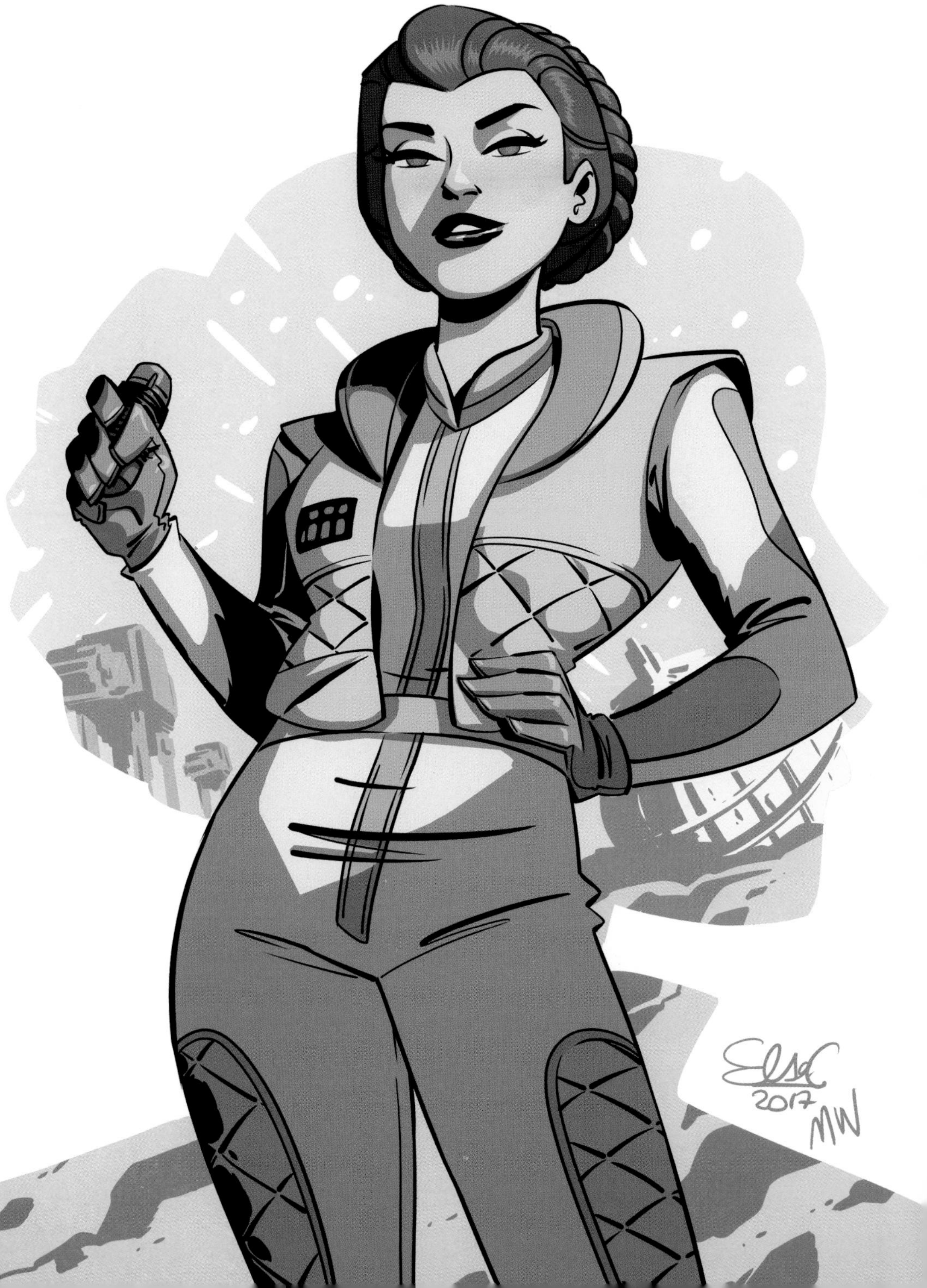
Elsa
2017
MW

Rey

Art by Arianna Florean

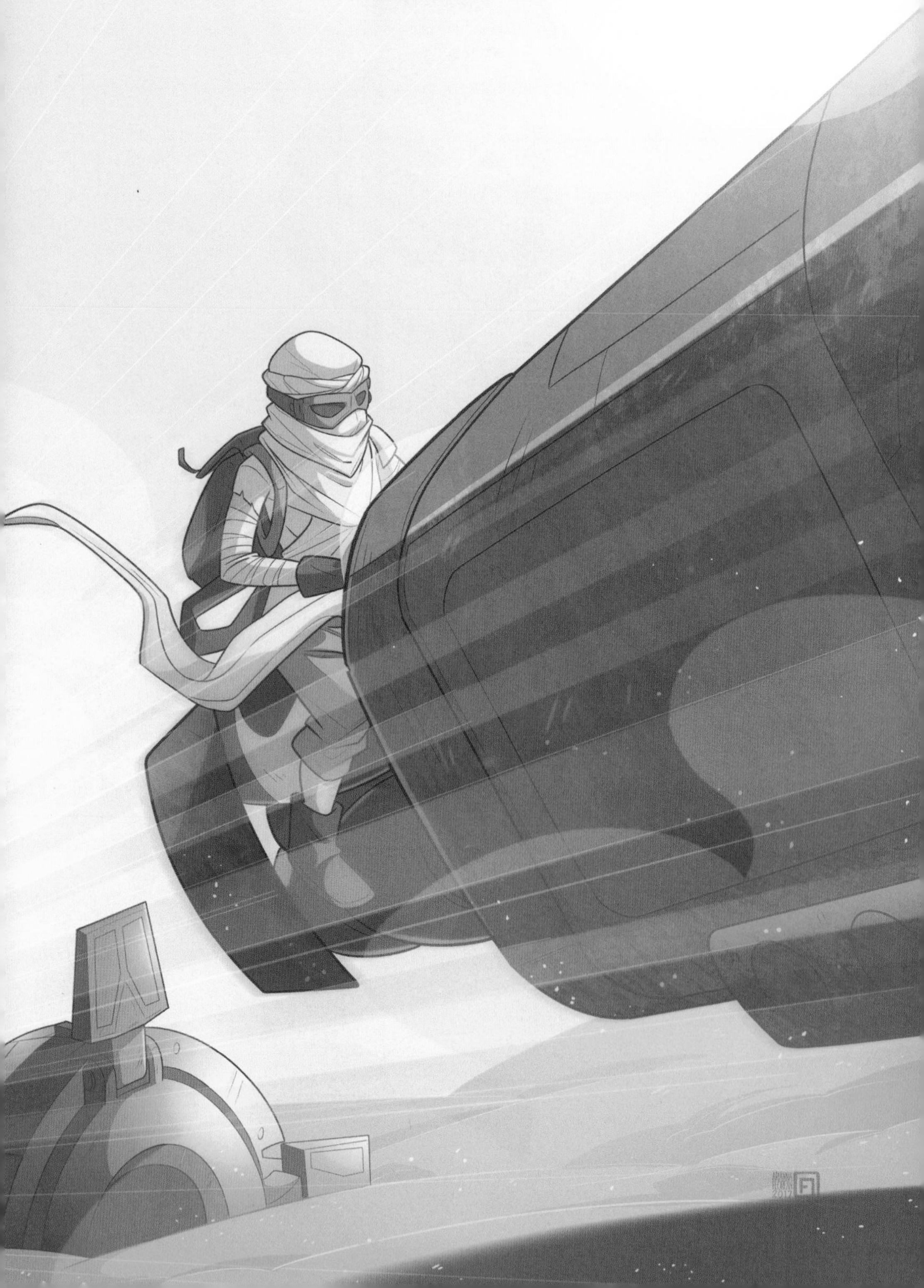

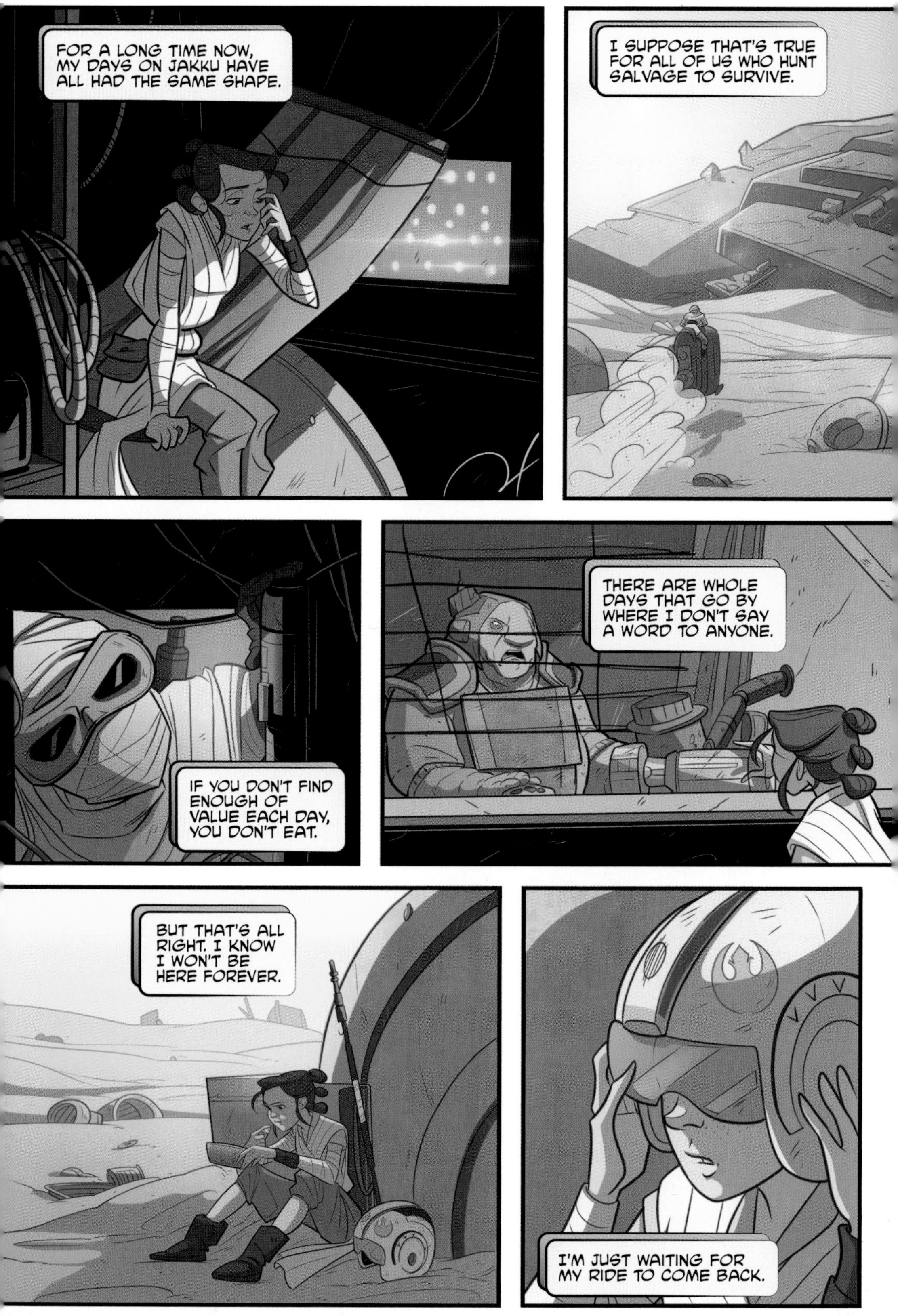
FOR A LONG TIME NOW, MY DAYS ON JAKKU HAVE ALL HAD THE SAME SHAPE.
I SUPPOSE THAT'S TRUE FOR ALL OF US WHO HUNT SALVAGE TO SURVIVE.
IF YOU DON'T FIND ENOUGH OF VALUE EACH DAY, YOU DON'T EAT.
THERE ARE WHOLE DAYS THAT GO BY WHERE I DON'T SAY A WORD TO ANYONE.
BUT THAT'S ALL RIGHT. I KNOW I WON'T BE HERE FOREVER.
I'M JUST WAITING FOR MY RIDE TO COME BACK.

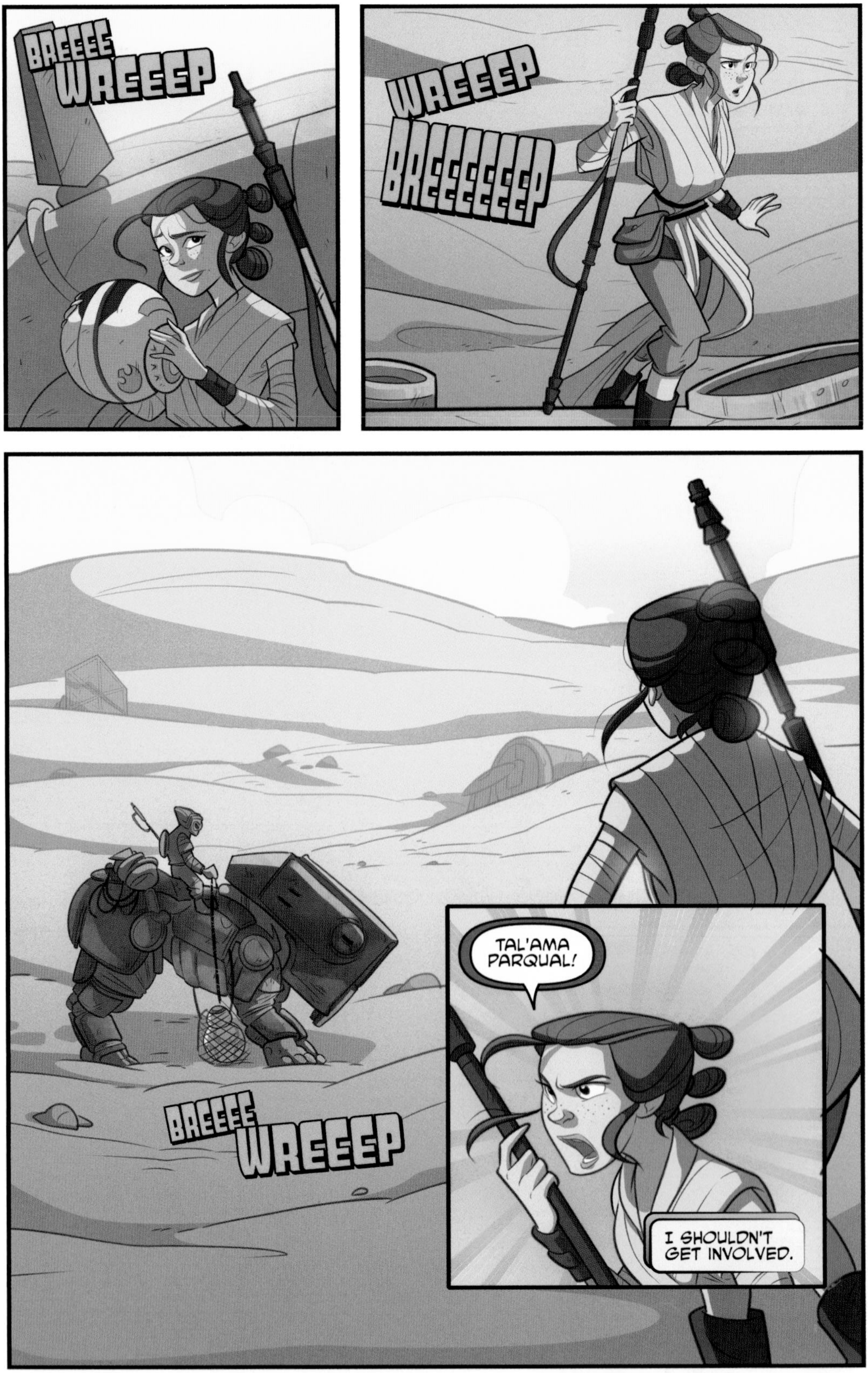
BREEEE
WREEEP
WREEEP
BREEEEEEP
TAL'AMA PARQUAL!
BREEEE
WREEEP
I SHOULDN'T GET INVOLVED.

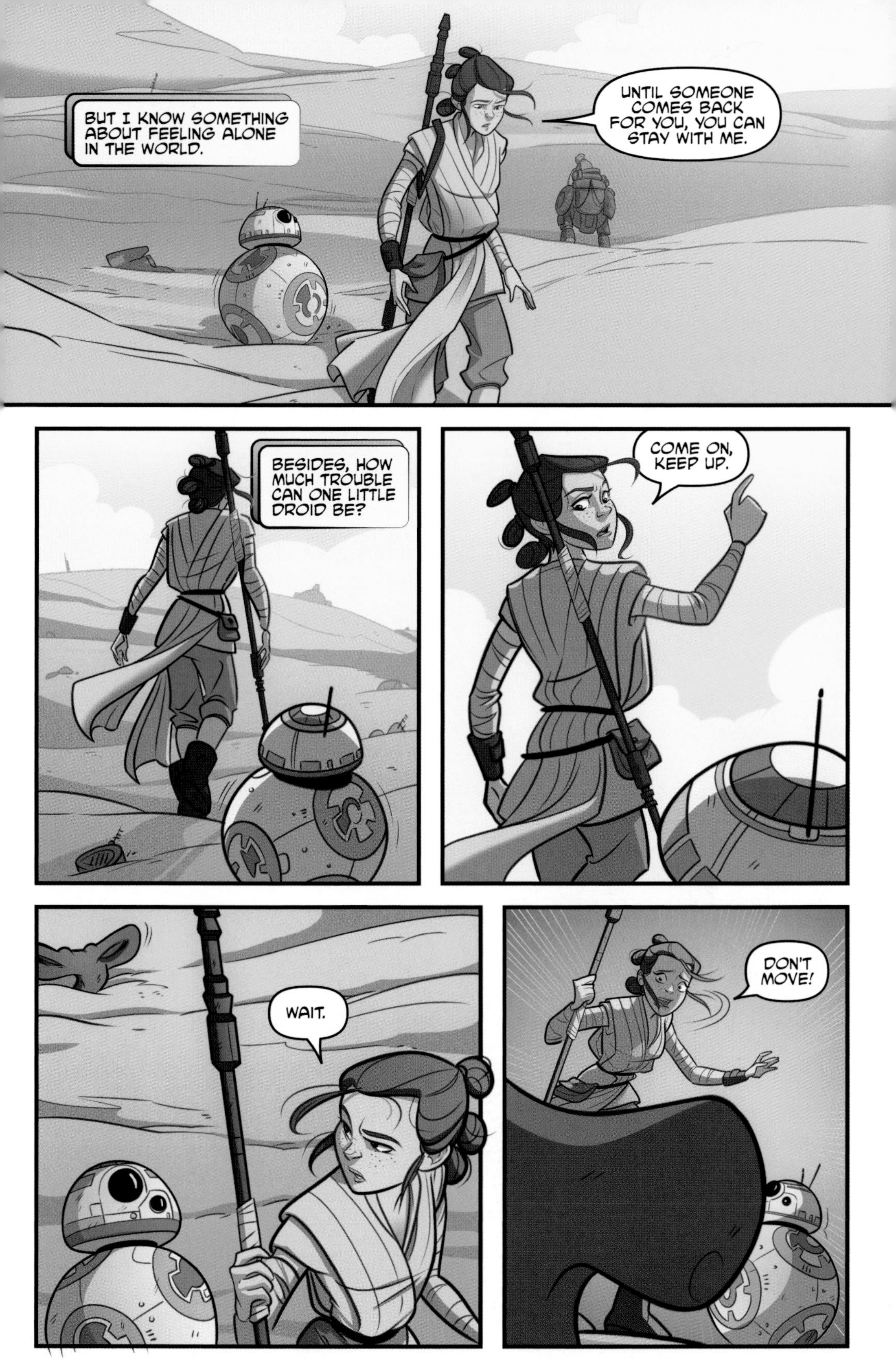
BUT I KNOW SOMETHING ABOUT FEELING ALONE IN THE WORLD.
UNTIL SOMEONE COMES BACK FOR YOU, YOU CAN STAY WITH ME.
BESIDES, HOW MUCH TROUBLE CAN ONE LITTLE DROID BE?
COME ON, KEEP UP.
WAIT.
DON'T MOVE!

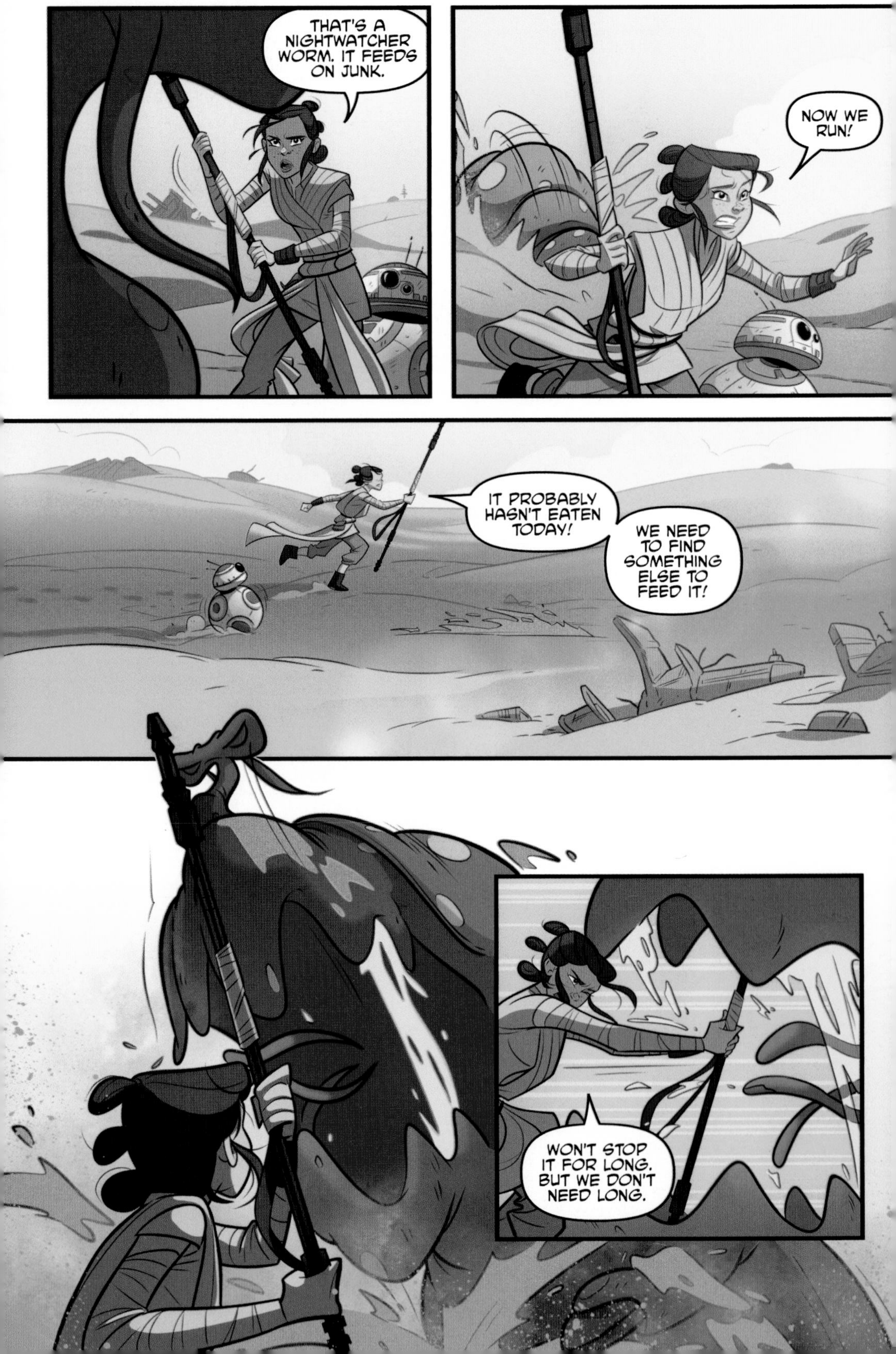
THAT'S A NIGHTWATCHER WORM. IT FEEDS ON JUNK.
NOW WE RUN!
IT PROBABLY HASN'T EATEN TODAY!
WE NEED TO FIND SOMETHING ELSE TO FEED IT!
WON'T STOP IT FOR LONG. BUT WE DON'T NEED LONG.

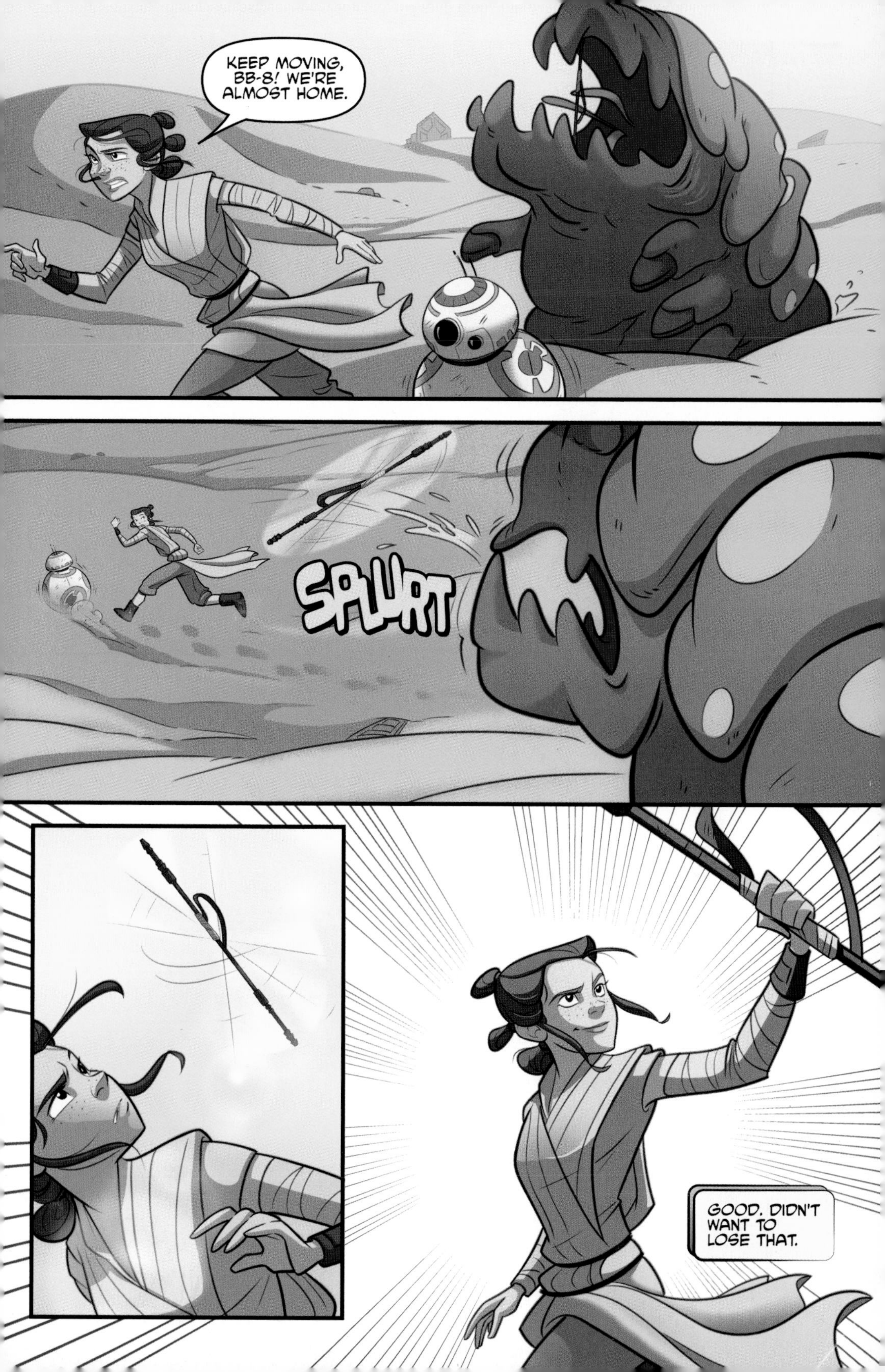
KEEP MOVING, BB-8! WE'RE ALMOST HOME.
SPLURT
GOOD. DIDN'T WANT TO LOSE THAT.

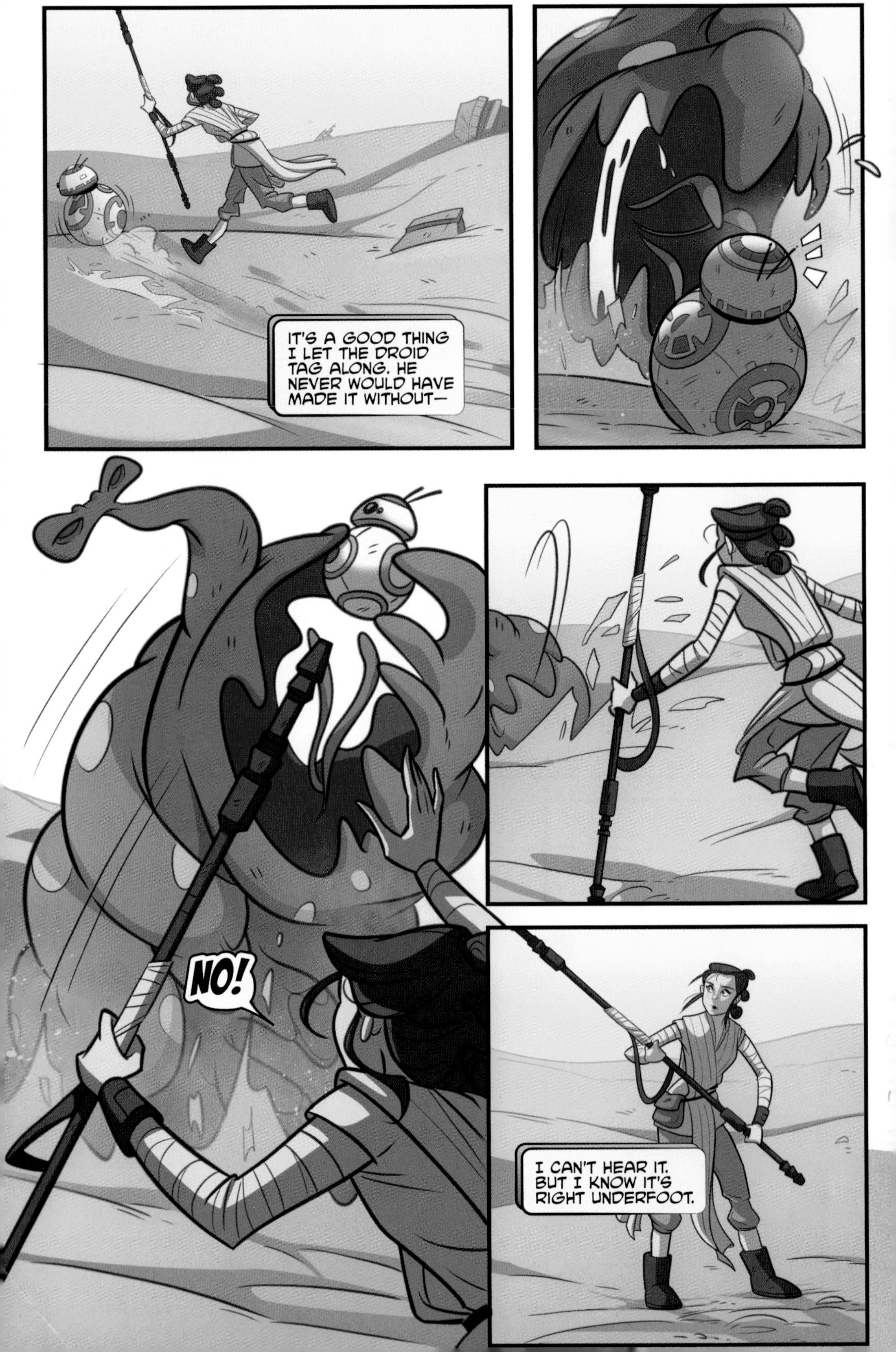
IT'S A GOOD THING I LET THE DROID TAG ALONG. HE NEVER WOULD HAVE MADE IT WITHOUT—
NO!
I CAN'T HEAR IT. BUT I KNOW IT'S RIGHT UNDERFOOT.

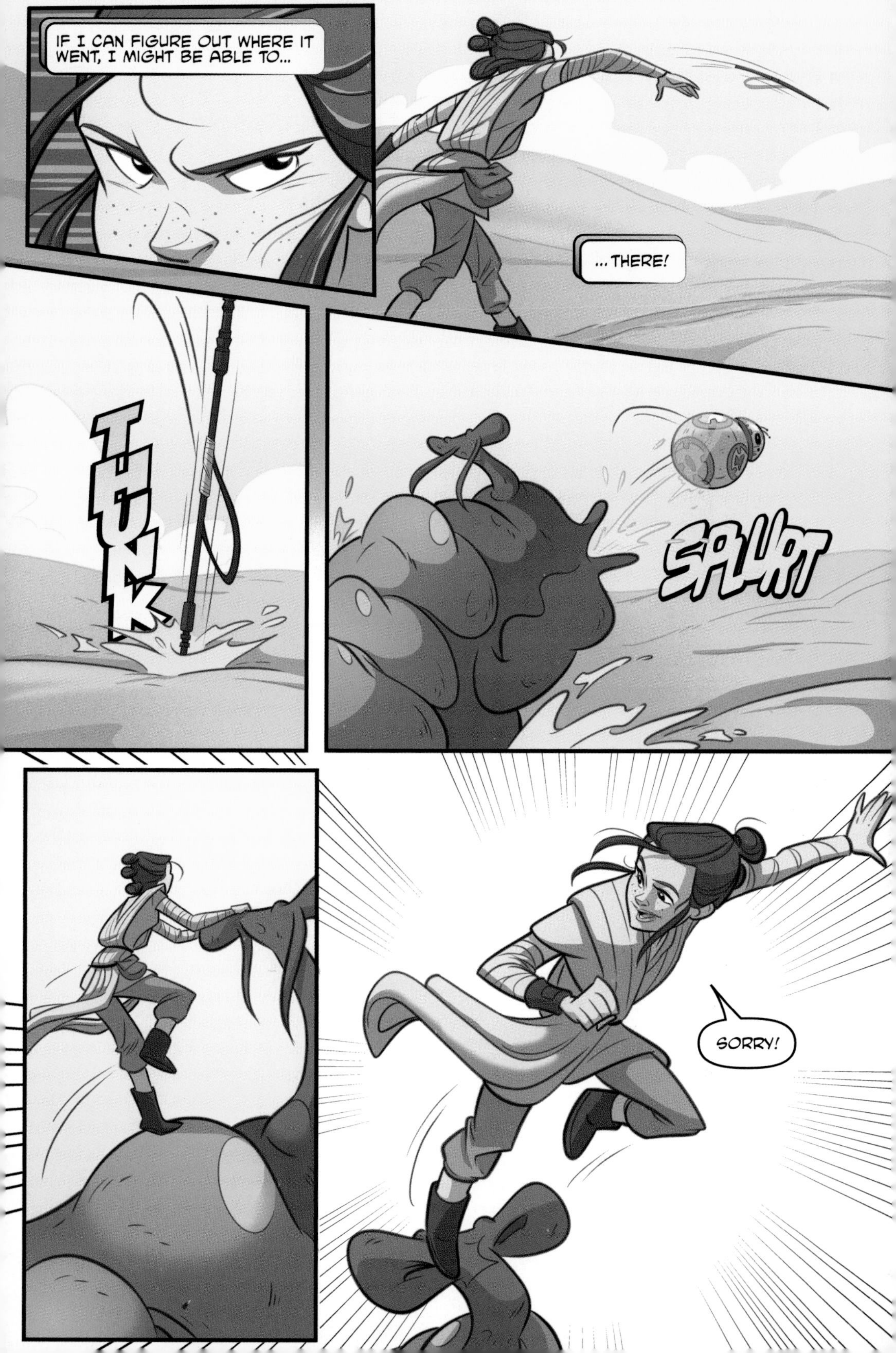
IF I CAN FIGURE OUT WHERE IT WENT, I MIGHT BE ABLE TO...
...THERE!
THUNK
SPLURT
SORRY!

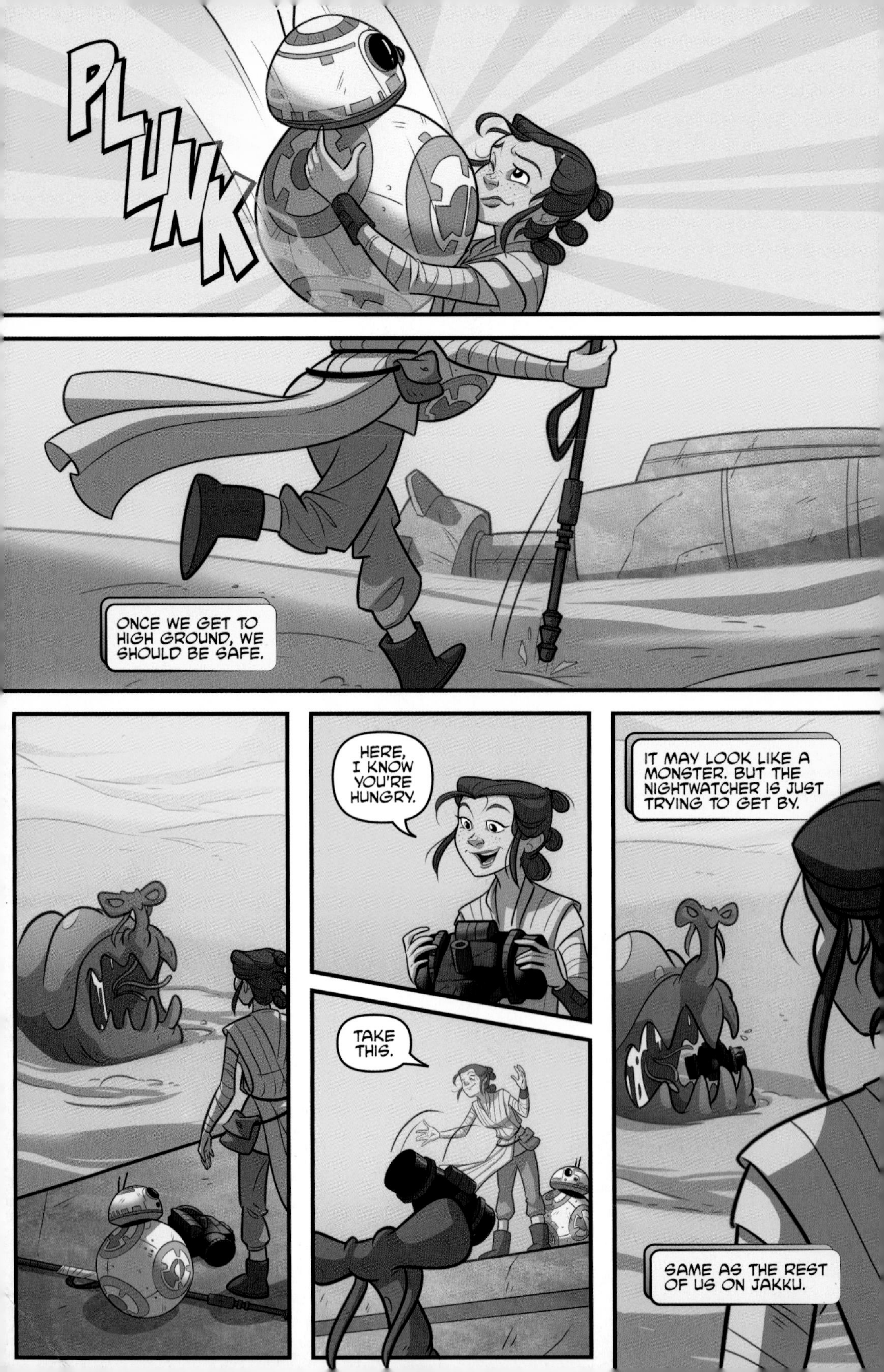
PLUNK
ONCE WE GET TO HIGH GROUND, WE SHOULD BE SAFE.
HERE, I KNOW YOU'RE HUNGRY.
TAKE THIS.
IT MAY LOOK LIKE A MONSTER. BUT THE NIGHTWATCHER IS JUST TRYING TO GET BY.
SAME AS THE REST OF US ON JAKKU.

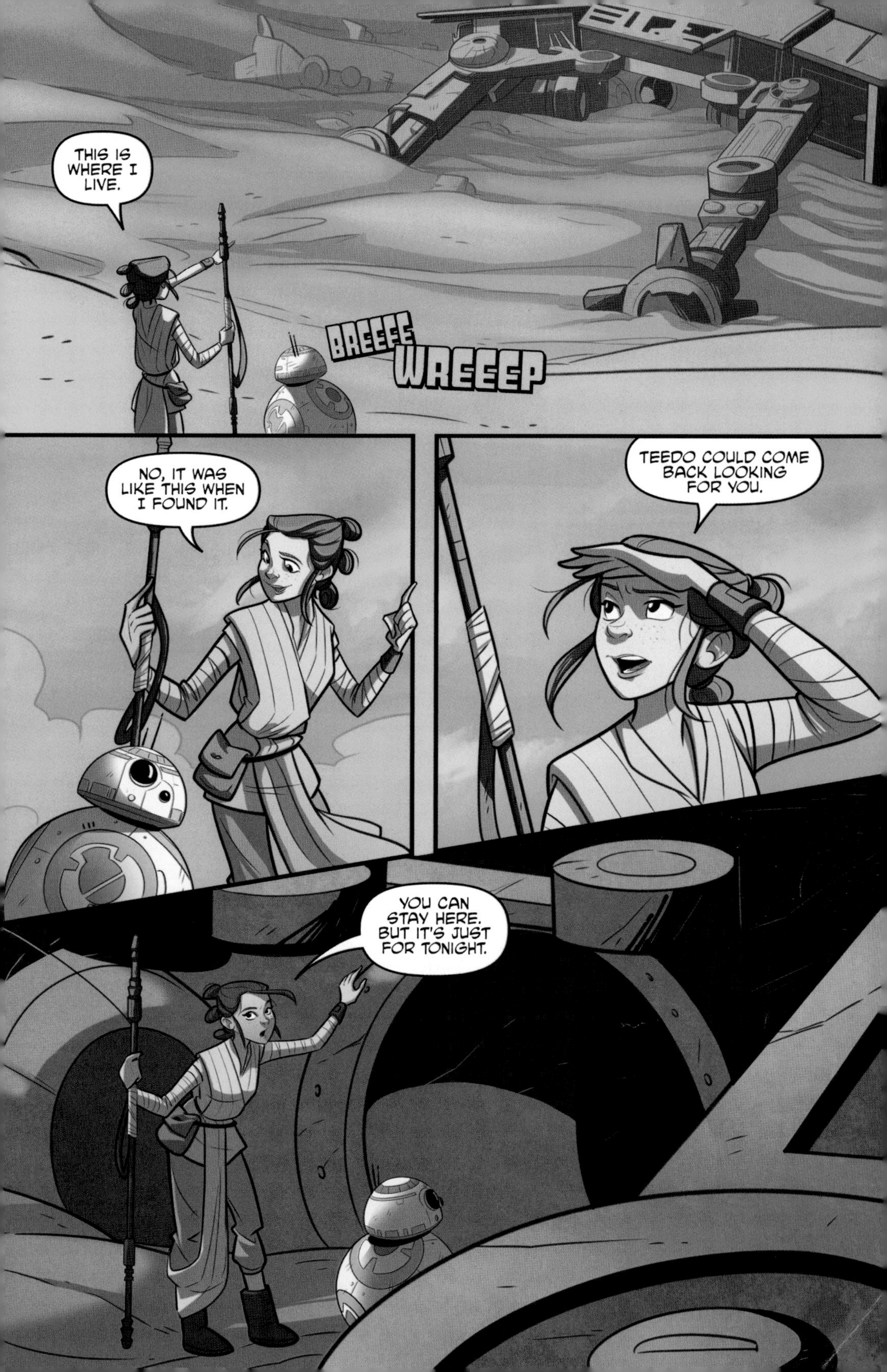
THIS IS WHERE I LIVE.
BREEEE
WREEEP
NO, IT WAS LIKE THIS WHEN I FOUND IT.
TEEDO COULD COME BACK LOOKING FOR YOU.
YOU CAN STAY HERE. BUT IT'S JUST FOR TONIGHT.

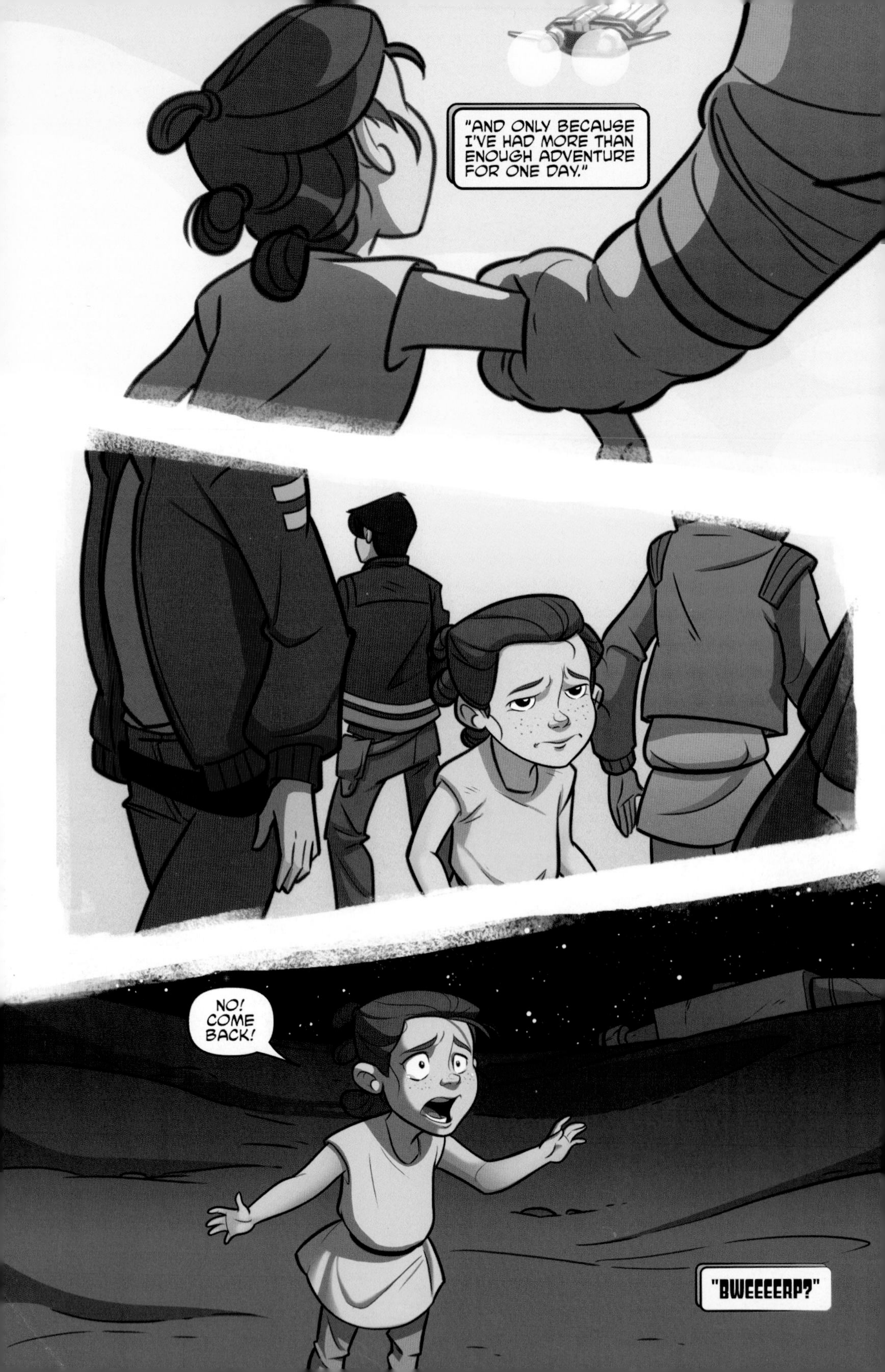
"AND ONLY BECAUSE I'VE HAD MORE THAN ENOUGH ADVENTURE FOR ONE DAY."
NO! COME BACK!
"BWEEEERP?"

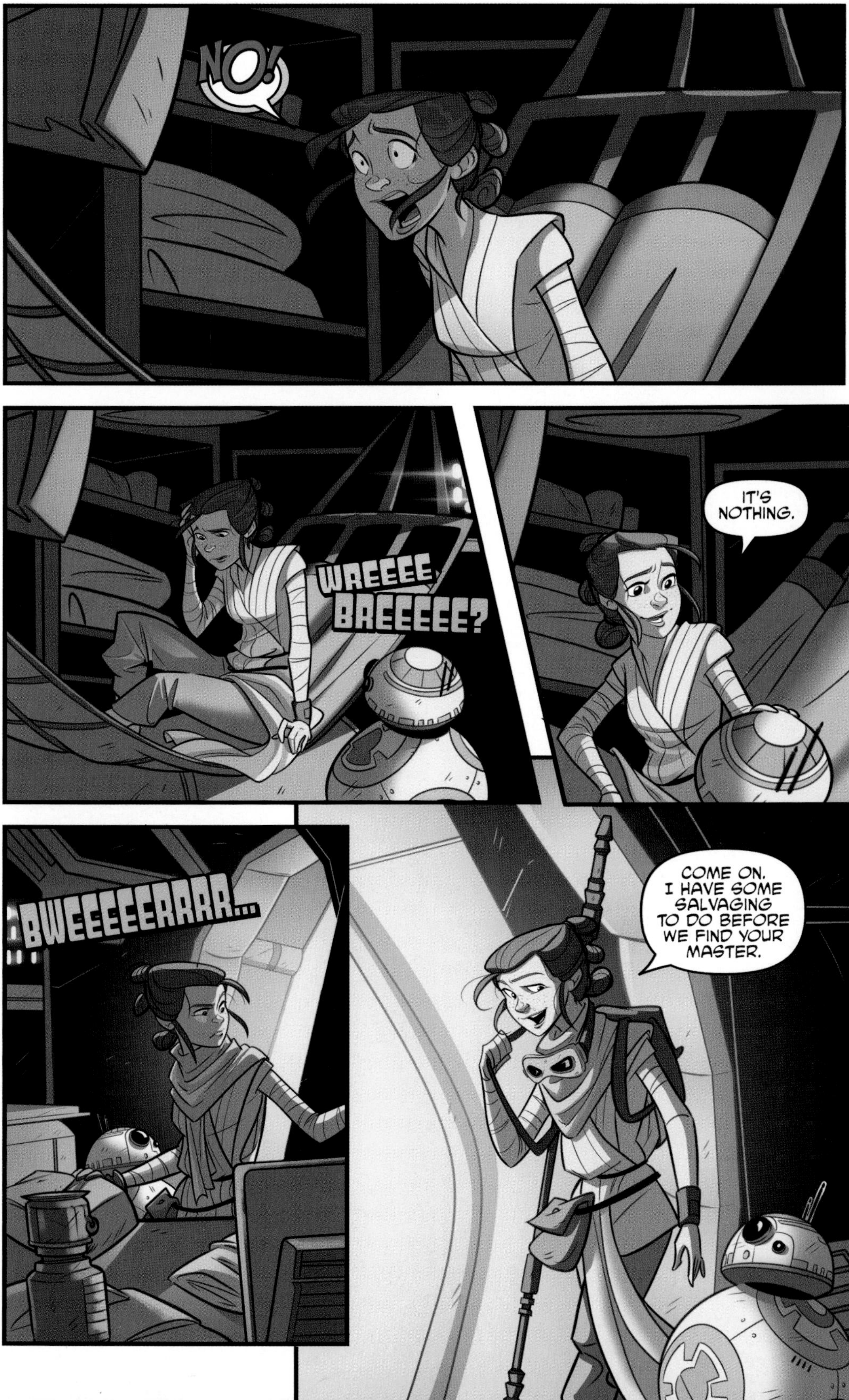
NO!
WREEEE BREEEEE?
IT'S NOTHING.
BWEEEEERRRR...
COME ON. I HAVE SOME SALVAGING TO DO BEFORE WE FIND YOUR MASTER.

IT'S STRANGE TO HAVE COMPANY.

BE CAREFUL. I DON'T THINK I'LL BE ABLE TO CATCH YOU IN HERE.

STRANGE, BUT RATHER NICE.

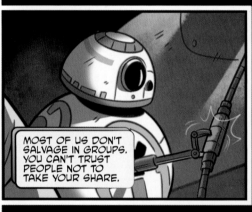

MOST OF US DON'T SALVAGE IN GROUPS. YOU CAN'T TRUST PEOPLE NOT TO TAKE YOUR SHARE.

HE JUST NEEDS TO FIND HIS WAY BACK.

THANK YOU.

BUT THIS LITTLE DROID DOESN'T NEED TO EAT.

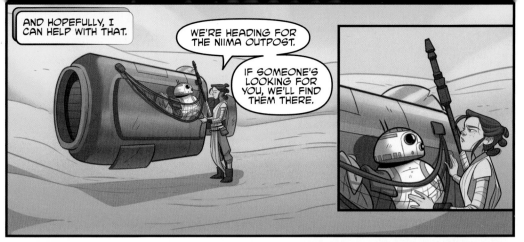

AND HOPEFULLY, I CAN HELP WITH THAT.

WE'RE HEADING FOR THE NIIMA OUTPOST.

IF SOMEONE'S LOOKING FOR YOU, WE'LL FIND THEM THERE.

TEEDO...

I WON'T LET HIM GET YOU.

BWREEEEP

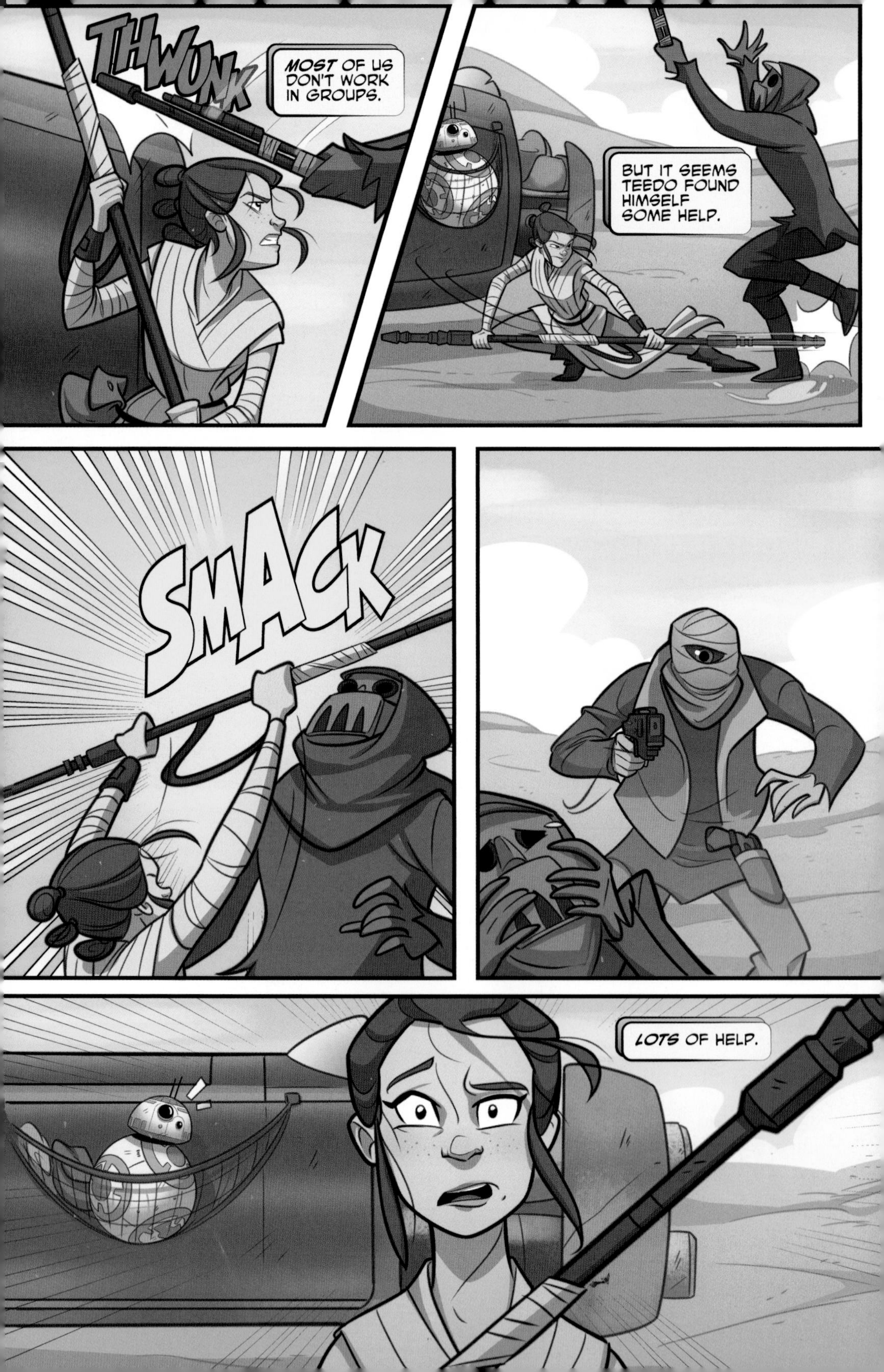
THWONK
MOST OF US DON'T WORK IN GROUPS.
BUT IT SEEMS TEEDO FOUND HIMSELF SOME HELP.
SMACK
LOTS OF HELP.

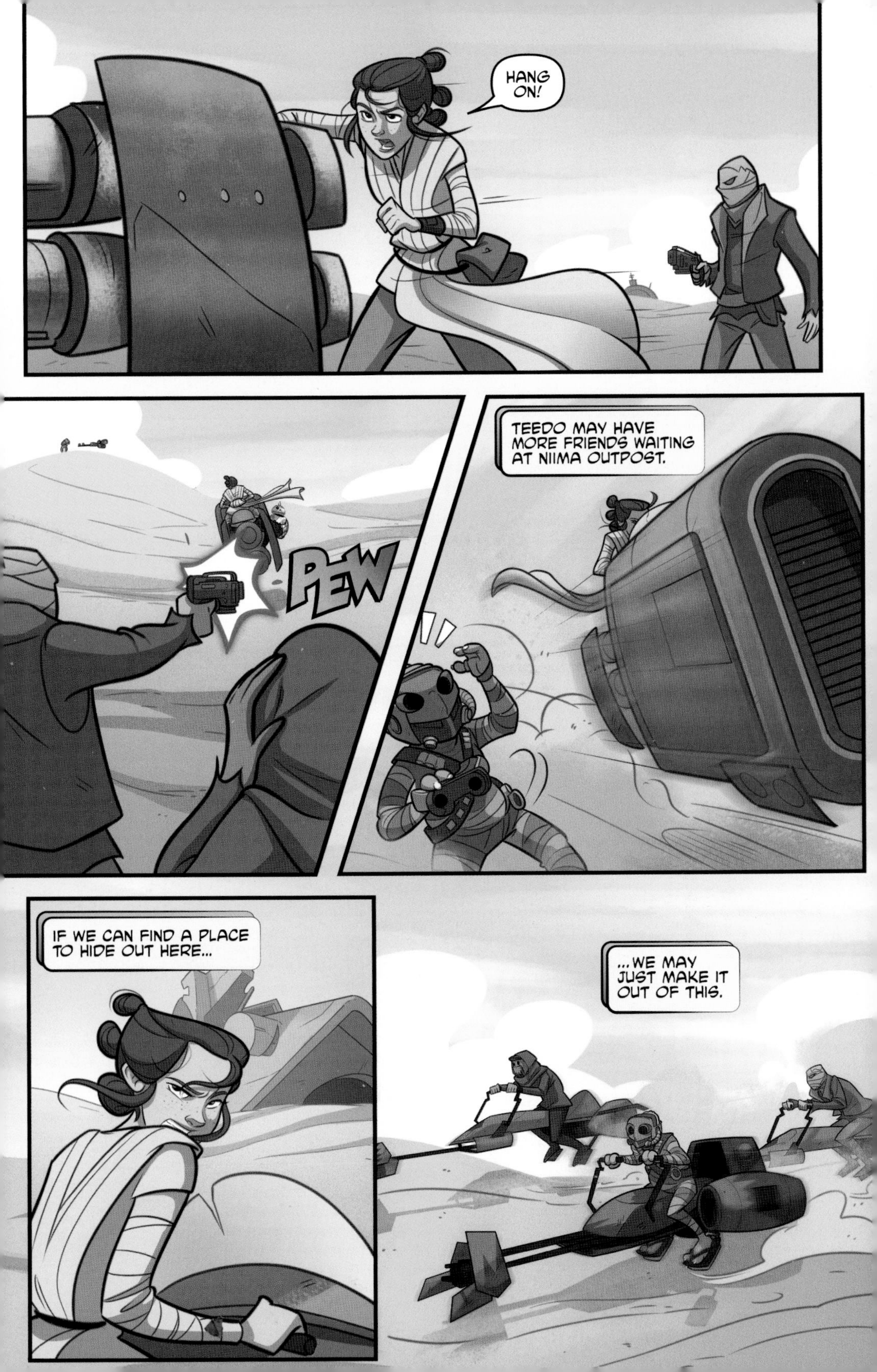
HANG ON!
PEW
TEEDO MAY HAVE MORE FRIENDS WAITING AT NIIMA OUTPOST.
IF WE CAN FIND A PLACE TO HIDE OUT HERE...
...WE MAY JUST MAKE IT OUT OF THIS.

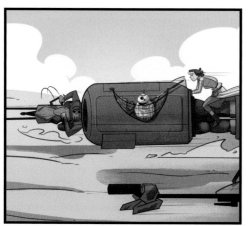

KLAAAANG

CRASH

TWO DOWN.

TURNS OUT, YOU'RE QUITE A POPULAR DROID.

WREEEP?

YES, YES! EXACTLY LIKE WITH THE NIGHTWATCHER WORM!

LET'S GO PAY HIM A VISIT...

CLEVER LITTLE DROID. HE MAY HAVE JUST SAVED US BOTH.

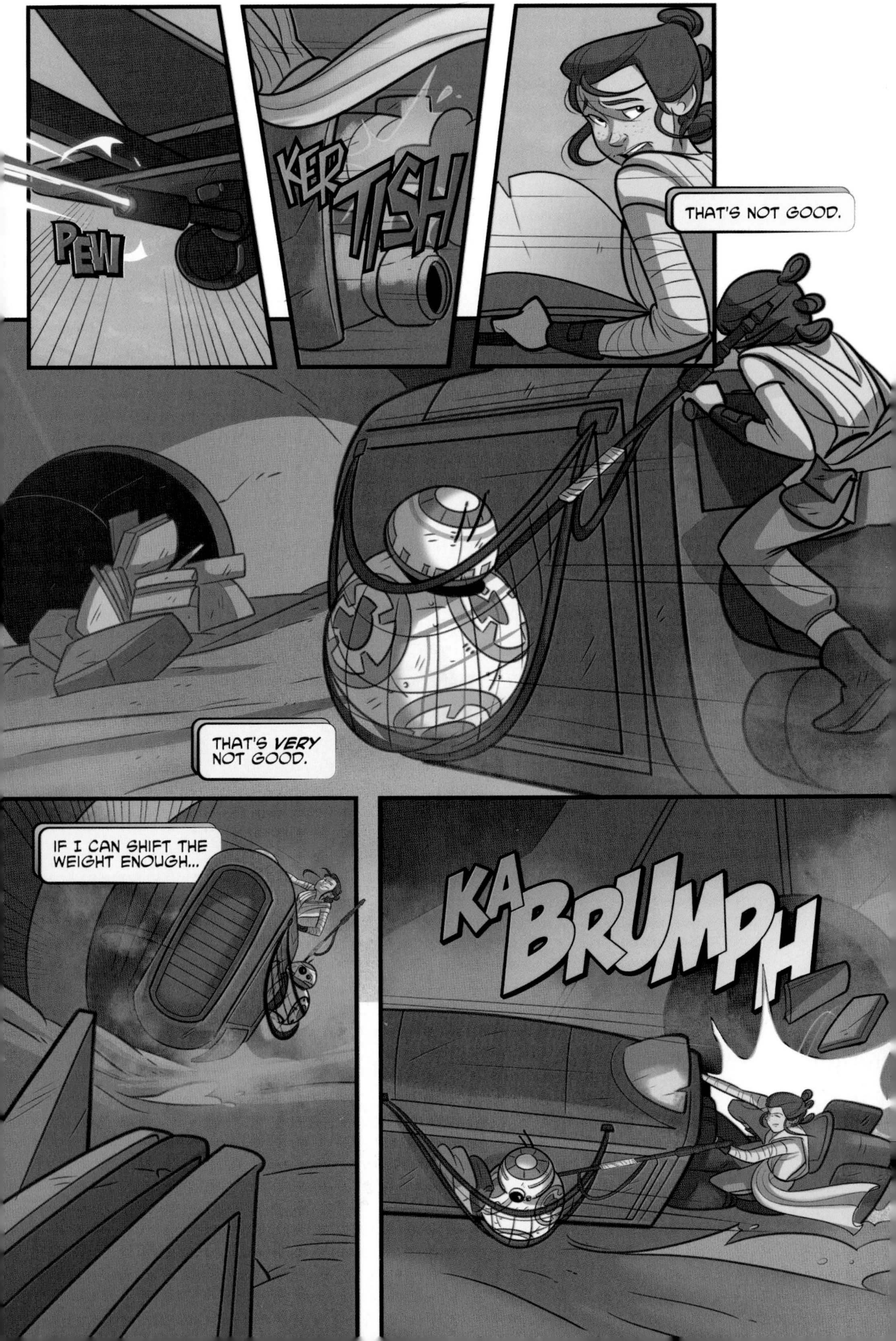
PEW
KER TISH
THAT'S NOT GOOD.
THAT'S VERY NOT GOOD.
IF I CAN SHIFT THE WEIGHT ENOUGH...
KA BRUMPH

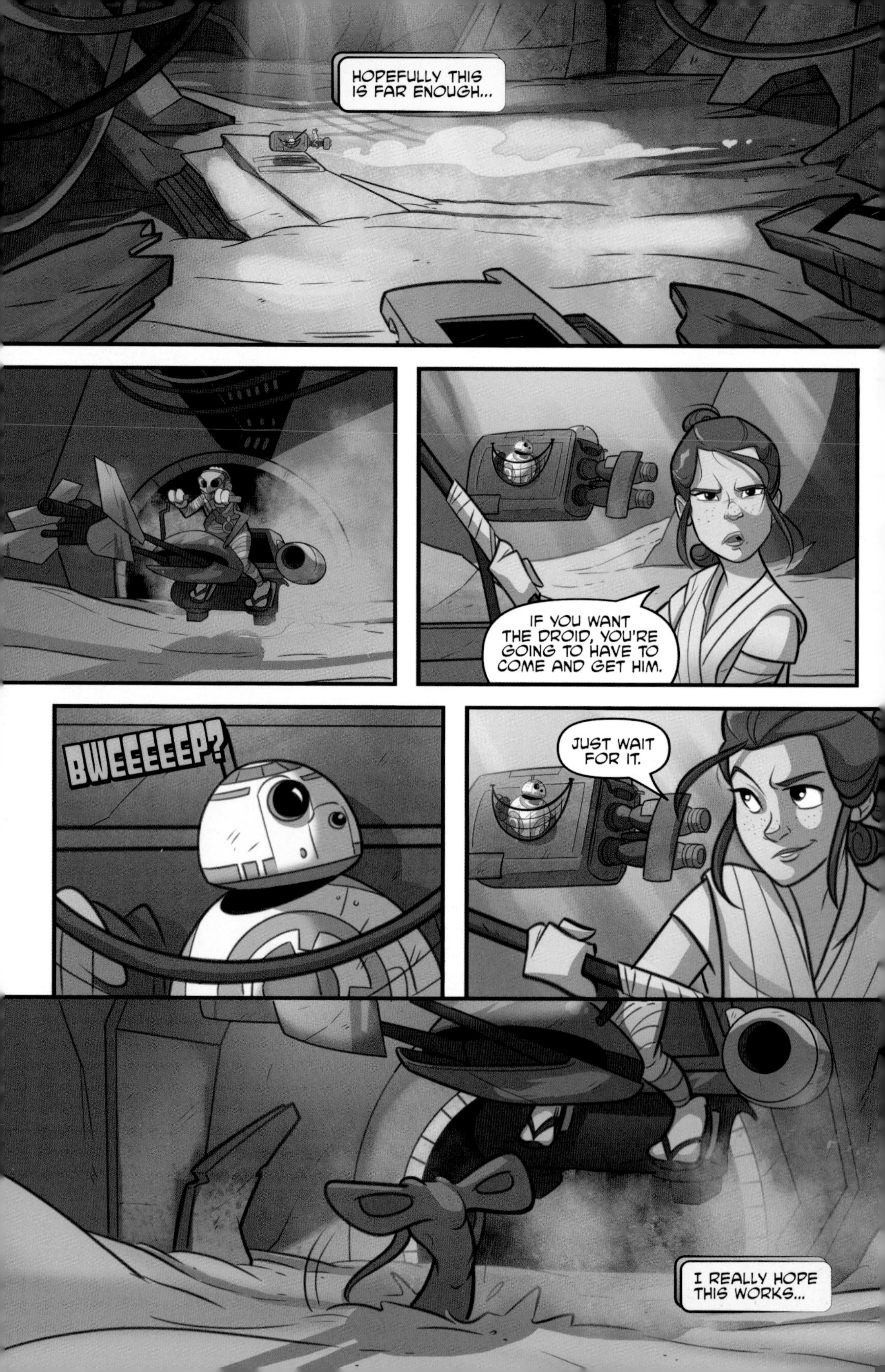
HOPEFULLY THIS IS FAR ENOUGH...
IF YOU WANT THE DROID, YOU'RE GOING TO HAVE TO COME AND GET HIM.
BWEEEEEP?
JUST WAIT FOR IT.
I REALLY HOPE THIS WORKS...

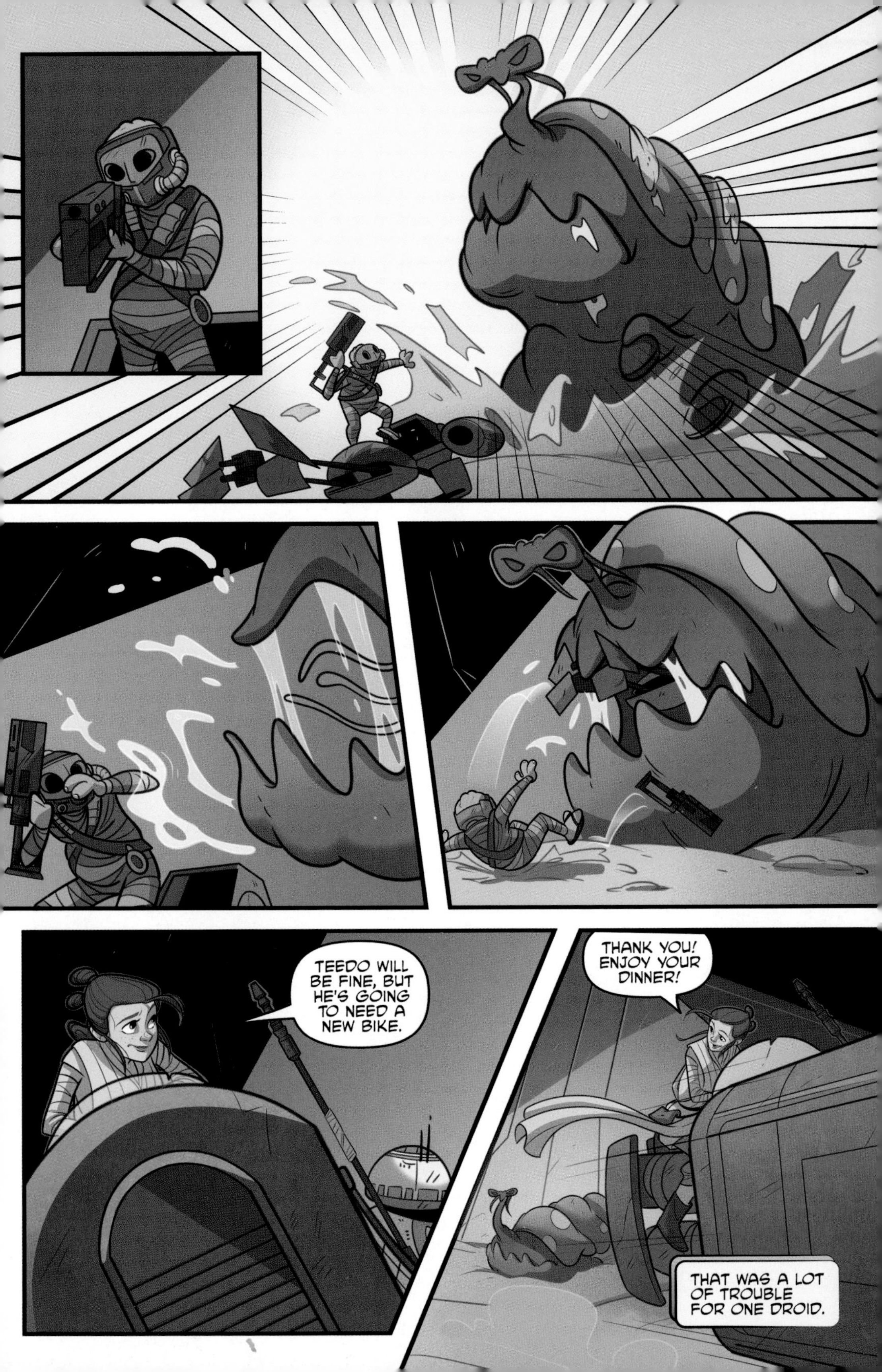
TEEDO WILL BE FINE, BUT HE'S GOING TO NEED A NEW BIKE.
THANK YOU! ENJOY YOUR DINNER!
THAT WAS A LOT OF TROUBLE FOR ONE DROID.

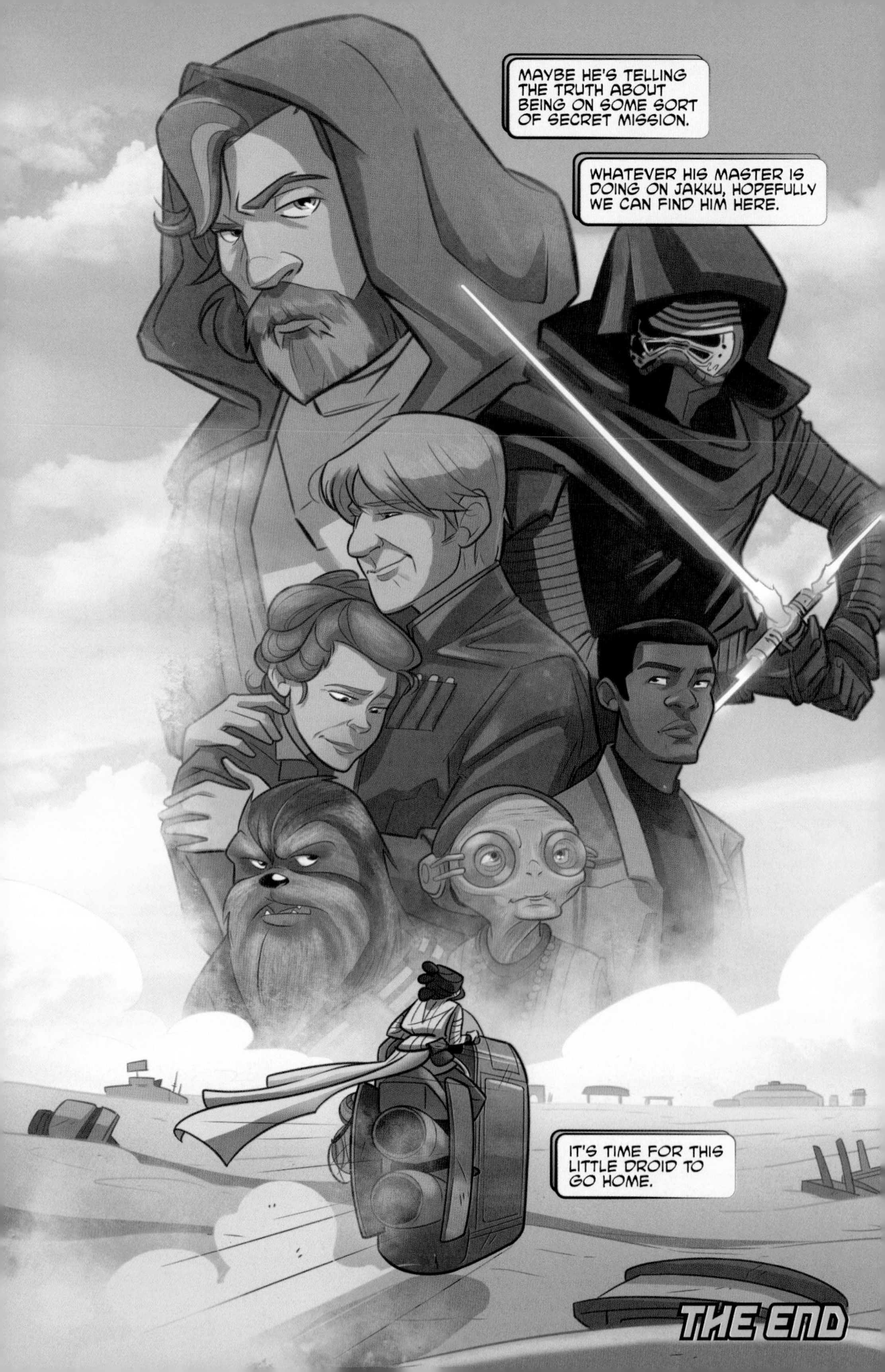
MAYBE HE'S TELLING THE TRUTH ABOUT BEING ON SOME SORT OF SECRET MISSION.
WHATEVER HIS MASTER IS DOING ON JAKKU, HOPEFULLY WE CAN FIND HIM HERE.
IT'S TIME FOR THIS LITTLE DROID TO GO HOME.
THE END

Art by Elsa Charretier, Colors by Matt Wilson

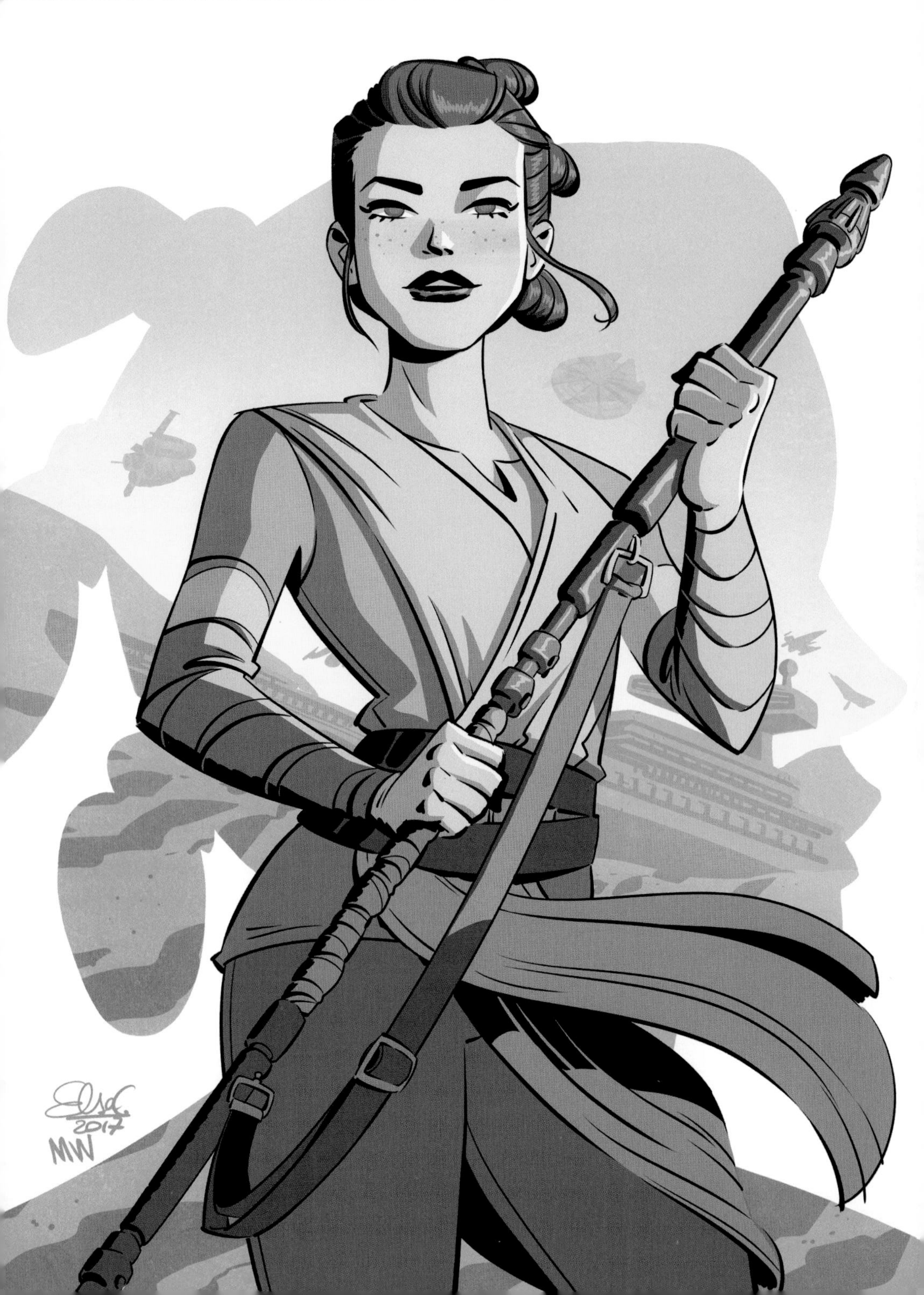

Hera

Art by Eva Widermann, Colors by Monica Kubina

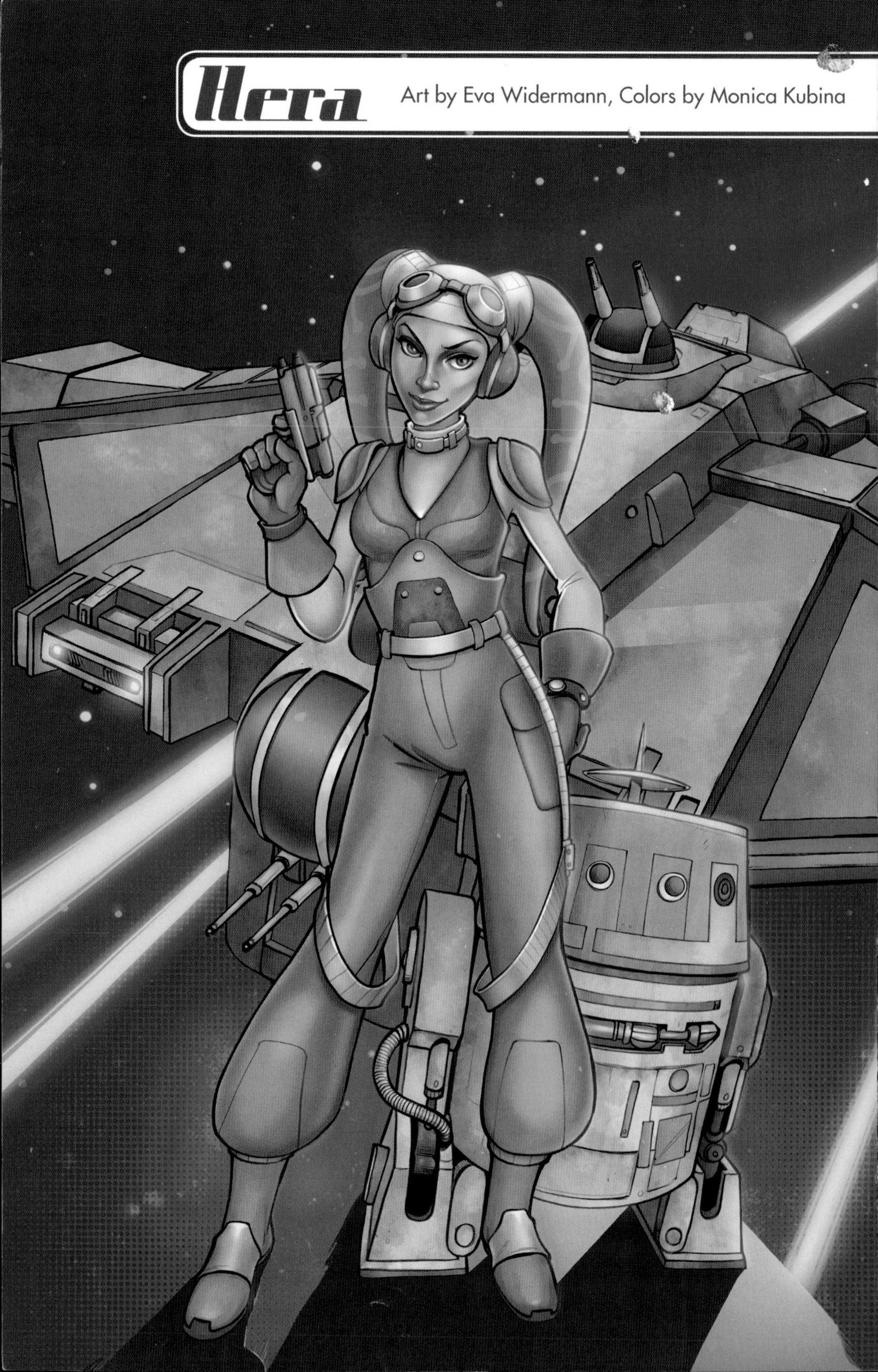

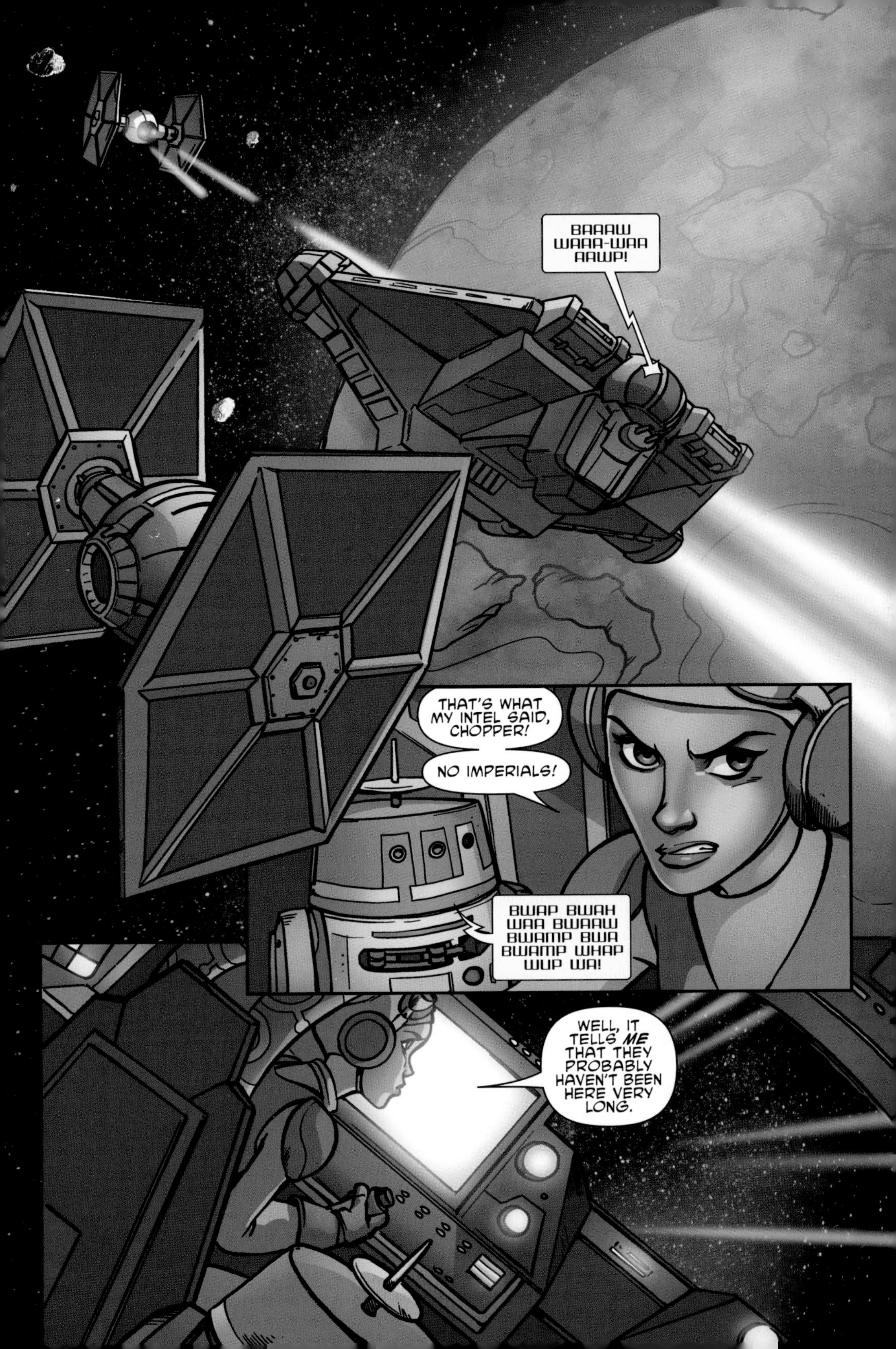
BAAAW WAAA-WAA AAWP!
THAT'S WHAT MY INTEL SAID, CHOPPER!
NO IMPERIALS!
BWAP BWAH WAA BWAAW BWAMP BWA BWAMP WHAP WUP WA!
WELL, IT TELLS *ME* THAT THEY PROBABLY HAVEN'T BEEN HERE VERY LONG.

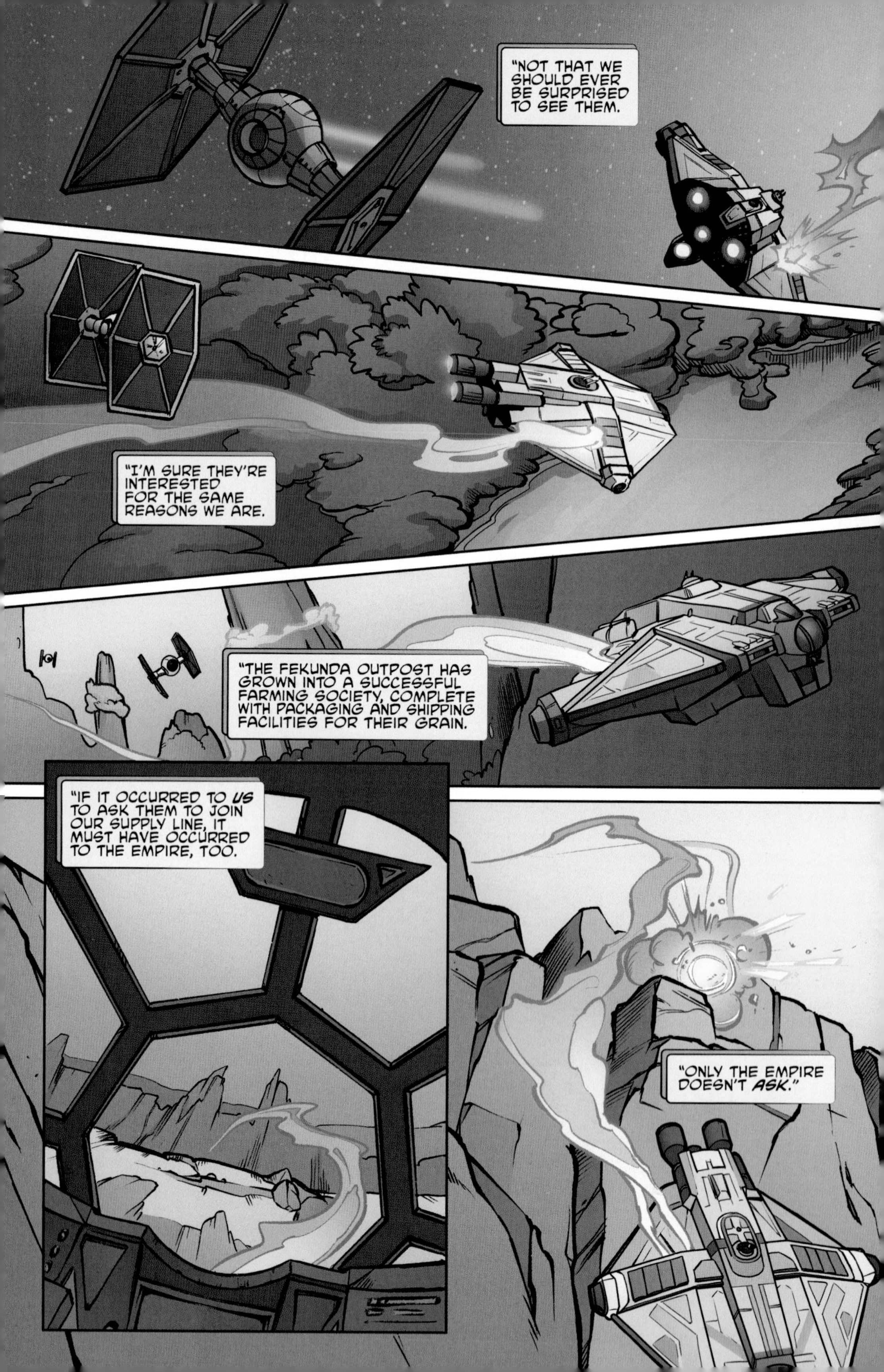
"NOT THAT WE SHOULD EVER BE SURPRISED TO SEE THEM.
"I'M SURE THEY'RE INTERESTED FOR THE SAME REASONS WE ARE.
"THE FEKUNDA OUTPOST HAS GROWN INTO A SUCCESSFUL FARMING SOCIETY, COMPLETE WITH PACKAGING AND SHIPPING FACILITIES FOR THEIR GRAIN.
"IF IT OCCURRED TO US TO ASK THEM TO JOIN OUR SUPPLY LINE, IT MUST HAVE OCCURRED TO THE EMPIRE, TOO.
"ONLY THE EMPIRE DOESN'T ASK."

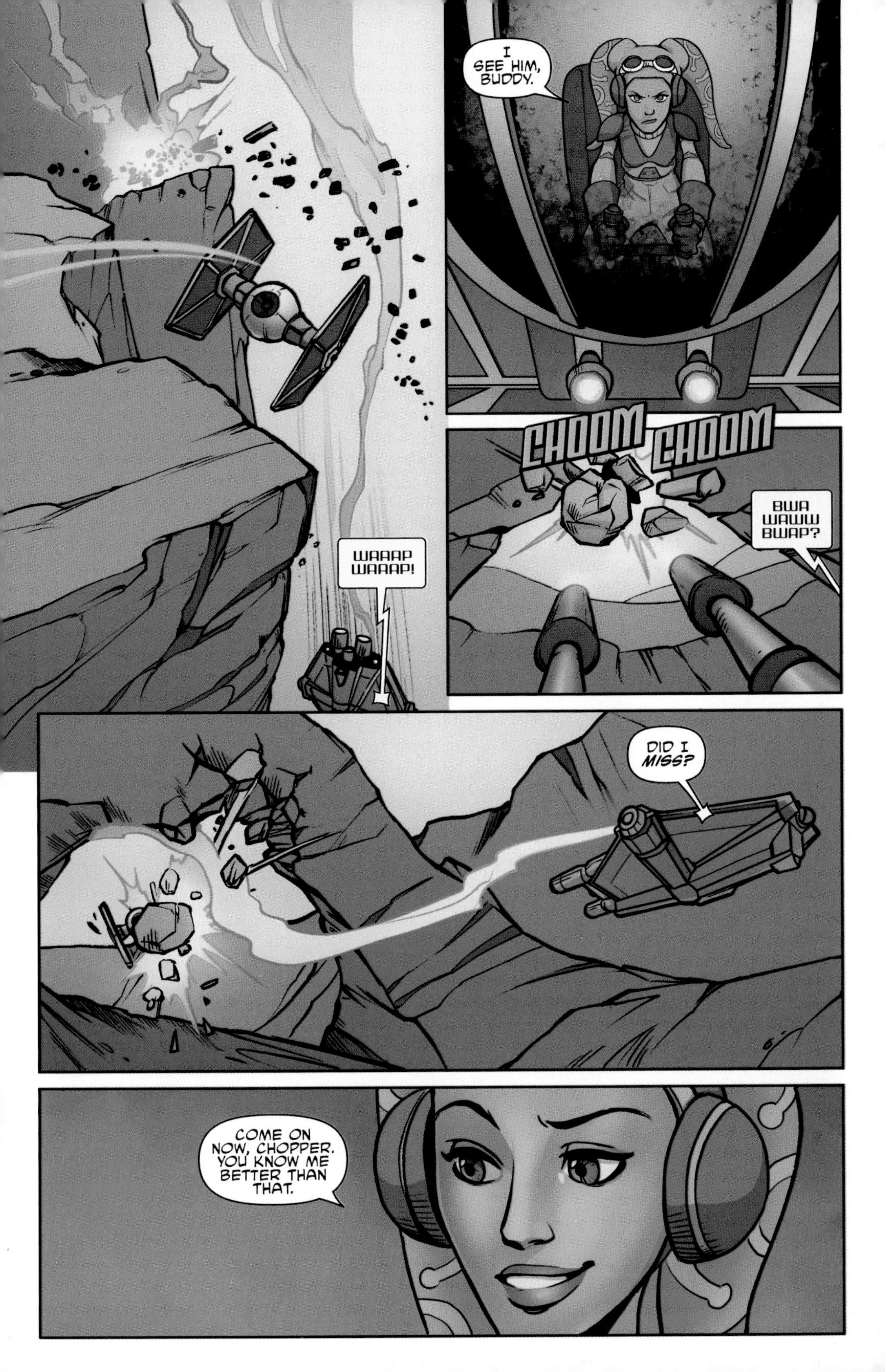
WAAAP WAAAP!
I SEE HIM, BUDDY.
CHOOM CHOOM
BWA WAWW BWAP?
DID I MISS?
COME ON NOW, CHOPPER. YOU KNOW ME BETTER THAN THAT.

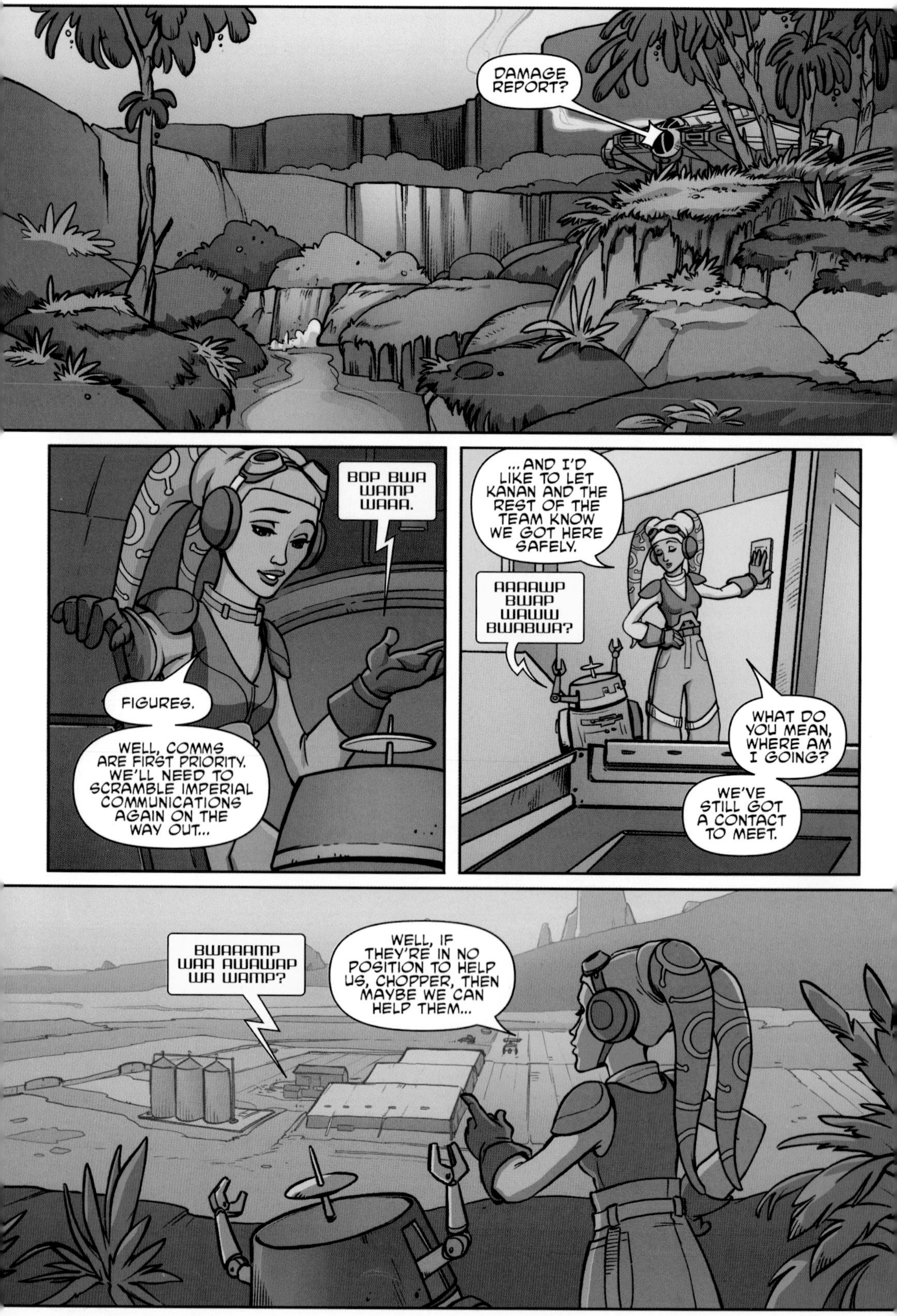
DAMAGE REPORT?
BOP BWA WAMP WAAA.
FIGURES.
WELL, COMMS ARE FIRST PRIORITY. WE'LL NEED TO SCRAMBLE IMPERIAL COMMUNICATIONS AGAIN ON THE WAY OUT...
...AND I'D LIKE TO LET KANAN AND THE REST OF THE TEAM KNOW WE GOT HERE SAFELY.
AAAAWP BWAP WAWW BWABWA?
WHAT DO YOU MEAN, WHERE AM I GOING?
WE'VE STILL GOT A CONTACT TO MEET.
BWAAAMP WAA AWAWAP WA WAMP?
WELL, IF THEY'RE IN NO POSITION TO HELP US, CHOPPER, THEN MAYBE WE CAN HELP THEM...

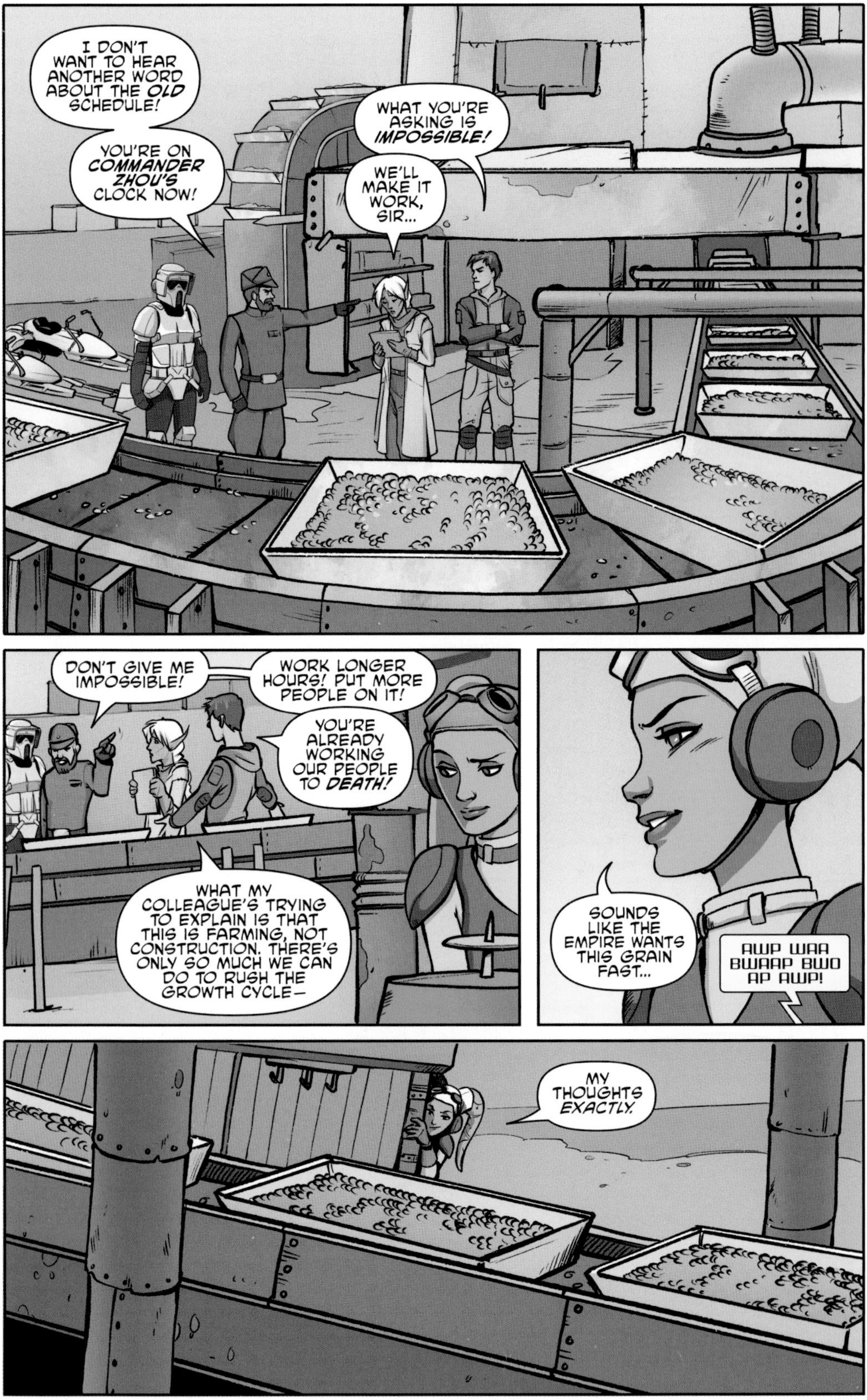
I DON'T WANT TO HEAR ANOTHER WORD ABOUT THE *OLD* SCHEDULE!
YOU'RE ON *COMMANDER ZHOU'S* CLOCK NOW!
WHAT YOU'RE ASKING IS *IMPOSSIBLE!*
WE'LL MAKE IT WORK, SIR...
DON'T GIVE ME IMPOSSIBLE!
WORK LONGER HOURS! PUT MORE PEOPLE ON IT!
YOU'RE ALREADY WORKING OUR PEOPLE TO *DEATH!*
WHAT MY COLLEAGUE'S TRYING TO EXPLAIN IS THAT THIS IS FARMING, NOT CONSTRUCTION. THERE'S ONLY SO MUCH WE CAN DO TO RUSH THE GROWTH CYCLE—
SOUNDS LIKE THE EMPIRE WANTS THIS GRAIN FAST...
AWP WAA BWAAP BWO AP AWP!
MY THOUGHTS *EXACTLY.*

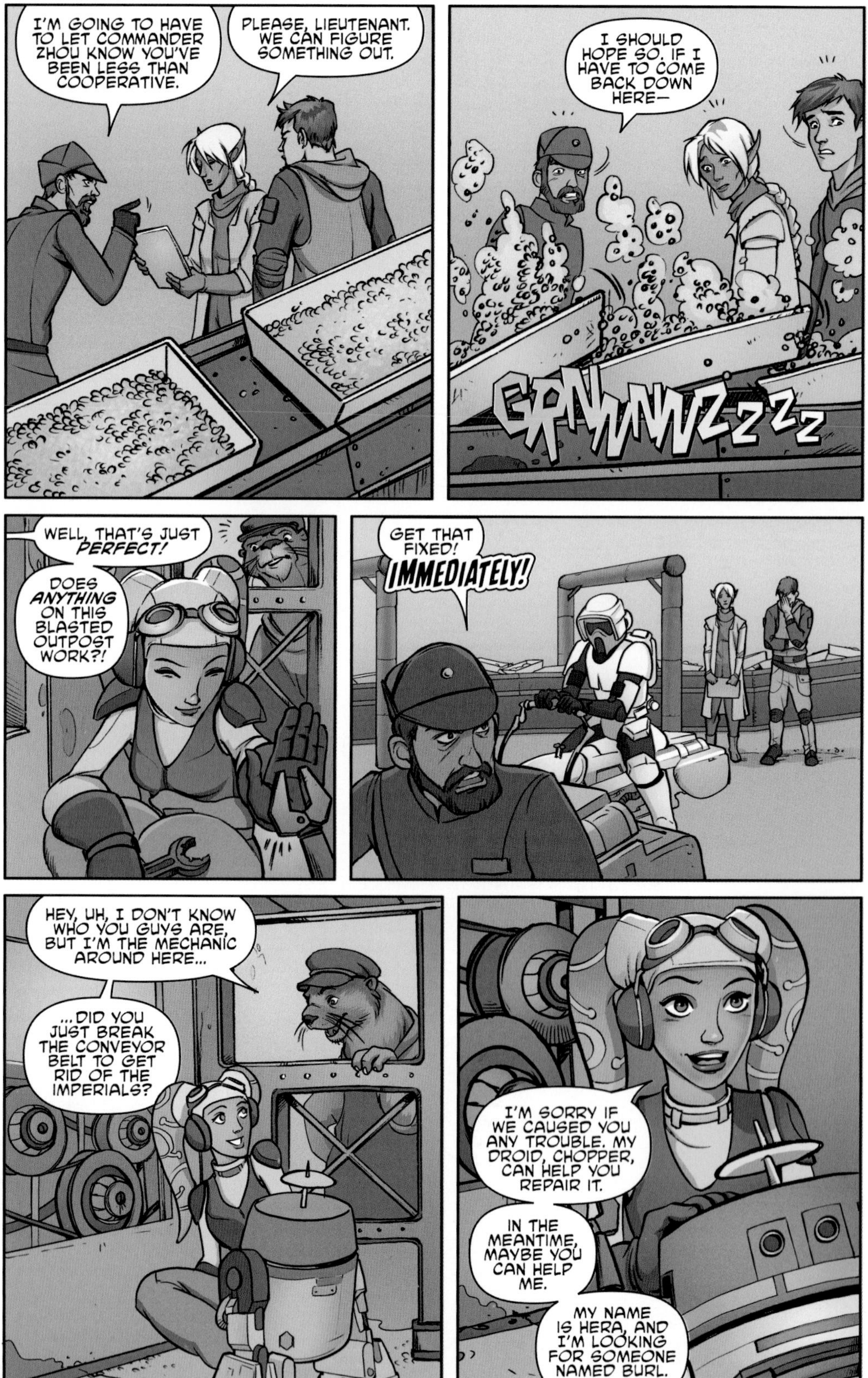
I'M GOING TO HAVE TO LET COMMANDER ZHOU KNOW YOU'VE BEEN LESS THAN COOPERATIVE.
PLEASE, LIEUTENANT. WE CAN FIGURE SOMETHING OUT.
I SHOULD HOPE SO. IF I HAVE TO COME BACK DOWN HERE—
GRNWWWZZZZ
WELL, THAT'S JUST *PERFECT!*
DOES *ANYTHING* ON THIS BLASTED OUTPOST WORK?!
GET THAT FIXED! *IMMEDIATELY!*
HEY, UH, I DON'T KNOW WHO YOU GUYS ARE, BUT I'M THE MECHANIC AROUND HERE...
...DID YOU JUST BREAK THE CONVEYOR BELT TO GET RID OF THE IMPERIALS?
I'M SORRY IF WE CAUSED YOU ANY TROUBLE. MY DROID, CHOPPER, CAN HELP YOU REPAIR IT.
IN THE MEANTIME, MAYBE YOU CAN HELP ME.
MY NAME IS HERA, AND I'M LOOKING FOR SOMEONE NAMED BURL.

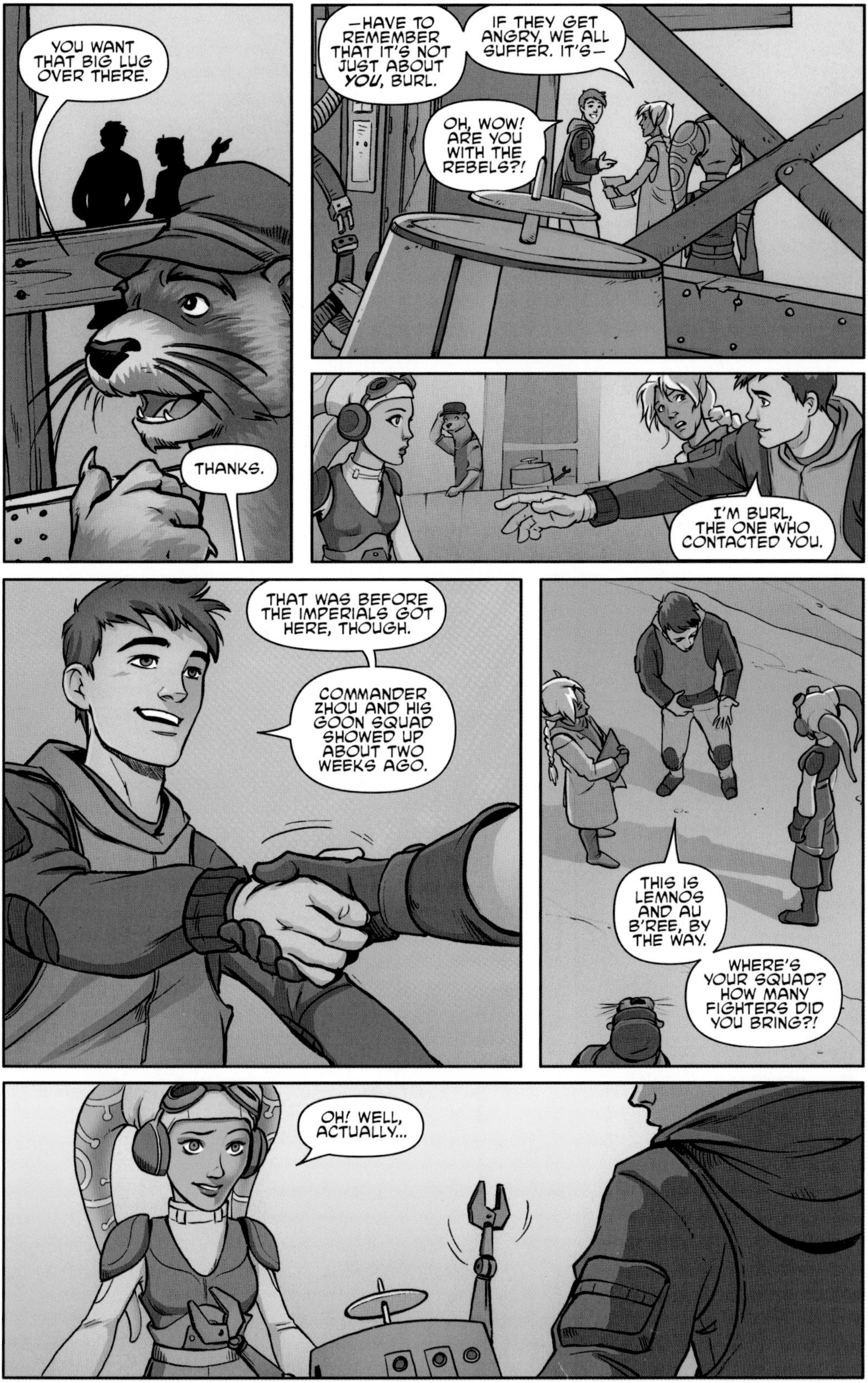
YOU WANT THAT BIG LUG OVER THERE.
THANKS.
—HAVE TO REMEMBER THAT IT'S NOT JUST ABOUT *YOU*, BURL.
IF THEY GET ANGRY, WE ALL SUFFER. IT'S—
OH, WOW! ARE YOU WITH THE REBELS?!
I'M BURL, THE ONE WHO CONTACTED YOU.
THAT WAS BEFORE THE IMPERIALS GOT HERE, THOUGH.
COMMANDER ZHOU AND HIS GOON SQUAD SHOWED UP ABOUT TWO WEEKS AGO.
THIS IS LEMNOS AND AU B'REE, BY THE WAY.
WHERE'S YOUR SQUAD? HOW MANY FIGHTERS DID YOU BRING?!
OH! WELL, ACTUALLY...

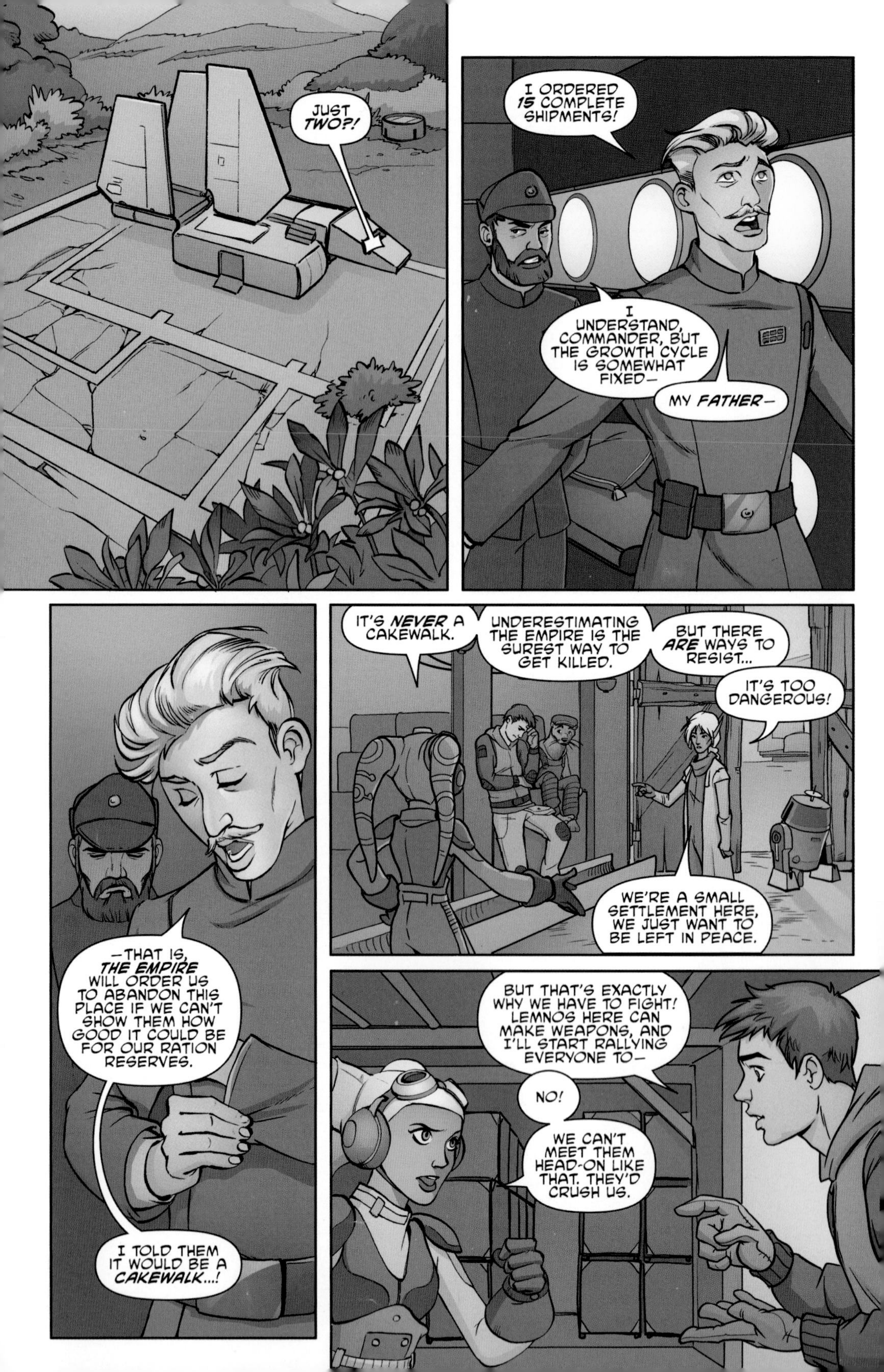
JUST *TWO?!*
I ORDERED *15* COMPLETE SHIPMENTS!
I UNDERSTAND, COMMANDER, BUT THE GROWTH CYCLE IS SOMEWHAT FIXED—
MY *FATHER*—
—THAT IS, *THE EMPIRE* WILL ORDER US TO ABANDON THIS PLACE IF WE CAN'T SHOW THEM HOW GOOD IT COULD BE FOR OUR RATION RESERVES.
I TOLD THEM IT WOULD BE A *CAKEWALK*...!
IT'S *NEVER* A CAKEWALK.
UNDERESTIMATING THE EMPIRE IS THE SUREST WAY TO GET KILLED.
BUT THERE *ARE* WAYS TO RESIST...
IT'S TOO DANGEROUS!
WE'RE A SMALL SETTLEMENT HERE, WE JUST WANT TO BE LEFT IN PEACE.
BUT THAT'S EXACTLY WHY WE HAVE TO FIGHT! LEMNOS HERE CAN MAKE WEAPONS, AND I'LL START RALLYING EVERYONE TO—
NO!
WE CAN'T MEET THEM HEAD-ON LIKE THAT. THEY'D CRUSH US.

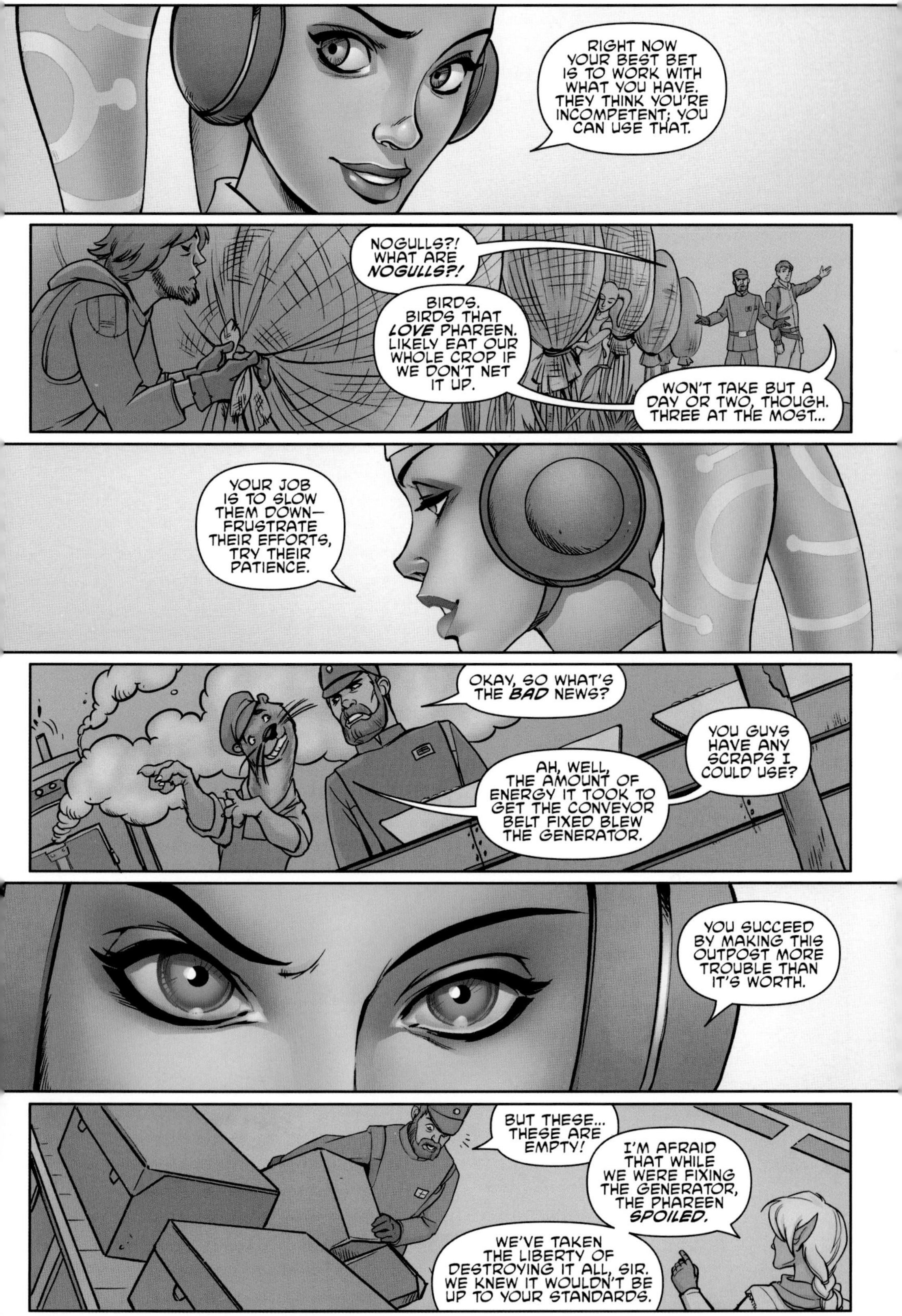
RIGHT NOW YOUR BEST BET IS TO WORK WITH WHAT YOU HAVE. THEY THINK YOU'RE INCOMPETENT; YOU CAN USE THAT.
NOGULLS?! WHAT ARE ***NOGULLS?!***
BIRDS. BIRDS THAT ***LOVE*** PHAREEN. LIKELY EAT OUR WHOLE CROP IF WE DON'T NET IT UP.
WON'T TAKE BUT A DAY OR TWO, THOUGH. THREE AT THE MOST...
YOUR JOB IS TO SLOW THEM DOWN— FRUSTRATE THEIR EFFORTS, TRY THEIR PATIENCE.
OKAY, SO WHAT'S THE ***BAD*** NEWS?
AH, WELL, THE AMOUNT OF ENERGY IT TOOK TO GET THE CONVEYOR BELT FIXED BLEW THE GENERATOR.
YOU GUYS HAVE ANY SCRAPS I COULD USE?
YOU SUCCEED BY MAKING THIS OUTPOST MORE TROUBLE THAN IT'S WORTH.
BUT THESE... THESE ARE EMPTY!
I'M AFRAID THAT WHILE WE WERE FIXING THE GENERATOR, THE PHAREEN ***SPOILED.***
WE'VE TAKEN THE LIBERTY OF DESTROYING IT ALL, SIR. WE KNEW IT WOULDN'T BE UP TO YOUR STANDARDS.

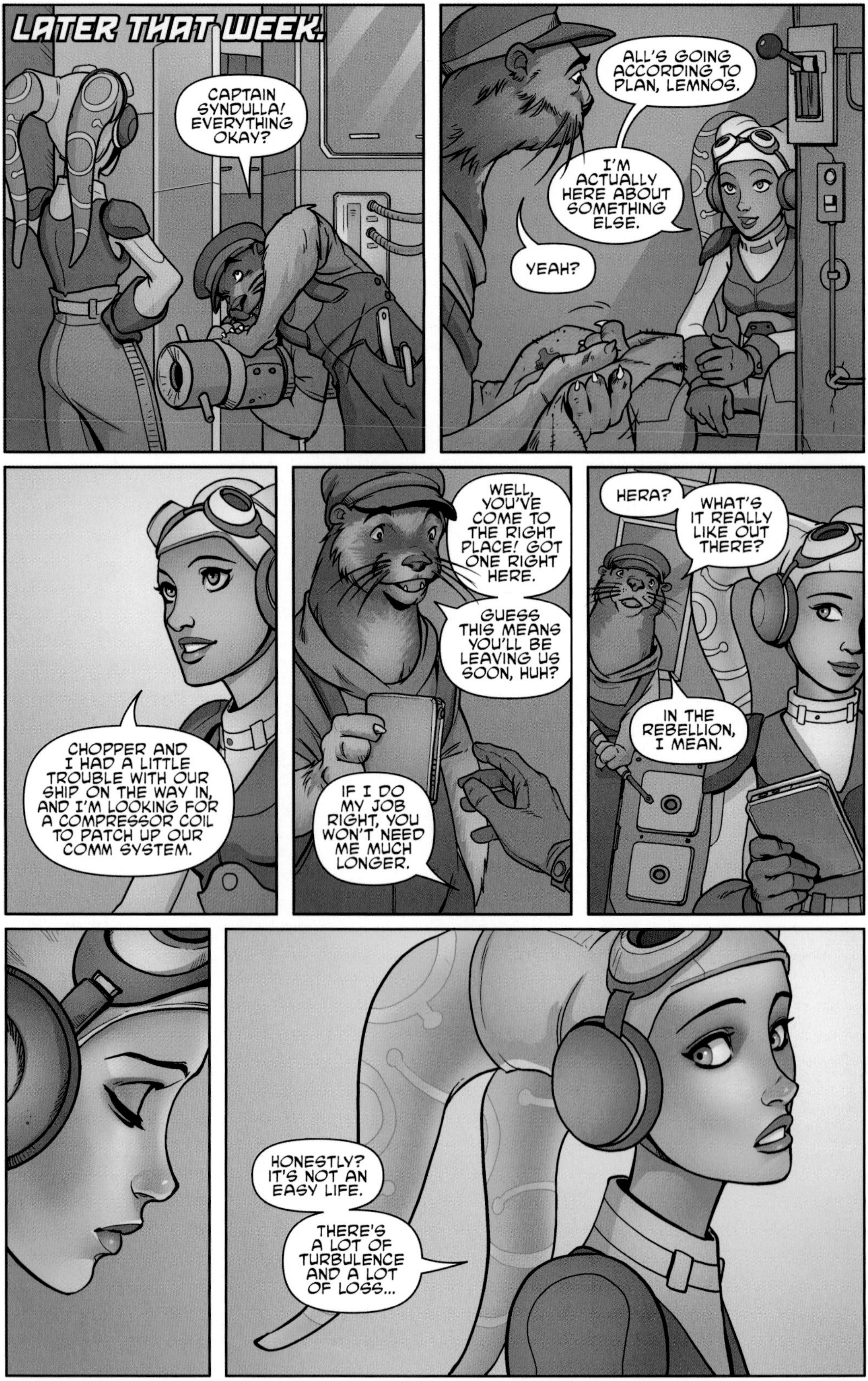
LATER THAT WEEK.
CAPTAIN SYNDULLA! EVERYTHING OKAY?
ALL'S GOING ACCORDING TO PLAN, LEMNOS.
I'M ACTUALLY HERE ABOUT SOMETHING ELSE.
YEAH?
CHOPPER AND I HAD A LITTLE TROUBLE WITH OUR SHIP ON THE WAY IN, AND I'M LOOKING FOR A COMPRESSOR COIL TO PATCH UP OUR COMM SYSTEM.
WELL, YOU'VE COME TO THE RIGHT PLACE! GOT ONE RIGHT HERE.
GUESS THIS MEANS YOU'LL BE LEAVING US SOON, HUH?
IF I DO MY JOB RIGHT, YOU WON'T NEED ME MUCH LONGER.
HERA?
WHAT'S IT REALLY LIKE OUT THERE?
IN THE REBELLION, I MEAN.
HONESTLY? IT'S NOT AN EASY LIFE.
THERE'S A LOT OF TURBULENCE AND A LOT OF LOSS...

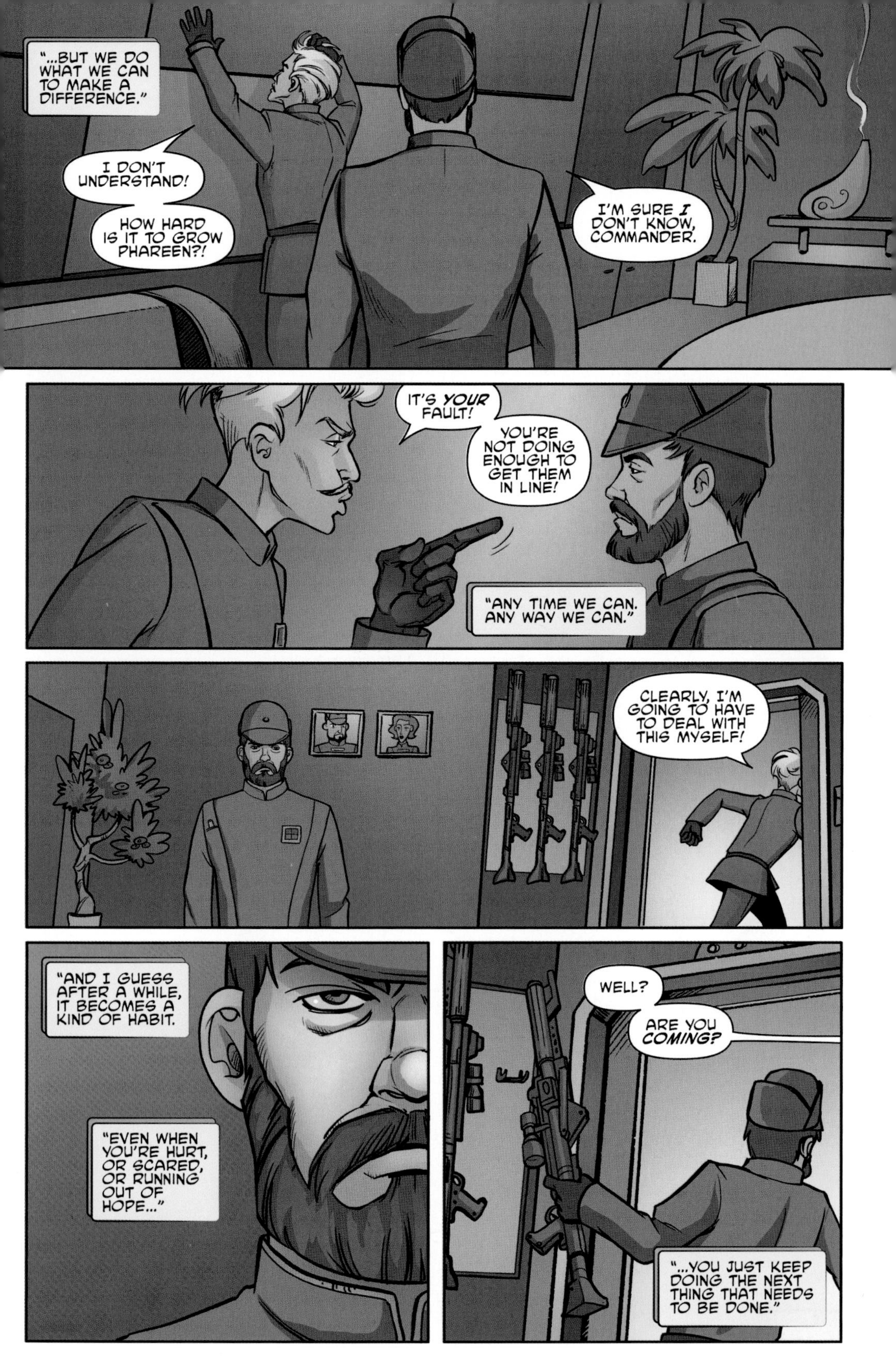
"...BUT WE DO WHAT WE CAN TO MAKE A DIFFERENCE."
I DON'T UNDERSTAND!
HOW HARD IS IT TO GROW PHAREEN?!
I'M SURE *I* DON'T KNOW, COMMANDER.
IT'S *YOUR* FAULT!
YOU'RE NOT DOING ENOUGH TO GET THEM IN LINE!
"ANY TIME WE CAN. ANY WAY WE CAN."
CLEARLY, I'M GOING TO HAVE TO DEAL WITH THIS MYSELF!
"AND I GUESS AFTER A WHILE, IT BECOMES A KIND OF HABIT.
"EVEN WHEN YOU'RE HURT, OR SCARED, OR RUNNING OUT OF HOPE..."
WELL?
ARE YOU *COMING?*
"...YOU JUST KEEP DOING THE NEXT THING THAT NEEDS TO BE DONE."

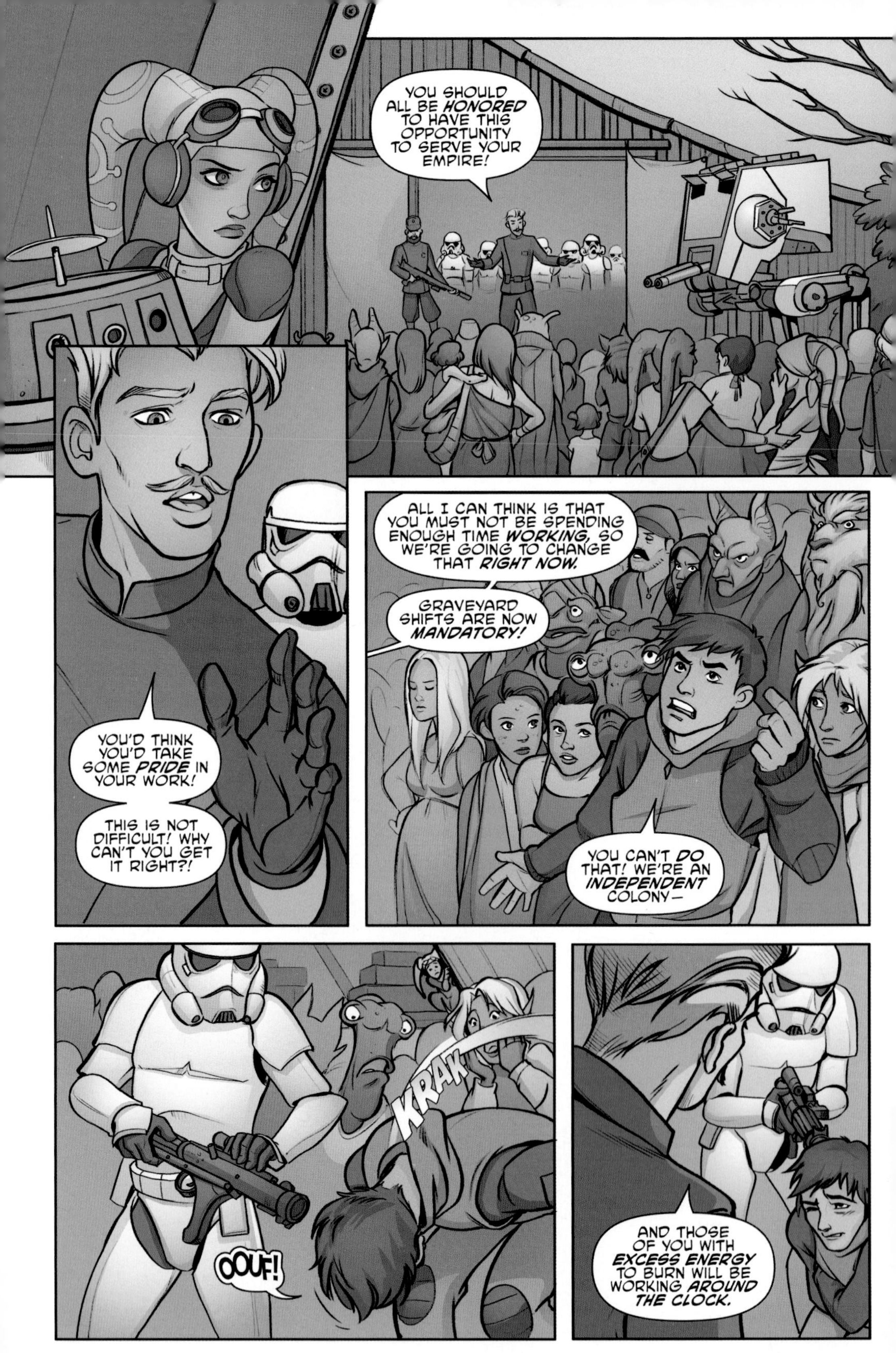
YOU SHOULD ALL BE *HONORED* TO HAVE THIS OPPORTUNITY TO SERVE YOUR EMPIRE!
YOU'D THINK YOU'D TAKE SOME *PRIDE* IN YOUR WORK!
THIS IS NOT DIFFICULT! WHY CAN'T YOU GET IT RIGHT?!
ALL I CAN THINK IS THAT YOU MUST NOT BE SPENDING ENOUGH TIME *WORKING*, SO WE'RE GOING TO CHANGE THAT *RIGHT NOW.*
GRAVEYARD SHIFTS ARE NOW *MANDATORY!*
YOU CAN'T *DO* THAT! WE'RE AN *INDEPENDENT* COLONY—
KRAK
OOUF!
AND THOSE OF YOU WITH *EXCESS ENERGY* TO BURN WILL BE WORKING *AROUND THE CLOCK.*

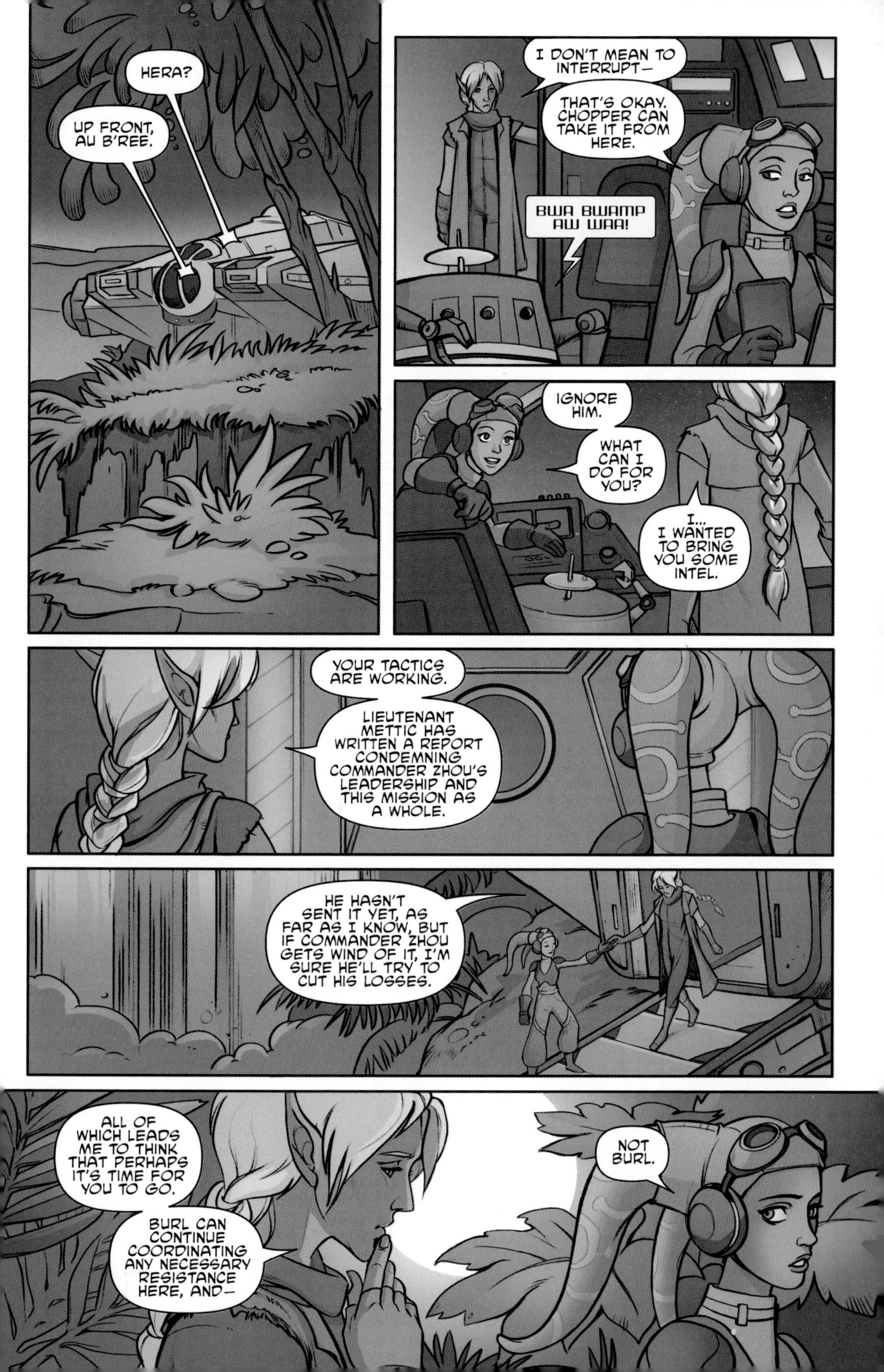
HERA?
UP FRONT, AU B'REE.
I DON'T MEAN TO INTERRUPT—
THAT'S OKAY. CHOPPER CAN TAKE IT FROM HERE.
BWA BWAMP AW WAA!
IGNORE HIM.
WHAT CAN I DO FOR YOU?
I... I WANTED TO BRING YOU SOME INTEL.
YOUR TACTICS ARE WORKING.
LIEUTENANT METTIC HAS WRITTEN A REPORT CONDEMNING COMMANDER ZHOU'S LEADERSHIP AND THIS MISSION AS A WHOLE.
HE HASN'T SENT IT YET, AS FAR AS I KNOW, BUT IF COMMANDER ZHOU GETS WIND OF IT, I'M SURE HE'LL TRY TO CUT HIS LOSSES.
ALL OF WHICH LEADS ME TO THINK THAT PERHAPS IT'S TIME FOR YOU TO GO.
BURL CAN CONTINUE COORDINATING ANY NECESSARY RESISTANCE HERE, AND—
NOT BURL.

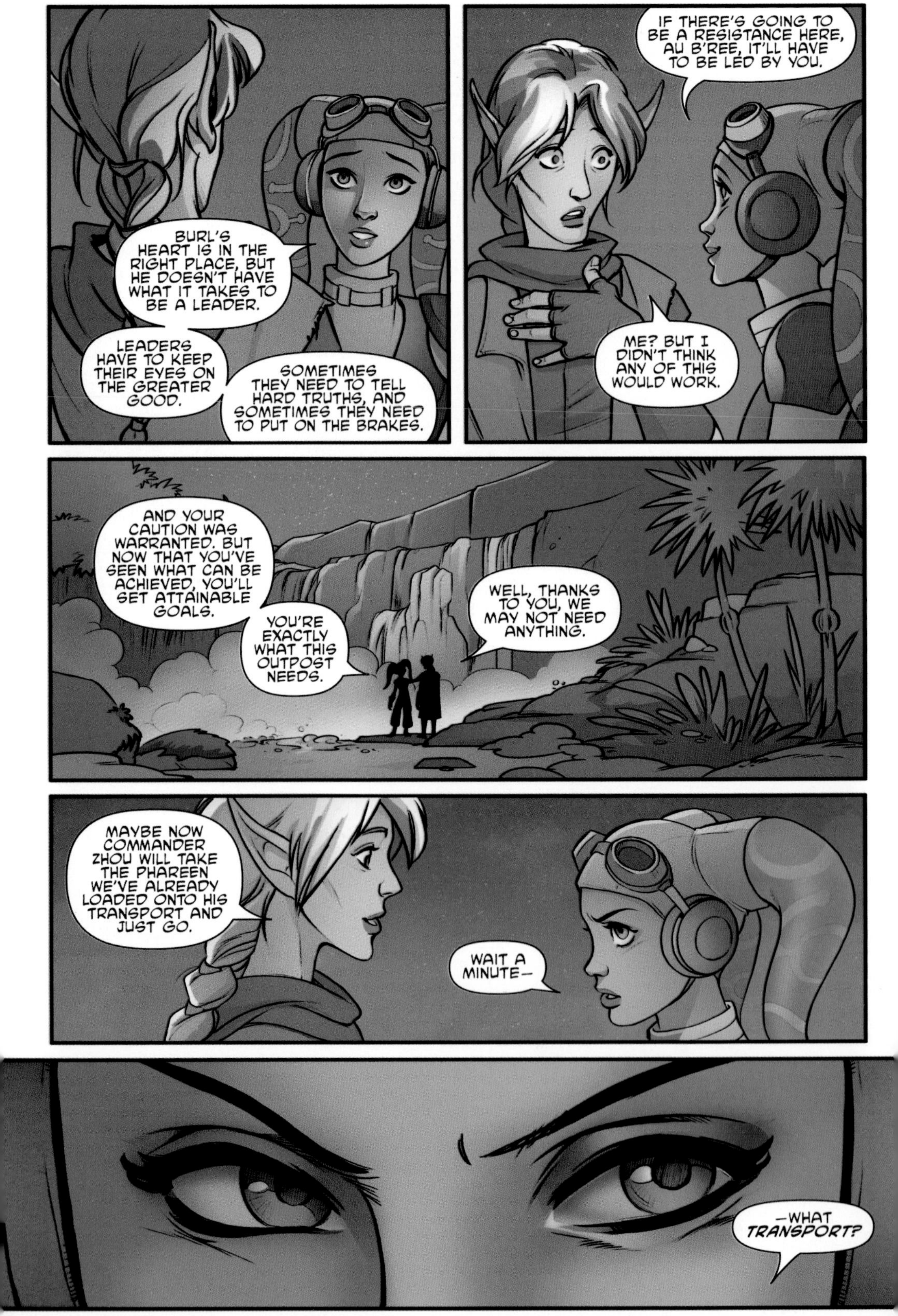
BURL'S HEART IS IN THE RIGHT PLACE, BUT HE DOESN'T HAVE WHAT IT TAKES TO BE A LEADER.
LEADERS HAVE TO KEEP THEIR EYES ON THE GREATER GOOD.
SOMETIMES THEY NEED TO TELL HARD TRUTHS, AND SOMETIMES THEY NEED TO PUT ON THE BRAKES.
IF THERE'S GOING TO BE A RESISTANCE HERE, AU B'REE, IT'LL HAVE TO BE LED BY YOU.
ME? BUT I DIDN'T THINK ANY OF THIS WOULD WORK.
AND YOUR CAUTION WAS WARRANTED. BUT NOW THAT YOU'VE SEEN WHAT CAN BE ACHIEVED, YOU'LL SET ATTAINABLE GOALS.
YOU'RE EXACTLY WHAT THIS OUTPOST NEEDS.
WELL, THANKS TO YOU, WE MAY NOT NEED ANYTHING.
MAYBE NOW COMMANDER ZHOU WILL TAKE THE PHAREEN WE'VE ALREADY LOADED ONTO HIS TRANSPORT AND JUST GO.
WAIT A MINUTE—
—WHAT *TRANSPORT?*

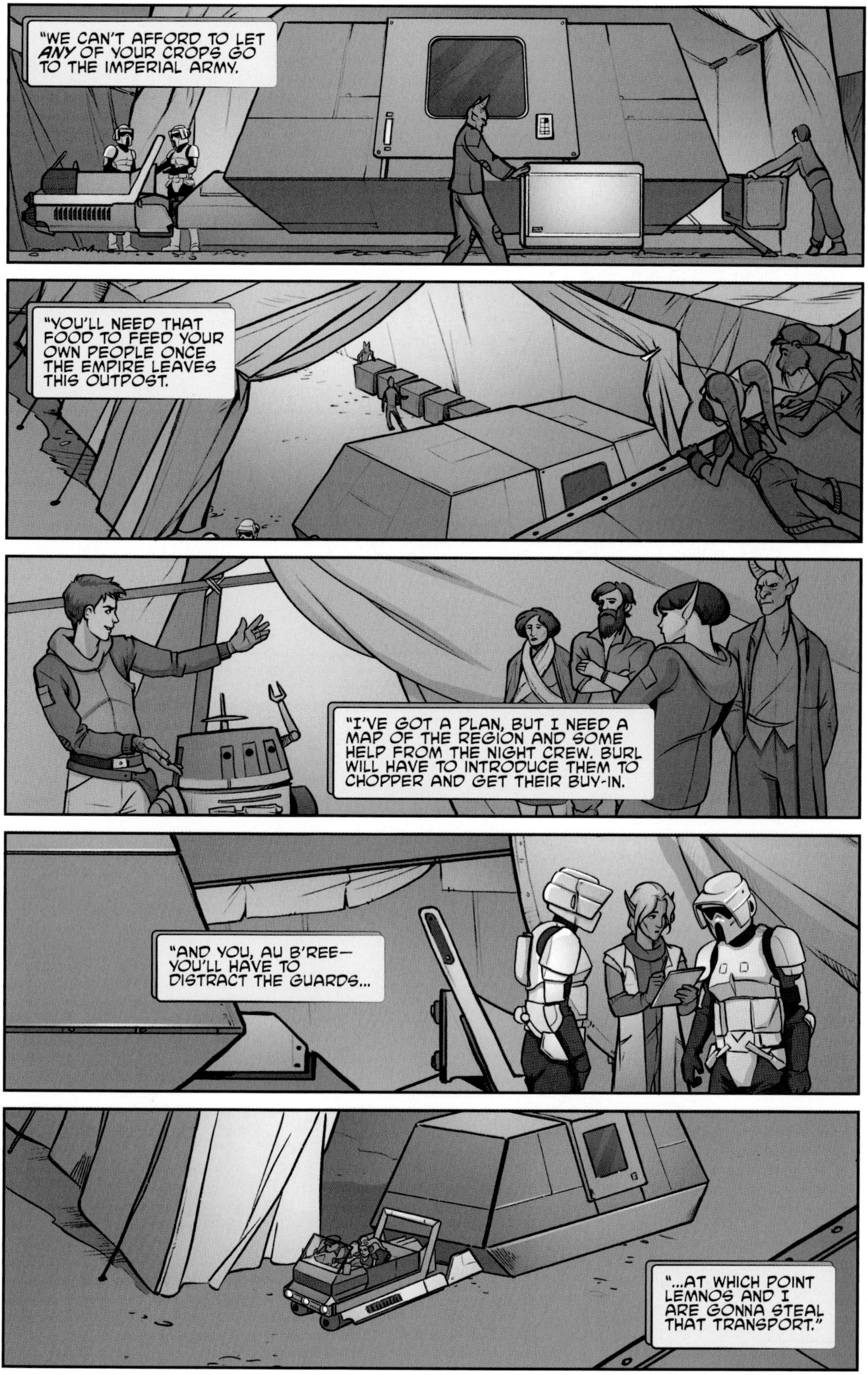
"WE CAN'T AFFORD TO LET ANY OF YOUR CROPS GO TO THE IMPERIAL ARMY.
"YOU'LL NEED THAT FOOD TO FEED YOUR OWN PEOPLE ONCE THE EMPIRE LEAVES THIS OUTPOST.
"I'VE GOT A PLAN, BUT I NEED A MAP OF THE REGION AND SOME HELP FROM THE NIGHT CREW. BURL WILL HAVE TO INTRODUCE THEM TO CHOPPER AND GET THEIR BUY-IN.
"AND YOU, AU B'REE— YOU'LL HAVE TO DISTRACT THE GUARDS...
"...AT WHICH POINT LEMNOS AND I ARE GONNA STEAL THAT TRANSPORT."

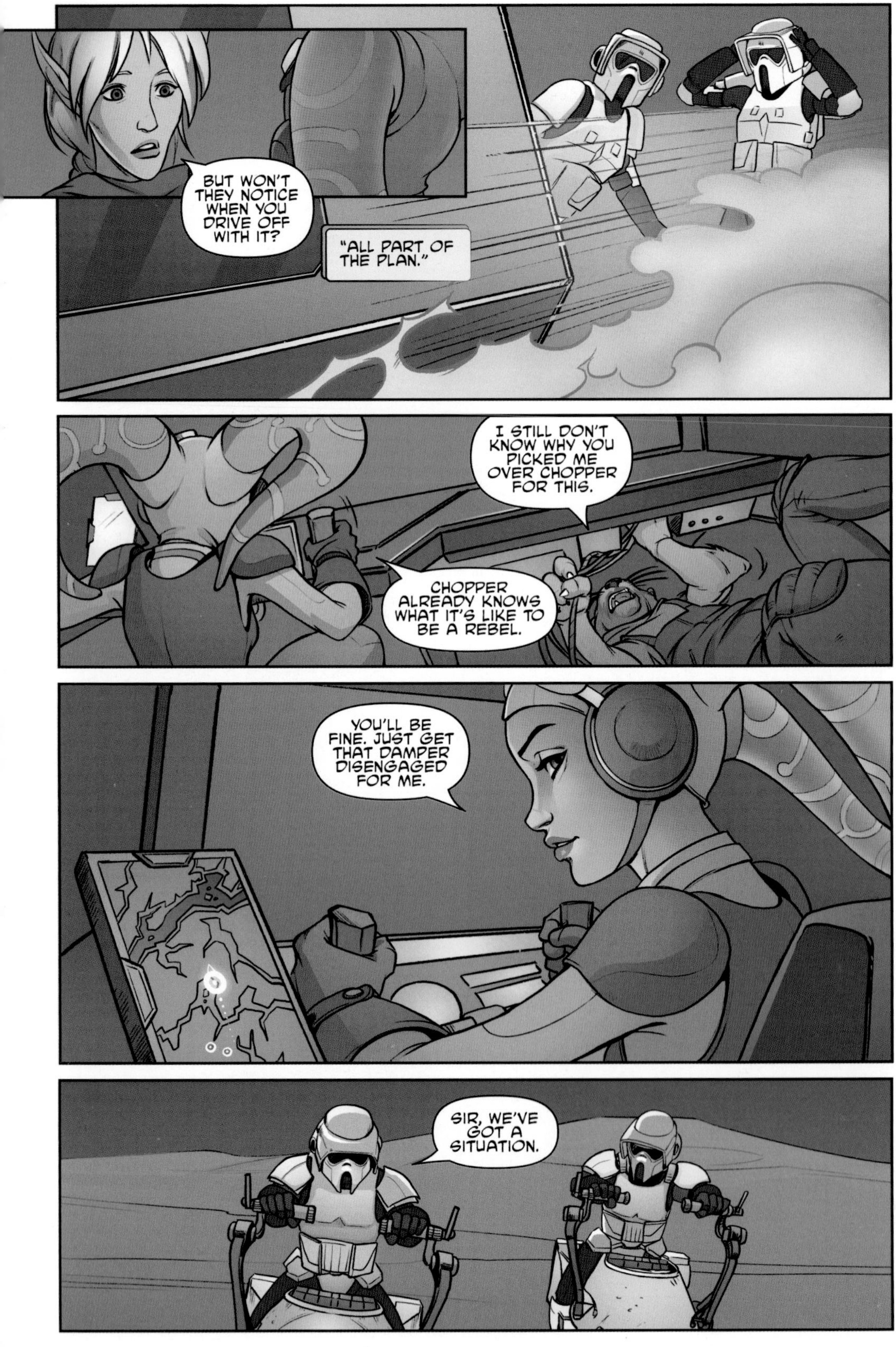
BUT WON'T THEY NOTICE WHEN YOU DRIVE OFF WITH IT?
"ALL PART OF THE PLAN."
I STILL DON'T KNOW WHY YOU PICKED ME OVER CHOPPER FOR THIS.
CHOPPER ALREADY KNOWS WHAT IT'S LIKE TO BE A REBEL.
YOU'LL BE FINE. JUST GET THAT DAMPER DISENGAGED FOR ME.
SIR, WE'VE GOT A SITUATION.

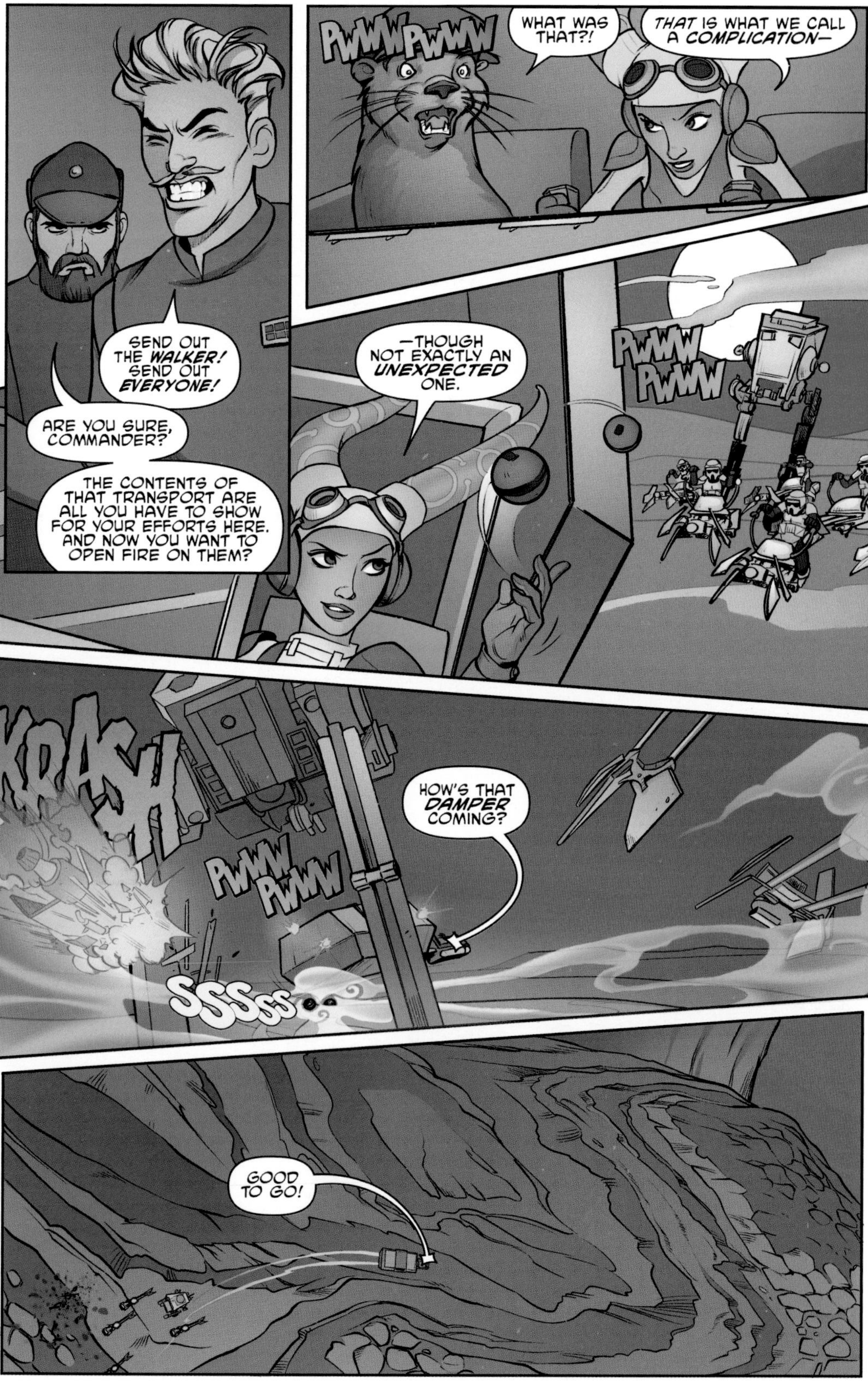
PWWW PWWW
WHAT WAS THAT?!
THAT IS WHAT WE CALL A COMPLICATION—
SEND OUT THE WALKER! SEND OUT EVERYONE!
ARE YOU SURE, COMMANDER?
THE CONTENTS OF THAT TRANSPORT ARE ALL YOU HAVE TO SHOW FOR YOUR EFFORTS HERE. AND NOW YOU WANT TO OPEN FIRE ON THEM?
—THOUGH NOT EXACTLY AN UNEXPECTED ONE.
PWWW PWWW
KRASH
PWWW PWWW
HOW'S THAT DAMPER COMING?
SSSss
GOOD TO GO!

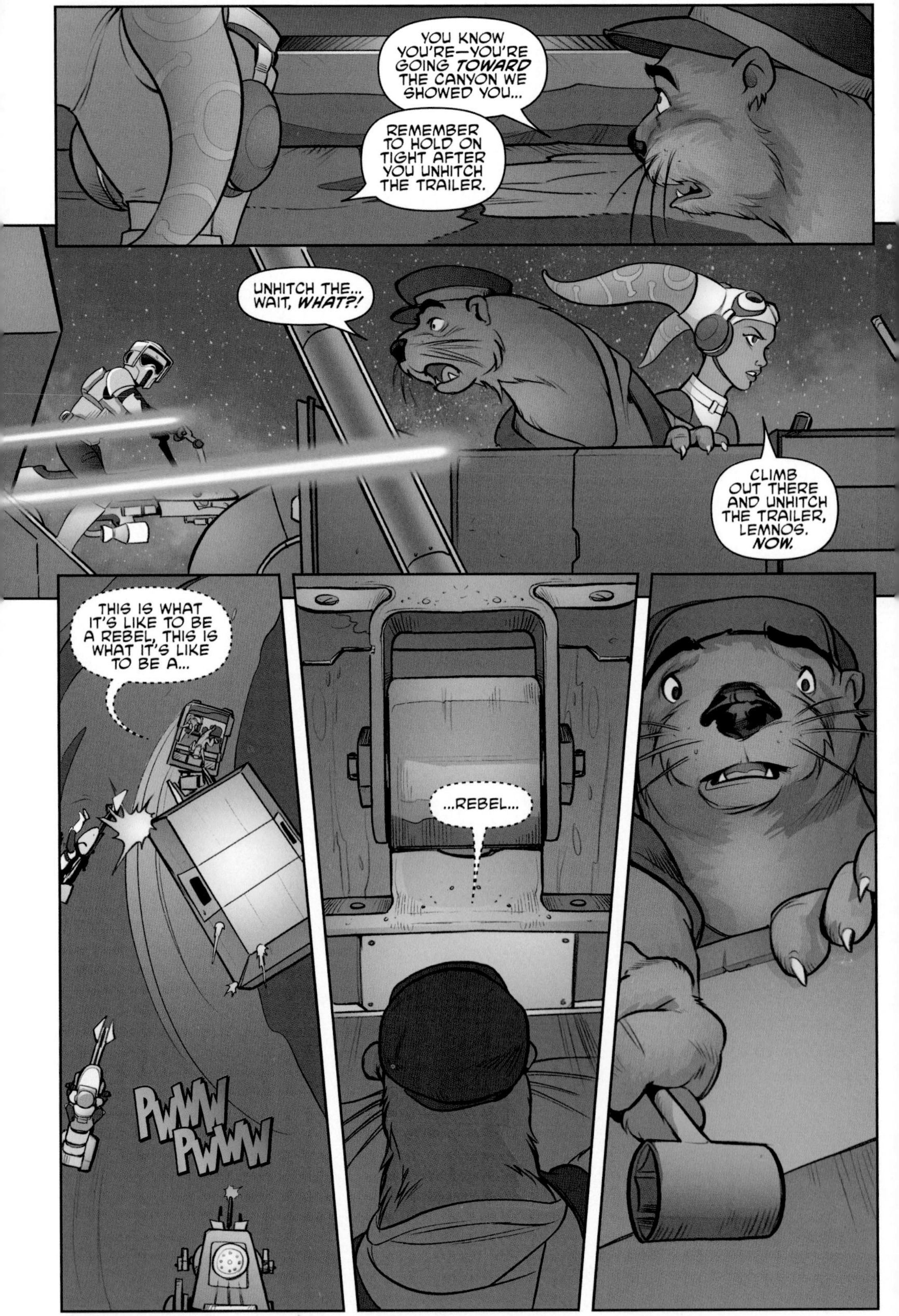

YOU KNOW YOU'RE—YOU'RE GOING *TOWARD* THE CANYON WE SHOWED YOU...
REMEMBER TO HOLD ON TIGHT AFTER YOU UNHITCH THE TRAILER.
UNHITCH THE... WAIT, *WHAT?!*
CLIMB OUT THERE AND UNHITCH THE TRAILER, LEMNOS. *NOW.*
THIS IS WHAT IT'S LIKE TO BE A REBEL, THIS IS WHAT IT'S LIKE TO BE A...
PWWW PWWW
...REBEL...

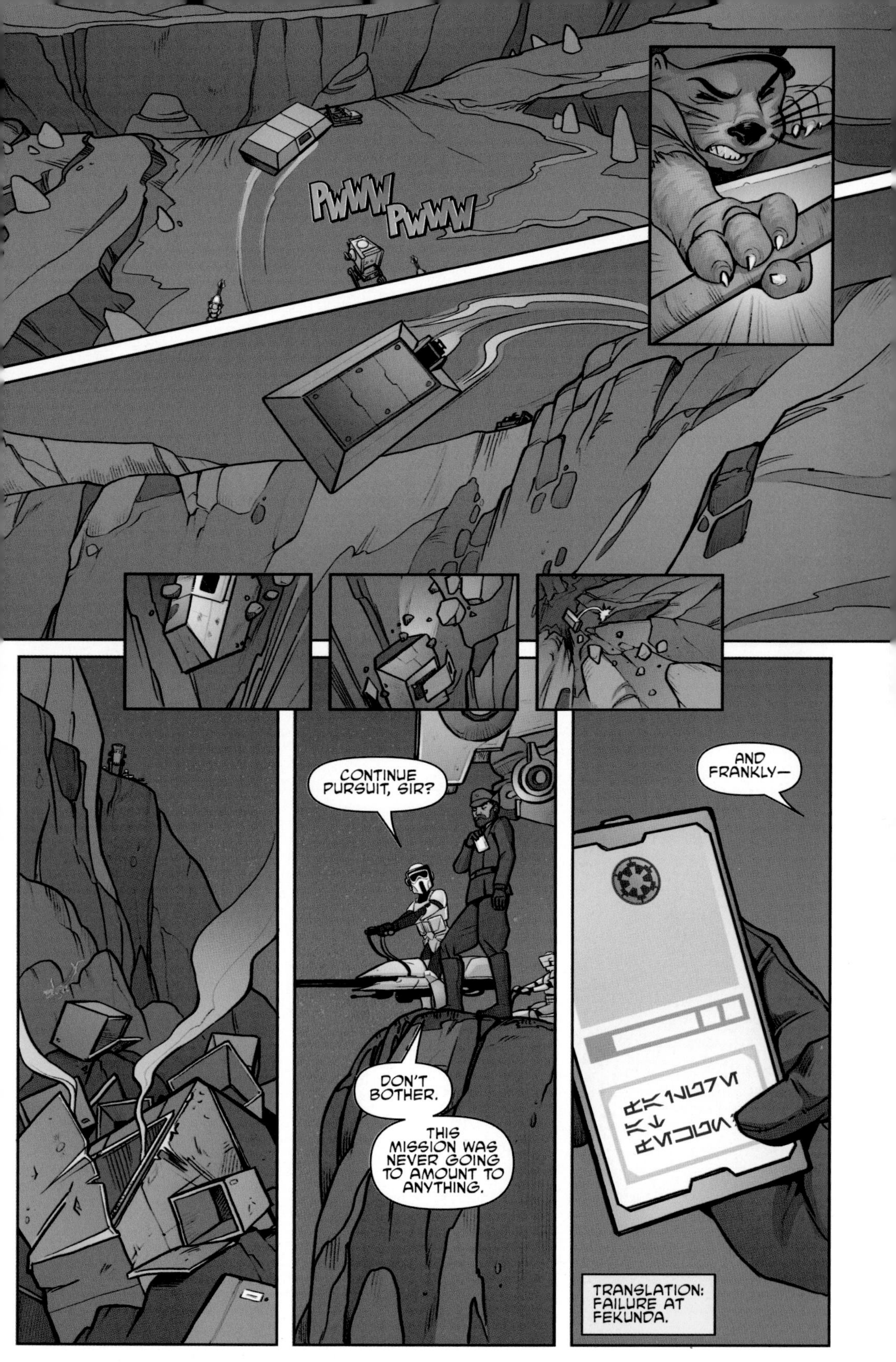
PWWW PWWW
CONTINUE PURSUIT, SIR?
DON'T BOTHER.
THIS MISSION WAS NEVER GOING TO AMOUNT TO ANYTHING.
AND FRANKLY—
TRANSLATION: FAILURE AT FEKUNDA.

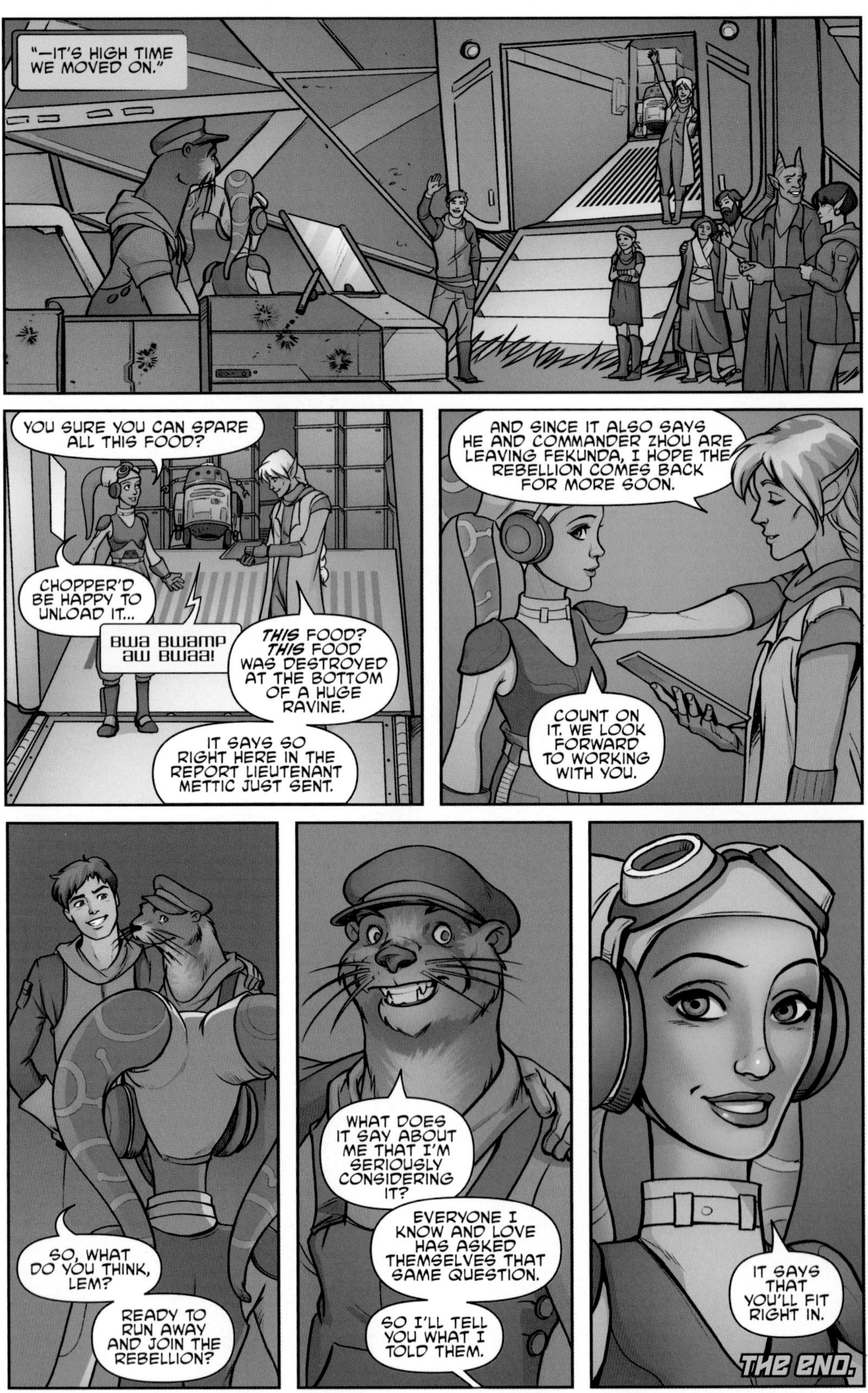
"—IT'S HIGH TIME WE MOVED ON."
YOU SURE YOU CAN SPARE ALL THIS FOOD?
CHOPPER'D BE HAPPY TO UNLOAD IT...
BWA BWAMP AW BWAA!
THIS FOOD? *THIS* FOOD WAS DESTROYED AT THE BOTTOM OF A HUGE RAVINE.
IT SAYS SO RIGHT HERE IN THE REPORT LIEUTENANT METTIC JUST SENT.
AND SINCE IT ALSO SAYS HE AND COMMANDER ZHOU ARE LEAVING FEKUNDA, I HOPE THE REBELLION COMES BACK FOR MORE SOON.
COUNT ON IT. WE LOOK FORWARD TO WORKING WITH YOU.
SO, WHAT DO YOU THINK, LEM?
READY TO RUN AWAY AND JOIN THE REBELLION?
WHAT DOES IT SAY ABOUT ME THAT I'M SERIOUSLY CONSIDERING IT?
EVERYONE I KNOW AND LOVE HAS ASKED THEMSELVES THAT SAME QUESTION.
SO I'LL TELL YOU WHAT I TOLD THEM.
IT SAYS THAT YOU'LL FIT RIGHT IN.
THE END.

Art by Elsa Charretier, Colors by Matt Wilson

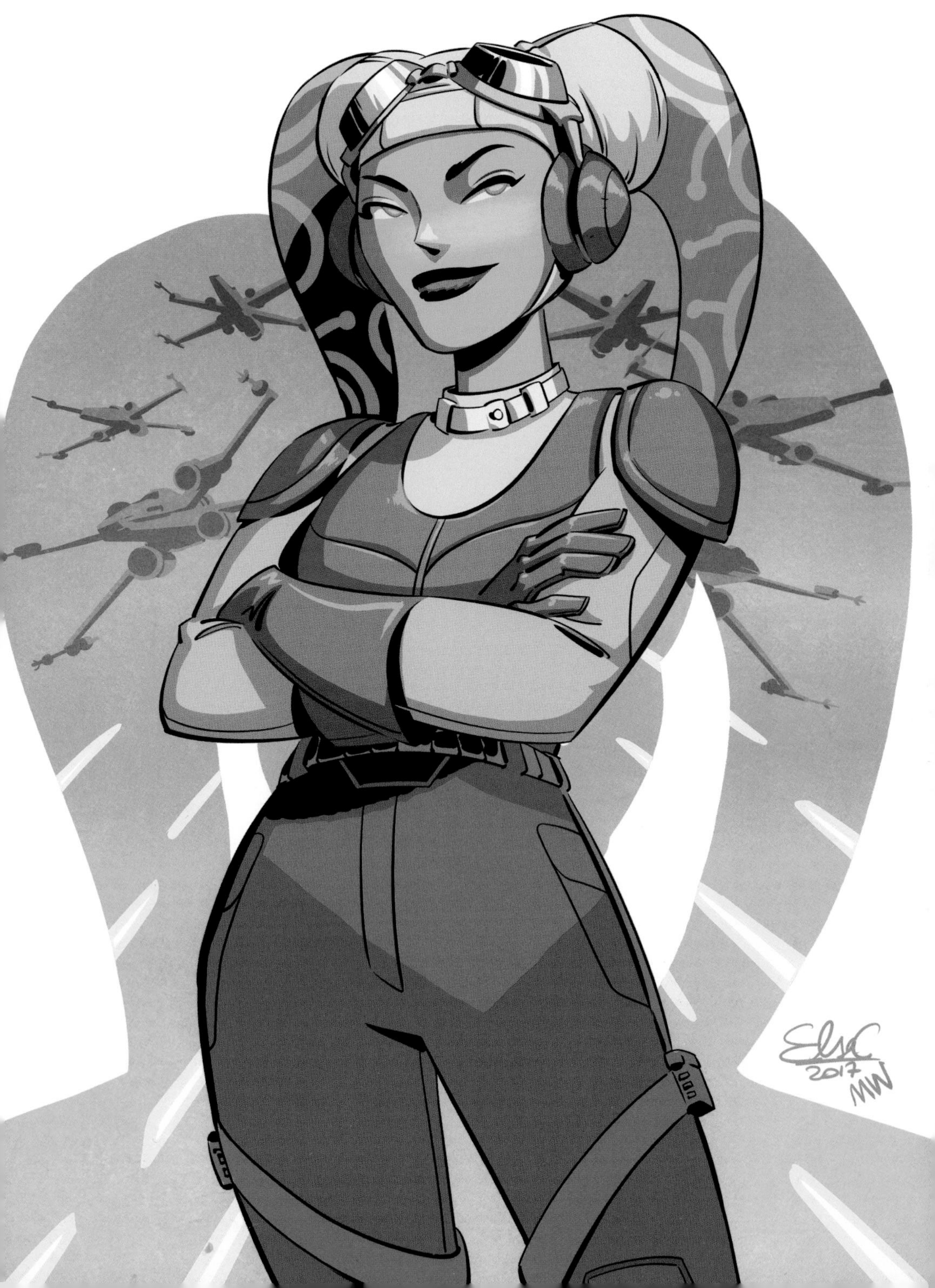
ElsaC
2017
MW

Ahsoka & Padmé

Art by Valentina Pinto

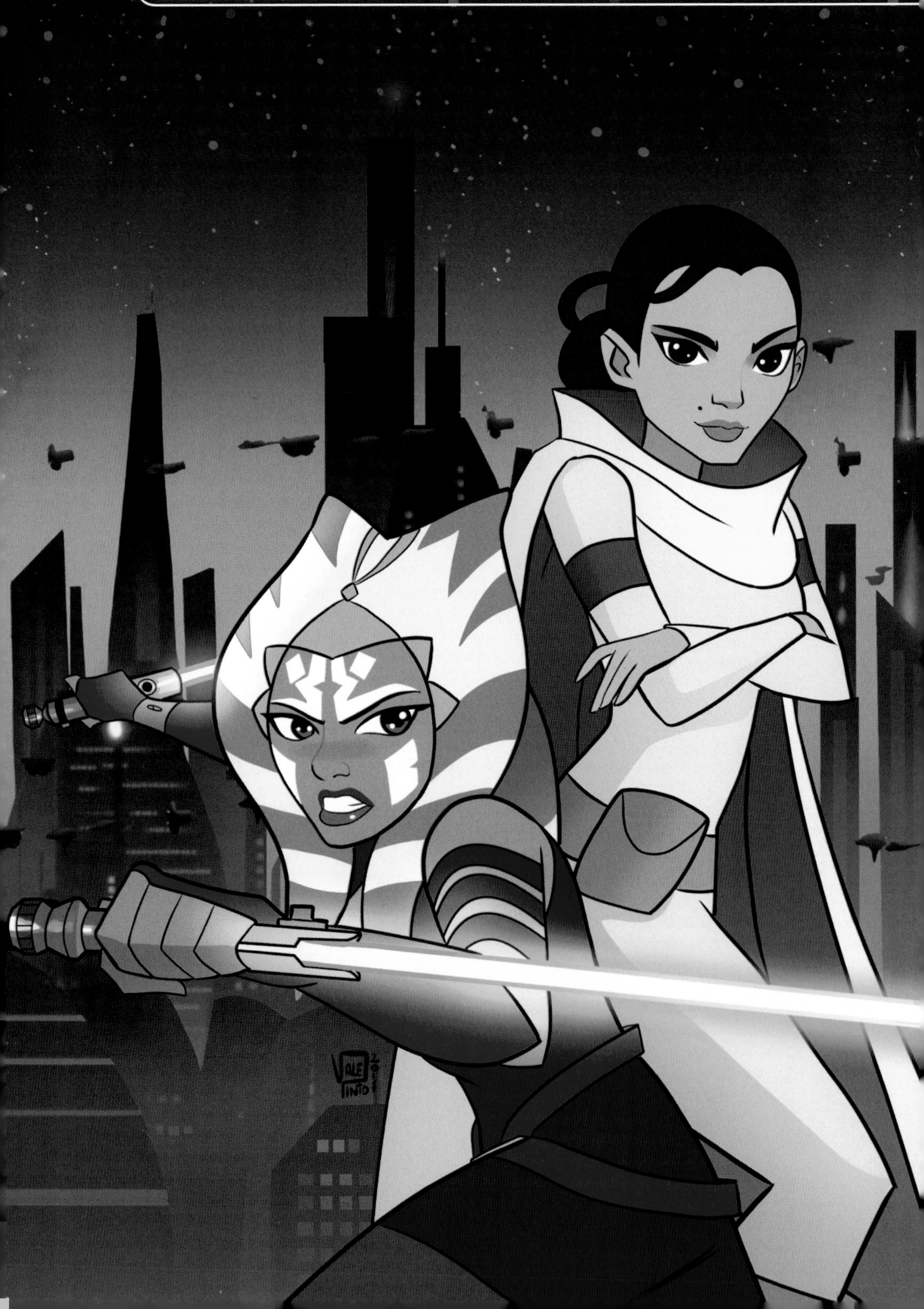

VALE PINTO

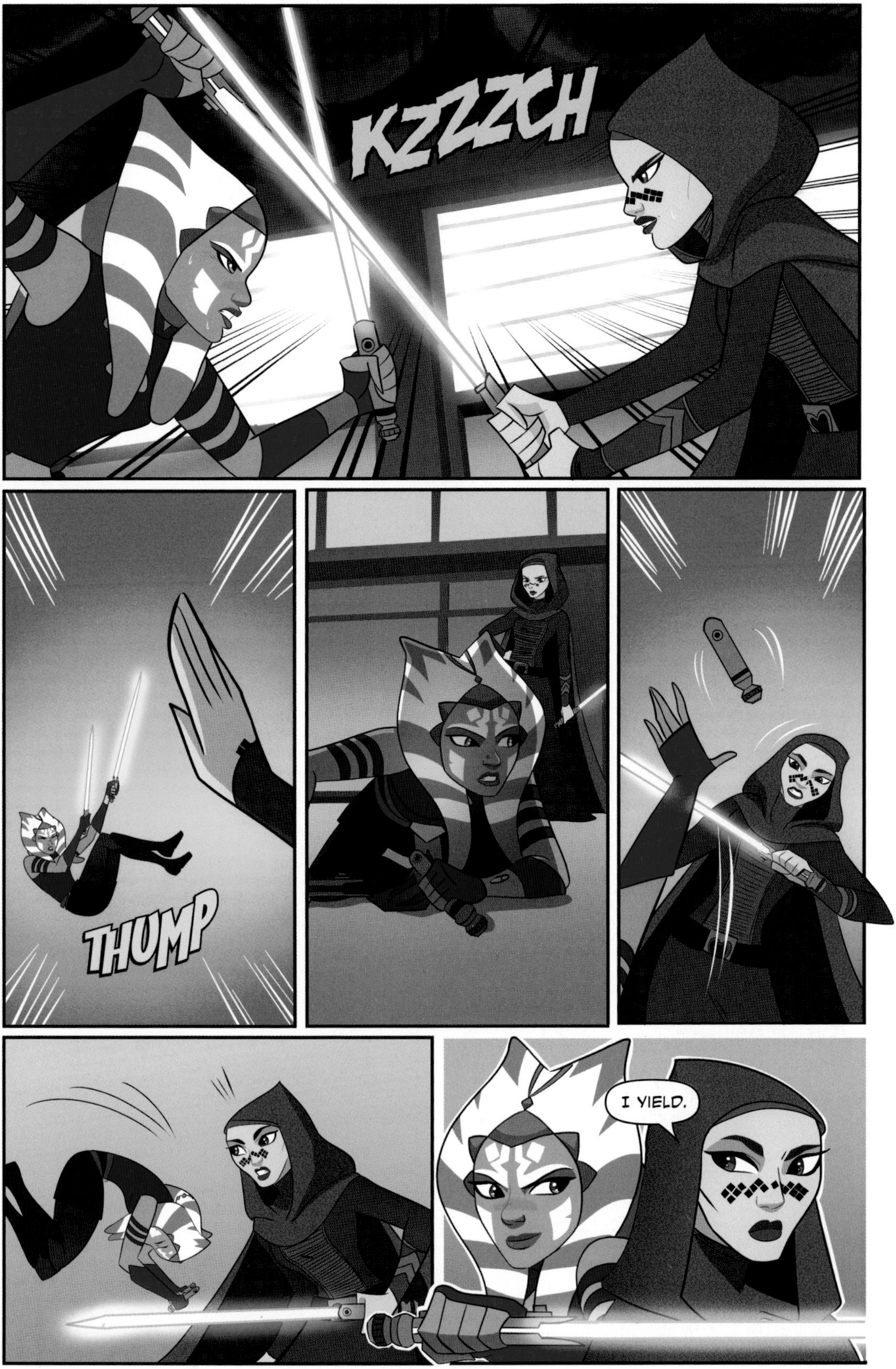
KZZZCH
THUMP
I YIELD.

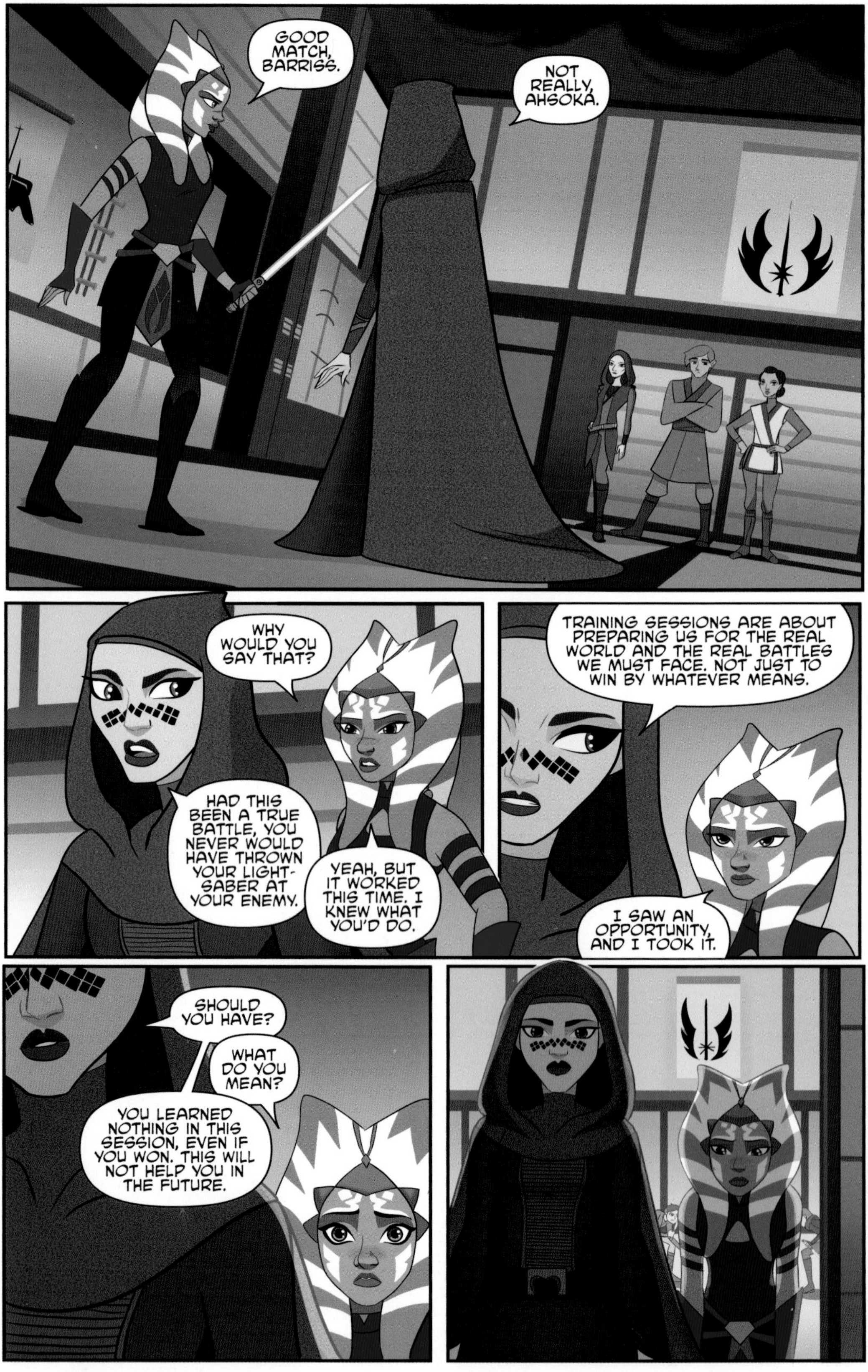
GOOD MATCH, BARRISS.
NOT REALLY, AHSOKA.
WHY WOULD YOU SAY THAT?
HAD THIS BEEN A TRUE BATTLE, YOU NEVER WOULD HAVE THROWN YOUR LIGHT-SABER AT YOUR ENEMY.
YEAH, BUT IT WORKED THIS TIME. I KNEW WHAT YOU'D DO.
TRAINING SESSIONS ARE ABOUT PREPARING US FOR THE REAL WORLD AND THE REAL BATTLES WE MUST FACE. NOT JUST TO WIN BY WHATEVER MEANS.
I SAW AN OPPORTUNITY, AND I TOOK IT.
SHOULD YOU HAVE?
WHAT DO YOU MEAN?
YOU LEARNED NOTHING IN THIS SESSION, EVEN IF YOU WON. THIS WILL NOT HELP YOU IN THE FUTURE.

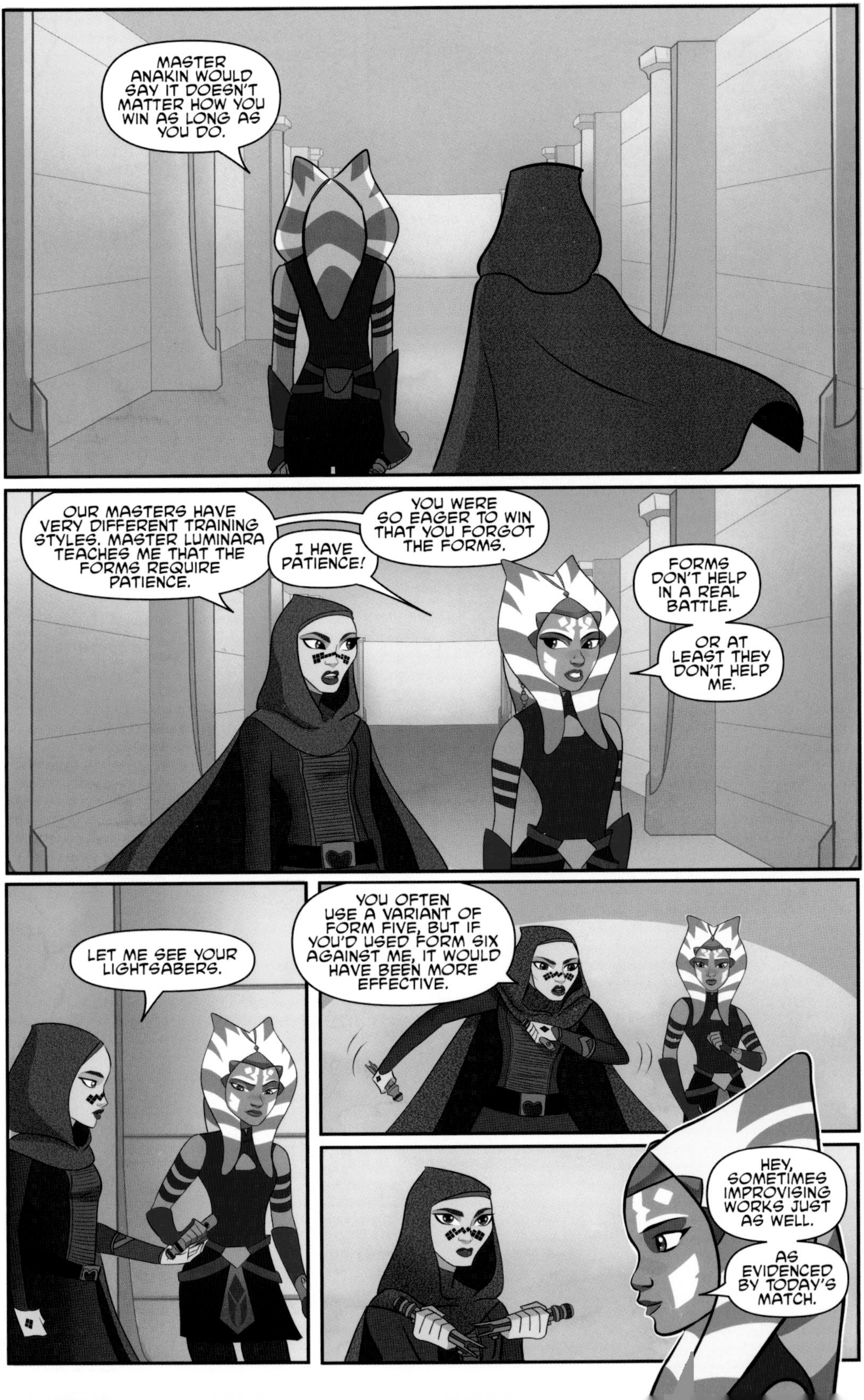
MASTER ANAKIN WOULD SAY IT DOESN'T MATTER HOW YOU WIN AS LONG AS YOU DO.
OUR MASTERS HAVE VERY DIFFERENT TRAINING STYLES. MASTER LUMINARA TEACHES ME THAT THE FORMS REQUIRE PATIENCE.
I HAVE PATIENCE!
YOU WERE SO EAGER TO WIN THAT YOU FORGOT THE FORMS.
FORMS DON'T HELP IN A REAL BATTLE.
OR AT LEAST THEY DON'T HELP ME.
LET ME SEE YOUR LIGHTSABERS.
YOU OFTEN USE A VARIANT OF FORM FIVE, BUT IF YOU'D USED FORM SIX AGAINST ME, IT WOULD HAVE BEEN MORE EFFECTIVE.
HEY, SOMETIMES IMPROVISING WORKS JUST AS WELL.
AS EVIDENCED BY TODAY'S MATCH.

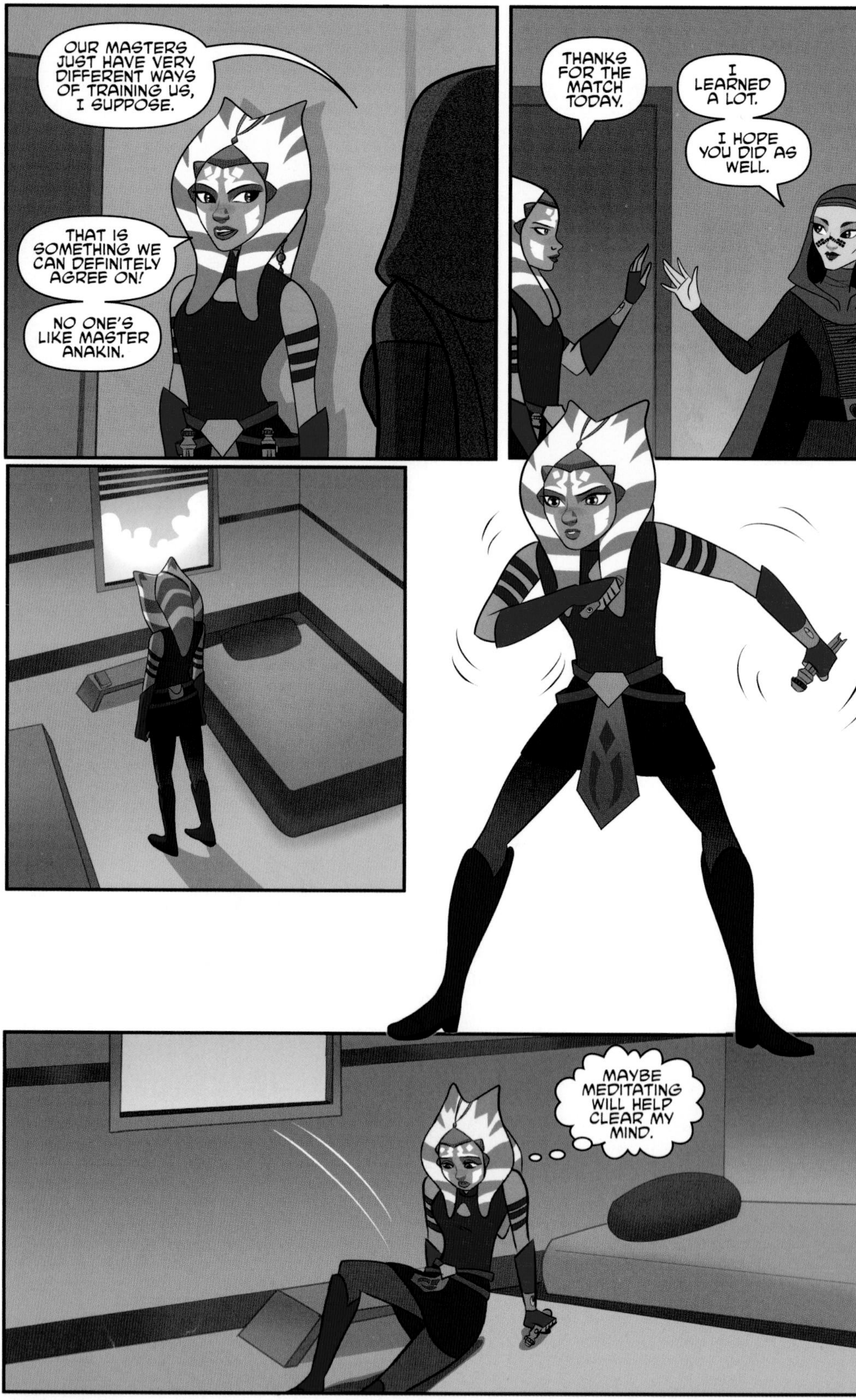
OUR MASTERS JUST HAVE VERY DIFFERENT WAYS OF TRAINING US, I SUPPOSE.
THAT IS SOMETHING WE CAN DEFINITELY AGREE ON!
NO ONE'S LIKE MASTER ANAKIN.
THANKS FOR THE MATCH TODAY.
I LEARNED A LOT.
I HOPE YOU DID AS WELL.
MAYBE MEDITATING WILL HELP CLEAR MY MIND.

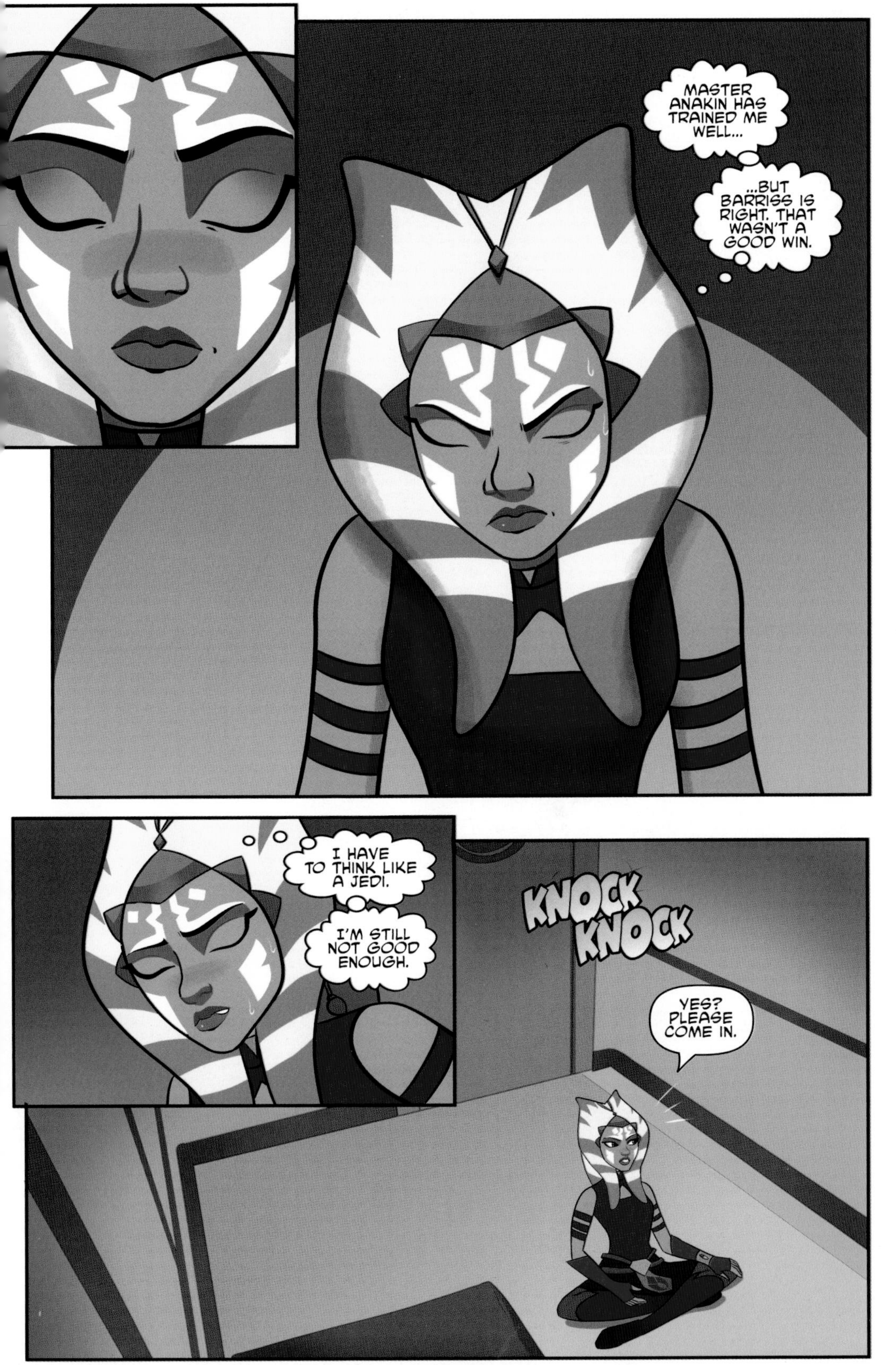
MASTER ANAKIN HAS TRAINED ME WELL...
...BUT BARRISS IS RIGHT. THAT WASN'T A GOOD WIN.
I HAVE TO THINK LIKE A JEDI.
I'M STILL NOT GOOD ENOUGH.
KNOCK KNOCK
YES? PLEASE COME IN.

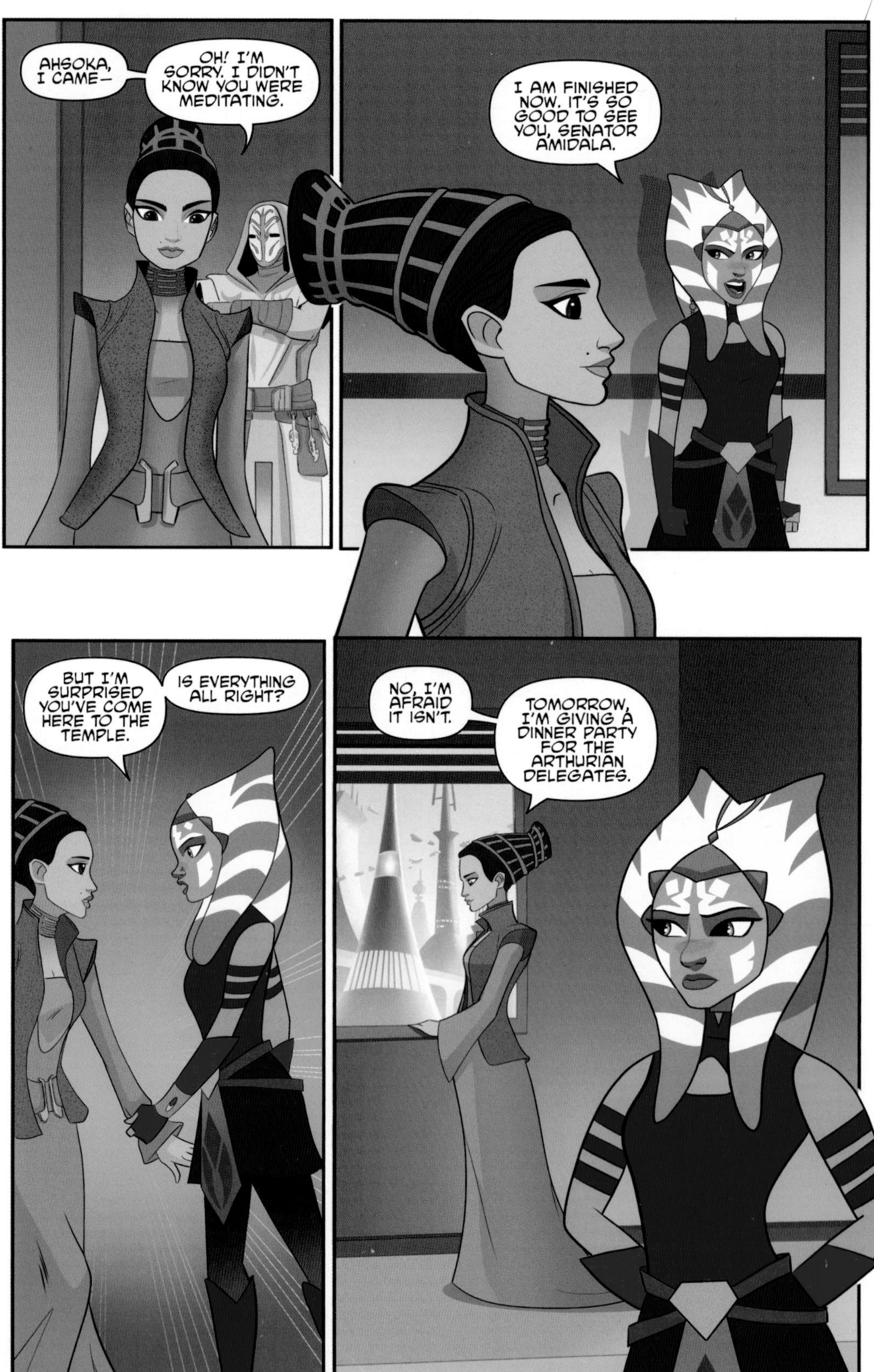
AHSOKA, I CAME—
OH! I'M SORRY. I DIDN'T KNOW YOU WERE MEDITATING.
I AM FINISHED NOW. IT'S SO GOOD TO SEE YOU, SENATOR AMIDALA.
BUT I'M SURPRISED YOU'VE COME HERE TO THE TEMPLE.
IS EVERYTHING ALL RIGHT?
NO, I'M AFRAID IT ISN'T.
TOMORROW, I'M GIVING A DINNER PARTY FOR THE ARTHURIAN DELEGATES.

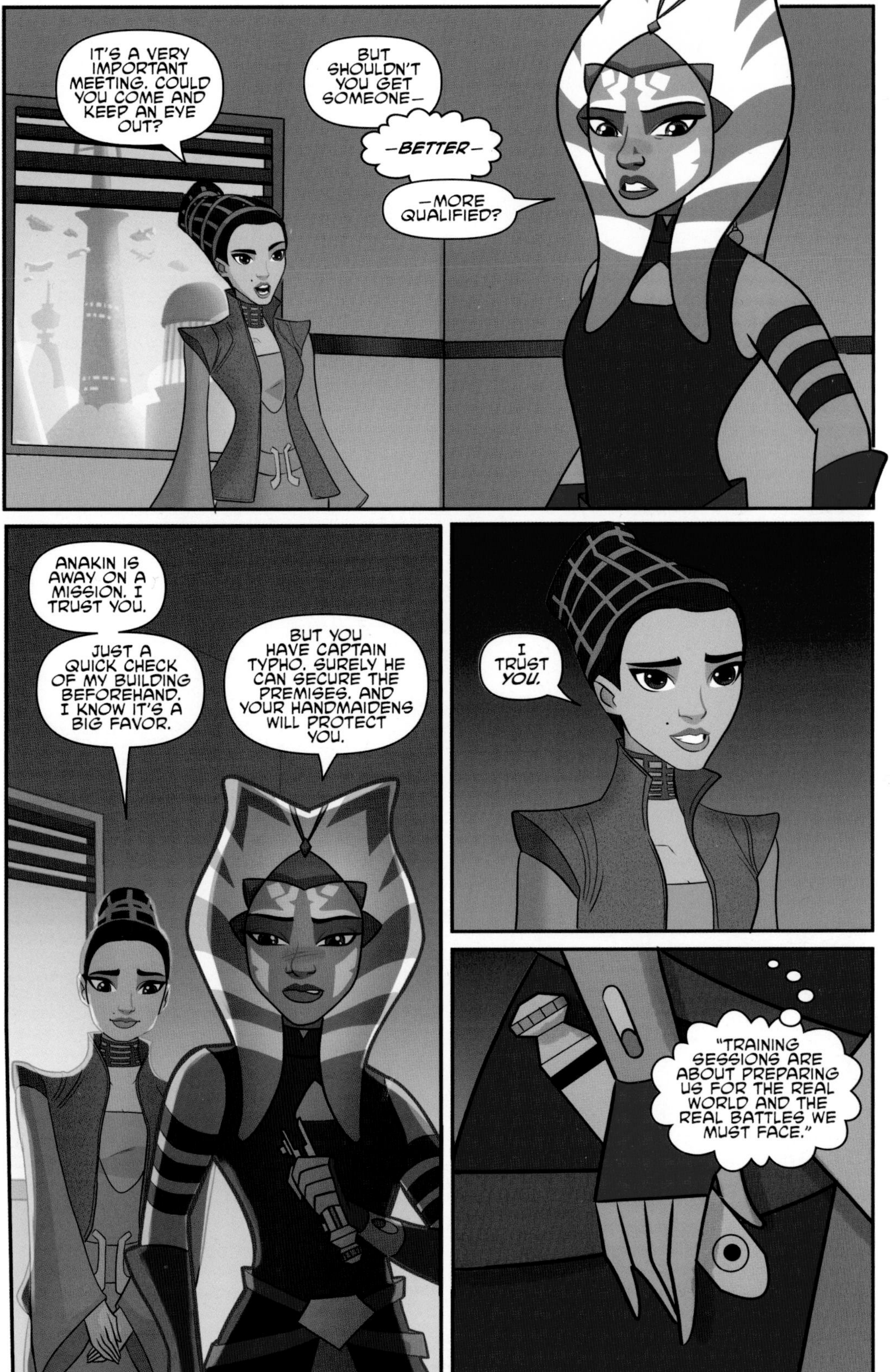
IT'S A VERY IMPORTANT MEETING. COULD YOU COME AND KEEP AN EYE OUT?
BUT SHOULDN'T YOU GET SOMEONE—
—BETTER—
—MORE QUALIFIED?
ANAKIN IS AWAY ON A MISSION. I TRUST YOU.
JUST A QUICK CHECK OF MY BUILDING BEFOREHAND. I KNOW IT'S A BIG FAVOR.
BUT YOU HAVE CAPTAIN TYPHO. SURELY HE CAN SECURE THE PREMISES. AND YOUR HANDMAIDENS WILL PROTECT YOU.
I TRUST YOU.
"TRAINING SESSIONS ARE ABOUT PREPARING US FOR THE REAL WORLD AND THE REAL BATTLES WE MUST FACE."

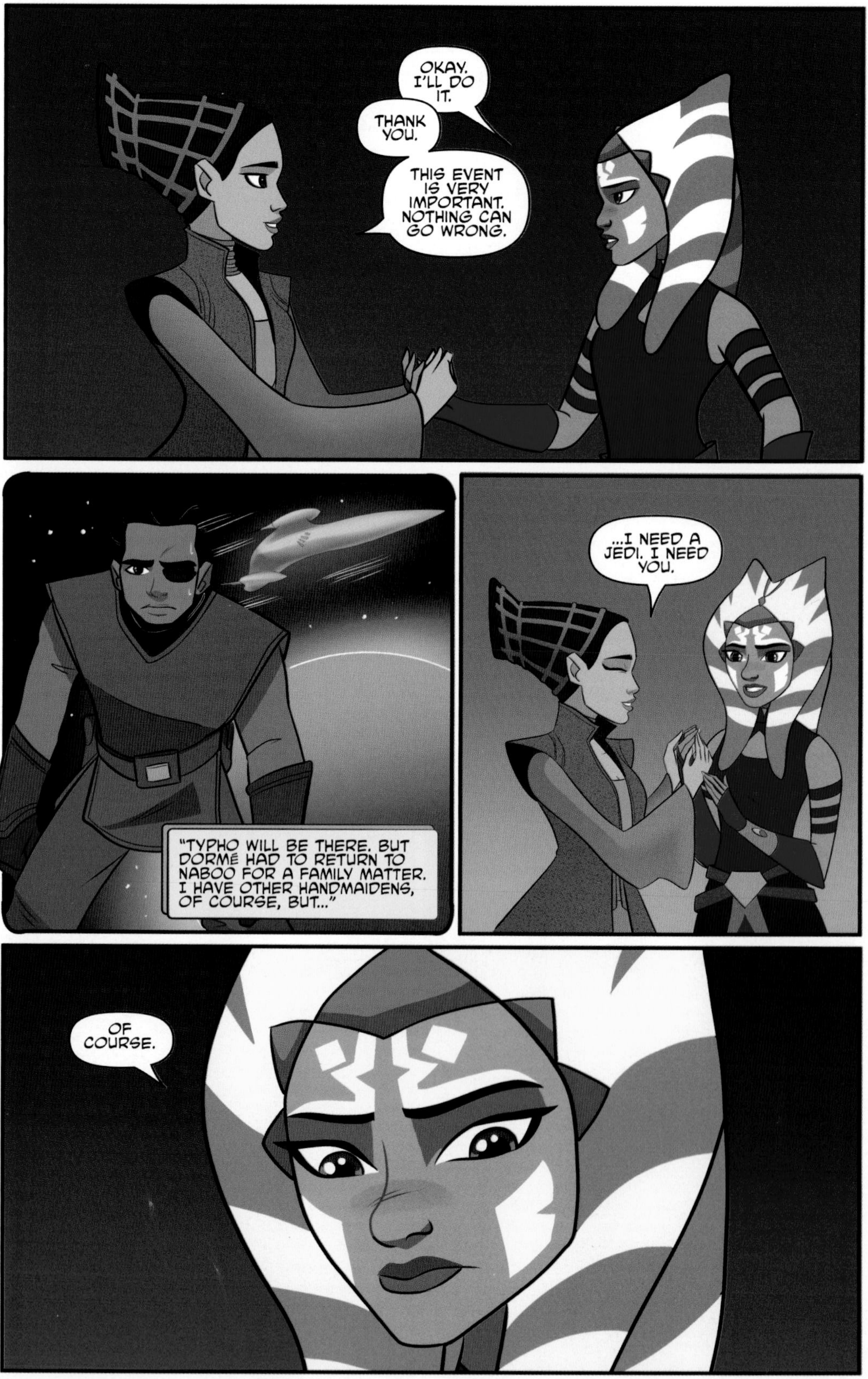
OKAY. I'LL DO IT.
THANK YOU.
THIS EVENT IS VERY IMPORTANT. NOTHING CAN GO WRONG.
"TYPHO WILL BE THERE. BUT DORMÉ HAD TO RETURN TO NABOO FOR A FAMILY MATTER. I HAVE OTHER HANDMAIDENS, OF COURSE, BUT..."
...I NEED A JEDI. I NEED YOU.
OF COURSE.

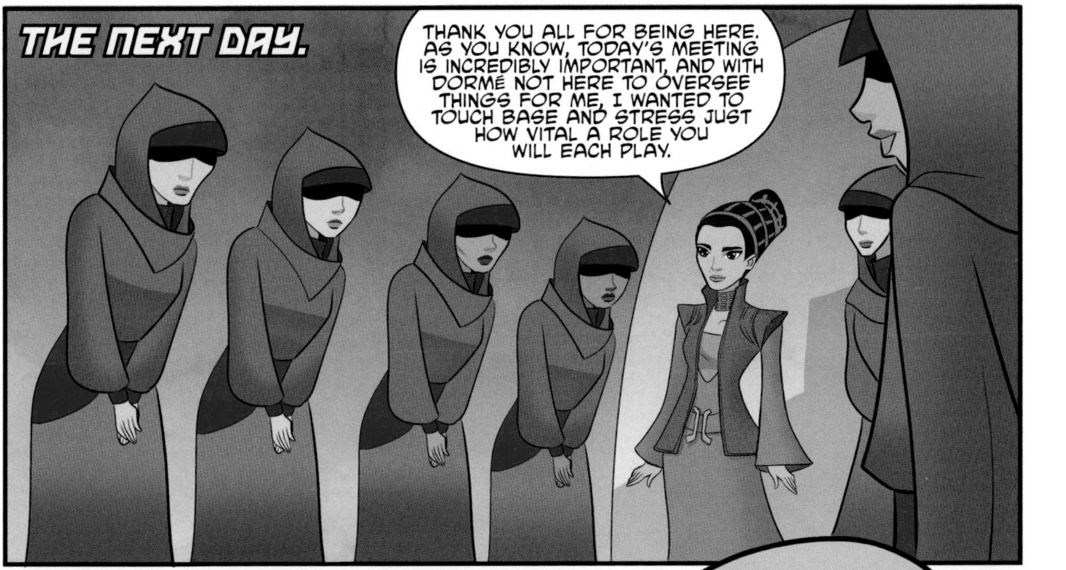
THE NEXT DAY.
THANK YOU ALL FOR BEING HERE. AS YOU KNOW, TODAY'S MEETING IS INCREDIBLY IMPORTANT, AND WITH DORMÉ NOT HERE TO OVERSEE THINGS FOR ME, I WANTED TO TOUCH BASE AND STRESS JUST HOW VITAL A ROLE YOU WILL EACH PLAY.

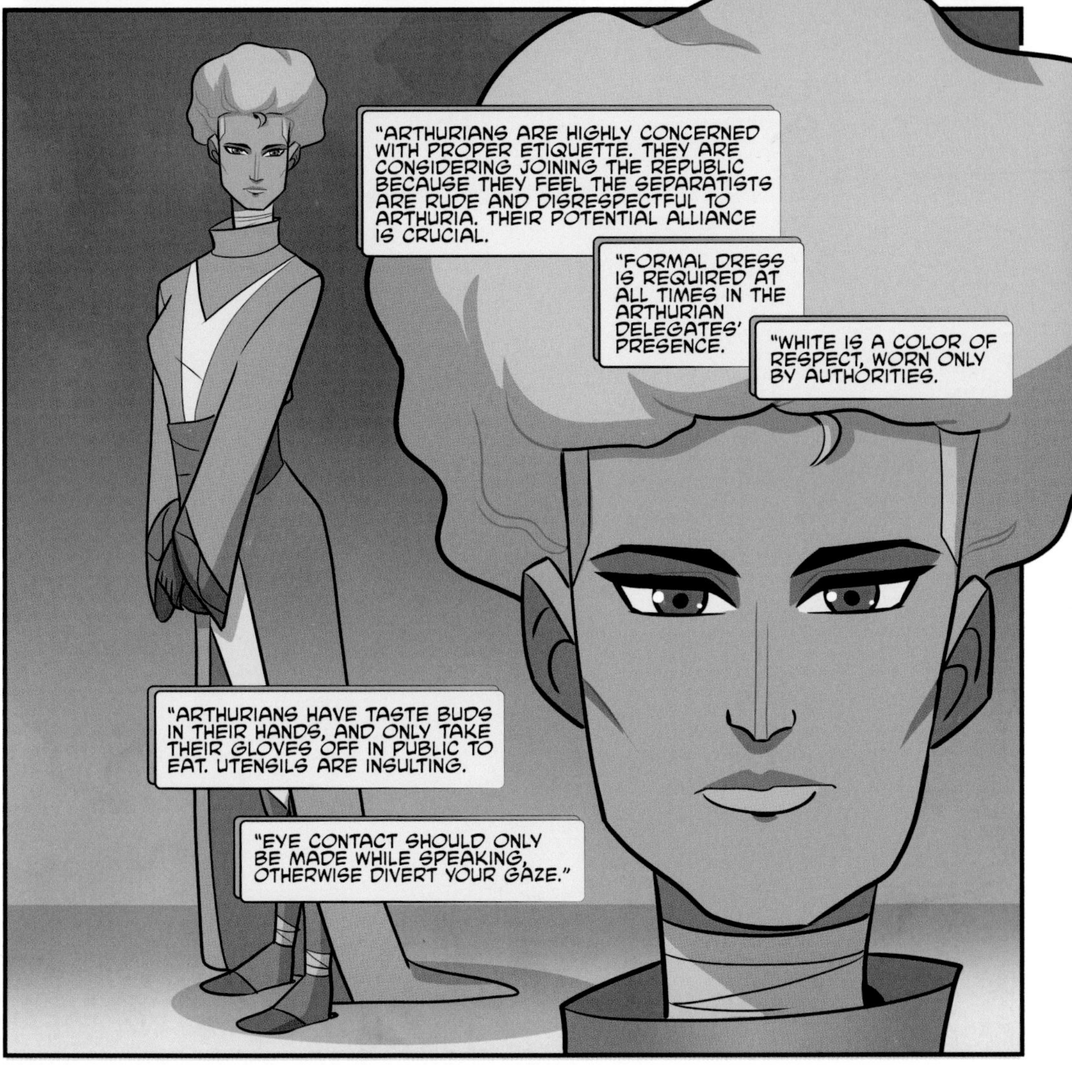
"ARTHURIANS ARE HIGHLY CONCERNED WITH PROPER ETIQUETTE. THEY ARE CONSIDERING JOINING THE REPUBLIC BECAUSE THEY FEEL THE SEPARATISTS ARE RUDE AND DISRESPECTFUL TO ARTHURIA. THEIR POTENTIAL ALLIANCE IS CRUCIAL.
"FORMAL DRESS IS REQUIRED AT ALL TIMES IN THE ARTHURIAN DELEGATES' PRESENCE.
"WHITE IS A COLOR OF RESPECT, WORN ONLY BY AUTHORITIES.
"ARTHURIANS HAVE TASTE BUDS IN THEIR HANDS, AND ONLY TAKE THEIR GLOVES OFF IN PUBLIC TO EAT. UTENSILS ARE INSULTING.
"EYE CONTACT SHOULD ONLY BE MADE WHILE SPEAKING, OTHERWISE DIVERT YOUR GAZE."

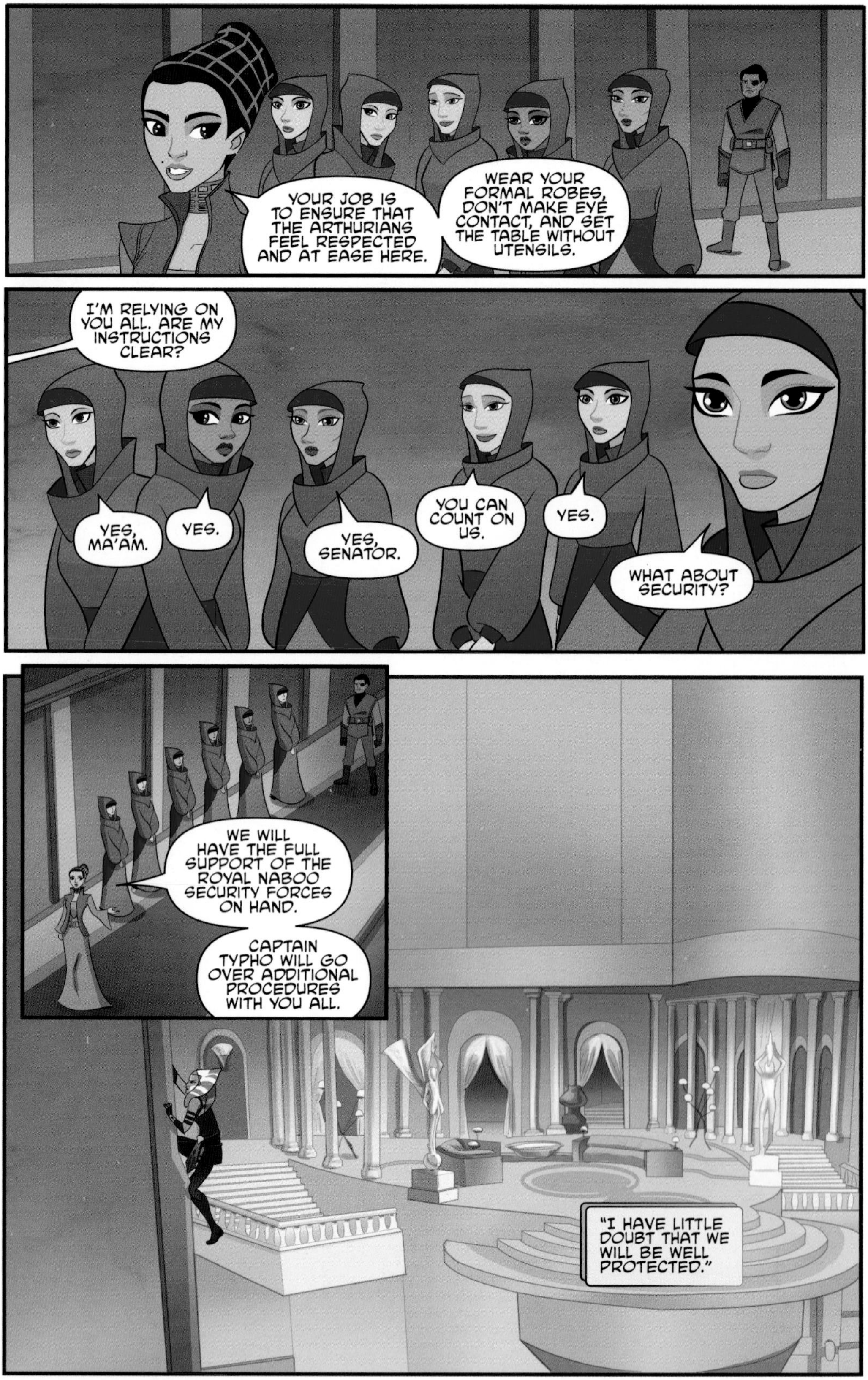
YOUR JOB IS TO ENSURE THAT THE ARTHURIANS FEEL RESPECTED AND AT EASE HERE.
WEAR YOUR FORMAL ROBES, DON'T MAKE EYE CONTACT, AND SET THE TABLE WITHOUT UTENSILS.
I'M RELYING ON YOU ALL. ARE MY INSTRUCTIONS CLEAR?
YES, MA'AM.
YES.
YES, SENATOR.
YOU CAN COUNT ON US.
YES.
WHAT ABOUT SECURITY?
WE WILL HAVE THE FULL SUPPORT OF THE ROYAL NABOO SECURITY FORCES ON HAND.
CAPTAIN TYPHO WILL GO OVER ADDITIONAL PROCEDURES WITH YOU ALL.
"I HAVE LITTLE DOUBT THAT WE WILL BE WELL PROTECTED."

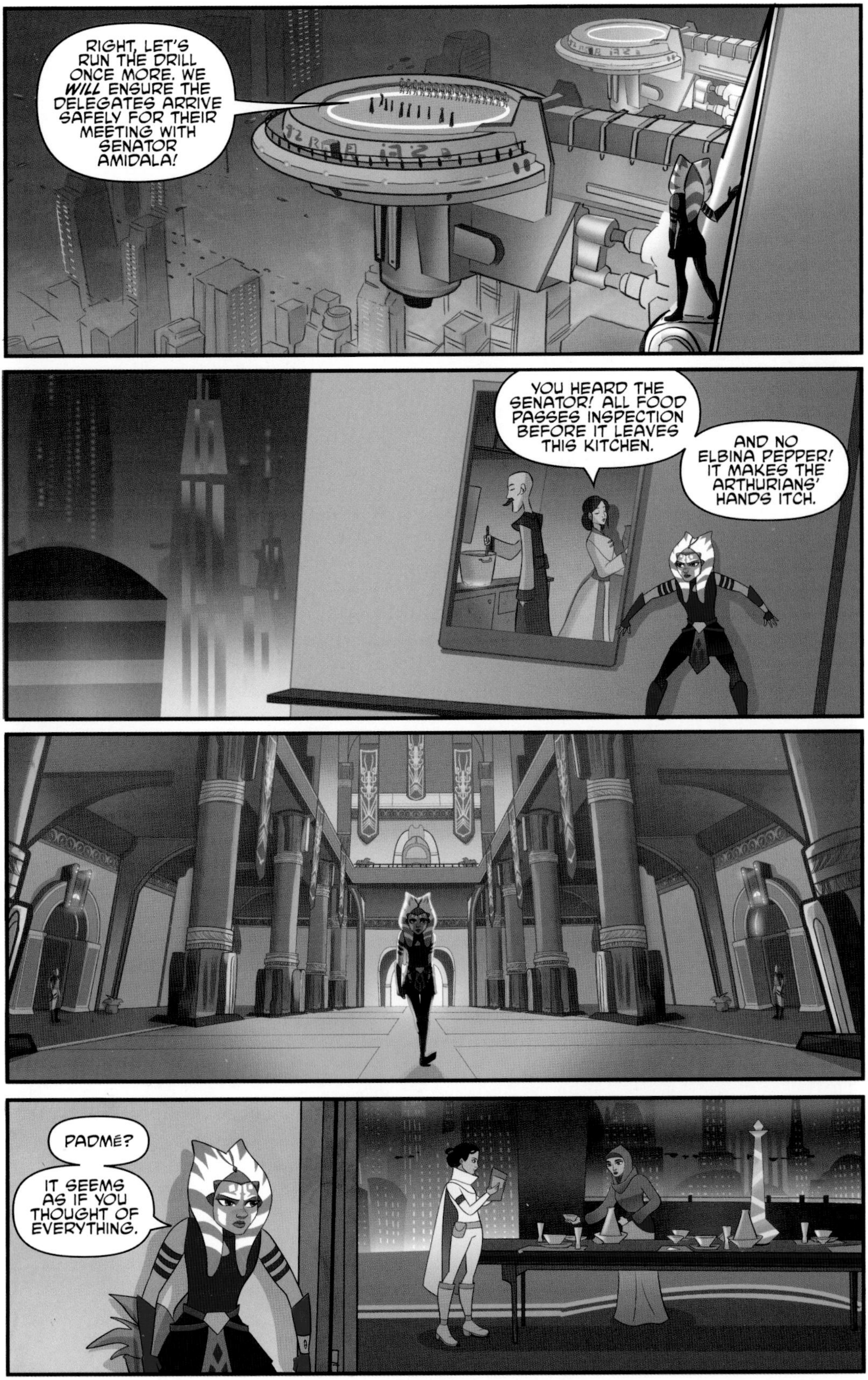
RIGHT, LET'S RUN THE DRILL ONCE MORE. WE *WILL* ENSURE THE DELEGATES ARRIVE SAFELY FOR THEIR MEETING WITH SENATOR AMIDALA!
YOU HEARD THE SENATOR! ALL FOOD PASSES INSPECTION BEFORE IT LEAVES THIS KITCHEN.
AND NO ELBINA PEPPER! IT MAKES THE ARTHURIANS' HANDS ITCH.
PADMÉ?
IT SEEMS AS IF YOU THOUGHT OF EVERYTHING.

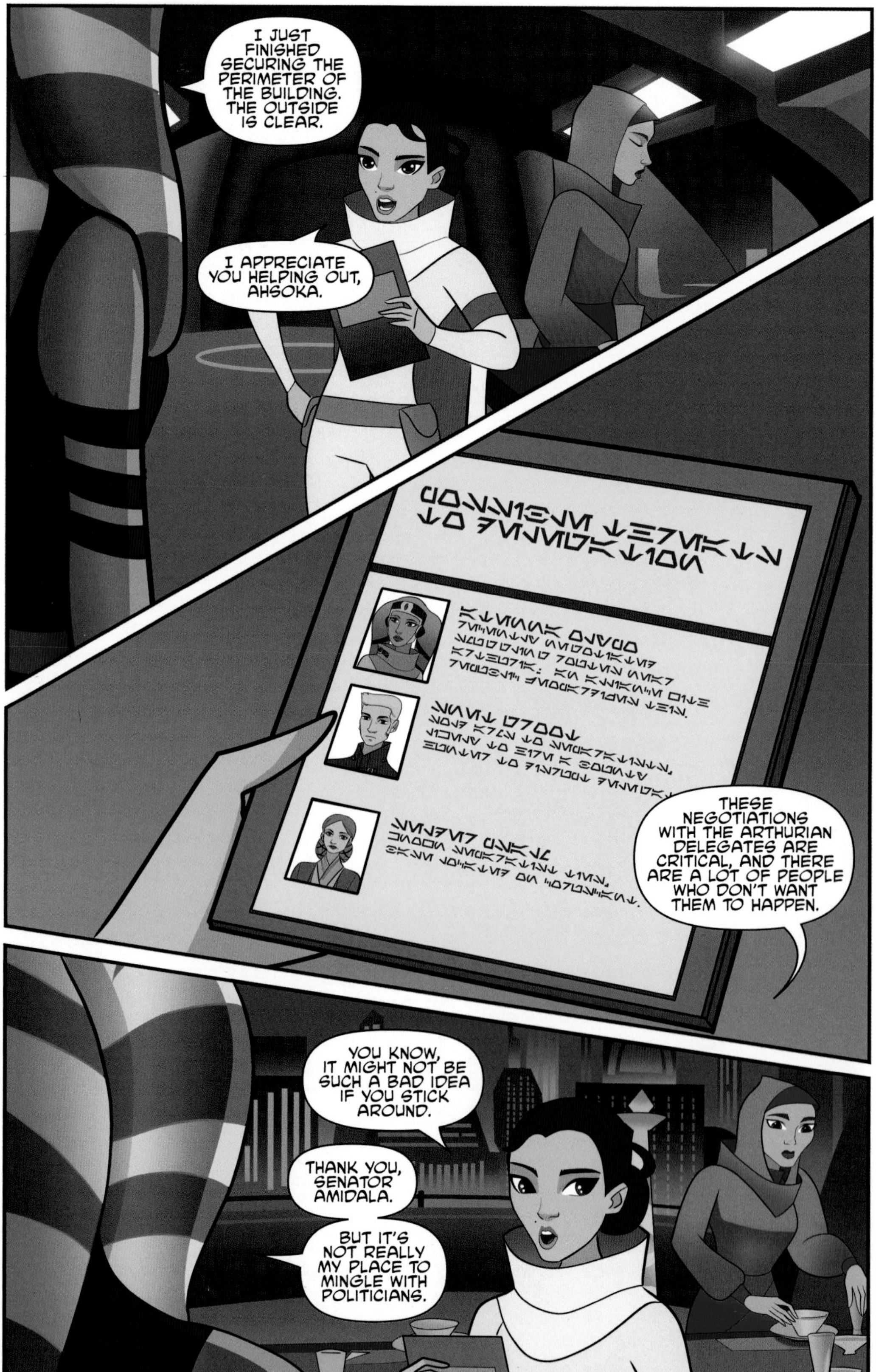
I JUST FINISHED SECURING THE PERIMETER OF THE BUILDING. THE OUTSIDE IS CLEAR.
I APPRECIATE YOU HELPING OUT, AHSOKA.
THESE NEGOTIATIONS WITH THE ARTHURIAN DELEGATES ARE CRITICAL, AND THERE ARE A LOT OF PEOPLE WHO DON'T WANT THEM TO HAPPEN.
YOU KNOW, IT MIGHT NOT BE SUCH A BAD IDEA IF YOU STICK AROUND.
THANK YOU, SENATOR AMIDALA.
BUT IT'S NOT REALLY MY PLACE TO MINGLE WITH POLITICIANS.

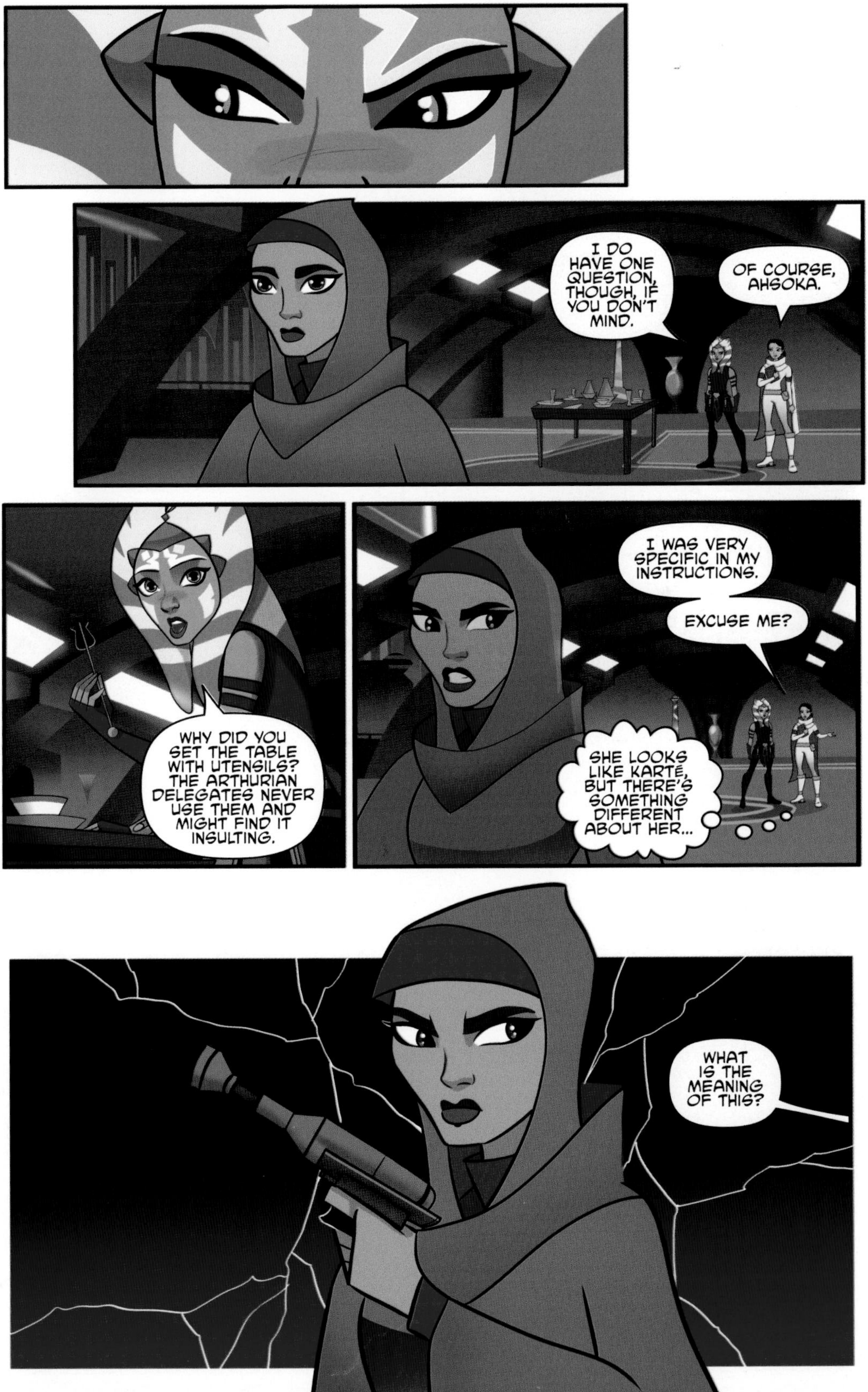
I DO HAVE ONE QUESTION, THOUGH, IF YOU DON'T MIND.
OF COURSE, AHSOKA.
WHY DID YOU SET THE TABLE WITH UTENSILS? THE ARTHURIAN DELEGATES NEVER USE THEM AND MIGHT FIND IT INSULTING.
I WAS VERY SPECIFIC IN MY INSTRUCTIONS.
EXCUSE ME?
SHE LOOKS LIKE KARTÉ, BUT THERE'S SOMETHING DIFFERENT ABOUT HER...
WHAT IS THE MEANING OF THIS?

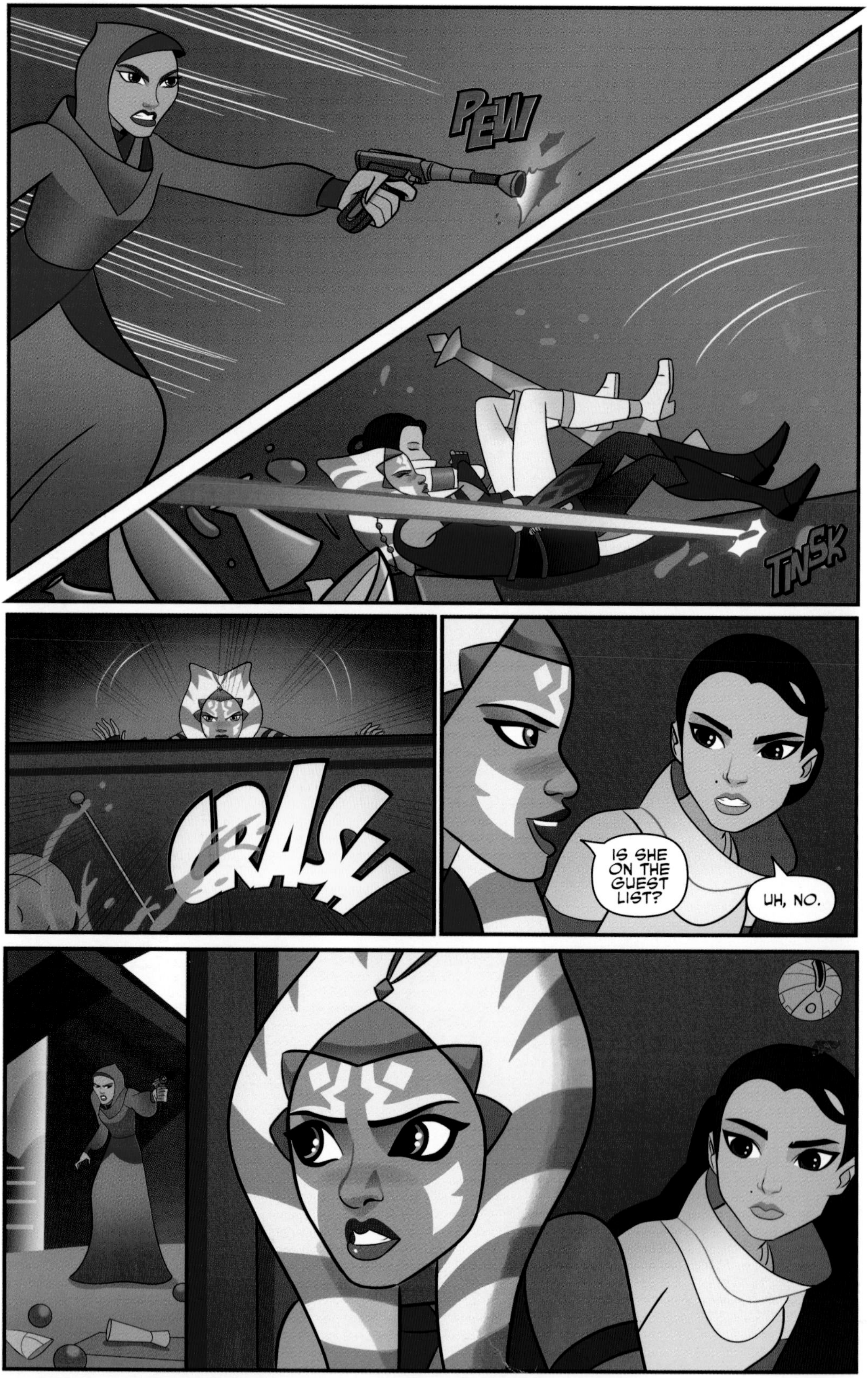
PEW
TNSK
CRASH
IS SHE ON THE GUEST LIST?
UH, NO.

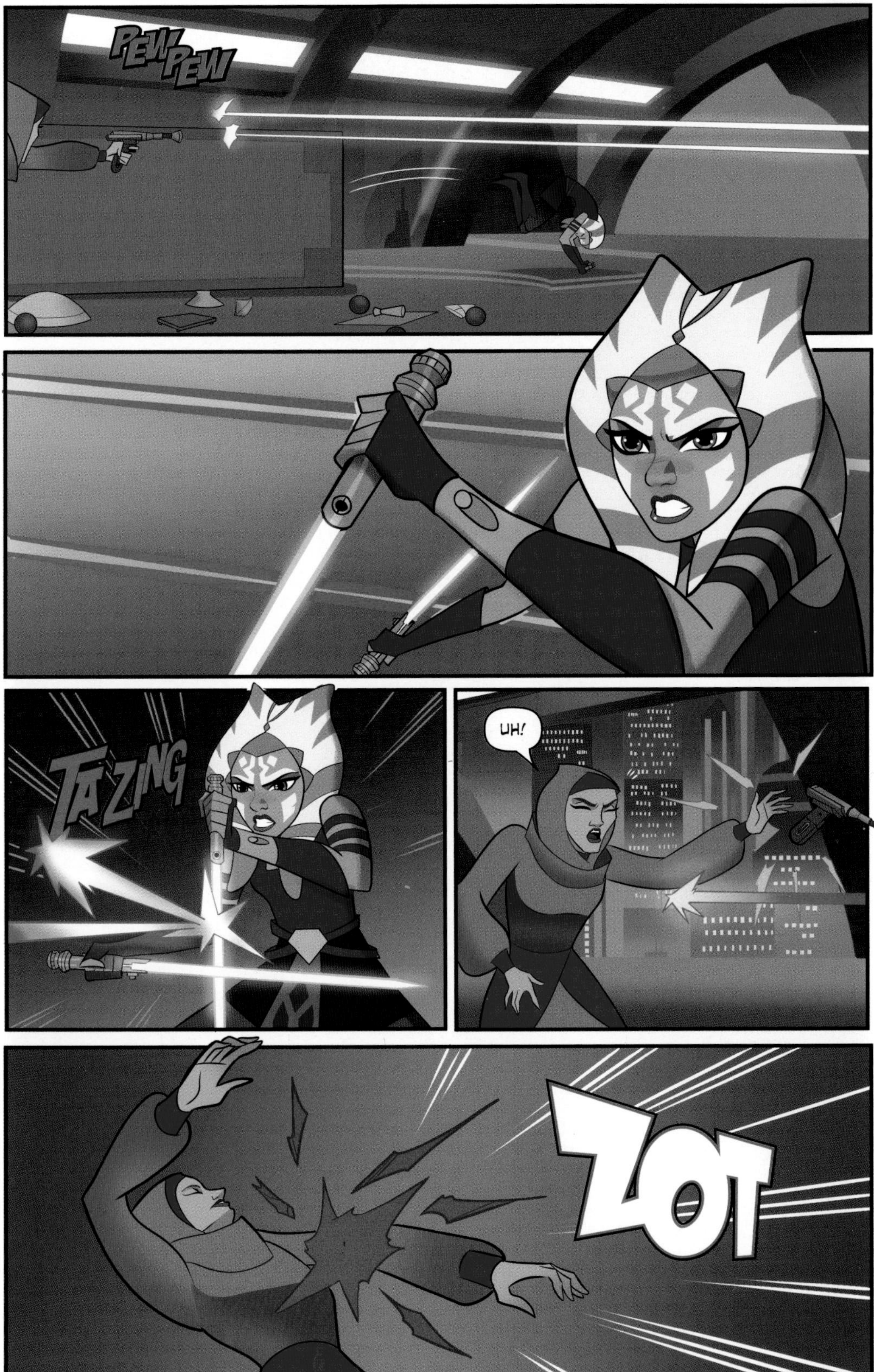
PEW PEW
TAZING
UH!
ZOT

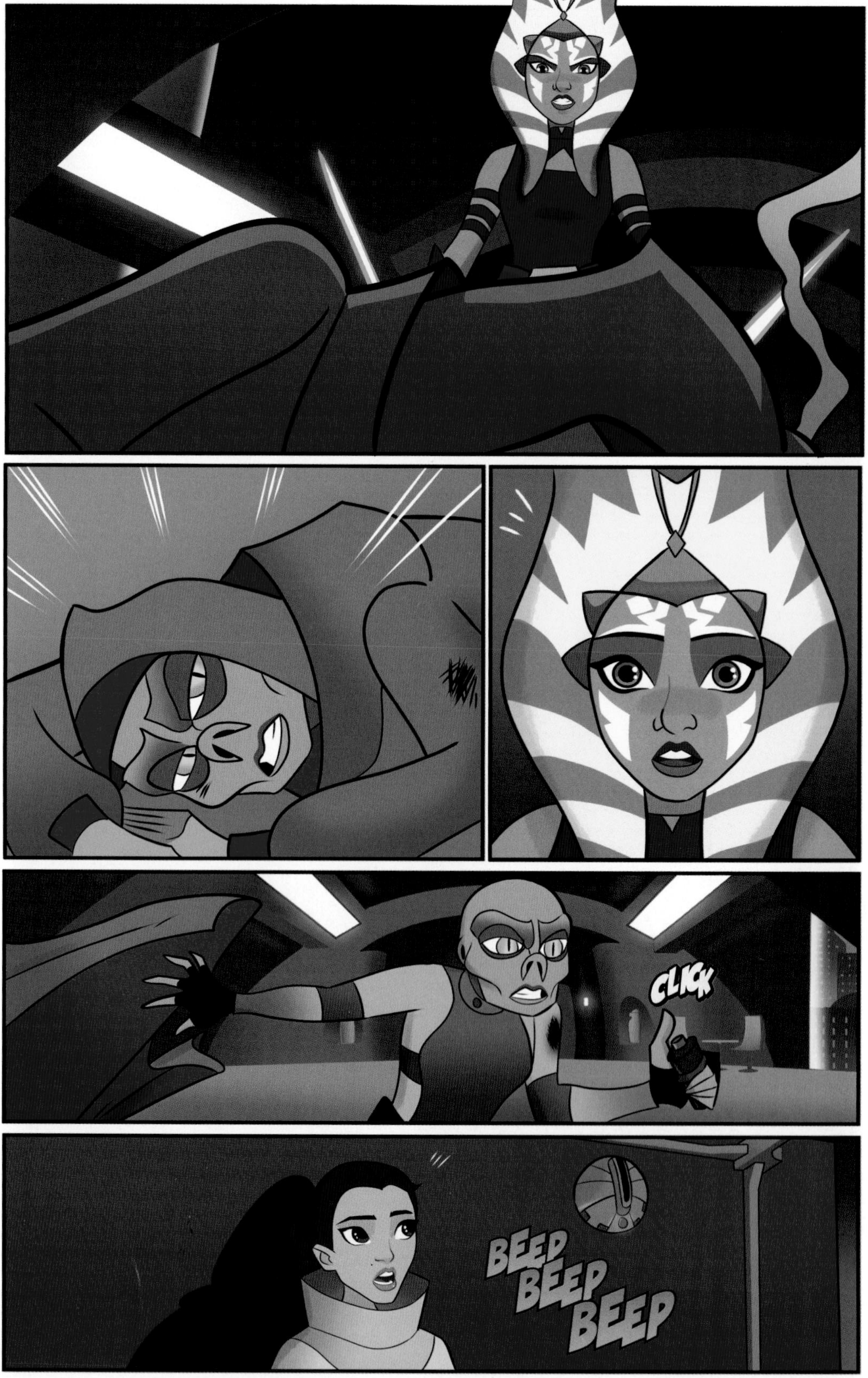
CLICK
BEEP
BEEP
BEEP

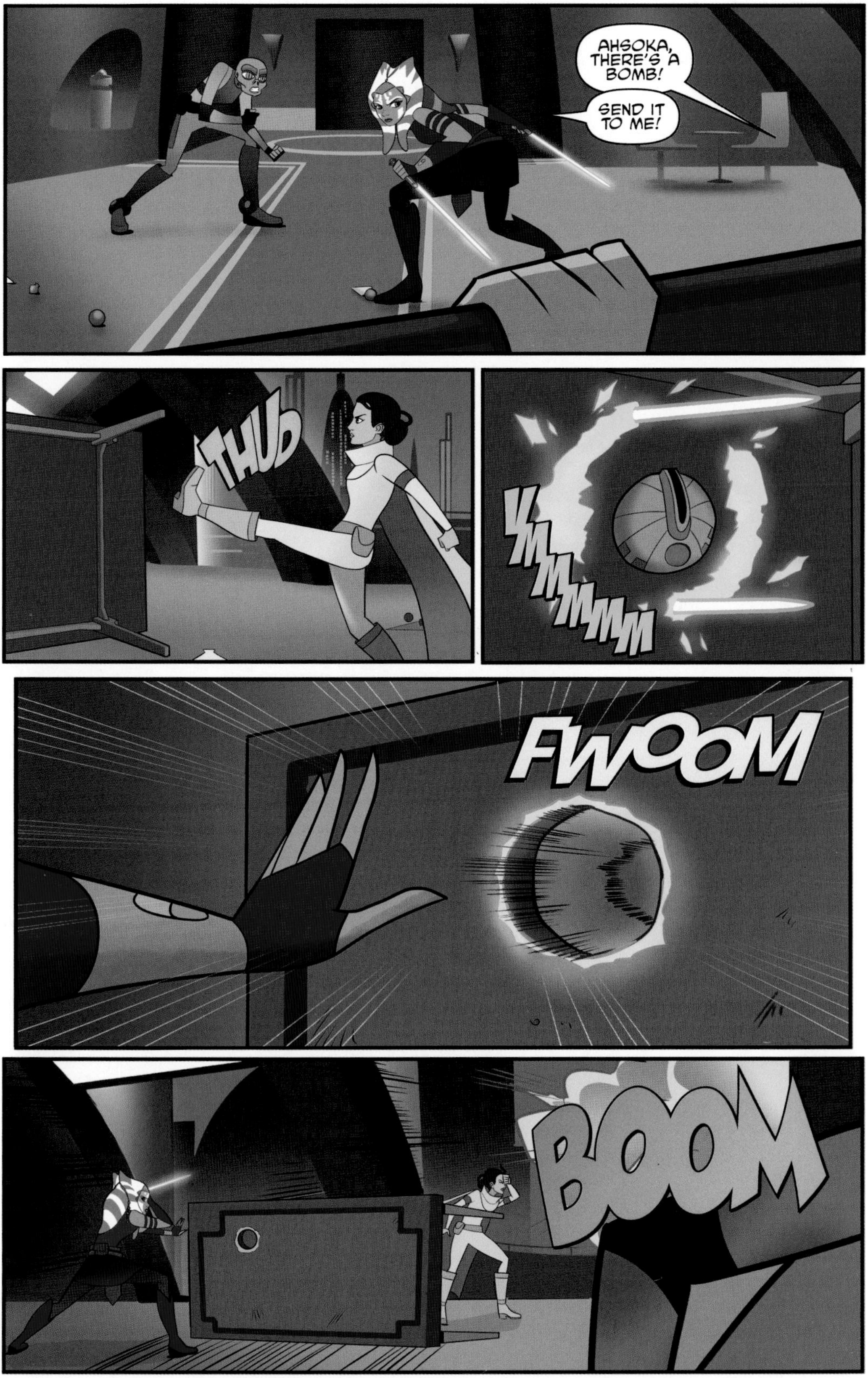
AHSOKA, THERE'S A BOMB!
SEND IT TO ME!
THUD
VMMMMMM
FWOOM
BOOM

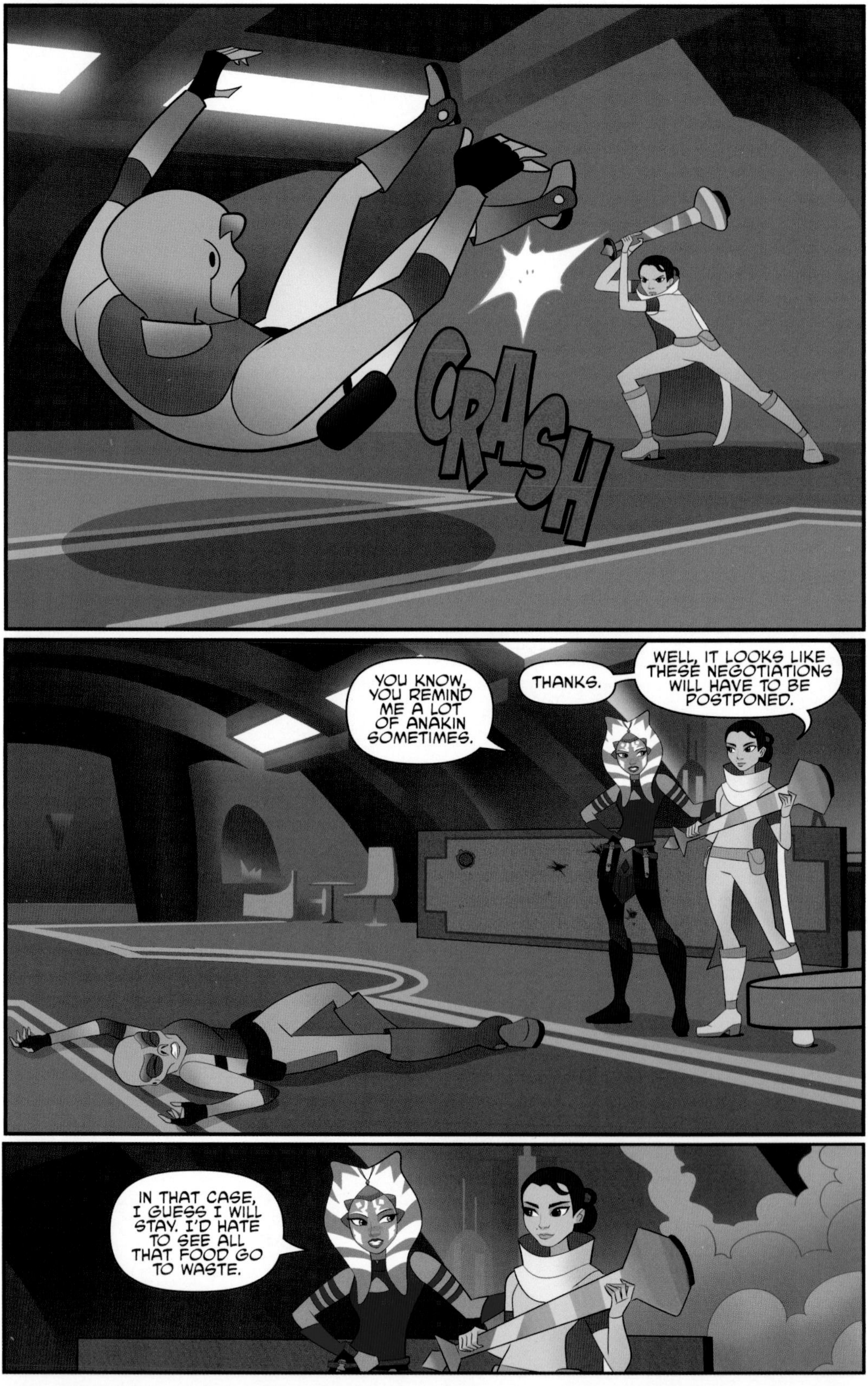
CRASH
YOU KNOW, YOU REMIND ME A LOT OF ANAKIN SOMETIMES.
THANKS.
WELL, IT LOOKS LIKE THESE NEGOTIATIONS WILL HAVE TO BE POSTPONED.
IN THAT CASE, I GUESS I WILL STAY. I'D HATE TO SEE ALL THAT FOOD GO TO WASTE.

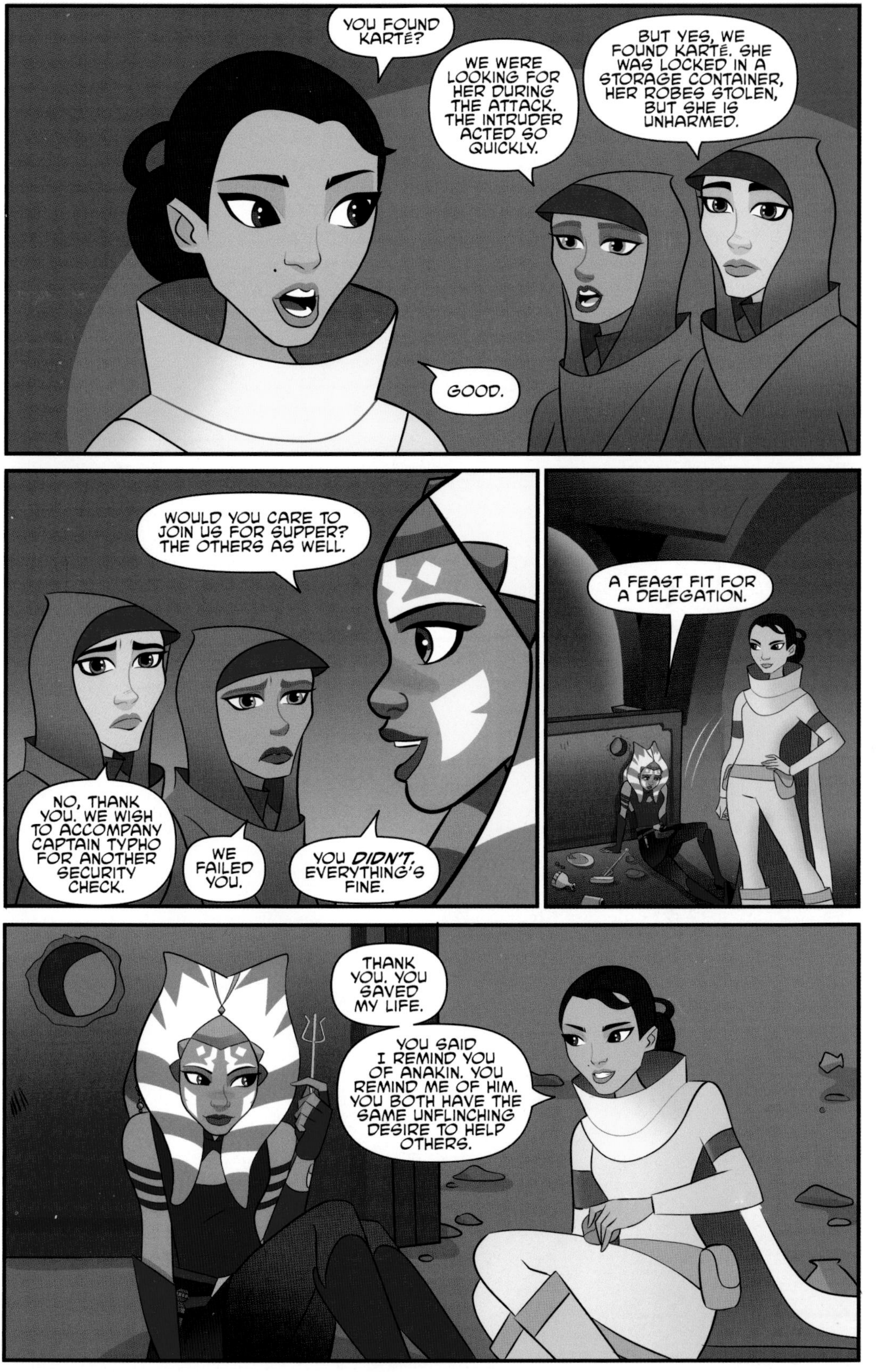

YOU FOUND KARTÉ?
WE WERE LOOKING FOR HER DURING THE ATTACK. THE INTRUDER ACTED SO QUICKLY.
BUT YES, WE FOUND KARTÉ. SHE WAS LOCKED IN A STORAGE CONTAINER, HER ROBES STOLEN, BUT SHE IS UNHARMED.
GOOD.
WOULD YOU CARE TO JOIN US FOR SUPPER? THE OTHERS AS WELL.
NO, THANK YOU. WE WISH TO ACCOMPANY CAPTAIN TYPHO FOR ANOTHER SECURITY CHECK.
WE FAILED YOU.
YOU *DIDN'T.* EVERYTHING'S FINE.
A FEAST FIT FOR A DELEGATION.
THANK YOU. YOU SAVED MY LIFE.
YOU SAID I REMIND YOU OF ANAKIN. YOU REMIND ME OF HIM. YOU BOTH HAVE THE SAME UNFLINCHING DESIRE TO HELP OTHERS.

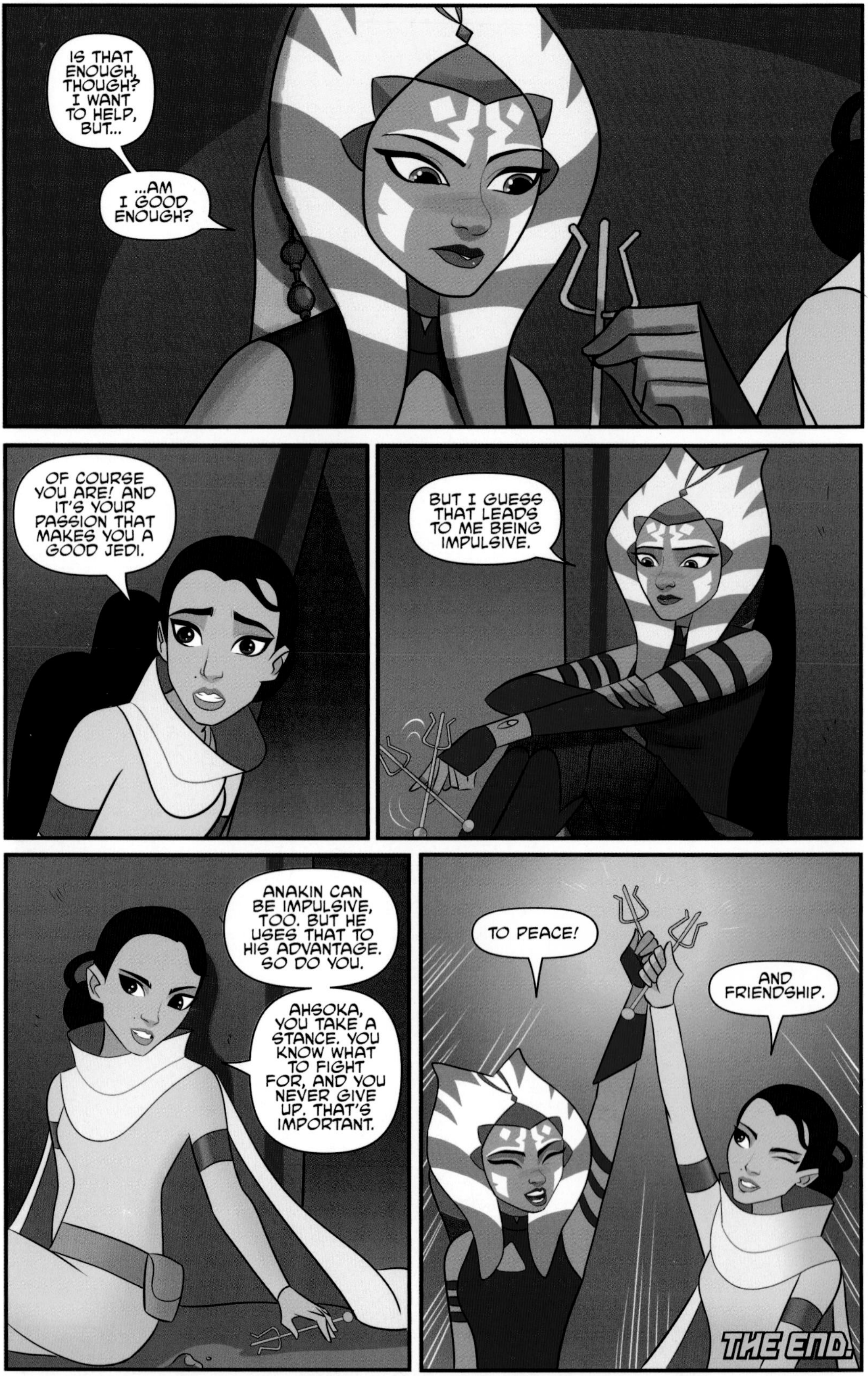
IS THAT ENOUGH, THOUGH? I WANT TO HELP, BUT...
...AM I GOOD ENOUGH?
OF COURSE YOU ARE! AND IT'S YOUR PASSION THAT MAKES YOU A GOOD JEDI.
BUT I GUESS THAT LEADS TO ME BEING IMPULSIVE.
ANAKIN CAN BE IMPULSIVE, TOO. BUT HE USES THAT TO HIS ADVANTAGE. SO DO YOU.
AHSOKA, YOU TAKE A STANCE. YOU KNOW WHAT TO FIGHT FOR, AND YOU NEVER GIVE UP. THAT'S IMPORTANT.
TO PEACE!
AND FRIENDSHIP.
THE END.

Art by Elsa Charretier, Colors by Matt Wilson

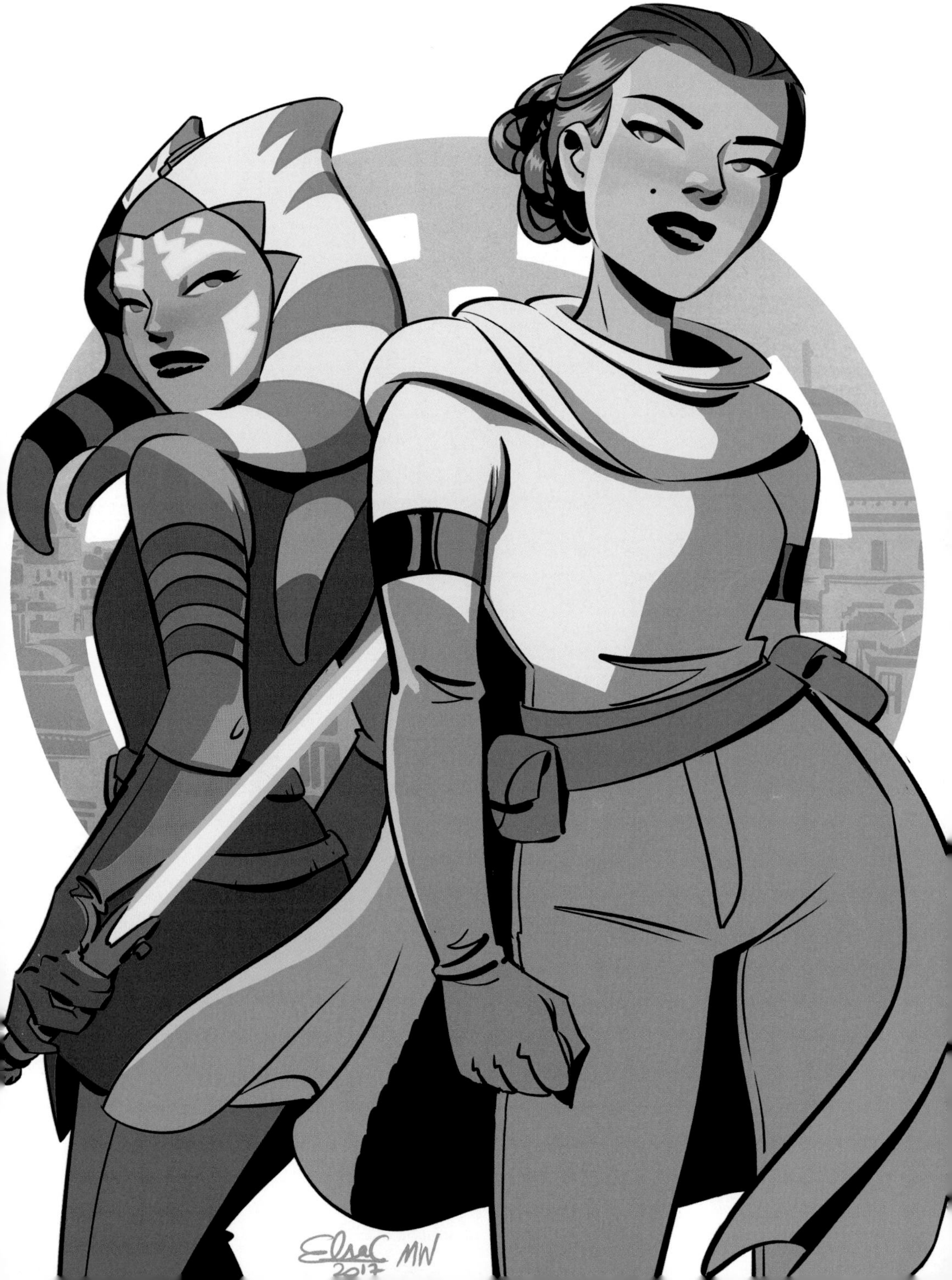
ElsaC MW
2017

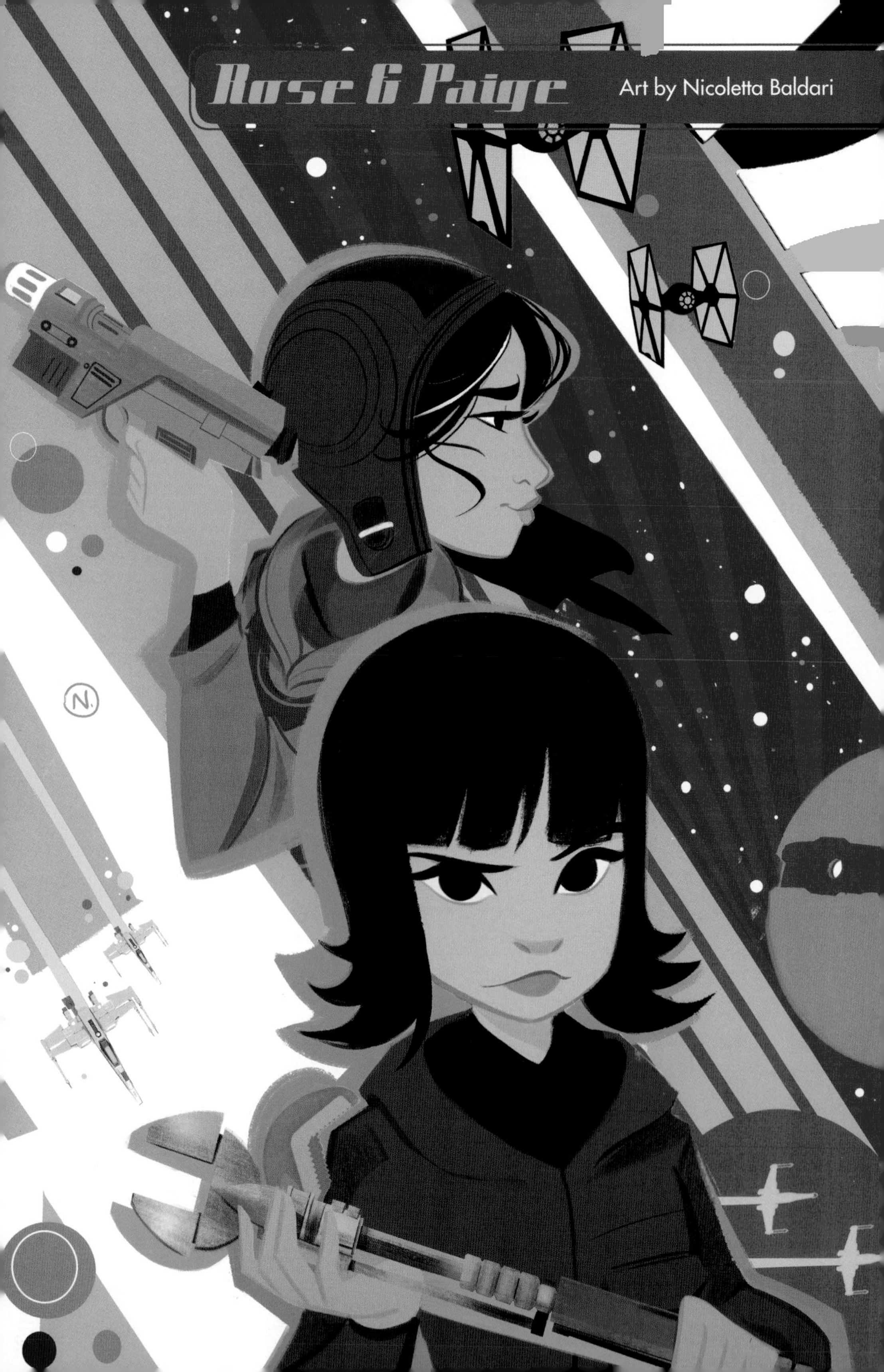
Rose & Paige
Art by Nicoletta Baldari
N.

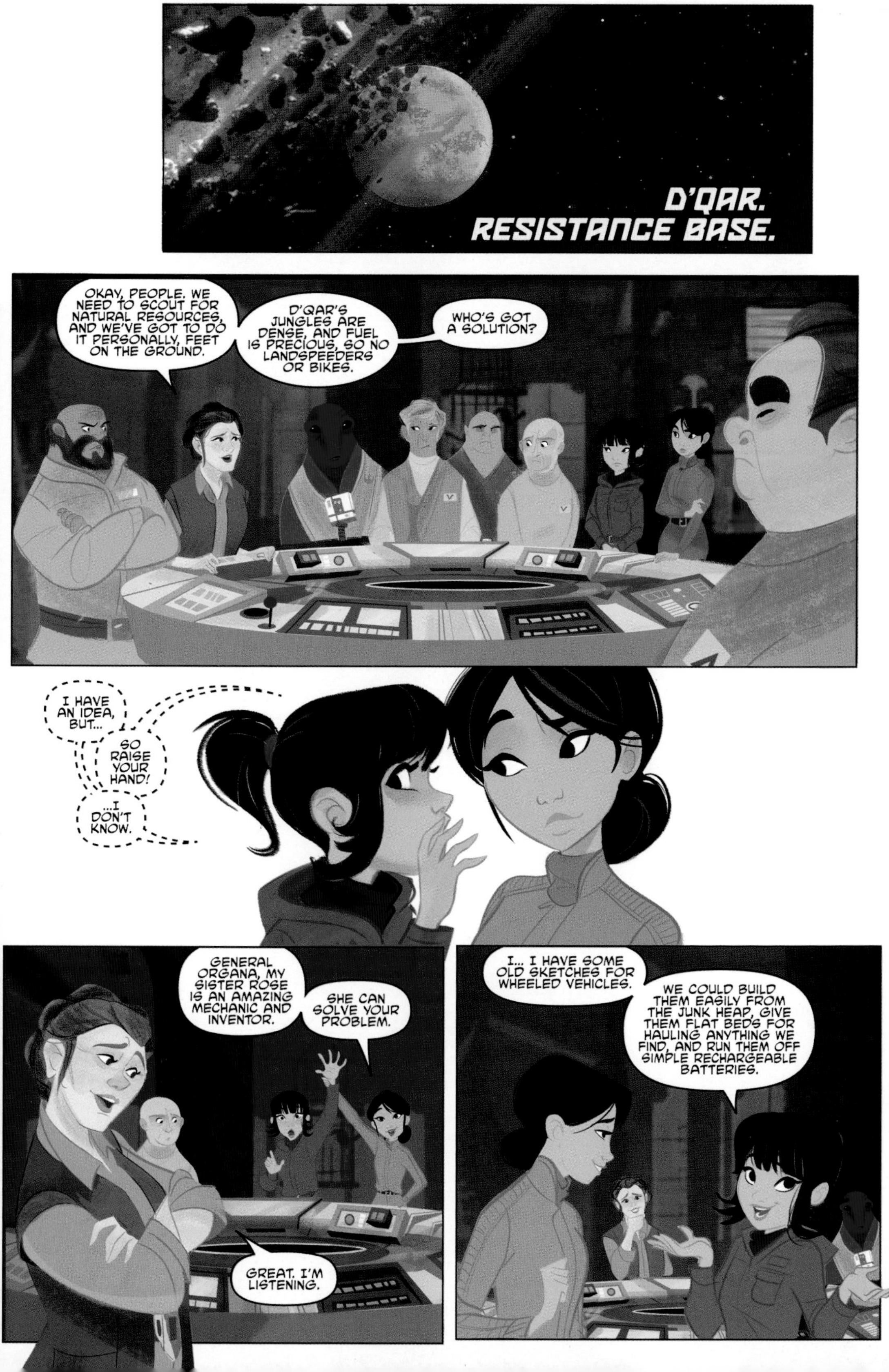
D'QAR. RESISTANCE BASE.
OKAY, PEOPLE. WE NEED TO SCOUT FOR NATURAL RESOURCES, AND WE'VE GOT TO DO IT PERSONALLY, FEET ON THE GROUND.
D'QAR'S JUNGLES ARE DENSE, AND FUEL IS PRECIOUS, SO NO LANDSPEEDERS OR BIKES.
WHO'S GOT A SOLUTION?
I HAVE AN IDEA, BUT...
SO RAISE YOUR HAND!
...I DON'T KNOW.
GENERAL ORGANA, MY SISTER ROSE IS AN AMAZING MECHANIC AND INVENTOR.
SHE CAN SOLVE YOUR PROBLEM.
GREAT. I'M LISTENING.
I... I HAVE SOME OLD SKETCHES FOR WHEELED VEHICLES.
WE COULD BUILD THEM EASILY FROM THE JUNK HEAP, GIVE THEM FLAT BEDS FOR HAULING ANYTHING WE FIND, AND RUN THEM OFF SIMPLE RECHARGEABLE BATTERIES.

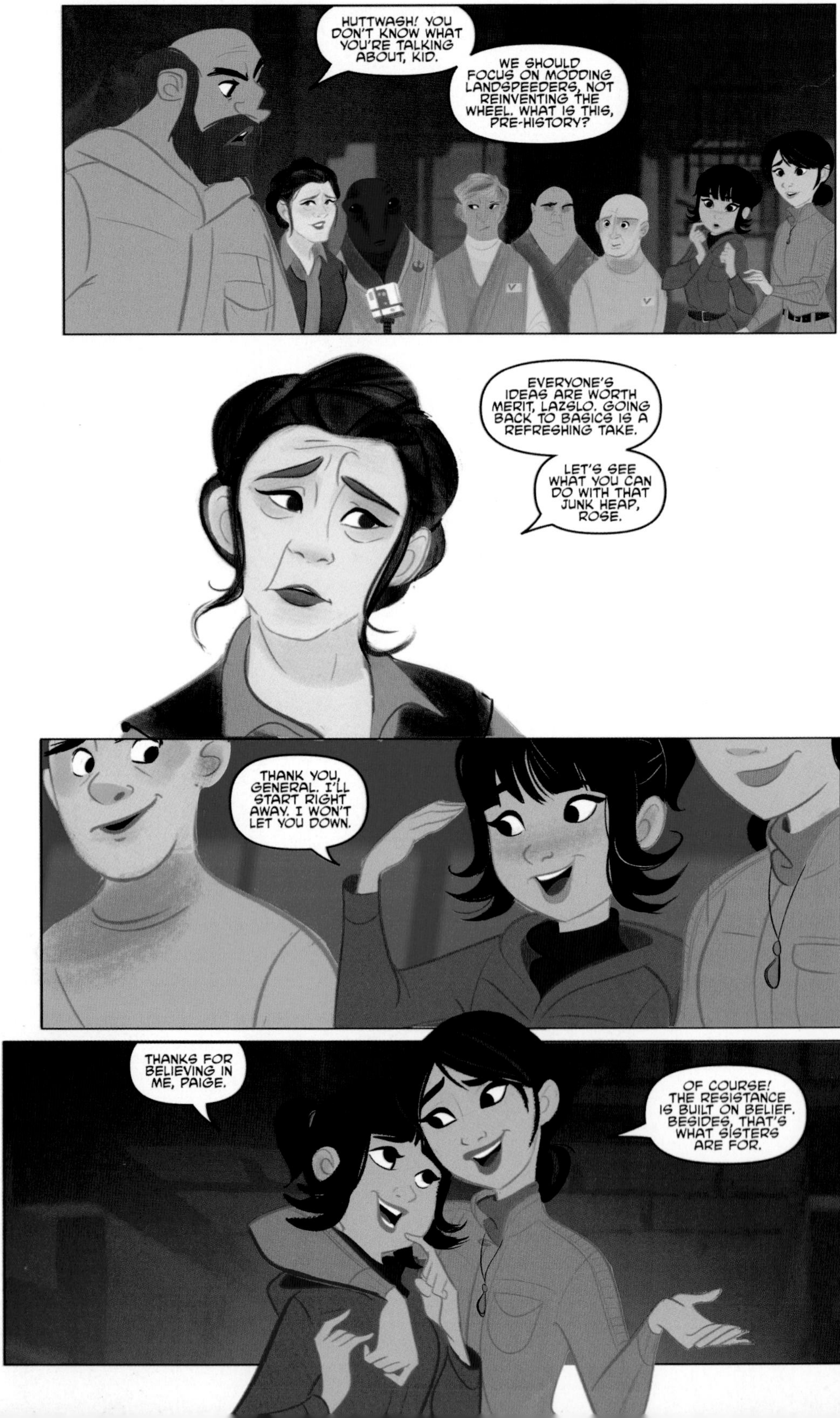
HUTTWASH! YOU DON'T KNOW WHAT YOU'RE TALKING ABOUT, KID.
WE SHOULD FOCUS ON MODDING LANDSPEEDERS, NOT REINVENTING THE WHEEL. WHAT IS THIS, PRE-HISTORY?
EVERYONE'S IDEAS ARE WORTH MERIT, LAZSLO. GOING BACK TO BASICS IS A REFRESHING TAKE.
LET'S SEE WHAT YOU CAN DO WITH THAT JUNK HEAP, ROSE.
THANK YOU, GENERAL. I'LL START RIGHT AWAY. I WON'T LET YOU DOWN.
THANKS FOR BELIEVING IN ME, PAIGE.
OF COURSE! THE RESISTANCE IS BUILT ON BELIEF. BESIDES, THAT'S WHAT SISTERS ARE FOR.

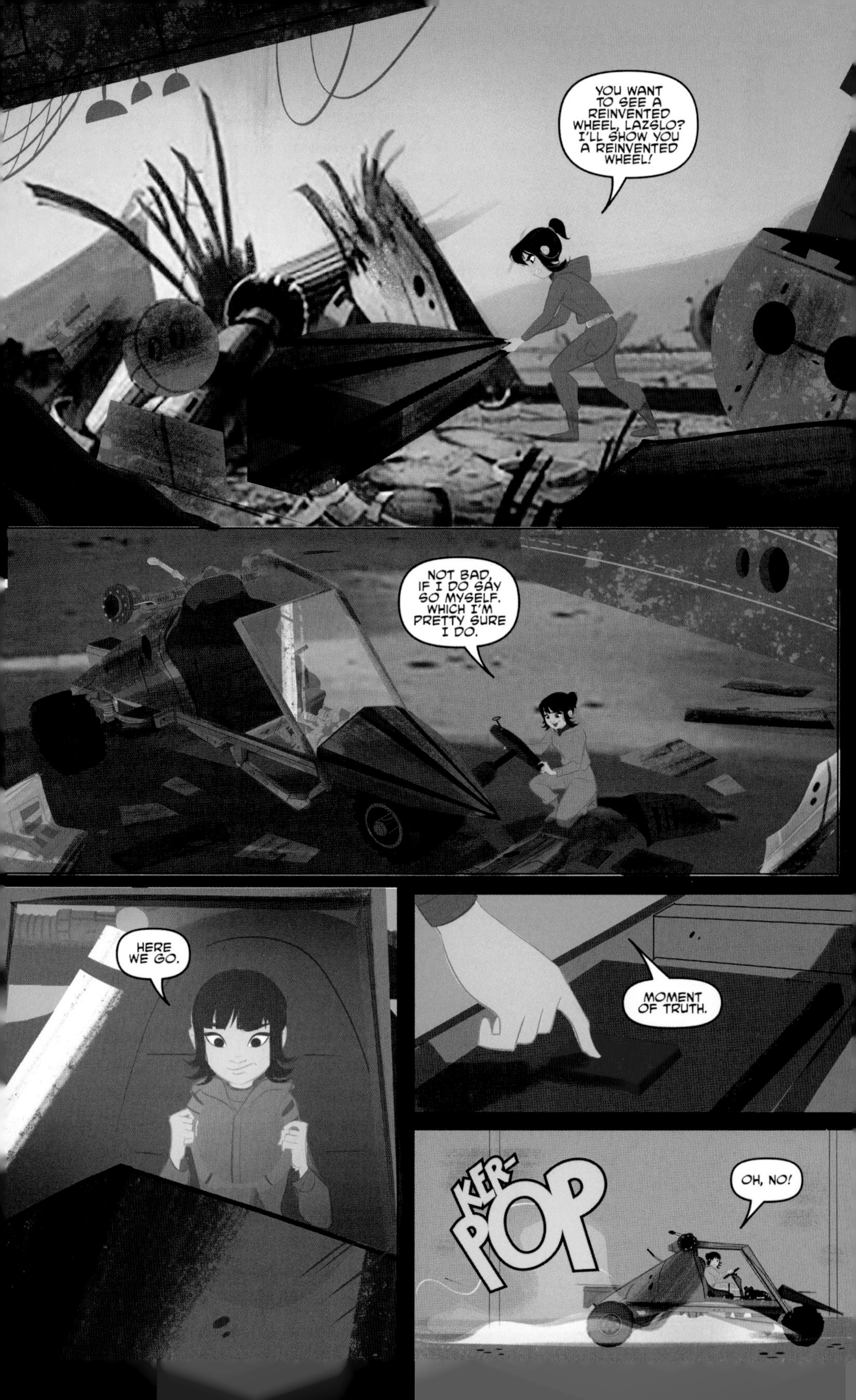
YOU WANT TO SEE A REINVENTED WHEEL, LAZSLO? I'LL SHOW YOU A REINVENTED WHEEL!
NOT BAD, IF I DO SAY SO MYSELF. WHICH I'M PRETTY SURE I DO.
HERE WE GO.
MOMENT OF TRUTH.
KER-POP
OH, NO!

HA! COULDN'T EVEN REINVENT SOMETHING THAT WAS ALREADY INVENTED.

NICE TRY, BUT MAYBE YOU SHOULD GO BACK TO YOUR REAL JOB INSTEAD OF TRYING TO IMPRESS THE GENERAL WITH WILD IDEAS.

I'M NOT TRYING TO IMPRESS ANYONE.

I'M TRYING TO HELP THE RESISTANCE. THERE'S A DIFFERENCE.

IGNORE HIM. I KNOW YOU CAN DO IT.

I KNOW THAT, TOO. I JUST WISH EVERYONE WASN'T WATCHING ME.

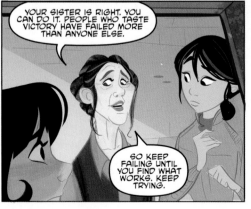

YOUR SISTER IS RIGHT. YOU CAN DO IT. PEOPLE WHO TASTE VICTORY HAVE FAILED MORE THAN ANYONE ELSE.

SO KEEP FAILING UNTIL YOU FIND WHAT WORKS. KEEP TRYING.

EVERY TIME SHE TALKS TO ME, I CAN BARELY FUNCTION.

SHE MIGHT BE OUR GENERAL, BUT I CAN NEVER FORGET THAT SHE'S ALSO A PRINCESS. AND SHE BELIEVES IN ME!

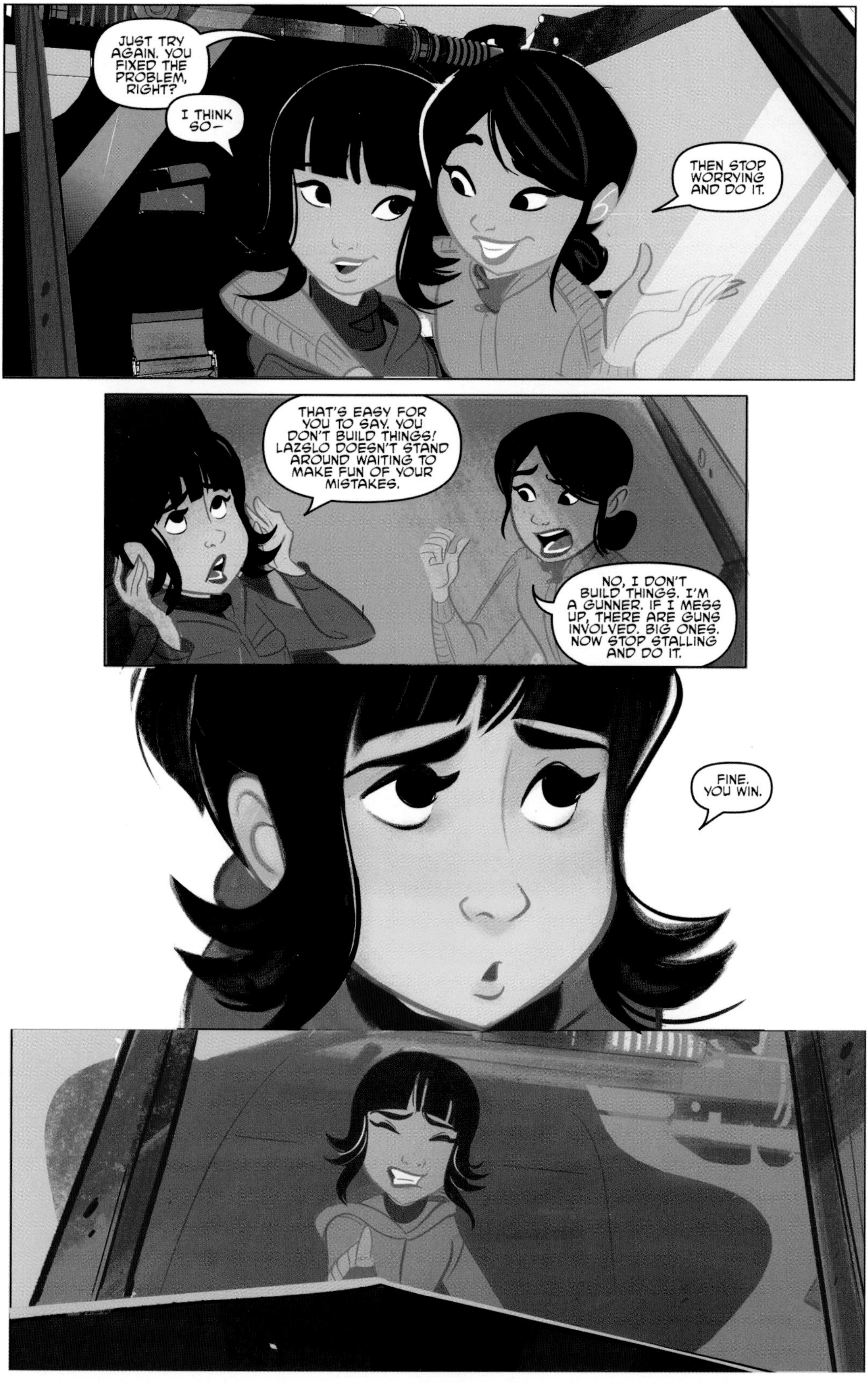
JUST TRY AGAIN. YOU FIXED THE PROBLEM, RIGHT?
I THINK SO—
THEN STOP WORRYING AND DO IT.
THAT'S EASY FOR YOU TO SAY. YOU DON'T BUILD THINGS! LAZSLO DOESN'T STAND AROUND WAITING TO MAKE FUN OF YOUR MISTAKES.
NO, I DON'T BUILD THINGS. I'M A GUNNER. IF I MESS UP, THERE ARE GUNS INVOLVED. BIG ONES. NOW STOP STALLING AND DO IT.
FINE. YOU WIN.

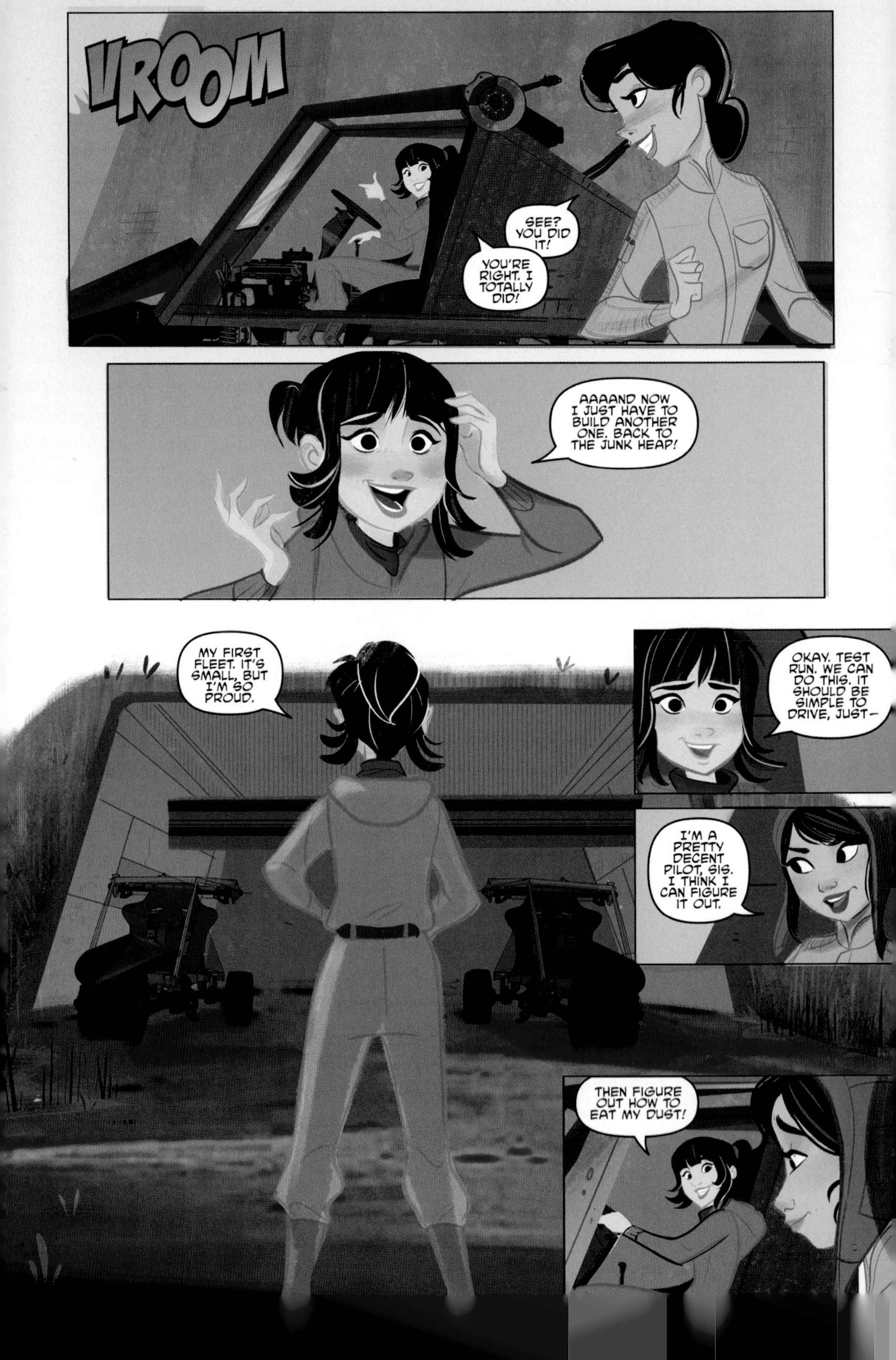
VROOM
SEE? YOU DID IT!
YOU'RE RIGHT. I TOTALLY DID!
AAAAND NOW I JUST HAVE TO BUILD ANOTHER ONE. BACK TO THE JUNK HEAP!
MY FIRST FLEET. IT'S SMALL, BUT I'M SO PROUD.
OKAY. TEST RUN. WE CAN DO THIS. IT SHOULD BE SIMPLE TO DRIVE, JUST—
I'M A PRETTY DECENT PILOT, SIS. I THINK I CAN FIGURE IT OUT.
THEN FIGURE OUT HOW TO EAT MY DUST!

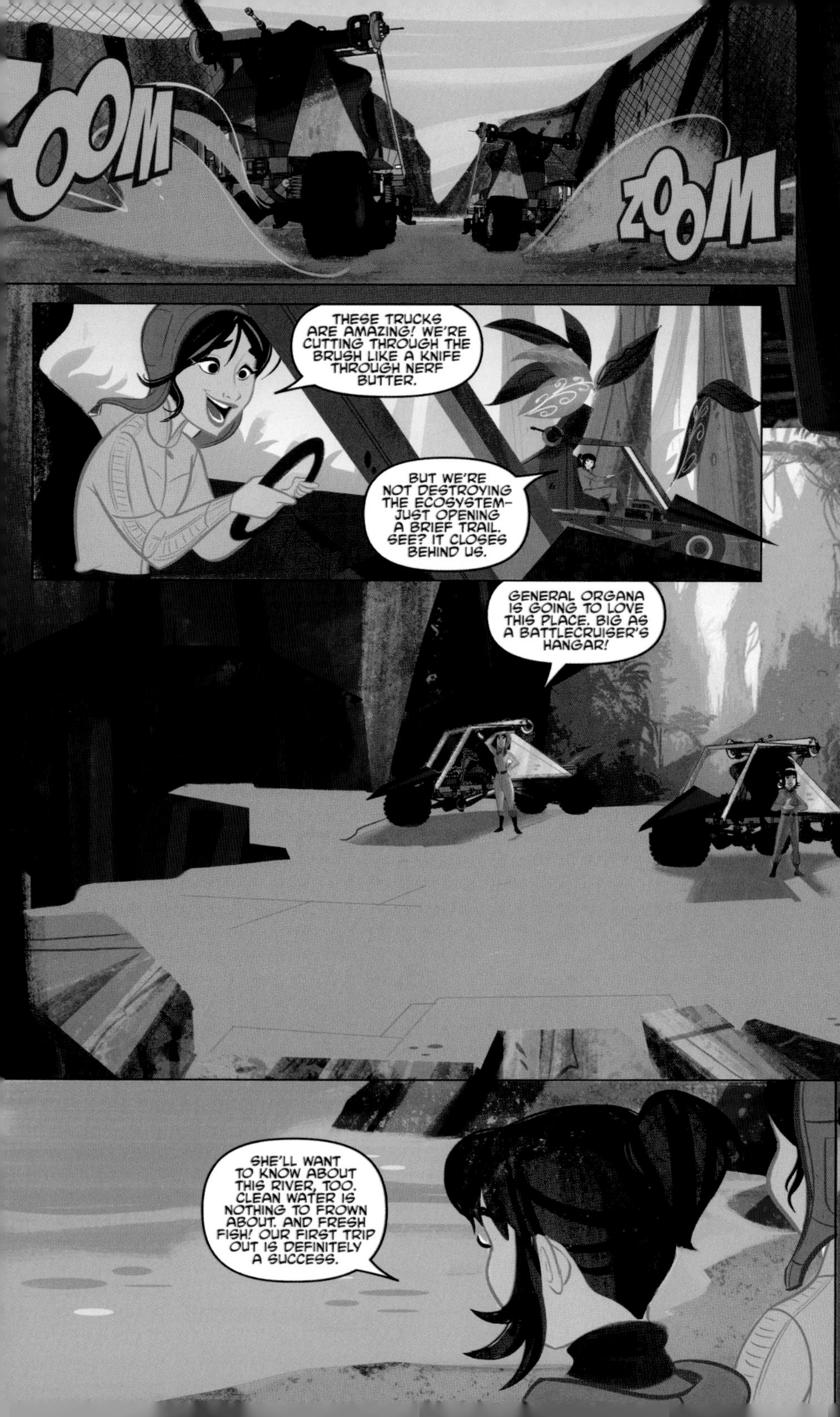
ZOOM
ZOOM
THESE TRUCKS ARE AMAZING! WE'RE CUTTING THROUGH THE BRUSH LIKE A KNIFE THROUGH NERF BUTTER.
BUT WE'RE NOT DESTROYING THE ECOSYSTEM– JUST OPENING A BRIEF TRAIL. SEE? IT CLOSES BEHIND US.
GENERAL ORGANA IS GOING TO LOVE THIS PLACE. BIG AS A BATTLECRUISER'S HANGAR!
SHE'LL WANT TO KNOW ABOUT THIS RIVER, TOO. CLEAN WATER IS NOTHING TO FROWN ABOUT. AND FRESH FISH! OUR FIRST TRIP OUT IS DEFINITELY A SUCCESS.

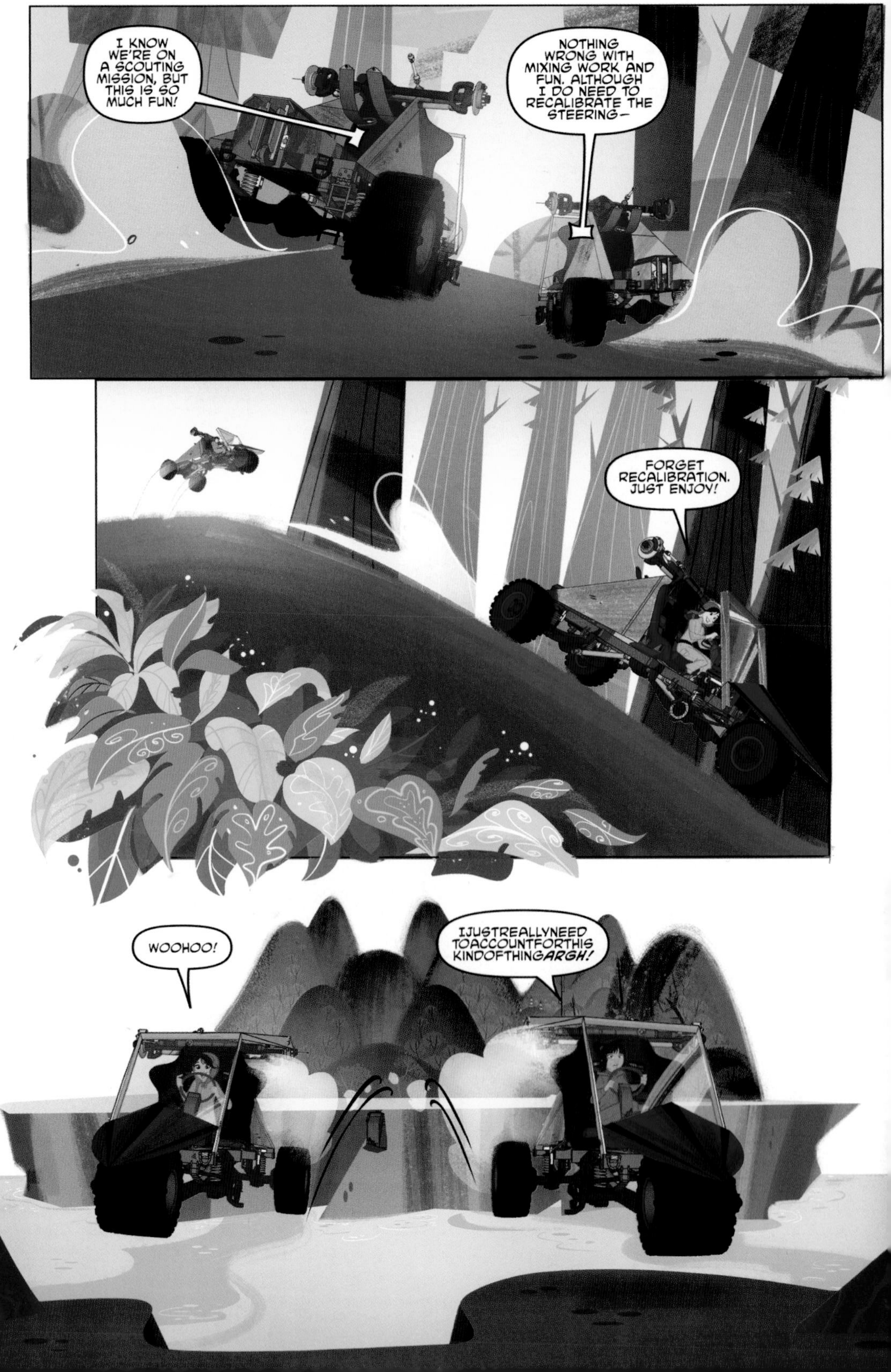
I KNOW WE'RE ON A SCOUTING MISSION, BUT THIS IS SO MUCH FUN!
NOTHING WRONG WITH MIXING WORK AND FUN. ALTHOUGH I DO NEED TO RECALIBRATE THE STEERING—
FORGET RECALIBRATION. JUST ENJOY!
WOOHOO!
IJUSTREALLYNEED TOACCOUNTFORTHIS KINDOFTHINGARGH!

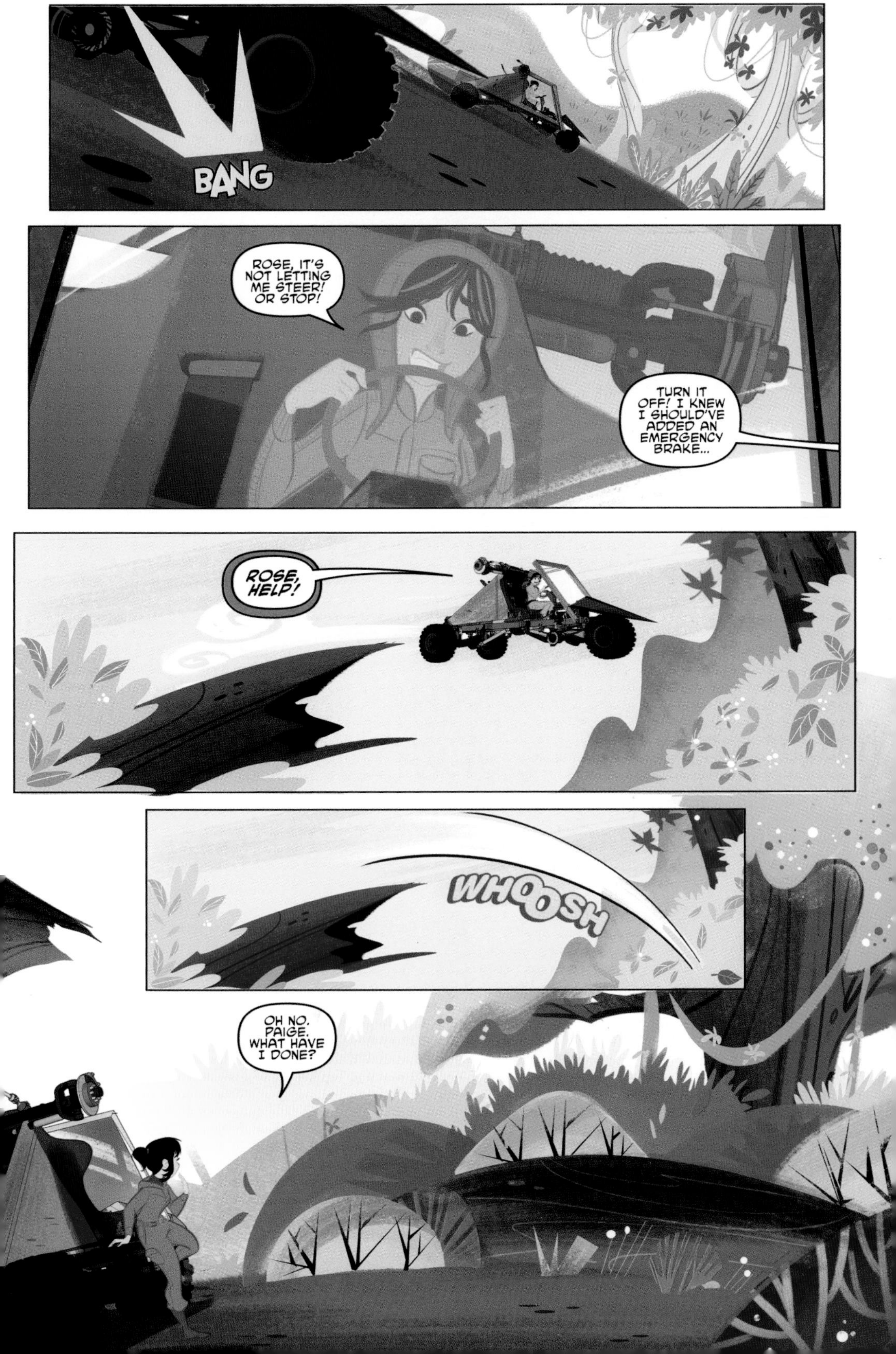
BANG
ROSE, IT'S NOT LETTING ME STEER! OR STOP!
TURN IT OFF! I KNEW I SHOULD'VE ADDED AN EMERGENCY BRAKE...
ROSE, HELP!
WHOOOSH
OH NO. PAIGE. WHAT HAVE I DONE?

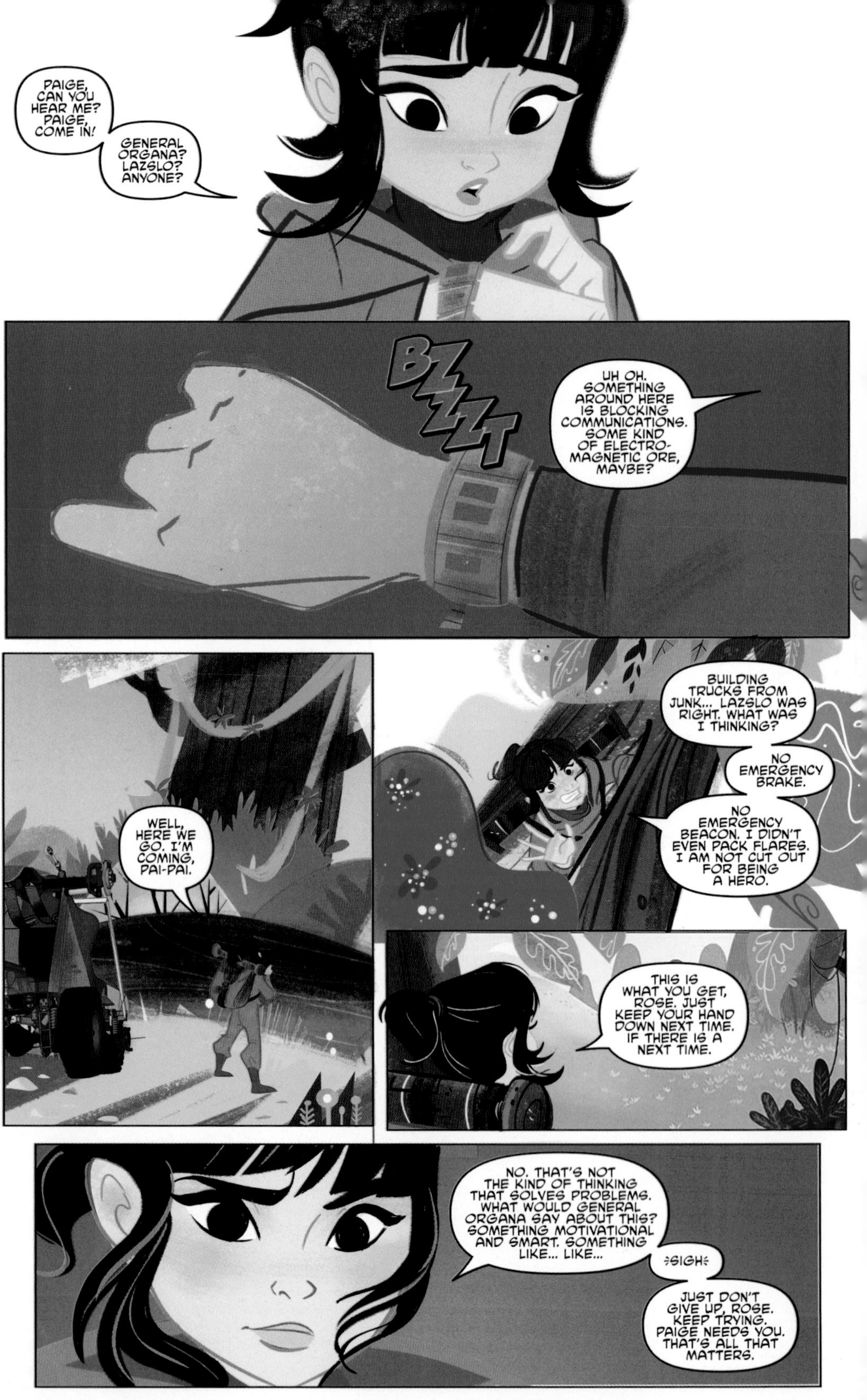
PAIGE, CAN YOU HEAR ME? PAIGE, COME IN!
GENERAL ORGANA? LAZSLO? ANYONE?
BZZZT
UH OH. SOMETHING AROUND HERE IS BLOCKING COMMUNICATIONS. SOME KIND OF ELECTRO-MAGNETIC ORE, MAYBE?
WELL, HERE WE GO. I'M COMING, PAI-PAI.
BUILDING TRUCKS FROM JUNK... LAZSLO WAS RIGHT. WHAT WAS I THINKING?
NO EMERGENCY BRAKE.
NO EMERGENCY BEACON. I DIDN'T EVEN PACK FLARES. I AM NOT CUT OUT FOR BEING A HERO.
THIS IS WHAT YOU GET, ROSE. JUST KEEP YOUR HAND DOWN NEXT TIME. IF THERE IS A NEXT TIME.
NO. THAT'S NOT THE KIND OF THINKING THAT SOLVES PROBLEMS. WHAT WOULD GENERAL ORGANA SAY ABOUT THIS? SOMETHING MOTIVATIONAL AND SMART. SOMETHING LIKE... LIKE...
SIGH
JUST DON'T GIVE UP, ROSE. KEEP TRYING. PAIGE NEEDS YOU. THAT'S ALL THAT MATTERS.

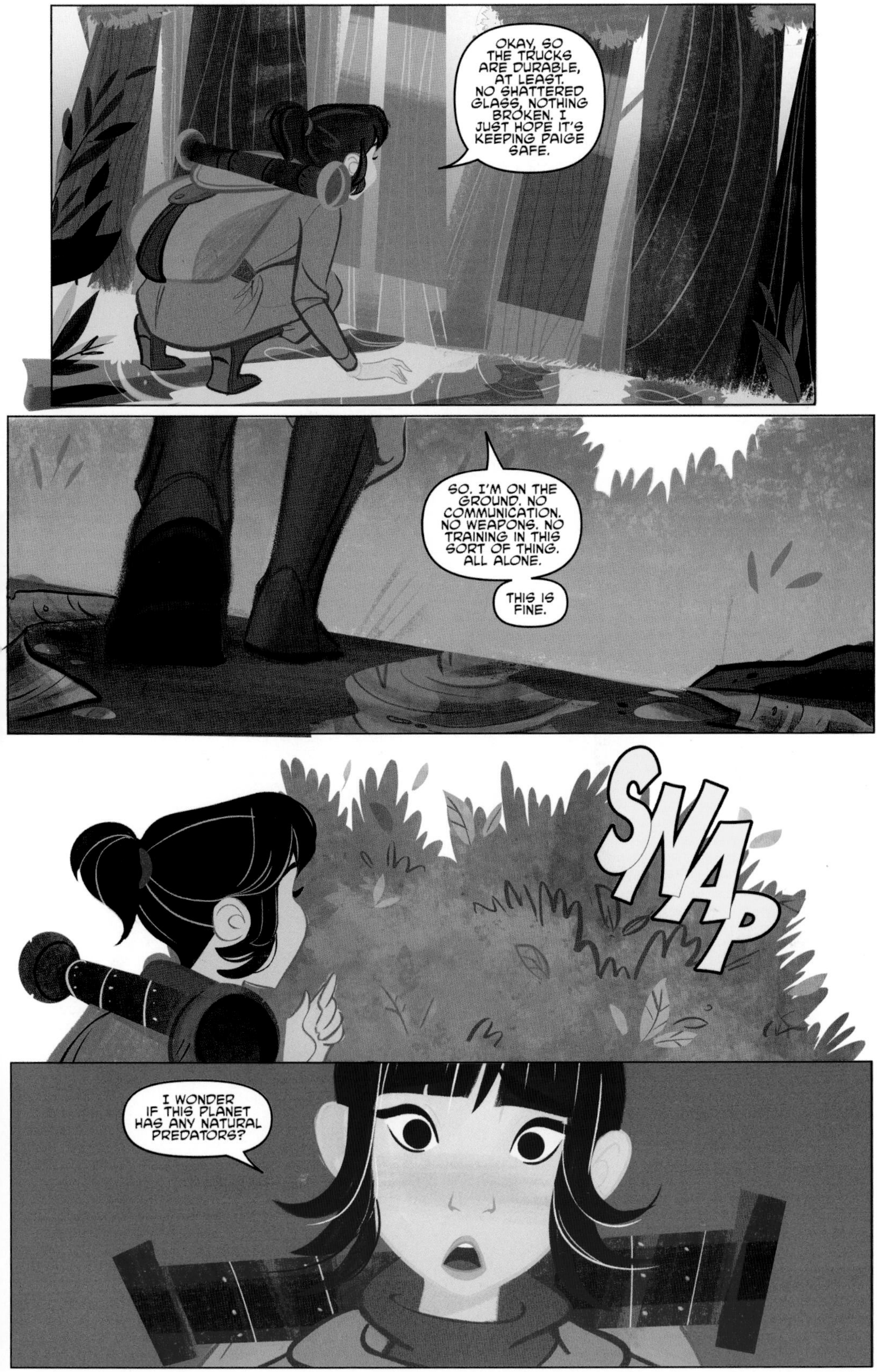
OKAY, SO THE TRUCKS ARE DURABLE, AT LEAST. NO SHATTERED GLASS, NOTHING BROKEN. I JUST HOPE IT'S KEEPING PAIGE SAFE.
SO. I'M ON THE GROUND. NO COMMUNICATION. NO WEAPONS. NO TRAINING IN THIS SORT OF THING. ALL ALONE.
THIS IS FINE.
SNAP
I WONDER IF THIS PLANET HAS ANY NATURAL PREDATORS?

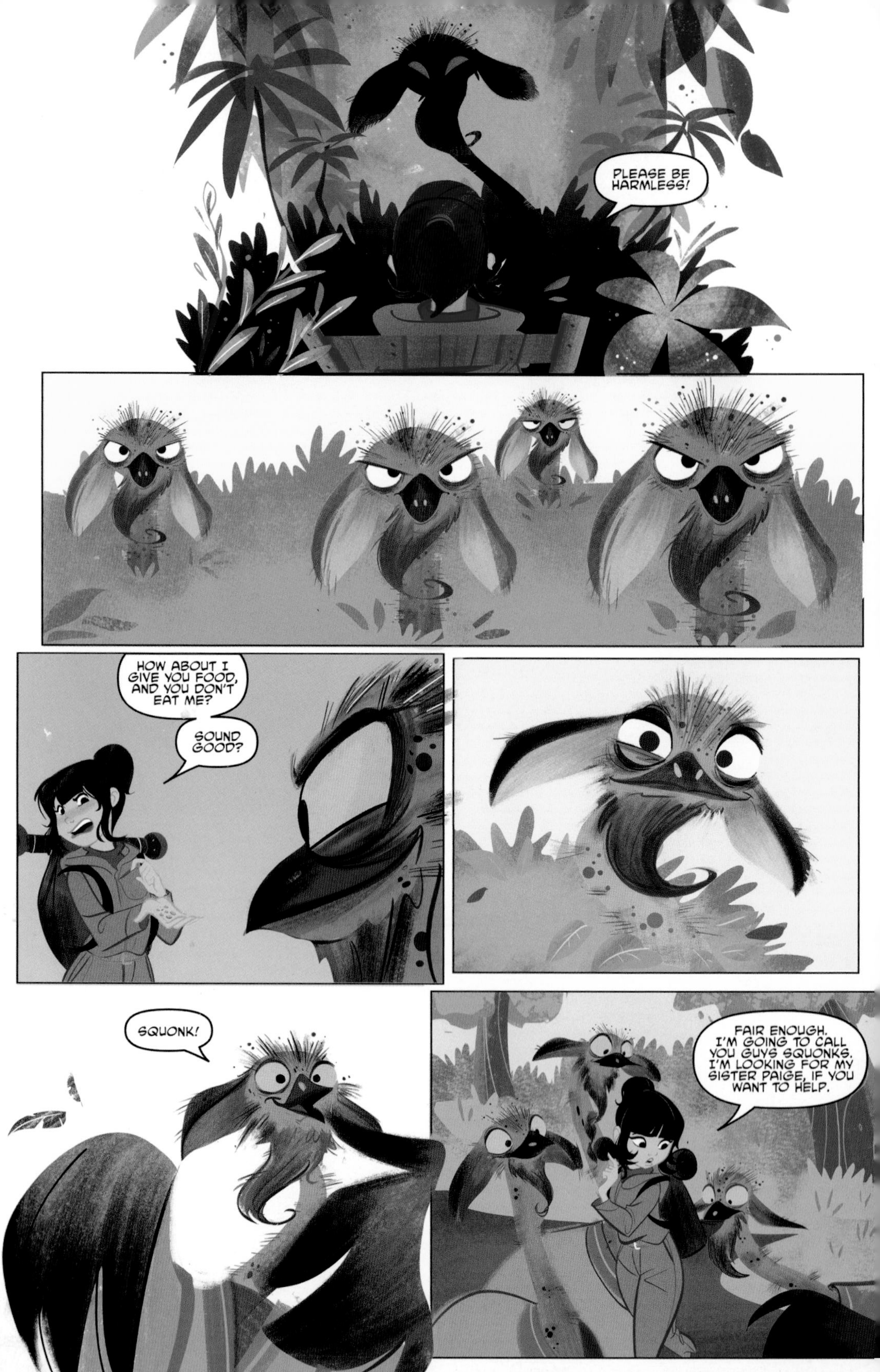
PLEASE BE HARMLESS!
HOW ABOUT I GIVE YOU FOOD, AND YOU DON'T EAT ME?
SOUND GOOD?
SQUONK!
FAIR ENOUGH. I'M GOING TO CALL YOU GUYS SQUONKS. I'M LOOKING FOR MY SISTER PAIGE, IF YOU WANT TO HELP.

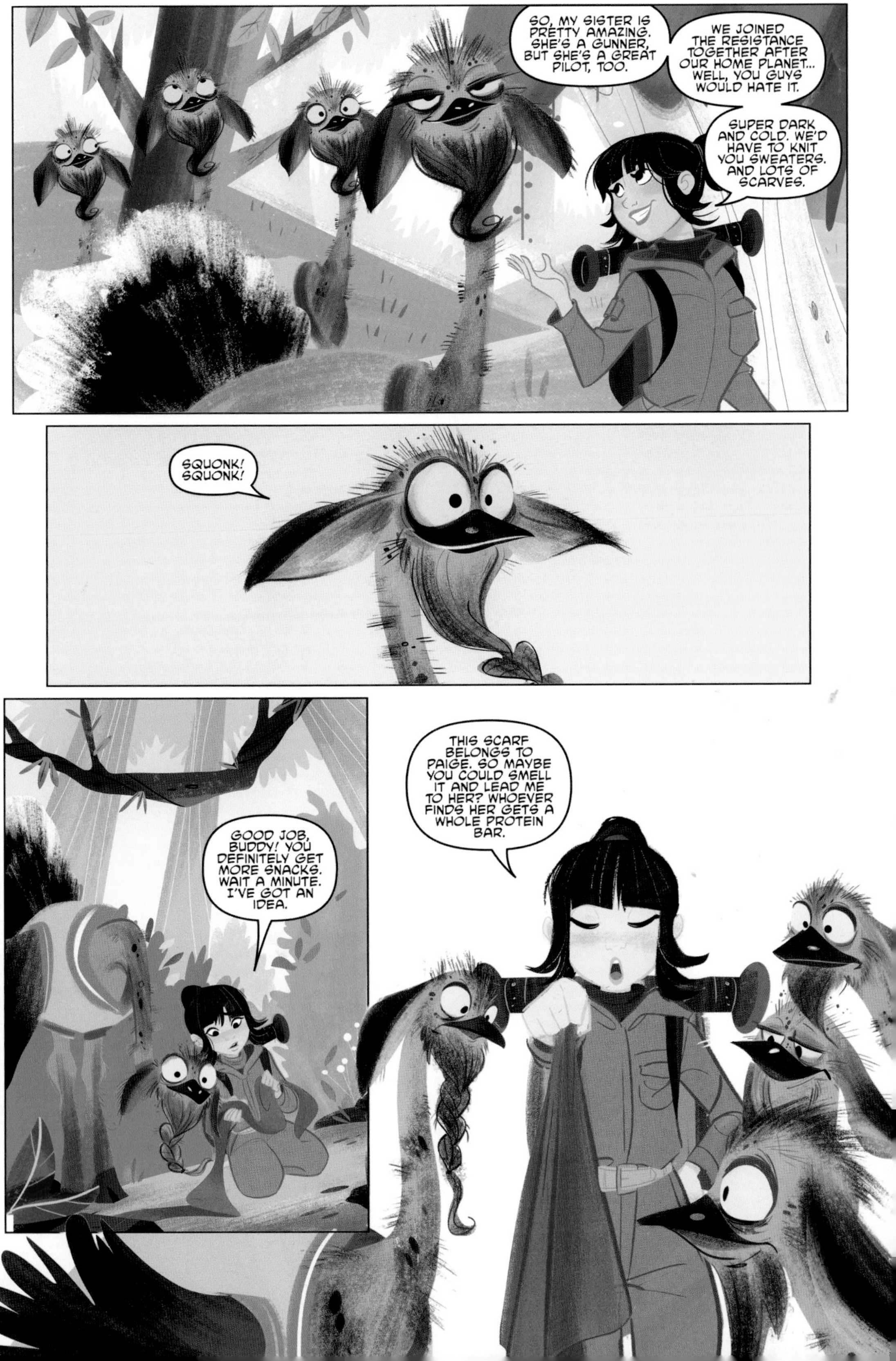

SO, MY SISTER IS PRETTY AMAZING. SHE'S A GUNNER, BUT SHE'S A GREAT PILOT, TOO.
WE JOINED THE RESISTANCE TOGETHER AFTER OUR HOME PLANET... WELL, YOU GUYS WOULD HATE IT.
SUPER DARK AND COLD. WE'D HAVE TO KNIT YOU SWEATERS. AND LOTS OF SCARVES.
SQUONK! SQUONK!
GOOD JOB, BUDDY! YOU DEFINITELY GET MORE SNACKS. WAIT A MINUTE. I'VE GOT AN IDEA.
THIS SCARF BELONGS TO PAIGE. SO MAYBE YOU COULD SMELL IT AND LEAD ME TO HER? WHOEVER FINDS HER GETS A WHOLE PROTEIN BAR.

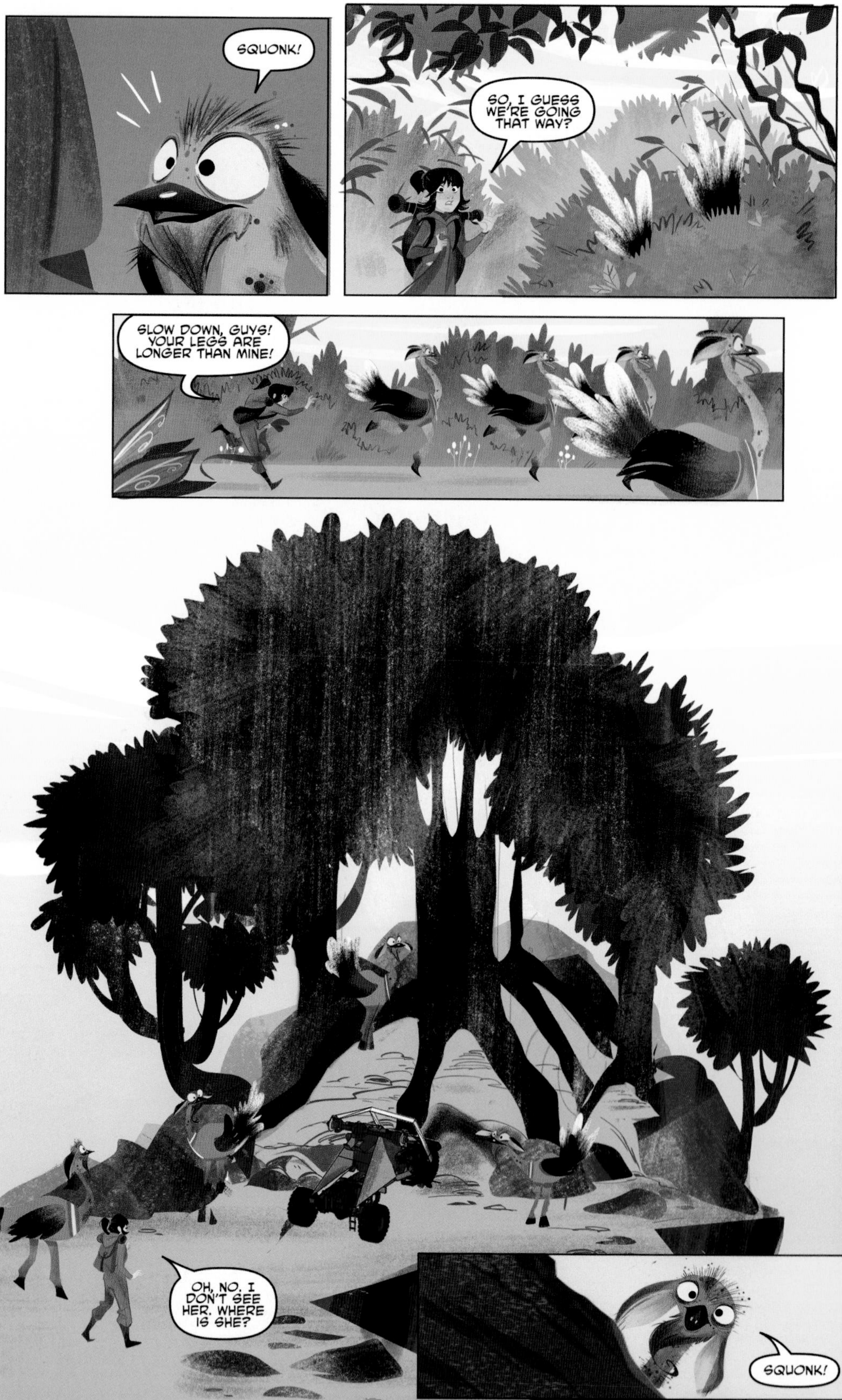
SQUONK!
SO, I GUESS WE'RE GOING THAT WAY?
SLOW DOWN, GUYS! YOUR LEGS ARE LONGER THAN MINE!
OH, NO. I DON'T SEE HER. WHERE IS SHE?
SQUONK!

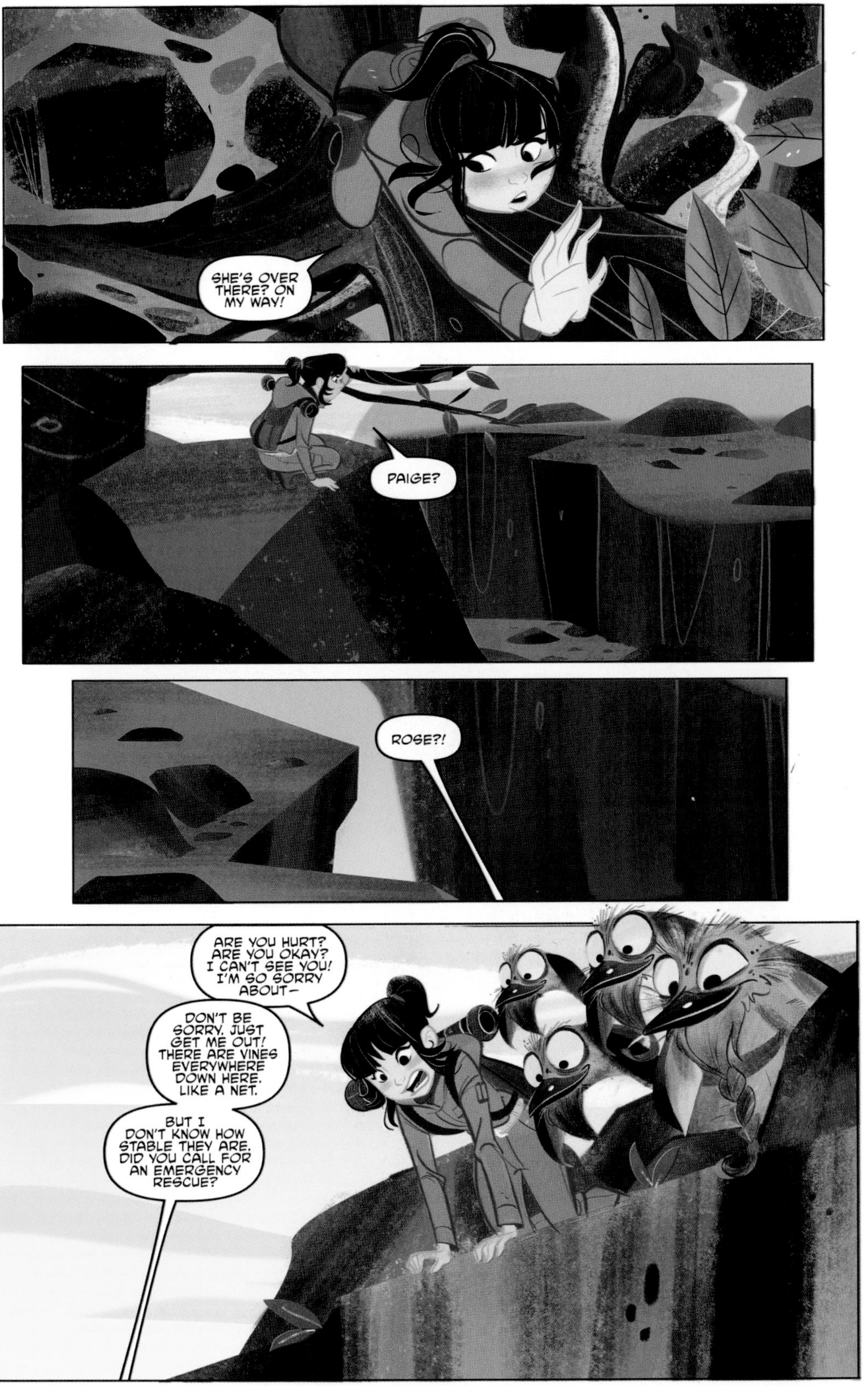
SHE'S OVER THERE? ON MY WAY!
PAIGE?
ROSE?!
ARE YOU HURT? ARE YOU OKAY? I CAN'T SEE YOU! I'M SO SORRY ABOUT–
DON'T BE SORRY. JUST GET ME OUT! THERE ARE VINES EVERYWHERE DOWN HERE. LIKE A NET.
BUT I DON'T KNOW HOW STABLE THEY ARE. DID YOU CALL FOR AN EMERGENCY RESCUE?

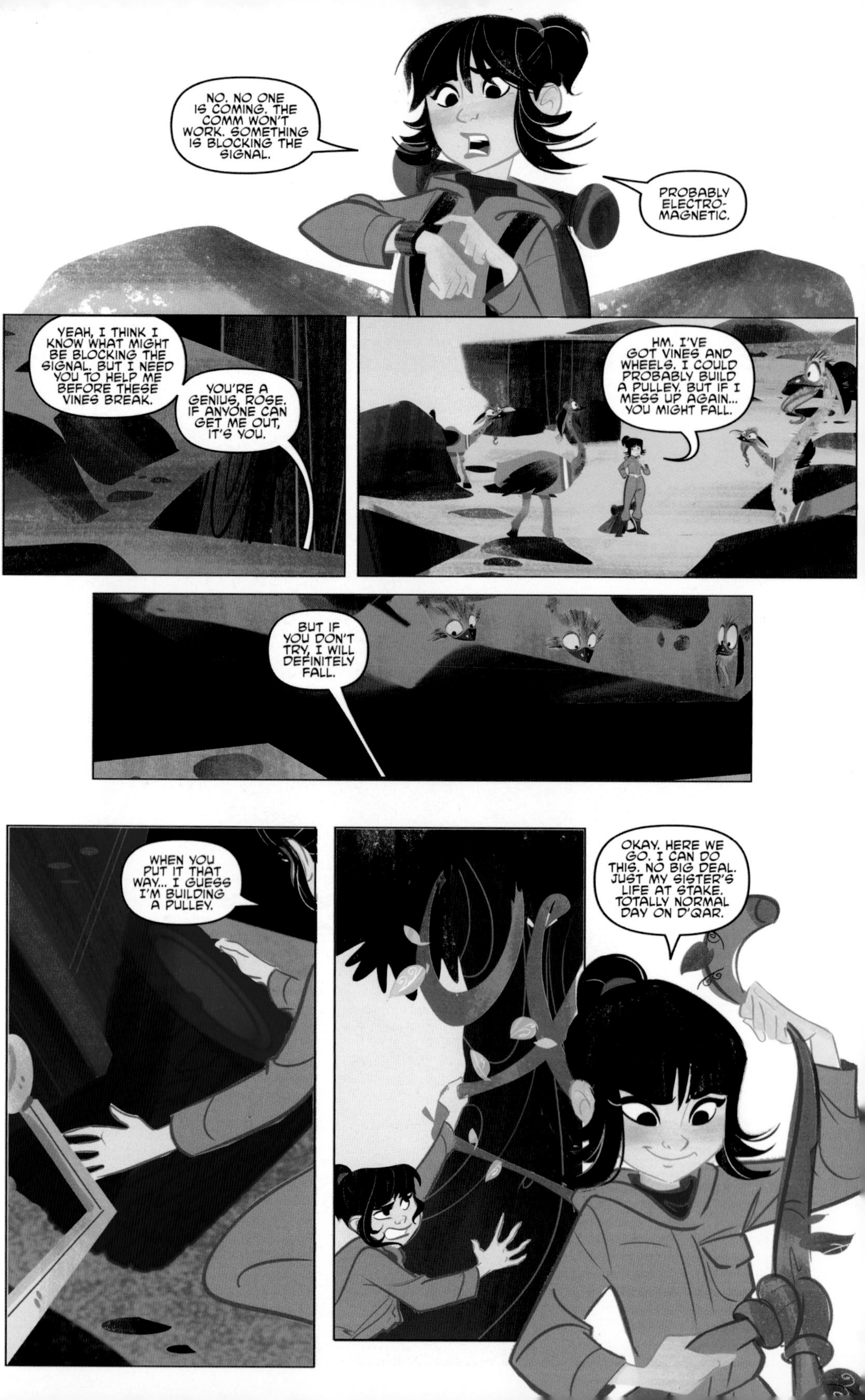
NO. NO ONE IS COMING. THE COMM WON'T WORK. SOMETHING IS BLOCKING THE SIGNAL.
PROBABLY ELECTRO-MAGNETIC.
YEAH, I THINK I KNOW WHAT MIGHT BE BLOCKING THE SIGNAL. BUT I NEED YOU TO HELP ME BEFORE THESE VINES BREAK.
YOU'RE A GENIUS, ROSE. IF ANYONE CAN GET ME OUT, IT'S YOU.
HM. I'VE GOT VINES AND WHEELS. I COULD PROBABLY BUILD A PULLEY. BUT IF I MESS UP AGAIN... YOU MIGHT FALL.
BUT IF YOU DON'T TRY, I WILL DEFINITELY FALL.
WHEN YOU PUT IT THAT WAY... I GUESS I'M BUILDING A PULLEY.
OKAY. HERE WE GO. I CAN DO THIS. NO BIG DEAL. JUST MY SISTER'S LIFE AT STAKE. TOTALLY NORMAL DAY ON D'QAR.

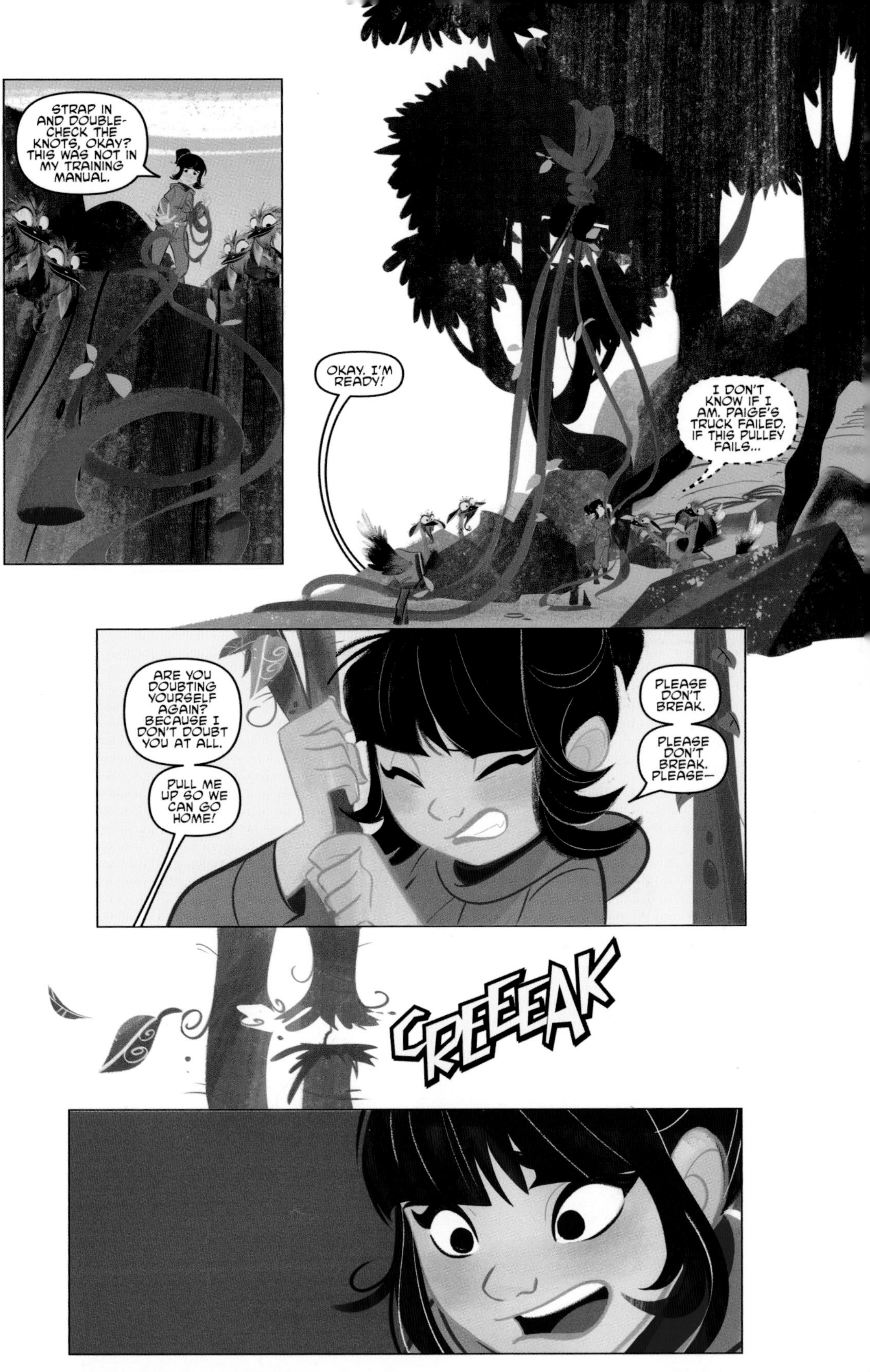
STRAP IN AND DOUBLE-CHECK THE KNOTS, OKAY? THIS WAS NOT IN MY TRAINING MANUAL.
OKAY. I'M READY!
I DON'T KNOW IF I AM. PAIGE'S TRUCK FAILED. IF THIS PULLEY FAILS...
ARE YOU DOUBTING YOURSELF AGAIN? BECAUSE I DON'T DOUBT YOU AT ALL.
PULL ME UP SO WE CAN GO HOME!
PLEASE DON'T BREAK.
PLEASE DON'T BREAK. PLEASE—
CREEEAK

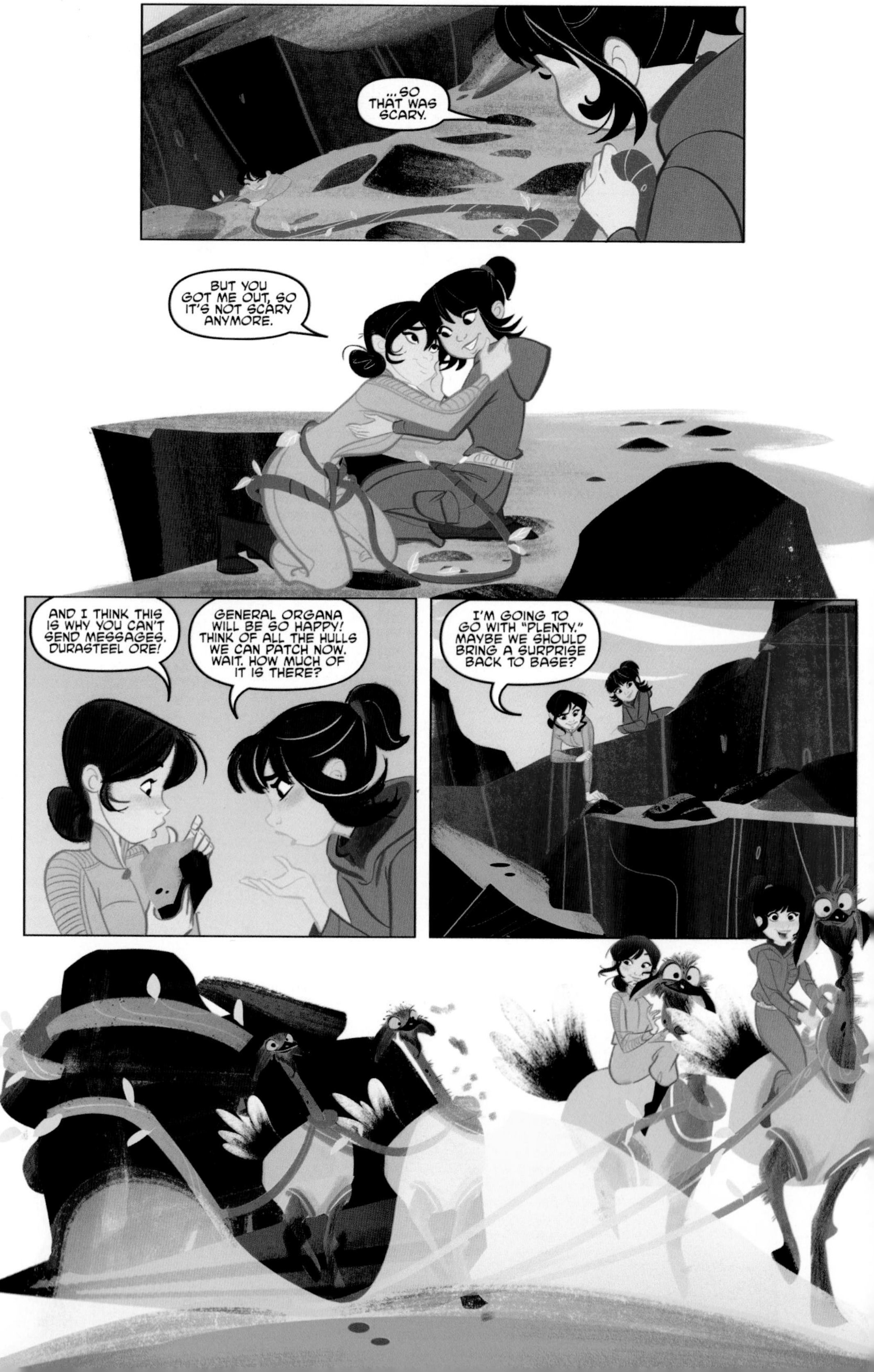
...SO THAT WAS SCARY.
BUT YOU GOT ME OUT, SO IT'S NOT SCARY ANYMORE.
AND I THINK THIS IS WHY YOU CAN'T SEND MESSAGES. DURASTEEL ORE!
GENERAL ORGANA WILL BE SO HAPPY! THINK OF ALL THE HULLS WE CAN PATCH NOW. WAIT. HOW MUCH OF IT IS THERE?
I'M GOING TO GO WITH "PLENTY." MAYBE WE SHOULD BRING A SURPRISE BACK TO BASE?

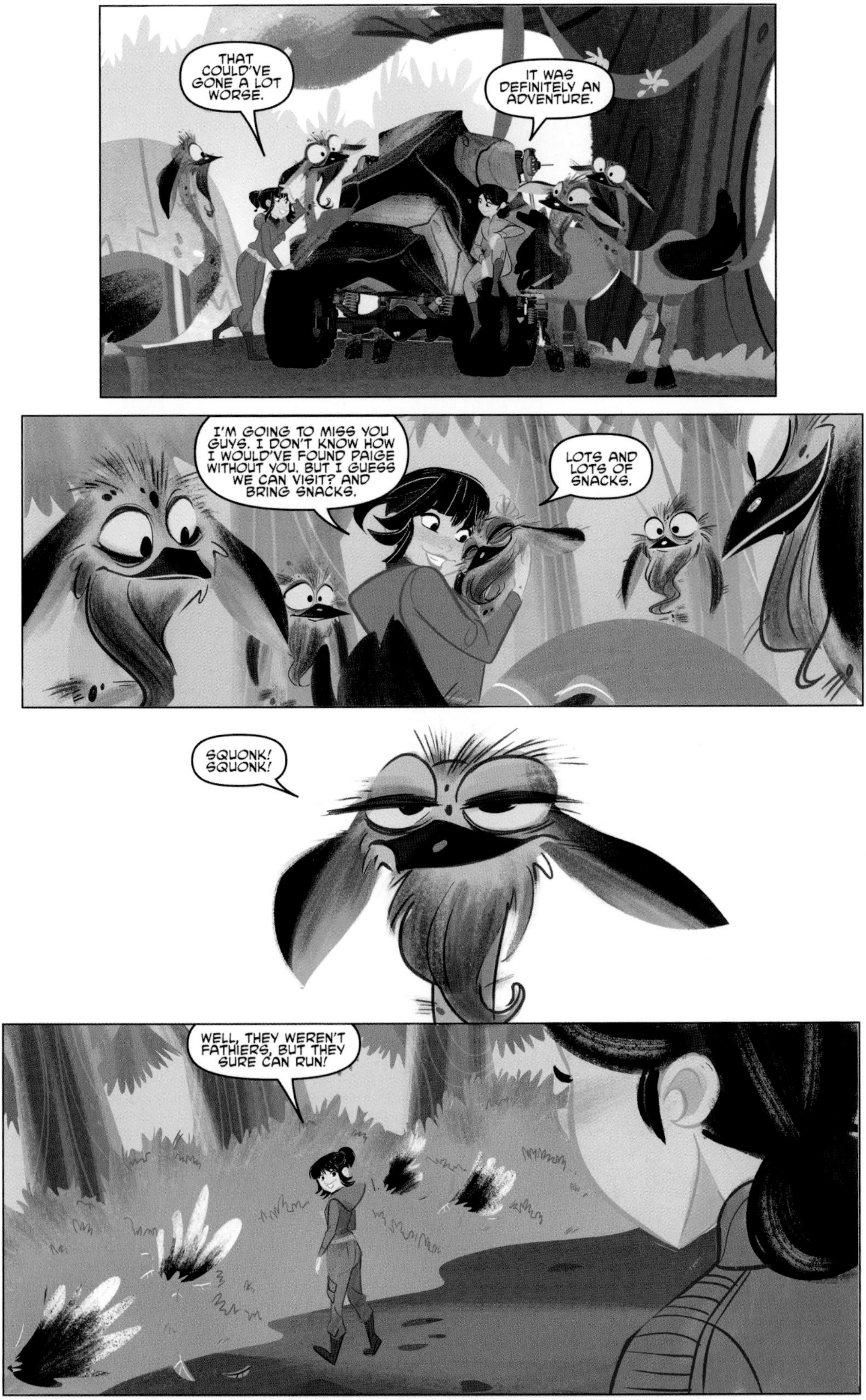
THAT COULD'VE GONE A LOT WORSE.
IT WAS DEFINITELY AN ADVENTURE.
I'M GOING TO MISS YOU GUYS. I DON'T KNOW HOW I WOULD'VE FOUND PAIGE WITHOUT YOU. BUT I GUESS WE CAN VISIT? AND BRING SNACKS.
LOTS AND LOTS OF SNACKS.
SQUONK! SQUONK!
WELL, THEY WEREN'T FATHIERS, BUT THEY SURE CAN RUN!

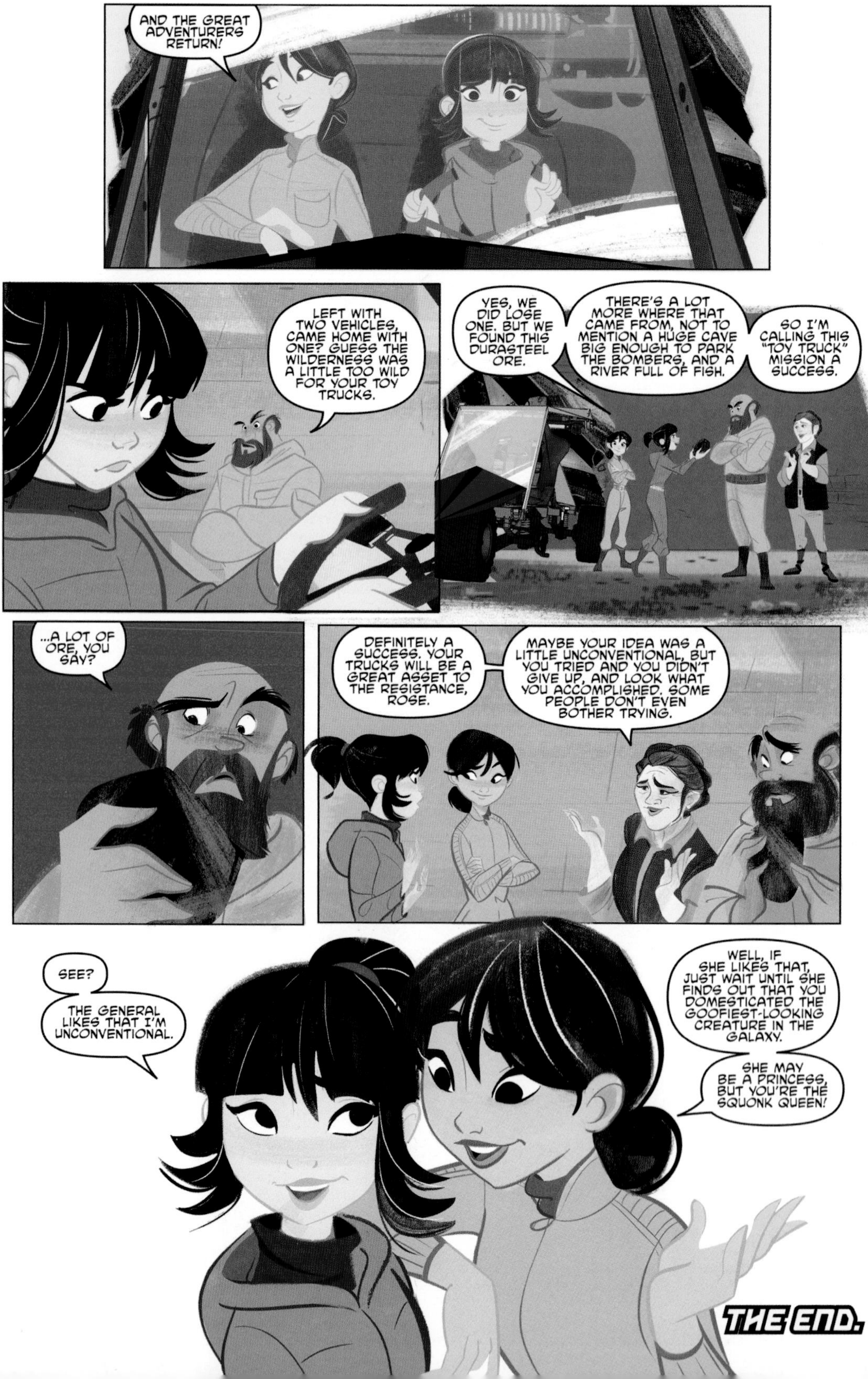

AND THE GREAT ADVENTURERS RETURN!
LEFT WITH TWO VEHICLES, CAME HOME WITH ONE? GUESS THE WILDERNESS WAS A LITTLE TOO WILD FOR YOUR TOY TRUCKS.
YES, WE DID LOSE ONE. BUT WE FOUND THIS DURASTEEL ORE.
THERE'S A LOT MORE WHERE THAT CAME FROM, NOT TO MENTION A HUGE CAVE BIG ENOUGH TO PARK THE BOMBERS, AND A RIVER FULL OF FISH.
SO I'M CALLING THIS "TOY TRUCK" MISSION A SUCCESS.
...A LOT OF ORE, YOU SAY?
DEFINITELY A SUCCESS. YOUR TRUCKS WILL BE A GREAT ASSET TO THE RESISTANCE, ROSE.
MAYBE YOUR IDEA WAS A LITTLE UNCONVENTIONAL, BUT YOU TRIED AND YOU DIDN'T GIVE UP, AND LOOK WHAT YOU ACCOMPLISHED. SOME PEOPLE DON'T EVEN BOTHER TRYING.
SEE?
THE GENERAL LIKES THAT I'M UNCONVENTIONAL.
WELL, IF SHE LIKES THAT, JUST WAIT UNTIL SHE FINDS OUT THAT YOU DOMESTICATED THE GOOFIEST-LOOKING CREATURE IN THE GALAXY.
SHE MAY BE A PRINCESS, BUT YOU'RE THE SQUONK QUEEN!
THE END.

Art by Elsa Charretier, Colors by Matt Wilson

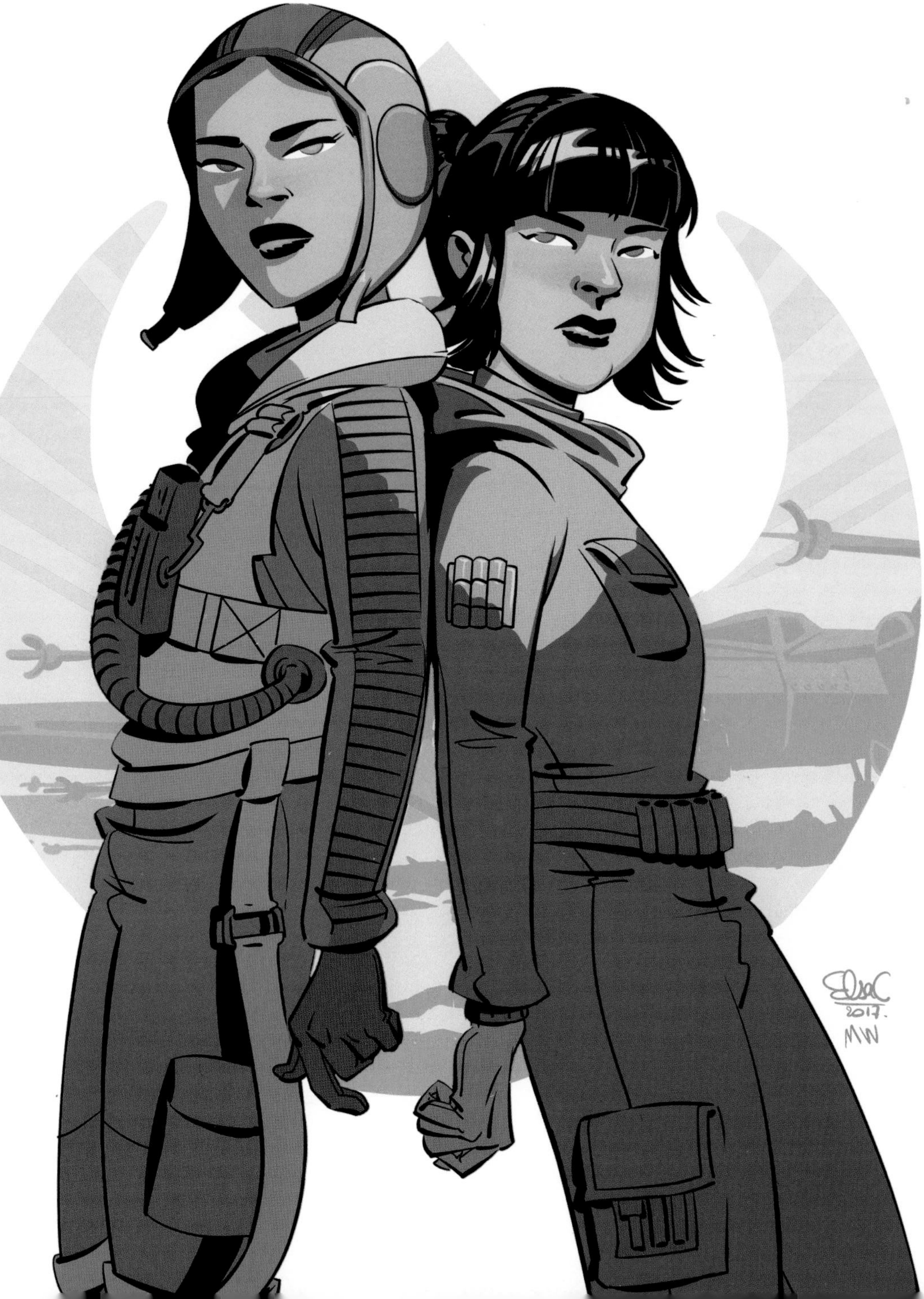
ElsaC
2017.
MW

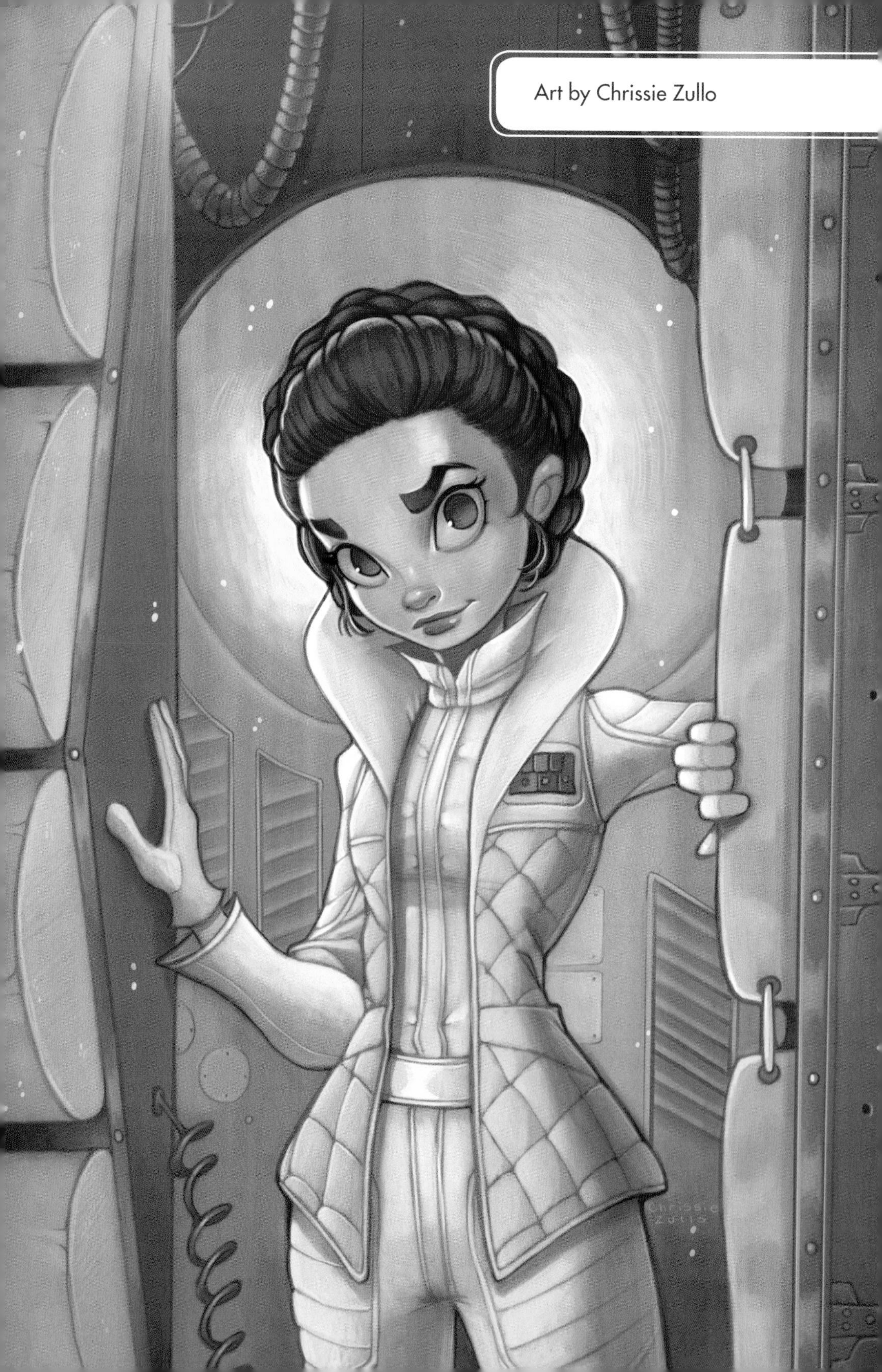
Chrissie
Zullo

Art by Chrissie Zullo

Art by Annie Wu

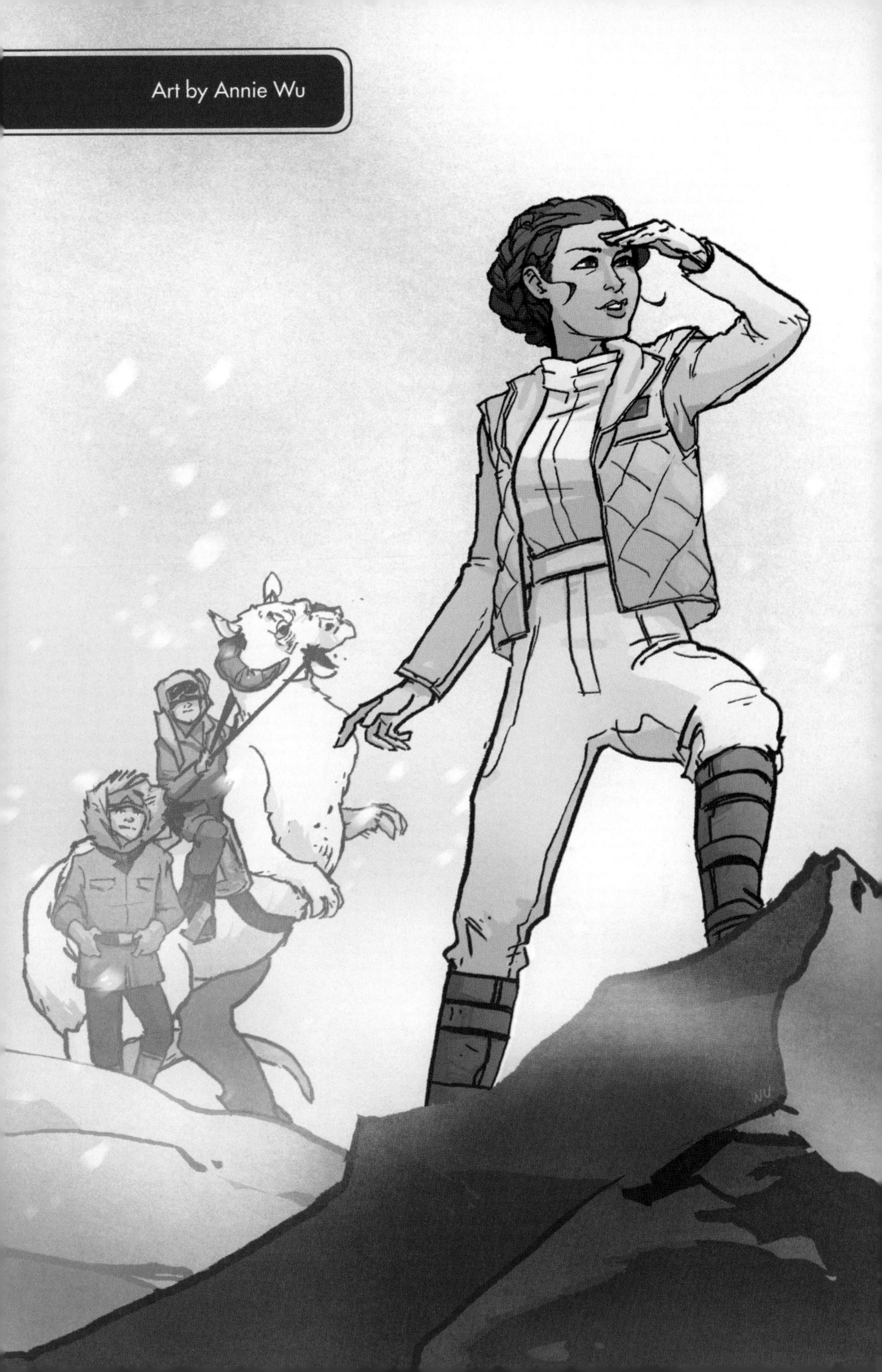
WU

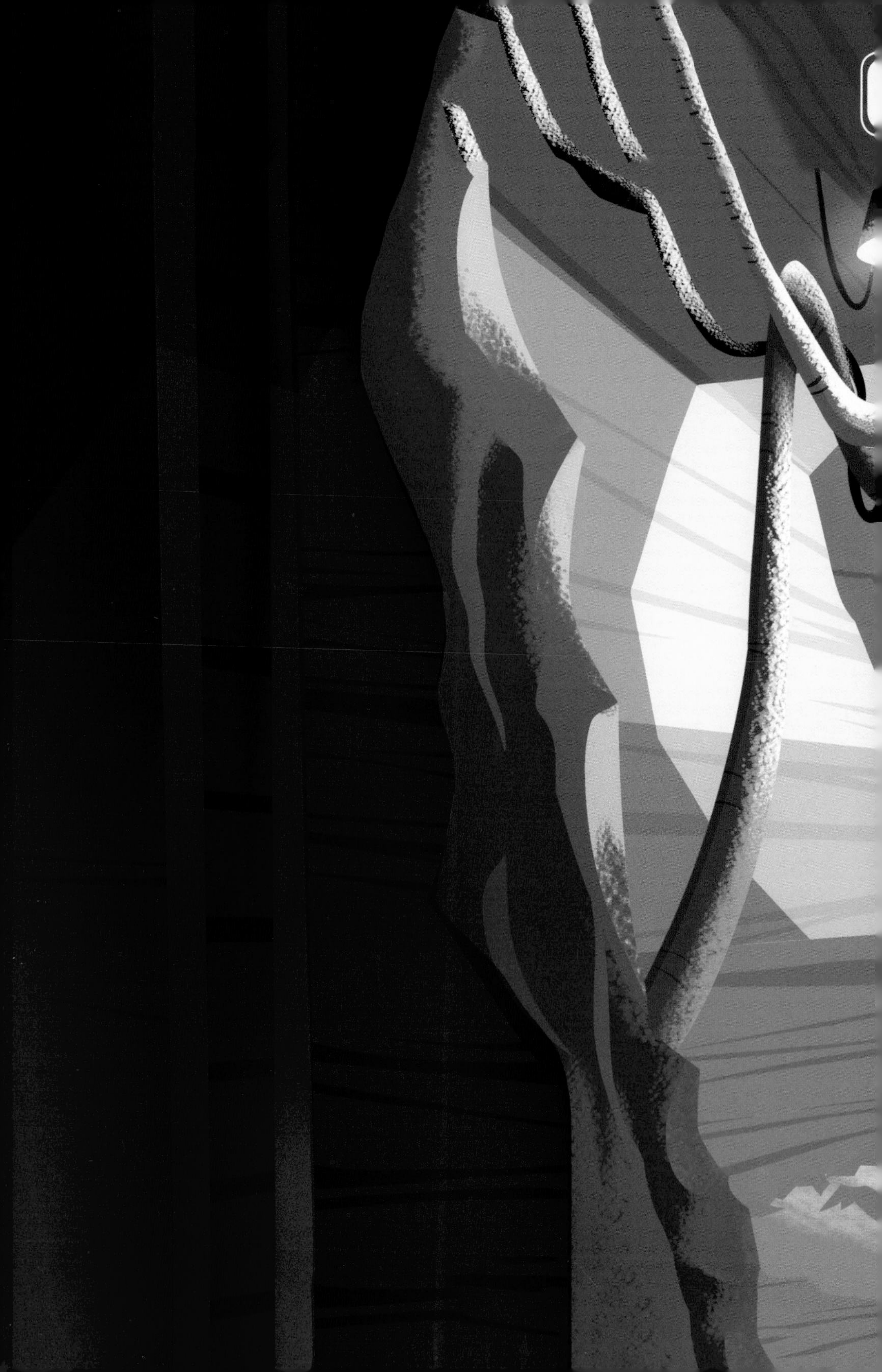

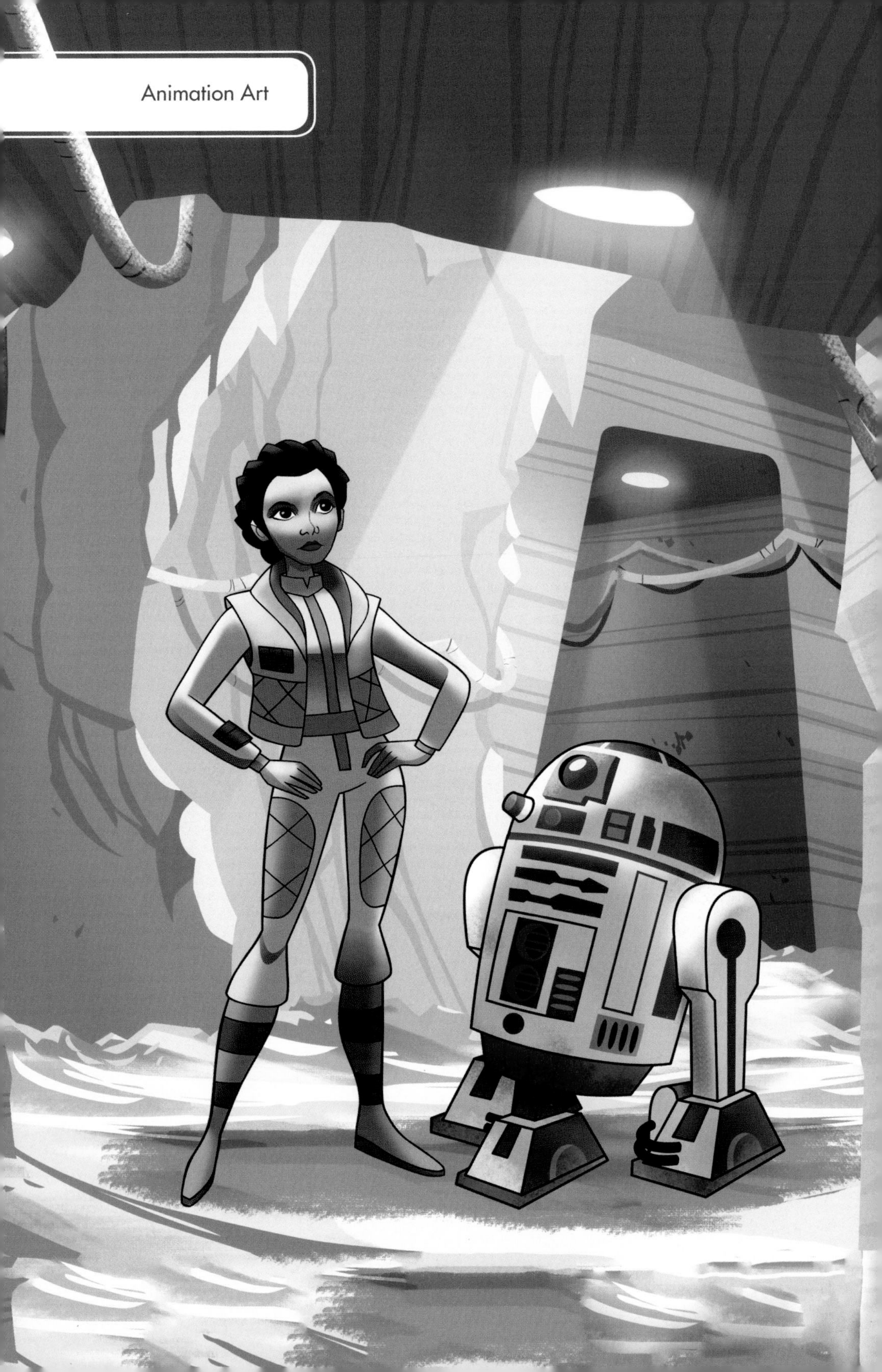

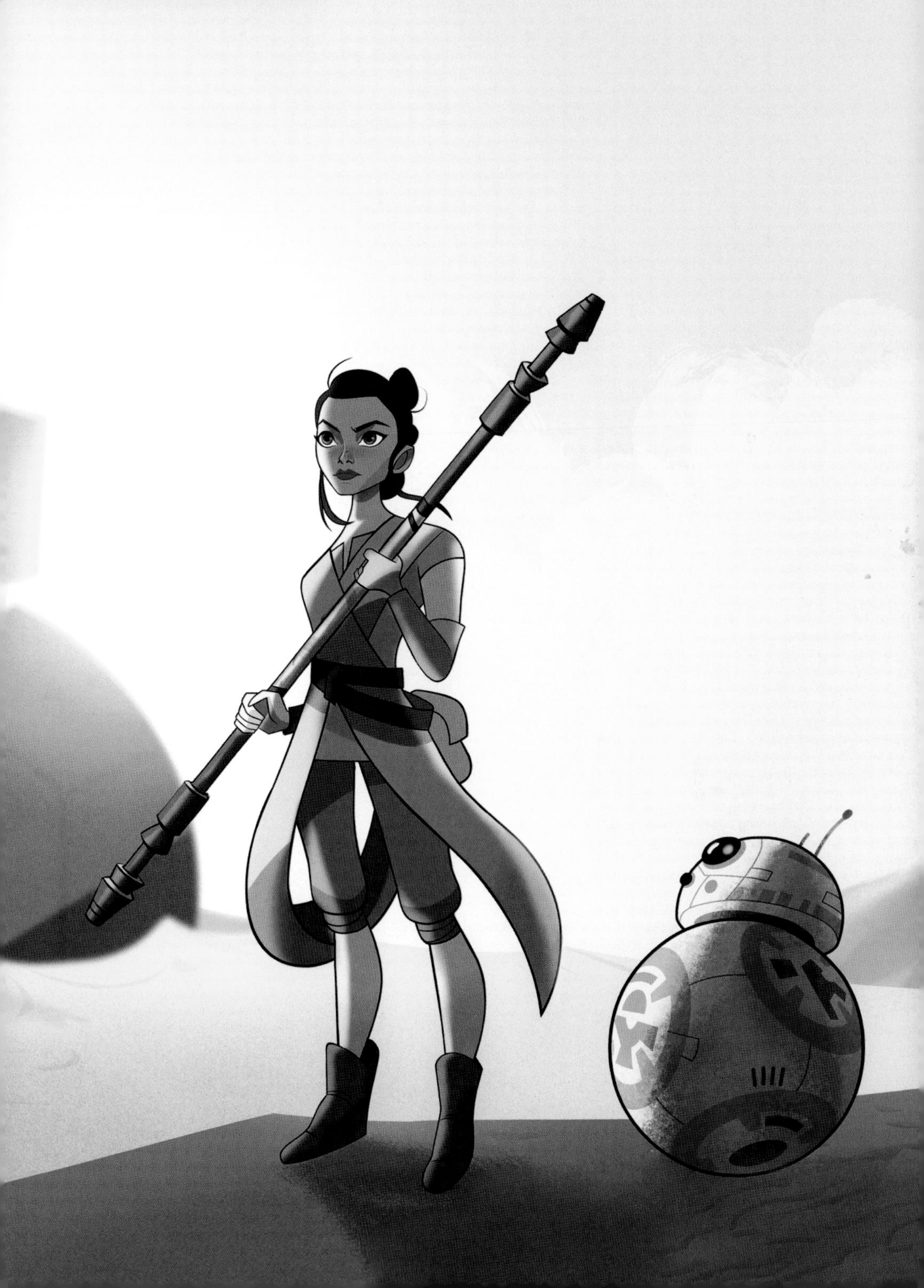

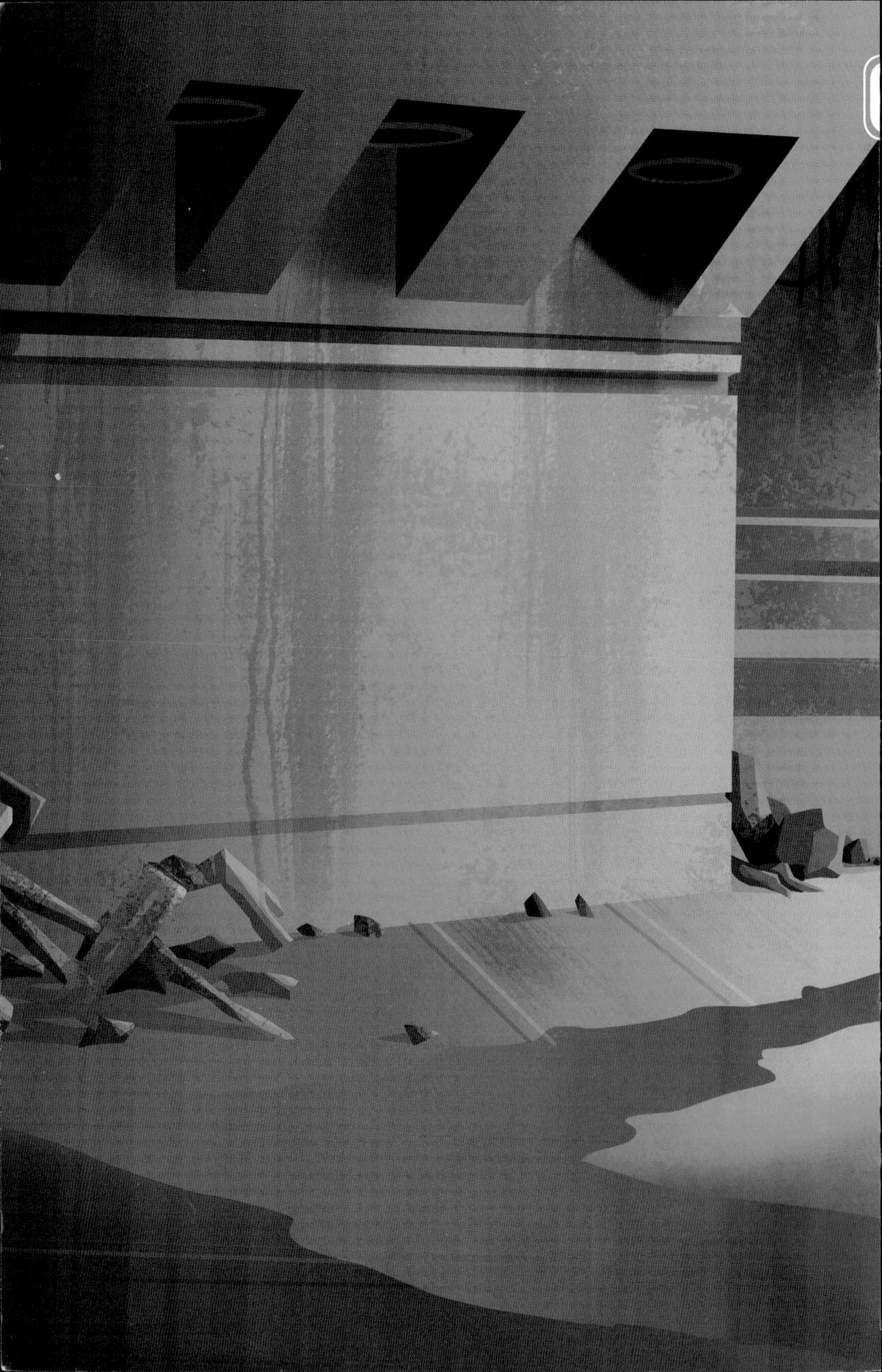

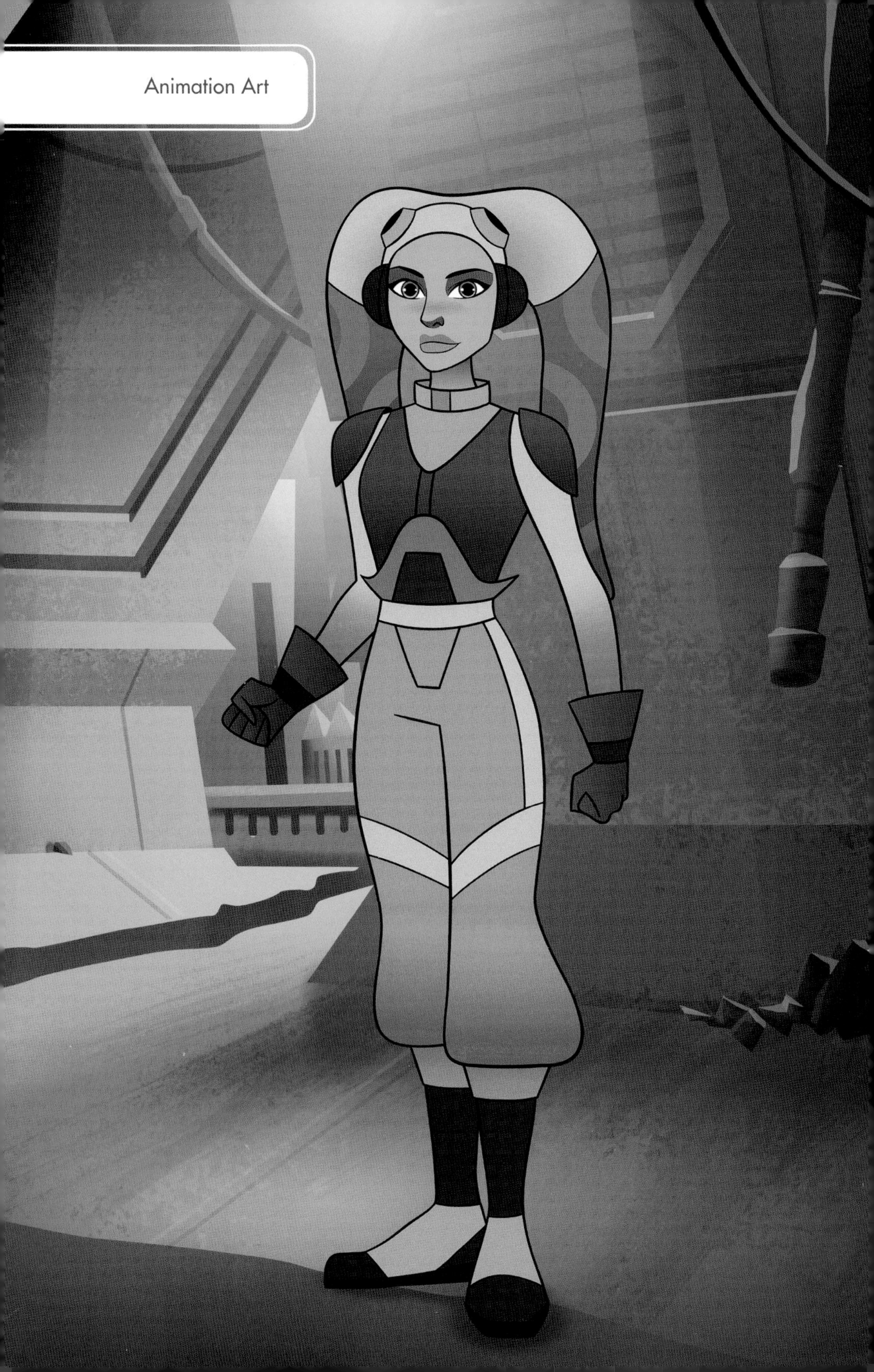

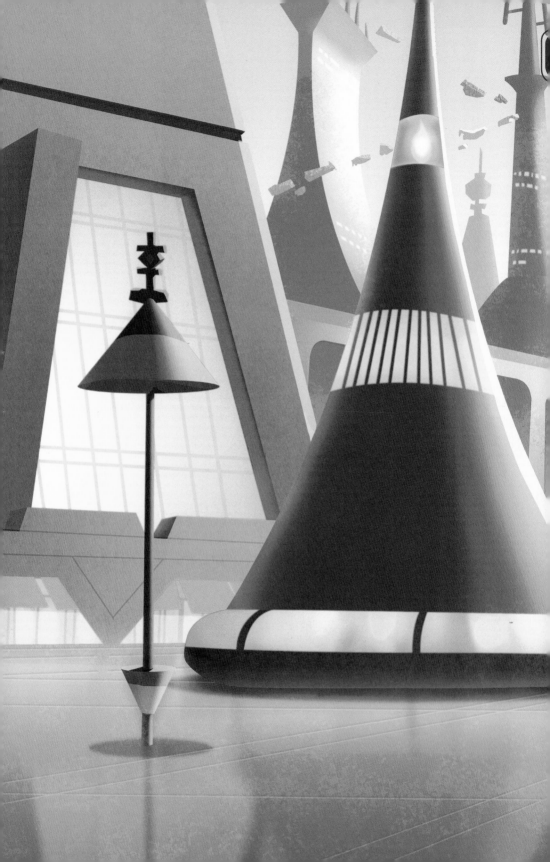

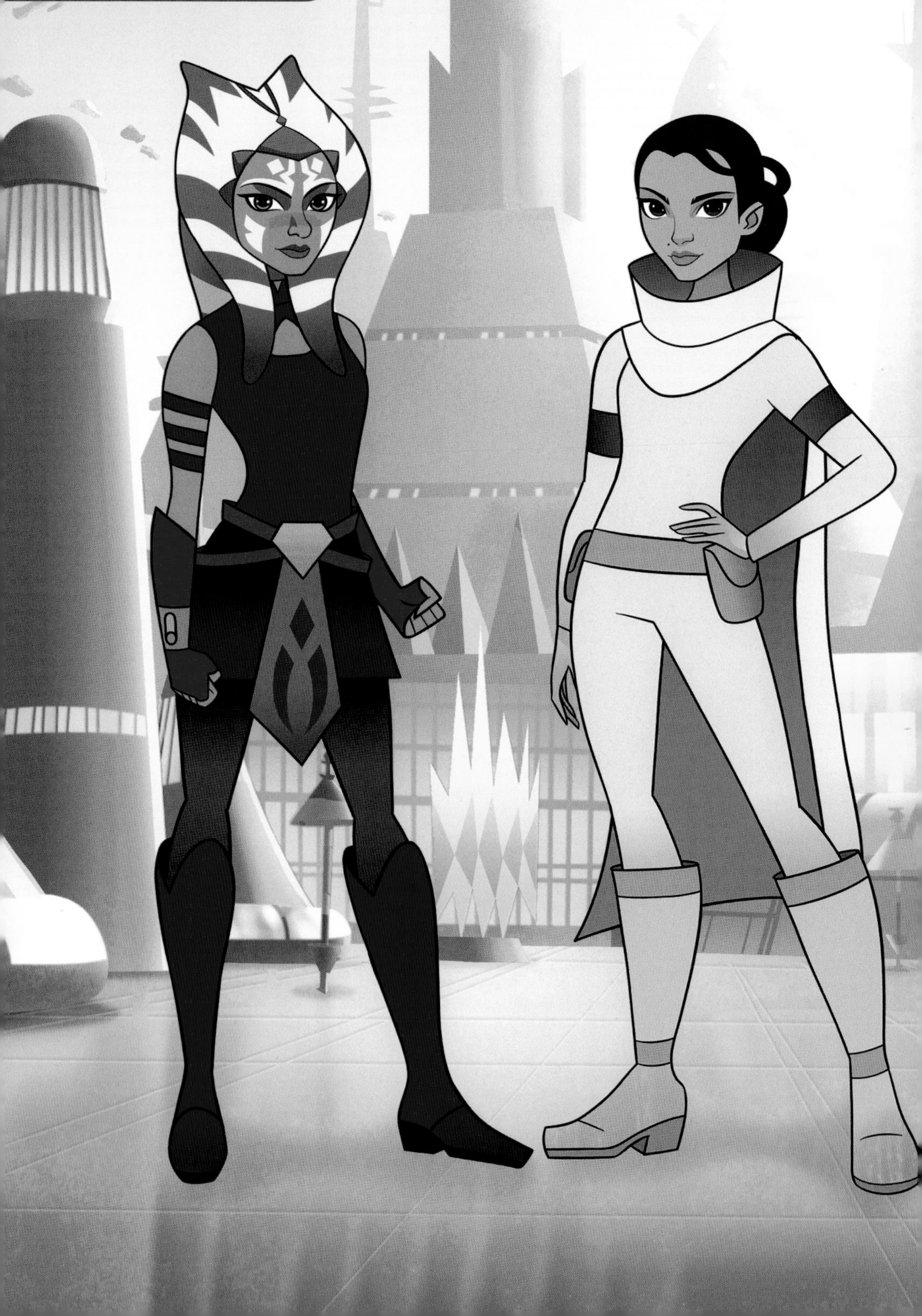

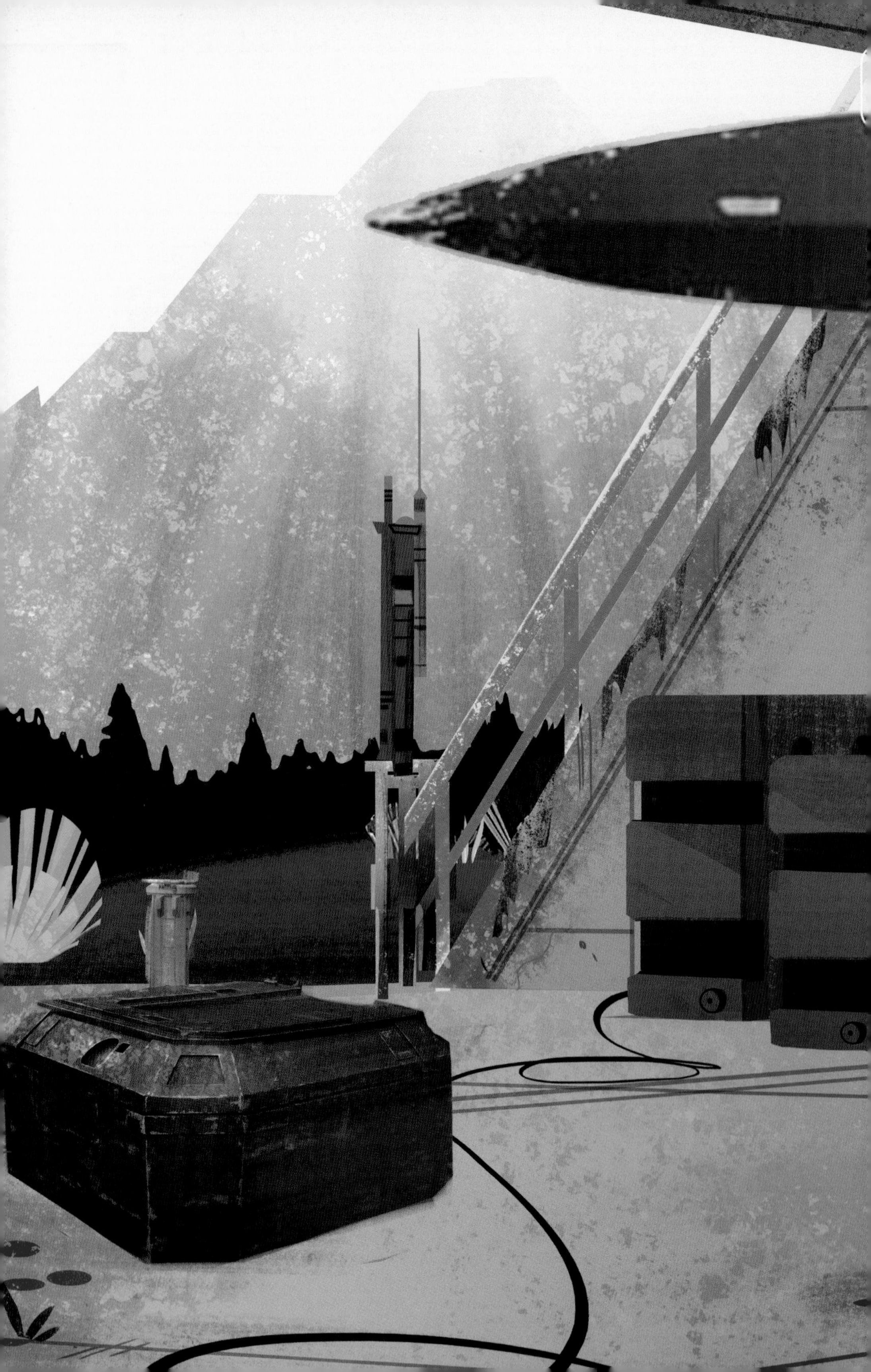

Art by Nicoletta Baldari

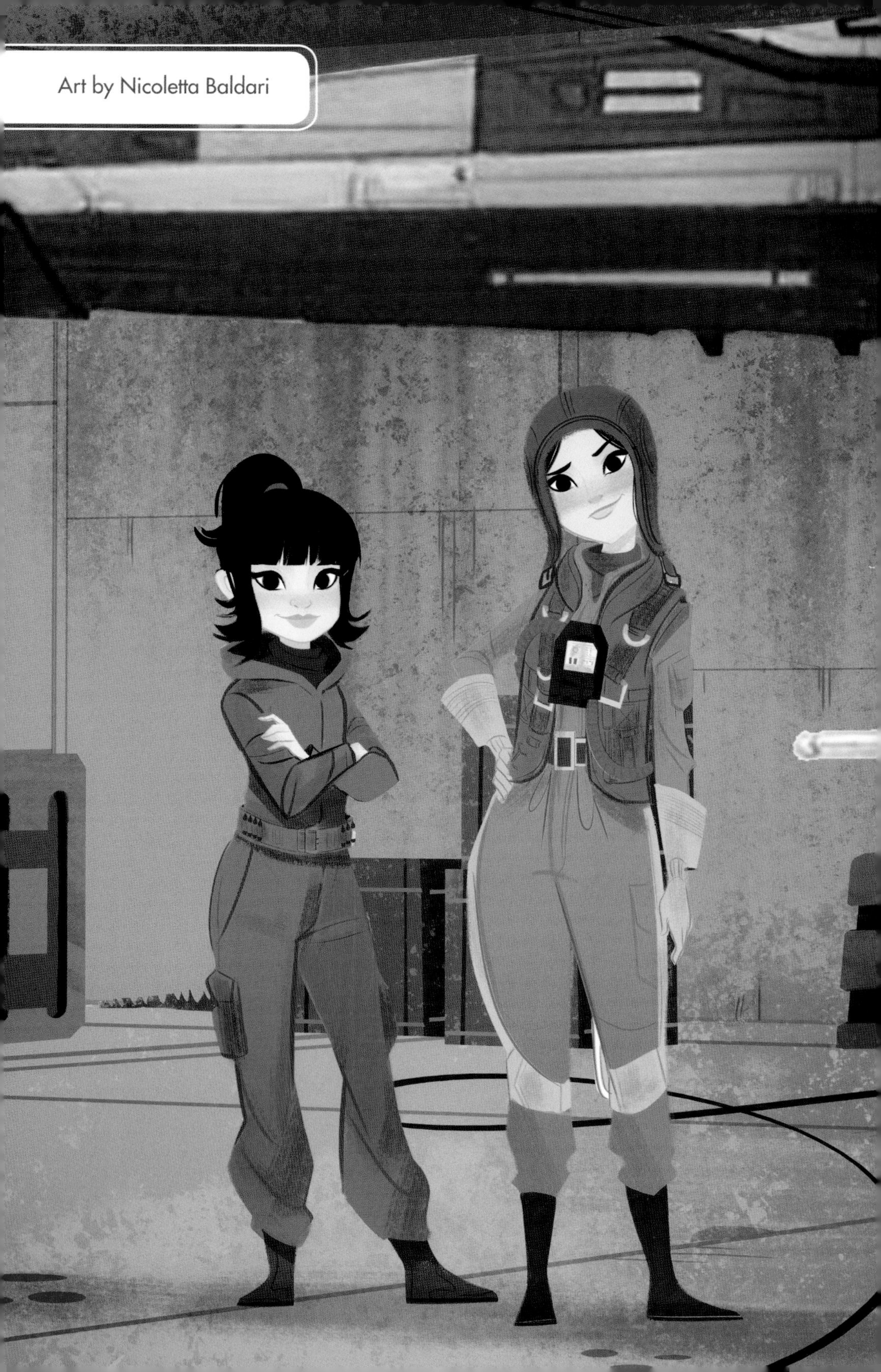

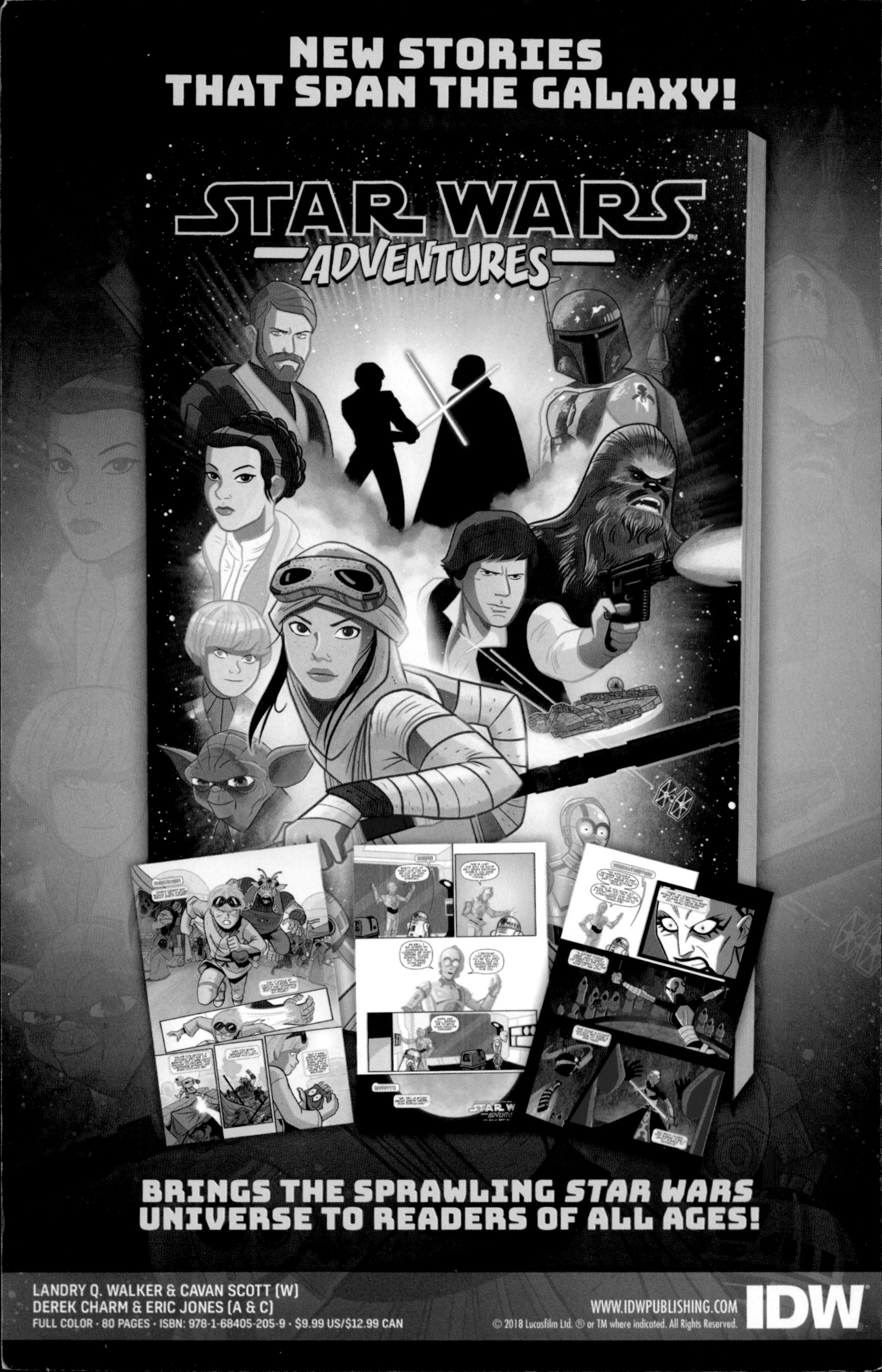
NEW STORIES
THAT SPAN THE GALAXY!
STAR WARS
ADVENTURES
BRINGS THE SPRAWLING *STAR WARS*
UNIVERSE TO READERS OF ALL AGES!
LANDRY Q. WALKER & CAVAN SCOTT (W)
DEREK CHARM & ERIC JONES (A & C)
FULL COLOR · 80 PAGES · ISBN: 978-1-68405-205-9 · $9.99 US/$12.99 CAN
WWW.IDWPUBLISHING.COM
© 2018 Lucasfilm Ltd. ® or TM where indicated. All Rights Reserved.
IDW

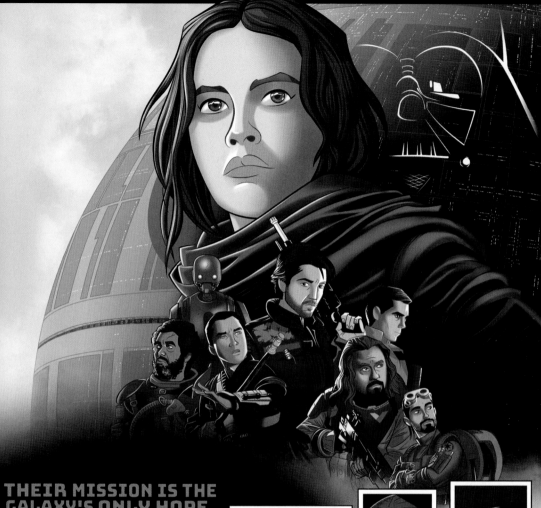

A **STAR WARS** STORY
GRAPHIC NOVEL ADAPTATION

**THEIR MISSION IS THE
GALAXY'S ONLY HOPE.**

ALESSANDRO FERRARI (W)
VARIOUS (A) ERIC JONES (C)

FULL COLOR • 80 PAGES • $9.99/$12.99 US/CAN
ISBN: 978-1-68405-220-2

WWW.IDWPUBLISHING.COM

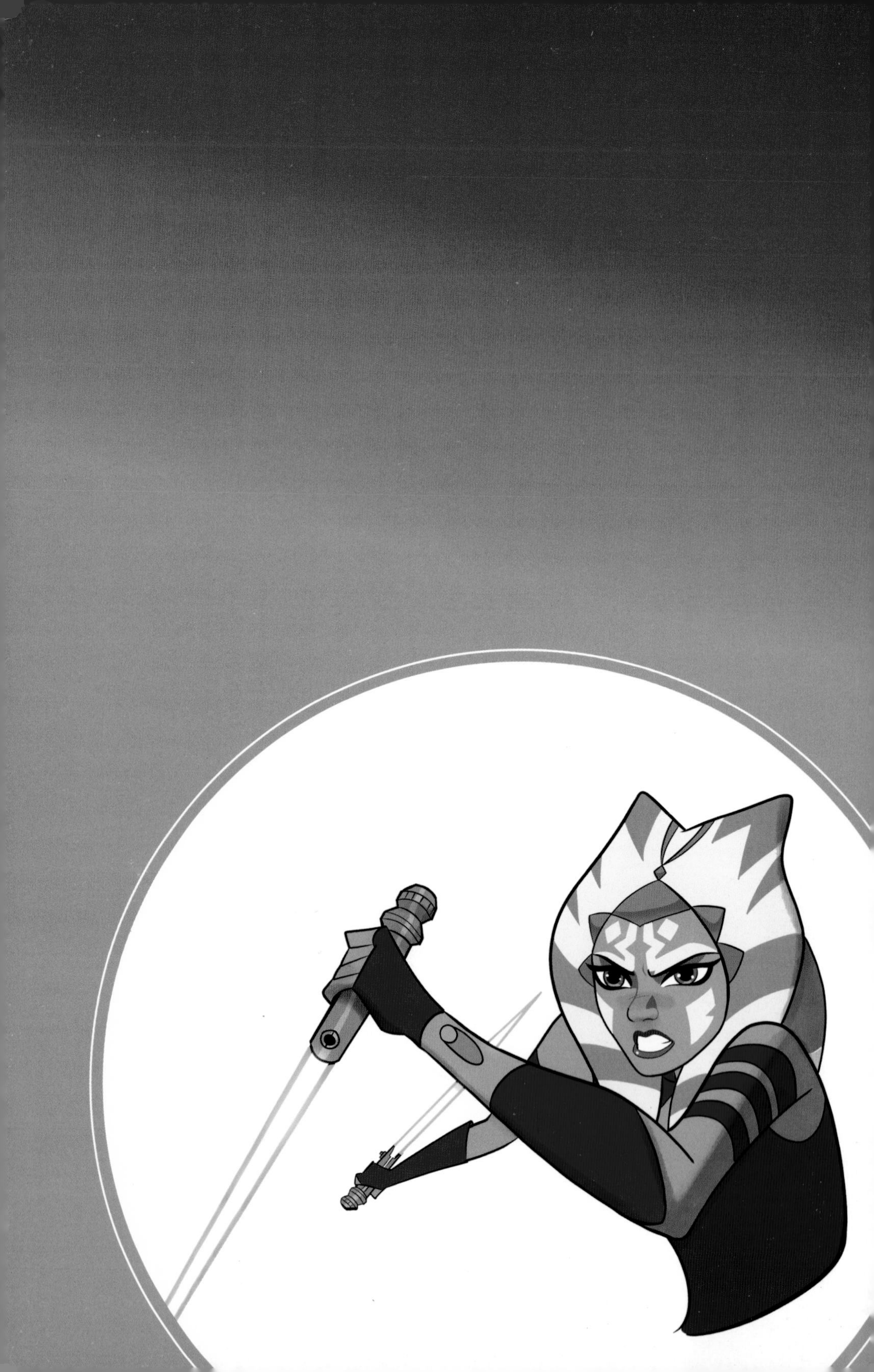